George Manvi

Fix Bay'nets

George Manville Fenn

Fix Bay'nets

1st Edition | ISBN: 978-3-75232-108-1

Place of Publication: Frankfurt am Main, Germany

Year of Publication: 2020

Outlook Verlag GmbH, Germany.

George Manville Fenn

"Fix Bay'nets"

Chapter One.

On the March.

Trrt—trrt—trrt. Just that little sound, as the sticks flirted with the drumheads to keep the men in step; for Her Majesty's 404th Fusiliers were marching "easy." So it was called; and it meant with the men smoking, and carrying their rifles as they pleased—shouldered, at the trail, slung muzzle up or muzzle down. But, all the same, it was a miserable fiction to call it marching easy, for it was impossible to make that march anything but hard. Why? Because of the road.

No; that is a fiction, too. It is absurd to call that stony shelf of rock, encumbered with stones of all sizes, full of cracks and holes, a road. It was almost in its natural state, with a smooth place here and there where it had been polished in bygone ages by avalanches of ice or stones.

But the sun shone brightly; the scenery was glorious, and grew in places awe-inspiring, as the regiment wound up and up the pass, and glimpses of snow-capped mountain and glowing valley were obtained.

To any one perched on high, as were a few scattered goats, the regiment, with its two mounted officers, its long train of mules, ambulance, and baggage-guard, and the native attendants, must have looked like a colony of marauding ants on their march, so wonderfully was everything dwarfed; even the grand deodar cedars growing far down the precipitous slopes below the track, which were stately trees, springing up to a hundred and a hundred and fifty feet, looking like groups of shrubs in the clear, pure air.

It was as much climbing as marching, and, as Bill Gedge said, "all agin the collar;" but the men did not seem to mind, as they mounted higher and higher in the expectation of finding that the next turn of the zigzag was the top of the pass.

"Here, I say," cried the owner of the just-mentioned name, a thin, wiry-looking fellow, whom so far drill and six months in the North-west Territory of Her Majesty's Indian dominions had not made muscular-

2

looking; though, for the matter of that, he did not differ much from his companions, who in appearance were of the thorough East-end Cockney type—that rather degenerate class of lads who look fifteen or sixteen at most when twenty. Stamina seemed to be wanting, chests looked narrow, and their tunics covered gaunt and angular bodies, while their spiked white helmets, though they fitted their heads, had rather an extinguisher-like effect over the thin, hollow-cheeked, beardless faces.

Defects, all these, that would naturally die out; but at the time now under consideration any newspaper writer would have been justified in calling them a regiment of boys.

But, boy-like, it did not trouble them, for, apparently as fresh as when they had started hours before, they seemed to be revelling in the wonderful air of the mountain region, and to be as full of antics as a party of schoolfellows out for a day. Songs had been sung, each with a roaring chorus; tricks had been surreptitiously played on the "pass it on" principle—a lad in the rear tilting the helmet of the file in front over his eyes, or giving him a sounding spank on the shoulder with the above admonition, when it was taken with a grin and passed on right away to the foremost rank; while the commissioned officers seemed to be peculiarly blind and deaf so long as their lads marched well, and there was no falling-out of done-up fellows waiting for the ambulance to overtake them for the rest of the march.

"Here, I say," cried Private Gedge, "I ain't a-going to drop no coppers in no blessed hats when that there band comes round. They don't 'arf play."

"Don't keep *on*," said the file on his left.

"Play? Yah! Why, we might jest as well have a dozen of them tom-tomming niggers in front saying 'Shallabala' as they taps the skins with their brown fingers."

"You are a chap, Bill," said another. "Talk about yer Syety for Cruelty to Hanimals! Why, yer orter be fined. It's all I can do to keep wind enough to climb up here, let alone having to blow a brass traction-engine, or even a fife."

"Gahn! They're used to it. They don't half play. Pass the word on for 'Brish Grannydiers.'"

Bang—bang—bang—bang! Four distinct beats of the big drum,

which were taken up by the echoes and repeated till they died away in the distance, in company with volleys of notes in a spirited crash from the brass instruments far in front, as the band struck up a rattling march, whose effect was to make breasts swell, heads perk up, and the lads pull themselves together and march on, many of them beginning to hum the familiar melody which had brightened many a long, up-country tramp.

"Talk about telly-phoning, Billy; they heered you without."

"Yes, that's your style," cried the first speaker, bursting out with a very good imitation of Punch in one of his vocal efforts, and supplementing it with a touch of the terpsichorean, tripping along in step with a suggestion of a nigger minstrel's jig.

Marching easy does not mean free and easy: and this was too much for one of the sergeants of the company, a tall, gaunt, particularly bony-faced fellow, frowning and full of importance, but almost as boyish of aspect as those who bore no chevrons on their sleeves.

He came up at the double, unnoticed by the dancer, and tried to range up alongside; but the rocky shelf was for some minutes not wide enough. Consequently he had time to grow redder in the face and more angry.

At last, though, he was in a position to speak.

"Here, you, sir," he shouted; "drop that. You're not on a cellar flap now. Recollect where you are."

Private Gedge gave a start, and squinted horribly for the benefit of his comrades right and left, as he pulled himself together, jerked his rifle over from one shoulder to the other, and marched on with his body stiff as a rifle-barrel.

"You're too full of these monkey-tricks, sir; and if there's any more of them I shall report you."

Private Gedge squinted more horribly than ever, as he marched on now as stiffly as if being drilled—too stiffly to satisfy the sergeant, who kept close behind.

"March easy, sir! march easy!" he cried importantly, and the offender dropped his rigidity, the result being that the sergeant returned to his place in the rear of the company, while Private Gedge relieved his feelings in a whisper.

"Yah! Gee up! Gee! Who wouldn't be a sergeant? Bless his heart! I love him 'most as much as my mother dear—my mother dear—my gee-yentle mother deear."

He sang the last words, but in a suppressed voice, to the great amusement of his fellows.

"Oh, I say, I wish I warn't a swaddy," he whispered.

"Why?" asked the lad on his left.

"So as to give old Gee one on the nose, and then have it out with him. I'd make him warm. It's this sort o' thing as makes me hate it all. The orficers don't mind us having a bit of a lark to make the march go light. They takes no notice so long as we're ready for 'tention and 'll fight. It's on'y chaps like Tommy Gee as has got his stripes that comes down upon you. Why, I was singing and doing that plantation song on'y yesterday, and Mr Bracy and Cap'en Roberts come along, and they both laughed. Bet sixpence the Colonel would have looked t'other way.—Oh, I say, ain't I hungry! Is it much farther?"

"I dunno," said another; "but ain't the wind cold up here?"

"Band's done again," said Gedge. "That was a short un. I s'pose if I was to cry 'Hongcore' old Gee 'd be down upon me again."

Ten minutes later the men had something more substantial to think about than music, for the shelf-like track came to an end in a great natural amphitheatre, whose walls were dwarfed mountains streaked with rifts and ravines which glistened white and sparkling as they scored the green grassy slopes, while the floor of the great hollow was a beautiful mead through which a fairly rapid torrent ran.

The halt was called upon a tolerably smooth level, arms were piled, and with the celerity displayed in a regiment on the march, the camp kitchens were formed, the smoke of fires rose, and videttes being thrown out after the fashion observed in an enemy's country, the men were free for a couple of hours' halt for rest and refreshment, to their great delight.

Pending the efforts of the regimental and camp follower cooks, some of the men began to roam about within bounds; and the group to which Private Gedge was joined made for one of the little ravines which glistened white in the sunshine, and the joker of the company soon made his voice heard.

"Oh, I say," he cried. "Only look! Here yer are, then. Here's yer hoky-poky. Here's yer real 'apenny ices laid on free gratis for nothing. Here yer are, sir; which 'll yer 'ave, strorbry or rarsbry? The real oridgenal 'stablishment, kep' by Billi Sneakino Pianni Organni. Who says hoky-poky?"

"Why, 'tis real ice, Bill," said one of the men.

"Snow," said another.

"Gahn!" cried Private Gedge, scooping up a couple of handfuls. "It's hailstones, that's what it is. You on'y get snow atop o' the high mountains."

"But it is snow, my lad," said a voice from behind, and the party started round, to see that a couple of their officers had followed to look at the glittering rift which ran right up hundreds of feet. "We're pretty high now."

"How high, sir?" said Gedge, saluting.

"We're at the top of the pass now," said the young officer who had spoken; "ten thousand feet above the sea."

"Why, that's higher than the top of Saint Paul's, sir," said one of the men.

"Top o' Saint Paul's," cried Gedge scornfully. "Why, it's higher than the Monniment atop o' that. Higher than 'Amstead, ain't it, sir?"

"Yes," said the young officer, smiling.—"Don't straggle away, my lads. Keep close in."

The speaker strolled away back with his companion towards where the native servants were busily preparing the mess meal, and their men looked after them.

"Ain't them two chummy?" said one.

"They jest are," said Gedge. "That Captain Roberts aren't a bad sort; but Mr Bracy's the chap for my money. He looks as if he could fight, too, if we had a row with the niggers."

"Oh, I don't know," said another superciliously; "you can't never tell. Some o' them nice-looking dossy chaps ain't up to much. They can talk, but they talk too fast. How could he know we were ten thousand foot high? Why, that must be miles, and that's all stuff."

"What do you know about it, stoopid?" cried Gedge fiercely. "Miles. Why, of course it is. Ain't we come miles this morning?"

"Longwise, but not uppards."

"Not uppards? Why, it's been sich a gettin' upstairs ever since we started this morning. Don't you be so jolly ready to kick again' your orficers. Mr Bracy's a reg'lar good sort; and if we comes to a set-to with the niggers he'll let some of yer see. I say, though, think we shall have a row?"

"You bet! I heered Sergeant Gee say we should be at it 'fore long, and that these here—what do they call 'em?"

"Dwats," said one of the men.

"Yes, that's it," cried Gedge. "That's right. I remember, because I said to myself if we did we'd jolly soon give 'em Dwat for."

Just then a bugle rang out, and the men doubled back for the lines, where, thanks to the clever native cooks, a hastily prepared meal was ready and made short work of, the keen mountain air and the long march having given the men a ravenous appetite.

Chapter Two.

The Colonel.

"Well, Colonel," said Dr Morton as the officers sat enjoying their lunch, breathing in the crisp mountain air and feasting their eyes at the same time upon the grand mountain scenery, "I must confess to being a bit lazy. You may be all athirst for glory, but after our ride this morning pale ale's good enough for me. I'm not a fighting man, and I hope when we get to the station we shall find that the what you may call 'em —Dwats—have dissolved into thin air like the cloud yonder fading away on that snow-peak. If, however, it does come to a set-to, here I am, my dear boys, at your service, and I'll do the best I can."

"Thank ye, Doctor," came in chorus from the officers; "but the less the better."

"We shall have something to do, for certain," said the Colonel, a keen-looking, deeply bronzed man of fifty, "for these hill-tribes will never believe in England's strength till they have been well thrashed; but a fight does not mean for certain that we shall want the doctor's help afterwards."

"So much the better," said that gentleman, laughing. "But, as I said, here I am if you want me, and I've got as well-arranged an ambulance as—"

"Oh, I say, Doctor, don't talk shop," cried the young officer spoken of as Captain Roberts, a handsome, carefully dressed young fellow of seven or eight and twenty. "They're regular curs, are they not, sir—these Dwats?" he added, turning to the Colonel.

"Certainly not," replied the latter gravely. "They are decidedly a brave, bold, fighting race. Tall, dark, big-bearded, just such fellows as hill-tribes are; restless, pugnacious fighting-men, always engaged in petty warfare with the neighbouring chiefs, and making plundering expeditions."

"I see, sir," said the Captain; "like our old Border chieftains used to be at home."

"Exactly," said the Colonel; "and each chief thinks he is one of the greatest monarchs under the sun. England is to them, in their ignorance, only a similar nation to their own, and the Empress a lady-chief."

"We shall have to teach them better," said the Major, a gentleman with an eyeglass and a disposition to become stout. "We shall soon do it. A good sharp lesson is all that's wanted. The only difficulty is that, though they are as a rule always busy cutting one another's throats, as soon as one of the tribes is attacked they all become friends and help one another."

"Save us trouble."

"What's that, Bracy?" said the Colonel.

"Save us trouble, sir," said the young man, laughing; "we can thrash half-a-dozen of the tribes together."

"With a regiment of raw boys?" said the Major, frowning so fiercely that he shot his glass out of his eye and replaced it angrily.

"Look here, Graham, you and I are going to quarrel."

8

"What about, sir?"

"Your bad habit of depreciating our lads."

"Yes," said the Doctor, nodding his head sharply. "You do, Major, and it isn't good form to cry bad fish."

"But it's true," said the Major sharply. "The War Office ought to be ashamed of itself for sending such a regiment of boys upon so arduous a task."

"The boys are right enough," said the Colonel. "What do you say, Bracy?"

"I say of course they are, sir."

"Yes, because you're a boy yourself," said the Major in a tone which made the young man flush.

"I wish I had some more boys like you, Bracy, my lad," said the Colonel warmly. "Graham's a bit touched in the liver with the change from warm weather to cold. He doesn't mean what he says—eh, Morton?"

"That's right, Colonel," said the Doctor. "I have my eye upon him. He'll be asking for an interview with me to-morrow, *re*, as the lawyers say, B.P. and B.D."

"Hang your B.P.s and B.D.s!" said the Major hotly. "I mean what I say, Colonel. These boys ought to have had three or four years in England before they were sent out here."

"But they are sent up into the hills here where the climate is glorious, sir," cried the Doctor, "and I'll answer for it that in a year's time they will have put on muscle in a wonderful way, while in a couple of years you'll be proud of them."

"I'm proud of the lads now," said the Colonel quietly.

"I'm not," said the Major. "I feel like old Jack Falstaff sometimes, ready to say, 'If I be not ashamed of my soldiers, I'm a soused gurnet.' They're boys, and nothing else."

"Nonsense," said the Colonel good-humouredly. "I've seen some service, and I never had men under me who marched better or more cheerfully than these lads have to-day."

"And not one fell out or came to me with sore feet," said the

9

Doctor stoutly. "Boys? Well, hang it all! they're not such boys as there were in the old 34th."

"What do you mean?" said the Major, shooting his eyeglass again.

"In the Peninsular War, sir," said the Doctor; "a regiment of boys, whose ages were from fourteen to sixteen, and they behaved splendidly."

"That's right," said the Colonel, nodding his head.

"Oh yes," cried the Major superciliously; "but they had only the French to fight against. Any English boy could thrash a Frenchman."

"Don't despise the French, Graham," said the Colonel quietly. "They are a very brave and gallant nation; and as to our lads, I certainly agree that they are very young; but when, as the Doctor says, they have been out here a bit, and put on more muscle—"

"But, hang it all, sir!" cried the Major, "they didn't come out here to put on muscle, but to fight. And as to your 34th, our fellows haven't got to fight Frenchmen, but these big hill-tribes. The boys are right enough in their place, and we shall make soldiers of them in time; but suppose to-morrow or next day we come plump upon the enemy—what then?"

"Our boys will make them run, sir," cried Bracy, flushing up.

"You mean they'll make our lads run," growled the Major.

"No, I don't, sir. I'll answer for our company. What do you say, Roberts?"

"Same as you do, old man. Go on; you can put it stronger than I can."

"No," said Bracy: "perhaps I've said too much, as the youngest officer in the regiment."

"Not a bit, my lad," cried the Colonel warmly. "I endorse all you say. They are terribly young-looking, but, take them all together, as bright and plucky a set of fellows as any officer could wish to command."

"Yes," said the Major through his teeth; "but look at them to-day. Hang me if they didn't at times seem like a pack of schoolboys out for a holiday—larking and shouting at one another, so that I got out of patience with them."

"Better like that than limping along, discontented and footsore," said the Colonel gravely. "The boys are as smart over their drill as they can be, and a note on the bugle would have brought every one into his place. I don't want to see the life and buoyancy crushed out of lads by discipline and the reins held too tightly at the wrong time. By the way, Graham, you dropped the curb-rein on your horse's neck coming up the rough pass, and thoroughly gave him his head."

"Yes," said the Major; "but we were talking about men, not horses."

"Bah! Don't listen to him," cried the Doctor, laughing. "He's a bit yellow in the eyes, and he'll be singing quite a different song soon. The boys are right enough, Colonel, and all the better for being young—they'll mould more easily into your ways."

"Humph!" growled the Major, frowning at the Doctor, who responded by raising his glass, nodding, and drinking to him.

It did not seem long before the bugle sounded, and the men fell in, every lad drawing himself well up, trying to look his best and as proud as a peacock, when the Colonel rode along the ranks, noting everything and ready to give boy after boy a look of recognition and a word of praise about something which had been improved; for Colonel Graves had one of those memories which seem never to forget, and it had long been borne in upon the lads in the ranks that their leader noted and remembered everything, ready for blame or praise.

In this case he drew rein opposite one very thin-looking fellow, making his sallow face turn red.

"Felt any more of that sprain, Smith?"

"No, sir; right as can be now. Ain't felt it a bit."

"That's right. Fall out, my lad, if it turns weak in the least, and get a ride."

"Yes, sir; thanky, sir. I will, sir."

A little farther on there was another halt.

"Those boots right, Judkins?"

"Yes, sir; fit splendid, sir."

"Good. Take care for the future; you and all of you. A man can't march well unless he has a comfortable boot, and a chafe once begun and neglected has sent many a good soldier into hospital."

"These are fust-rate, sir," said the man quickly. "Easy as a glove."

And so on as the Colonel rode along the ranks, making every man feel that his officer had a real interest in his welfare.

The inspection over, the advance-guard set off, then the order, "Band to the front," was given, and the regiment filed off past the Colonel's horse, making for a narrow opening between two hills which seemed to overlap, and sent back the strains of the musical instruments in a wonderful series of echoes which went rolling among the mountains, to die away in the distance.

Half-an-hour later the only signs left of the occupation of the pass were a few birds hovering about and stooping from time to time after some fragment of food. But all at once the birds took flight, as if in alarm, and the cause was not far to seek; for there was a flash in the afternoon sunshine among the rugged masses of half-frozen rocks on one side of the amphitheatre; then another flash, and a looker-on would have seen that it came from the long barrel of a gun.

Directly after appeared a tall, swarthy man in white which looked dingy by comparison with the beds of snow lying on the northern side of the mountains.

The man stole cautiously from stone to stone, and after making sure that the last soldier forming the baggage and rear-guard had disappeared, he ran quickly back to one of the snow-filled ravines and made a signal by holding his gun on high.

This he did three times, and then turned and ran steadily across the meadow-like bottom of the halting-ground, till he was near the narrow gap through which the regiment had passed, to recommence his furtive movements, seeking the shelter of stone after stone till he disappeared between the folding rocks, while in his track came in a straggling body quite a hundred active-looking men of the same type—strongly built, fierce-looking, bearded fellows, each carrying a long jezail, powder-horn, and bullet-bag, while a particularly ugly curved knife was thrust through the band which held his cotton robe tightly about his waist.

By this time the last of the rear-guard was well on its way, and the hill-men followed like so many shadows of evil that had been waiting till the little English force had passed, and were now about to seek an opportunity for mischief, whether to fall upon the rear or cut up stragglers remained to be seen. Possibly they were but one of many similar parties which would drop down from the rugged eminences and valleys which overlooked the track, completely cutting off the retreat of Colonel Graves's regiment of boys, of whose coming the tribes had evidently been warned, and so were gathering to give them a warm reception when the right time came.

Chapter Three.

First Troubles.

"Steady, my lads! steady!" said Lieutenant Bracy. "Not too fast, or we shall leave the baggage behind."

Warnings like this had to be given again and again; for, though the track was as bad as ever, it was for the most part downhill, and the patches of snow lying in the jagged hollows on either side of the pass were less frequent, while the sheltered slopes and hollows were greener with groves of stunted fir and grass, and, far below, glimpses were obtained of deep valleys branching off from the lower part of the pass, whose sides were glorious in the sunshine with what seemed to be tiny shrubs.

For the men required checking. They were growing weary, in spite of their midday halt, and longing to get to the ground below the snow-line, where they were to camp for the night.

Colonel Graves was no less eager; for, though his little force was safe enough on the right, where the side of the pass sloped precipitately down, the track lay along a continuation of the shelf which ran upon the steep mountain-side, the slope being impossible of ascent, save here and there where a stream tumbled foaming down a crack-like gully and the rocks above them rose like battlements continued with wonderful regularity, forming a dangerous set of strongholds ready to conceal an enemy who could destroy them by setting loose stones in motion, or, perfectly safe themselves, pick the men off at their leisure.

"I shall be heartily glad to get on to open ground again, Graham," said the Colonel.

"My heart has been in my mouth for the last two hours," was the reply. "We can do nothing but press on."

"And trust to the rocks up there being impassable to the enemy, if there is one on the stir."

"Yes; I don't think he could get up there," replied the Major; "but there is an enemy astir, you may be sure."

"I suppose so. The fact of a force like ours being at their mercy would set all the marauding scoundrels longing. Well, we have done everything possible. We're safe front and rear, and we can laugh up here at any attack from below on the right."

Just about the same time Bracy and his friend Roberts were tripping and stumbling along with their company, the slowness of the baggage giving them time to halt now and then to gaze in awe and wonder at the stupendous precipices around and the towering snow-mountains which came more and more into sight at every turn of the zigzag track.

"I suppose the Colonel knows what he's about," said Bracy during one of these halts.

"I suppose so," replied Roberts. "Why?"

"Because we seem to me to be getting more and more into difficulties, and where we must be polished off if the enemy lies in wait for us in force. Why in the world doesn't he try another way to Ghittah?"

"For the simple reason, my boy, that there is no other way from the south. There's one from the north, and one from the east."

"That settles the question, then, as to route; but oughtn't we to have flankers out?"

"Light cavalry?" said the Captain grimly.

"Bosh! Don't talk to me as if I were a fool. I mean skirmishers out right and left."

"Look here, young fellow, we have all we can do to get along by the regular track."

"Irregular track," said Bracy, laughing.

"Right. How, then, do you think our lads could get along below there?"

"Yes; impossible," said Bracy, with a sigh; and then glancing upward at the towering perpendicular rocks, he added, "and no one could get along there even with ropes and scaling-ladders. Well, I shall be precious glad to be out of it."

"There, don't fret. I expect we shall find any amount of this sort of country."

"Then I don't see how any manoeuvring's to be done. We shall be quite at the mercy of the enemy."

"Oh! one never knows."

"Well, I know this," said Bracy; "if I were in command I should devote my attention to avoiding traps. Hallo! what's amiss?"

The conversation had been cut short by the sharp crack of a rifle, which set the echoes rolling, and the two young officers hurried forward past their halted men, who, according to instructions, had dropped down, seeking every scrap of shelter afforded by the rocks.

"What is it?" asked Bracy as he reached the men who were in front, the advance-guard being well ahead and a couple of hundred feet below.

Half-a-dozen voices replied, loud above all being that of Private Gedge:

"Some one up there, sir, chucking stones down at us."

"No," replied Bracy confidently as he shaded his eyes and gazed up; "a stone or two set rolling by a mountain sheep or two. No one could be up there."

"What!" cried the lad excitedly. "Why, I see a chap in a white nightgown, sir, right up there, shove a stone over the edge of the parrypit, and it come down with a roosh."

"Was it you who fired?"

"Yes, sir; I loosed off at him at once, but I 'spect it was a rickershay."

"Keep down in front there, my lads," said Captain Roberts. "Did any one else see the enemy?"

A little chorus of "No" arose.

"Well, I dunno where yer eyes must ha' been, pardners," cried Gedge in a tone full of disgust; and then, before a word of reproof or order for silence could be uttered, he was standing right up, shaking his fist fiercely and shouting, "Hi, there! you shy that, and I'll come up and smash yer."

The words were still leaving his lips when Bracy had a glimpse of a man's head, then of his arms and chest, as he seemed to grasp a great stone, out of a crack five hundred feet above them, and as it fell he disappeared, the sharp cracks of half-a-dozen rifles ringing out almost together, and the stone striking a sharp edge of the precipitous face, shivering into a dozen fragments, which came roaring down, striking and splintering again and again, and glancing off to pass the shelf with a whirring, rushing sound, and strike again in a scattering volley far below.

"Any one touched?" cried the Captain.

"No, sir; no, sir."

"I think that chap were, sir," whispered Gedge, who was reloading close to Bracy's side. "I didn't have much time to aim, sir, and the smoke got a bit before my eyes, but he dropped back precious sudden. But oh, dear me, no!" he went on muttering, and grinning the while at his comrades, "I didn't see no one up there. I'd got gooseb'ries in my head 'stead of eyes. Now then, look out, lads; it's shooting for nuts, and forty in the bull's-eye."

"Hold yer row; here's the Colonel coming," whispered the man next him.

"Keep well under cover, my lads," said Bracy as the clattering of hoofs was heard.

"Right, sir," said one of the men.

"Why don't you, then?" muttered Gedge.

"Silence, sir!" snarled Sergeant Gee, who was close behind.

"All right," said Gedge softly; "but I don't want to see my orficer go down."

For, regardless of danger, while his men were pretty well in shelter, Bracy was standing right out, using a field-glass.

"Cover, cover, Mr Bracy," cried the Colonel sharply, and as he reined up he was put quickly in possession of the facts.

"Shall we have to go back, Sergeant?" whispered Gedge.

"You will—under arrest, sir, if you don't keep that tongue between your teeth."

"All right, Sergeant," muttered Gedge. "I only wanted to know."

He knew directly after, for the Colonel cried sharply:

"That's right, my lads; keep close, and fire the moment you see a movement. You six men go over the side there, and fire from the edge of the road."

The section spoken to rose and changed their positions rapidly, and as they did so a couple more blocks of stone were set in motion from above, and struck as the others had done, but did not break, glancing off, and passing over the men's heads with a fierce *whir*.

"Cover the advance with your company, and change places with the rear-guard when they have passed. Steady, there, my lads," continued the Colonel to the next company of the halted regiment; "forward!"

He took his place at their head, and advanced at a walk as coolly as if on parade; and the first movement seemed like a signal for stone after stone to be sent bounding down, and to be passed on their way by the long, thin, bolt-like bullets from the covering company's rifles, which spattered on the rocks above and kept the enemy from showing themselves, till, finding that every stone touched in the same place and glanced off the projecting shoulder half-way up, they became more bold, irritated without doubt by seeing the soldiers continue their course steadily along the track in spite of their efforts to stop their progress.

"That's got him," cried Bracy excitedly as he watched a man, who at the great height looked a mere dwarf, step into full view, carrying a block upon his shoulder.

This he heaved up with both hands above his head, and was in the act of casting it down when three rifles cracked, and he sprang out into space, diving down head first and still grasping the stone, to pass close over the marching men, strike the stony edge of the shelf, and shoot off into the deep valley below.

The horrible fall seemed to impress the covering party strangely, and for a brief space nothing was heard but the irregular tramp of the passing men.

"That's put a stop to their little game," whispered Gedge.

"Look out! fire!" growled the Sergeant; and a couple more of the enemy fell back, after exposing themselves for a few seconds to hurl down stones.

"Serve 'em right, the cowards," said Gedge, reloading. "If they want to fight, why don't they come down and have it out like men?"

"I say," whispered his neighbour on the left, "you hit one of them."

"Nay, not me," replied Gedge.

"You did."

"Don't think so. Fancy I hit that beggar who pitched down, stone and all. I felt like hitting him. But don't talk about it, pardner. One's got to do it, but I don't want to know."

"No," said Bracy, who overheard the words and turned to the lad, "it's not pleasant to think about, but it's to save your comrades' lives."

"Yes, sir, that's it, ain't it?" said the lad eagerly.

"Of course," replied Bracy.

"And I ought to shoot as straight as I can, oughtn't I?"

"Certainly."

"Hah!" ejaculated Gedge, and then to his nearest comrade, "I feel a deal better after that."

The stony bombardment continued, and Bracy watched every dislodged block as it fell, feeling a strange contraction about the heart, as it seemed certain that either it or the fragments into which it splintered must sweep some of the brave lads steadily marching along the shelf, horribly mutilated, into the gulf below.

But it was not so; either the stones were a little too soon or too late, or they struck the side and glanced off to fly whirring over the line of men and raise echoes from far below. For, after certainly losing four, the enemy grew more cautious about exposing themselves; and as the minutes glided by it began to appear as if the regiment would get past the dangerous spot without loss, for the baggage mules and heavily-laden camels were now creeping along, and the covering party at a word from Captain Roberts became, if possible, more watchful.

It was about this time that Bill Gedge, who tired seldom, but with the effect of keeping the stones from one special gap from doing mischief, drew the Sergeant's attention to that particular spot, and, hearing his remarks, Bracy lay back and brought his field-glass to bear upon it.

"It ain't no good firing at a pair o' hands coming and going," said Gedge. "I want to ketch the chap as is doing that there bit o' brick laying."

"Bit of what!" cried Bracy.

"Well, I calls it bricklaying, sir. You see, I've watched him ever so long, sticking stones one above another, ready to shove down all together. I think he means to send 'em down on the squelchy-welchies."

"The what?" cried Bracy, laughing.

"He means the camels, sir."

"Oh. Yes, I can see," continued Bracy. "Looks more like a breastwork."

Even as he spoke there was a puff of smoke, a dull report, and a sharp spat on the rock close to the young officer's hand, and he started up, looking a little white, while Sergeant Gee picked up a flattened-out piece of lead.

"Right, sir," he said; "it is a breastwork, and there's a couple o' long barrels sticking out."

"Let them have it there," cried Captain Roberts. "They're opening fire with their jezails."

"Yes, sir," said Gedge in a whisper; "we've just found that out for ourselves."

He drew trigger as he spoke, and as the smoke rose and he looked up, loading mechanically the while, he caught sight of a long gun dropping swiftly down, barrel first, to fall close by one of the camels, grunting and moaning as it bore its balanced load along the shelf.

"Mine," cried Gedge. "I hit the chap as he was looking down. I wants that there long gas-pipe to take home."

"Thank you, Gedge," said Bracy in a low voice. "I believe you've saved my life."

"Not me, sir; he shot first, but it did look near."

"Horribly, my lad, and he'd have had me next time."

"Think so, sir?" said the lad, taking aim again. "Well, there's another on 'em shooting, and I want to get him if I can. Stop him from committing murder, too."

Gedge took a long aim, and his finger trembled about the trigger for nearly a minute, but he did not fire; and all the while, evidently set in motion by a good strong party of the enemy, the stones came crashing and thundering down, in spite of the firing kept up by the covering sections, whose rifle-bullets spattered and splashed upon the rocks, and often started tiny avalanches of weathered débris.

Then all at once Gedge fired, and the long barrel, which had been thrust out from the little breastwork and sent down dangerous shots time after time, was suddenly snatched back, and the lad reloaded, looking smilingly at the lieutenant the while.

"Good shot," said Sergeant Gee importantly. "You didn't do your firing-practice for nothing, my man."

"Did you hit him, Gedge?" cried Bracy eagerly.

"Yes, sir; he had it that time. I could ha' done it afore if he'd ha' showed hisself."

"But he did at last."

"That he didn't, sir, on'y his shadder on the stone, and I aimed at that."

"Nonsense!" cried the Sergeant.

"Ah, well, you'll see," said Gedge, and he turned with a grin to his officer. "I foun' as I should never hit him strite forrard, sir, so I thinked it out a bit, and then aimed at his shadder, and it was like taking him off the cushion—fired at the stone where I could see the shadder of his head."

"Ah! a ricochet," cried Bracy.

"That's it, sir; a rickyshay."

The stones continued to fall without effect; but no one above attempted to expose himself again to the deadly fire from below.

Suddenly Bracy started from his place.

"Up with you, my lads; forward!"

Waving his sword, he made a rush, leading his men along the deadly-looking piece of road swept by the stones from above, for the rear-guard had passed in safety; and, with his breath coming thick and fast, he dashed forward, knowing full well that their first movement would be the signal for the stones to come down thick and fast. He was quite right; for, as the men cheered and dashed after their two officers, block after block came whirring down, crashing, bounding, shivering, and seeming to fill the air with fragments so thickly that it was quite impossible to believe the passage of that hundred exposed yards could be accomplished in safety. But they got across untouched, and the men cheered again as they clustered about their officers, the precipitous spot where they now stood being sheltered from the danger, apparently inaccessible even to the enemy.

"Bravo, my lads!" cried the Captain.

"Splendidly done," said Bracy, breathless, "and not a man hurt."

"All here?" said Captain Roberts.

"Yes, sir;" "Yes, sir," came in a scattered volley of words. "No—

stop!" said Bracy excitedly. "Where's Gedge?"

There was a dead silence, the men looking at one another and then back along the stone-strewed track, only a third of which was visible. But there was no sign of the missing man, and after a word or two with his brother officer Bracy doubled back, followed by Sergeant Gee, till they had rounded a bend of the track and could command the whole distance. As they halted to examine the road, another stone fell from above, struck the road, and then bounded off into the valley.

"There he is," cried Bracy excitedly, thrusting his sword back in its scabbard. "Just beyond where that stone fell."

"Yes, sir; I see him now. It's all over with the poor lad. Here, sir; don't, sir. What are you going to do?"

"Do? Fetch him in," said Bracy sharply.

"No, sir; don't, sir. It's like going to a 'orrid death," faltered the

Sergeant, whose face was of a clayey hue. "You mustn't go, sir. You ought to order me to fetch him in, and I will if you tell me."

"I'm not going to tell our lads to do what I daren't do myself," said Bracy coldly. "They can't see us here—can they?"

The Sergeant glanced upward, but the view in that direction was cut off by projecting masses of stone.

"No, sir; they can't see us here."

"Then here goes," cried the young officer, drawing a deep breath and pressing his helmet down upon his head.

"No, sir; don't—" began the Sergeant in tones of expostulation; but he did not finish, for before the second word had left his lips Bracy was bounding along as if running in an impediment race, leaping masses of stone, avoiding others, and making for where he could see the motionless figure; of Gedge still grasping his rifle and lying face downward among the stones.

A yell arose from above as Bracy bounded into view, and stones began to fall again; while, upon reaching the fallen man, the young officer, completely ignoring the terrible peril in which he stood, bent down, passed his arms about the waist, raised him, and with a big effort threw him over his shoulder;

It was more perilous to stand still than to go on.
PAGE 29.

and then turned and started back, carrying the poor fellow's rifle in his right hand.

The yells from above increased, and before Bracy had gone half-a-dozen yards of the return journey there was a loud *whish*, and he stopped short, for a block of stone struck the path not a yard before him, and then bounded off. For a moment or two Bracy felt mentally stunned by the close approach of a horrible death; then, recovering himself, he strode on again, feeling strongly that it was more perilous to stand still than to go on, with every step taking him nearer to safety.

There was an intense desire burning within him to try and run, but the rugged path forbade that, and he tramped slowly on with his load, with the air seeming to his heated imagination to be thick with the falling missiles which came hurtling around.

"The next must do it," he found himself muttering, as he went on with what, though only a matter of minutes, seemed to be a long journey, before, coming confusedly as it were out of a dream, he heard the cheering of his men, and Sergeant Gee and three more relieved him of his load, while the crash and rattle of the falling stones seemed to be far behind.

"Hooray!" A tremendously hearty British cheer—only that of a company, but as loud it seemed as if given by the whole regiment; and the next thing out of the confused dream was the feeling of his hand being grasped, and the hearing of his brother officer's voice.

"Splendid, old man!" he whispered. "Talk about pluck! But what's the matter? Don't say you're hurt?"

"No—no, I think not. Only feel a bit stunned."

"Then you're hit by a stone?"

"No, no. There, I'm better now. Here! That poor fellow Gedge! I hope he isn't killed."

They turned to the little group of men who surrounded poor Gedge, now lying on his back, with Gee upon one knee bending over him, and trying to give him some water from his canteen.

"Dead?" cried Bracy excitedly.

"'Fraid so, sir," replied the Sergeant. "Stone hit him on the 'elmet, and I expect his head's caved in."

"Bathe his face with a handful of the water," said Bracy sadly. "Poor lad! this was horribly sudden."

Both he and Roberts looked down sadly at the stony face so lately full of mischievous animation, and in view of the perilous position in which they stood and the duty he had to do, the Captain was about to order the men to make an extempore stretcher of their rifles and the Sergeant's strong netted sash, so that the retreat could be continued, when Gee dashed some water in the prostrate lad's face.

The effect was marvellous. In an instant a spasm ran through the stony features. There was a fit of coughing and choking, and as the men around, always ready for a laugh, broke out, the supposed dead opened his eyes, stared blankly, and gasped out:

"Stow that! Here, who did it? Here, I'll just wipe some one's eye for that, here, I know—I—here—I s'y—I—er—Mr Bracy, sir! You wouldn't play tricks with a fellow like that? Ah, I recklect now!"

The poor fellow's hand went to his bare head, and he winced at the acute pain the touch gave him.

"I say, sir," he said, "ketched me a spank right there.—Is my 'elmet spoiled?"

"Never mind your helmet, Gedge, my lad," cried Bracy, who was bending over him. "There, you must lie still till we get something ready to carry you to the ambulance."

"Kerry me, sir! What for? Ain't going to croak, am I? Not me. Here, I'm all right, sir. Give's a drink outer my bottle.—Hah! that's good.—Drop more, please, Sergeant,—Thanky.—Hah! that is good. Feel as if I could drink like a squelchy-welchy.—Here, I s'y, where's my rifle?"

"I've got it, pardner," said one of the lads.

"Oh, that's right. Ain't got the stock skretched, hev it?"

"No, no; that's all right, Bill."

"Glad o' that. Here, I s'y; I went down, didn't I?"

"Yes, my lad; just in the middle of the worst bit where the stones were falling."

"That was it—was it? Well, I did wonder they never hit nobody, sir, but I didn't expect they'd hit me."

"What are you going to do, my lad?" said the Captain sharply.

"Get up, sir.—Can't lie here. 'Tain't soft enough. I'm all right. Only feel silly, as if I'd been heving my fust pipe.—Thanky, Sergeant.—Here, it's all right; I can stand. Who's got my 'elmet?"

The poor fellow tottered a little, but the British pluck of his nature made him master the dizzy feeling, and the old familiar boyish grin broke out over his twitching white face as he took hold of the helmet handed to him and tried to put it on.

"Here, I s'y," he cried, "no larks now; this ain't in me."

"Yes, that's yours, Gedge," said the Sergeant.

"Got such a dint in it, then, that it won't go on."

"No, my lad," said Bracy. "Here, Sergeant, tie my handkerchief round his head."

"Yes, sir; thank ye, sir. Here, hold still, Gedge," cried the Sergeant.

"Well, I'm blest!" muttered the poor fellow; "there's all one side puffed out like arf a bushel basket. Here, I've often heard of chaps having the swelled head when they've got on a bit; but I won't show it, mateys. I won't cut your company.—Thank ye, Sergeant."

"Fall in," cried the Captain. "Gedge, you'll have to be carried. Two men. Sergeant, and change often."

"I can walk, sir, please," cried Gedge. "Let me try. If I can't some un can carry me then."

"Very well, try.—Forward."

The march was resumed, but after a few steps the injured lad was glad to grasp the arm offered him by Gee.

"Thanky, Sergeant," he said. "Just a bit dizzy now, and I don't want to go over the side. Better soon; but, I say, did you fetch me in?"

"No: it was Mr Bracy," said Gee gruffly.

"Oh, him!" said the lad quietly, and with a curious look in his eyes as he gazed in the young lieutenant's direction. "Well, thank ye, sir; much obliged," he said in an undertone. "I'll say so to you some time. But I say, Sergeant, talk about having a head on; I've got it now."

"Yes; but don't talk. Hullo! they're up above us again yonder."

"What, the Dwat you may call 'ems?"

"I s'pose so," said the Sergeant gruffly, as a stone crashed down close to the foremost man.

"And me not able to shoot!" muttered Gedge. "Well, of all the hard luck! But I owe some on 'em something for that shy at my coco-nut; and oh! I s'y, Sergeant, it's just as if some one was at work at it with a pick."

Chapter Four.

Wounded Men.

The Sergeant was right, for, after turning a rib-like mass of stone forming an angle in the path, it was to find that either a fresh party of the enemy were waiting for them, or the others had by taking a short cut reached an eminence commanding the path; and as soon as the company came in sight they were saluted with an avalanche of stones, on a spot where they were terribly exposed, there being no shelter that could be seized upon by a few picked marksmen to hold the stone-throwers in check while the rest got by.

Matters looked bad, for the whole; of the baggage with the guard had disappeared, and, to make matters worse, shot after shot came whistling by from behind, indicating that the hill-men had come down to the track, and were closely following them in the rear.

"We must make a rush for it, Bracy," said Captain Roberts, as he gazed up at the heights from which the invisible enemy were bombarding the path. "We'll hold them back for a few minutes, and then you take half the company and dash across to yonder rocks. As soon as you are in shelter open fire and cover, as I fancy you can get a sight of them from there. It's waste of ammunition to fire from here, and —Who's that down?"

For there was a sharp cry from one of the men, who staggered forward a few yards, fell, and sprang up again minus his helmet, which had been struck by a bullet from behind.

"All right; not much hurt, sir," cried the sufferer, rejoining his companions, after picking up his helmet, the back of which had been scored by a nearly spent rugged missile, whose track was marked in a long jagged cut across the man's right cheek-bone, from which the blood was trickling down.

The rear men were on the alert, watching for a chance to retaliate upon their troublesome enemy, but holding their fire, for not a man was visible, and it seemed useless to fire at the rocks they had just left.

"The sooner we are out of this the better," said the Captain quietly. "You know your work.—Wait a minute, and then at the word rush across to the rocks."

The minute had nearly passed, the time filled up by the rattle and roar of falling stones, and Bracy's half-company, though at rest, were panting hard with excitement like greyhounds held by a leash. Then, just as the falling stones were beginning to slacken as if the throwers grasped the fact that they were wasting their strength, and were reserving their discharge till the half-company made its rush, there was a sudden quick movement among the rocks they were to try and reach, and Bracy's blood ran cold as, puff, puff, puff, and then crack, crack, fire was opened.

"Hah!" ejaculated Roberts excitedly; "they've got down somehow to cut us off. We're between two fires, Bracy, man. There's nothing for it now but to dash forward. You must clear them out of that. Don't stop to pick up your men who go down. We shall be close behind, and will see to them. Get across, and then turn and cover us if you can."

Bracy nodded, and drew his revolver, just giving one glance upward at the heights from whence the stones came, and then fixing his eyes upon the rocks on the other side of the curve of the track, from which fresh puffs of smoke arose, making their position look desperate with the enemy in front and rear, supplemented by those hidden among the rugged natural battlements of their stronghold.

"How many men shall I lose?" thought the young officer; and then, "Shall I get across alive?"

The next moment all was changed.

"Why, Roberts," he cried, "it's our own men yonder, firing up instead of at us, to cover our advance."

"Forward, then," cried Roberts. "We shall be close behind."

Bracy dashed ahead, waving his sword, and his half-company of boys cheered as they followed him; while as soon as they started there was a tremendous crashing of dislodged masses of rock, which came thundering down, fortunately sent too soon to injure the charging soldiery, who were saved from a second discharge by a sharp crackling fire from the rocks which they were to have occupied, the rapid repetitions telling that a strong company of their friends were at work, and the bullets spattering and flicking among the enemy, driving them at once into cover.

There was a hearty cheer to greet Bracy and his half-company as they successfully crossed the stone-swept track and reached the shelter of the rocks, ready to turn on the instant and help to keep down the stone-throwing as Roberts and his men came along at the double.

But Bracy's lads did not fire a shot aloft, for a glance at the second half of the company revealed a new danger, and his men dropped into position, ready to repel that with a volley. For no sooner had the second half started than the track, a quarter of a mile in their rear, suddenly seemed to become alive with white-garbed hill-men, who came bounding along in a little crowd.

"Steady, steady! make every shot tell, boys," cried Bracy. "Fire!"

A ragged volley was the result; the hill-men stopped suddenly as if petrified, and were hesitating still as to what they should do, when a second volley sent them to the right-about, leaving several of their number on the track, while half-a-dozen more were seen to drop before their comrades were out of sight.

There was another burst of cheering as the second half-company pressed on without the loss of a man, Gedge having so far recovered that he was able to double with one of his comrades, who came steadily on with him, arm-in-arm. As the young officers stood breathless and panting with their exertions, the stern, keen face of Colonel Graves suddenly loomed above the smoke, and his horse bore him into their midst.

"How many men down?" was his first eager question.

"Two slightly wounded; that's all, sir," was the reply.

"Forward, then," he said, and he signed to Roberts and Bracy to come to his side.

"You've done well," he said. "Retain your places as rear-guard. I'll keep in touch with you.—Hark!"

"Firing, sir," said Captain Roberts.

"Yes; the Major must be clearing the way for us. We must get off this shelf and on to open ground before dark."

He turned his horse's head and made his way towards the front as rapidly as the nature of the wretched rock-strewn shelf would allow; and the two young officers tramped on at a fair distance from the rear of the baggage-guard, keeping a sharp lookout for enemies in pursuit, feeling little anxiety about the rugged eminences up to their left, knowing as they did that they would have ample warning of danger by an attack being made somewhere along the line whose extreme rear they were protecting.

Their task was comparatively easy now, for their two wounded men had been passed on to the baggage-train, so that they could be in charge of the ambulance men and have the benefit of the Doctor's help. A shot came now and then from behind, showing that the enemy were in pursuit; but no mischief was done, a return shot or two from the rear files, who retired in skirmishing order, silencing the firing at every outbreak. Every step taken, too, now was more and more downward, and the keen winds, sharpened by the ice and snow, which had cut down the ravines at the higher part of the pass, were now tempered by the warm afternoon sunshine, which bathed the tops of the shrubs they had looked down upon from above, the said shrubs having developed into magnificent groves of cedars, grand in form and towering in height.

These last were for the most part on the farther side of the now verdant valley—verdant, for its rocky harshness was rapidly becoming softened; even the shelf along which they tramped began to be dotted with alpine flowers, which gave the march the appearance of having lasted for months, for the morning; had been in part among mountains whose atmosphere was that of a sunny day in February. Now they were in May, and according to appearances they were descending into an evening that would be like June.

Matters were going on so quietly now that the two officers found time for a chat at intervals, one of which was as they passed a formidable-looking spot where the thickly scattered stones and marks of lead upon the rocks showed that it must have been the scene of one of the attacks made by the enemy from the rocks above. But there was no sign of them now, the only suggestion of danger being the presence of a score of their men left to keep any fresh attack in check, and who retired as soon as the rear-guard came in sight.

"This must be where the Major had to clear the way," said Roberts as he scanned the heights with his glass.

"Yes," replied Bracy; "and I hope he was as well satisfied with the boys as we were."

"Shame if he wasn't," cried Roberts. "Pooh! don't take any notice of what he said. You know his way."

"Yes; he must have something to grumble at," replied Bracy. "If he were with a regiment of veterans—"

"Yes, of course; he'd be snarling because they were what he'd call worn-out, useless cripples, only fit for Chelsea Hospital. The Doctor was right: it's his liver."

"Yes," said Bracy; "and when we are in camp to-night and at dinner he'll be in the highest of glee, and do nothing but brag about how he made the enemy run."

"Well, yes; a bit of work always does him good. It isn't brag, though, for I believe the Major to be a splendid officer, and if we have much to do he'll begin showing us greenhorns what a soldier ought to be. But, I say, don't talk about dinner. I didn't think of it before; now I feel famished. My word! I shall punish it to-night."

"If we get safely into camp," cried Bracy excitedly. "Down with you, my lads, and look out. It came from across the valley there, from among those trees."

Even as he spoke, pat, pat, pat came as many bullets, to strike against the bare face of the rock over their heads and fall among the stones at their feet, while the reports of the pieces fired were multiplied by the echoes till they died away.

"Nothing to mind," said Roberts coolly. "They're trying to pick us off! We can laugh at any attack if they try to cross the depths below there."

"Nothing to mind so long as we are not hit," replied Bracy; "but I object to being made a mark for their practice. What have you got there, Jones?"

"One of their bullets, sir," said the man, who had picked up a messenger which had come whizzing across the valley.

"Bullet—eh? Look here, Roberts," and Bracy handed his brother officer a ragged piece of iron which looked as if it had been cut off the end of a red-hot iron rod.

"Humph! Nice tackle to fire at us. Lead must be scarce. Now, that's the sort of thing that would make a wound that wouldn't heal, and delight old Morton."

Pat, pat, again overhead, and the missiles fell among the stones.

"We must stop this," said Roberts.—"Hold your fire, my lads, till you have a good chance. One telling shot is worth a hundred bad ones."

"Ah! Look out," cried Bracy, who was scanning the distant grove of large trees across the valley a quarter of a mile away. "There they go, breaking cover to take up ground more forward, to have at us again."

For, all at once, some fifty white-coats became visible, as their owners dashed out of one of the patches of cedars and ran for another a furlong ahead. The lads were looking out, and rifle after rifle cracked. Then there was quite a volley to teach the enemy that a quarter of a mile was a dangerous distance to stand at when British soldiers were kneeling behind rocks which formed steady rests for the rifles they had carefully sighted.

Five or six men, whose white-coats stood out plainly in the clear mountain air against the green, were seen to drop and not rise again; while the rest, instead of racing on to the cover in front, turned off at right-angles and made for a woody ravine higher up the right face of the valley; but they did not all reach it in safety.

The firing brought back the Colonel, who nodded thoughtfully on hearing Roberts's report.

"Hurry on," he said; "the shelf descends to quite an opening of the valley a quarter of a mile farther on, and there is a patch of wood well out of reach of the hills, where I shall camp to-night. The advance-guard have cleared it of a similar party to that you describe."

"It was getting time," said Bracy to Roberts as the Colonel rode on. "I shouldn't have liked for us to pass the night on this shelf. Think they'll attack us after dark?"

"Can't say, my son. If they do—"

"Well, what?" asked Bracy.

"We shall have to fight; but not, I hope, till we have had a comfortable meal."

"I hope the same; but I suppose there'll be no rest till we've had a good set-to and thrashed the ruffians. Why, the country seems to be up in arms against us."

"Yes," said Roberts; "it's a way these genial hill-men have."

"Fortunately for us it is very thinly peopled," observed Bracy as they tramped along, seemingly as fresh as when they started.

"Don't be too sure. We've been up among the mountains. Wait till we see the vales."

But the troubles of the day ceased at sunset, one which was made wonderful with the hues which dyed the mountains of the vast Karakoram range; and when the cooking-fires were out in the cedar grove and the watches were set, officers and men slept well in the aromatic air; even the mules did not squeal and kick so very much in their lines, while the weary camels groaned and sighed and sobbed in half-tones, as if bemoaning their fate as being rather better than usual, for none had been riddled by bullets, fallen, or been beaten overmuch, and their leaders had taken care that they were not overloaded, and that they had plenty to eat and drink. The only men who slept badly were Gedge and Symons, the man whose cheek-bone had been furrowed by a bullet. But even they were cheerful as they talked together in the shelter of a canvas tent, and passed the time comparing notes about their ill-luck in being the first down, and calculating how long it would be before they were back in the ranks.

"Hurt much, matey?" said Gedge.

"Pretty tidy, pardner. How's your nut?"

"Been easier since the Doctor put the wet rag on it soaked with some stuff or another. Oh, I shouldn't care a bit, only it keeps on swelling up like a balloon, and it'll make a fellow look such a guy."

"Hist!" said the other; "some one coming. The Doctor."

"Are you asleep in there?" said a low voice.

"Mr Bracy, sir," cried Gedge eagerly. "No, sir; we're wido."

"How are you, my lads—in much pain?"

"Oh no, sir; we're all right."

"I came just to see how you are. Good-night. Try and get to sleep."

"Yes, sir; thank ye, sir. Good-night, sir."

"Good-night."

There was a faint rustle as of feet passing over cedar needle, and then a faint choky sound as if some one in the dark were trying to swallow something.

"I like that," said Symons at last in a whisper; "makes yer feel as if yer orficers do think o' something else besides making yer be smart."

"Like it?" said Gedge huskily. "I should just think you do. Oh, I say, though, what a guy I shall look in the morning! Wish we'd got a box o' dominoes and a bit o' candle."

Chapter Five.

Boys in Action.

"Look at those boys," said Bracy the next morning on meeting his brother officers at their attractive-looking mess breakfast, spread by the native servants beneath a magnificent cedar. "Yes, they look cheery and larky enough, in spite of yesterday's experience."

"As full of fun as if this were a holiday," said another.

"Ah," said Roberts, "no one would think that we were surrounded by the enemy."

"Are we?" asked Bracy.

"Are we?—Just, hark at him.—Where have you been?"

"Having a glorious bath in that torrent. The water was as clear as crystal."

"And cold as ice," said the Major, with a shudder. "I tried it in my gutta-percha wash-basin."

"Oh yes, it was cold," said Bracy; "but it was like a shower-bath squared and cubed. It came down on my head in tubfuls, sent an electric thrill through one's muscles, and a good rub sent every trace of stiffness out of my legs. Feel as if I could walk any distance to-day."

"Well, be patient, old man," said Roberts, laughing. "I dare say you'll have a chance."

"But what's that you were saying about the enemy?"

"Why, every hill's covered with them, and they evidently mean to attack."

"Oh, very well," said Bracy, beginning upon his breakfast; "then I suppose we must fight."

There was a laugh behind him, a hand was laid upon his shoulder, and the young man looked up sharply, to see that the Colonel had come up silently over the thick carpet of cedar needles.

"Good-morning, sir."

"Good-morning—all," said the Colonel quietly. "All well?"

A chorus of assent ran round the group, and the Colonel continued:

"That's the spirit to take it in, Bracy. Of course we must fight; and the sooner the scoundrels give us the chance the better—eh, Graham?"

"Yes; we've come to give them a lesson, and they'll get it. We ought to reach the station by evening. The poor fellows there must be anxiously looking out for us."

"Yes; I've sent three different messengers to say that we shall be there by night, and I hope one out of the three will get there with the news."

"Then you mean to go on at once?"

"Of course. Did you think I meant to stay here?"

"I only thought it possible that, as this was a strong place, and we have plenty of provisions and good water, you might hold on and let them attack us."

"Oh no," replied the Colonel, taking his seat on the ground with the rest. "If we do that the enemy will take it for granted that we fear him. It must be forward, and plenty of dash."

"Yes; but while our lads are raw they would be more steady behind such a breastwork, or zareba, as we could soon make round us."

"I thought the boys were steady enough yesterday," said the Colonel quietly; "and we shall be far better off in the open than drawn out in a line on that narrow shelf."

"Oh, then we shall have a better road to-day?"

"Yes," said the Colonel, going on calmly enough with his meal. "As far as I can gather from our guides, who all agree as to the character of the road, we have wide, open valleys, with forest till within a couple of miles of Ghittah; then the mountains close in again, and we have a narrow shelf to traverse high above the bottom of a gorge."

"With plenty of places for stone-throwers?" said the Major.

"Plenty," replied the Colonel; "so you know what you have to expect, gentlemen. But I hope and believe that unless they are too closely beleaguered the little garrison at the station will make a sally to meet us, and help to clear the way."

"What a jolly old humbug Graham is!" whispered Roberts. "It's all to belittle our lads. He knew that as well as the Colonel."

"I suppose so," replied Bracy. "Ah, here's the Doctor."

For that gentleman came bustling up, smiling and nodding to all in turn.

"Morning, Doctor," said the Colonel. "What do you think of your patients this morning?"

"My patients? Seen them?"

"Yes," said the Colonel quietly. "Bracy and I had a look at them as soon as it was light."

"Getting on splendidly," said the Doctor, rubbing his hands. "Narrow escape for that boy whose cheek is scratched; an inch or two more to the left, and—"

"Ah! Bah! The old story, Doctor," said the Major contemptuously.

"Yes, sir," replied the Doctor tartly, as he fixed his eyes on the portly, middle-aged officer on the opposite side of the cloth. "You didn't take those pills, then?"

"How do you know?"

"By the way you talk," said the Doctor, chuckling, and screwing up one eye and glancing round at the rest.

"No, sir, I did not take the rubbish," said the Major angrily, as he saw every one smiling. "Was it likely that I should take them at a time like this?"

"No, I suppose not," said the Doctor coolly; "but I should. But, as I was going to say, Colonel, it's wonderful what a deal the human skull can bear. Now, for instance, that boy Gedge: a great stone comes down many hundred feet, increasing in velocity with the earth's attraction, strikes him on the head, and down he goes, insensible, with his skull crushed in, you would expect; but no: it is the old story of the strength of the arch and the difficulty in cracking an egg-shell from outside, though the beak of a tiny chicken can do it from within."

"Then there's no fracture?" said Bracy eagerly.

"Not so much as a faint crack, sir. Fellow was too thick-headed."

The Colonel sprang to his feet the next minute, for one of the officers appeared to announce the appearance of three several bodies of men descending from the distant heights.

"How near?" asked the Colonel.

"The nearest about a mile and a half, sir."

"Another live minutes for you to finish your breakfast, gentlemen, and then we march."

The bugles were sounding directly after, and in less time than their leader had given out, the officers were with their companies, the native servants had replaced the camp equipage, and at the end of the quarter of an hour the march was resumed in the most orderly way, the baggage-train being strongly guarded, and the men well rested, flushed, and eager for the coming fray.

It was like a glorious late spring morning in England, and the wide valley the regiment was traversing presented a lovely series of landscapes, backed up in front and to right and left with mighty snow-capped mountains, whose peaks looked dazzling in the early morning sun. But though every breast breathed in the crisp air with a strange sense of exhilaration, no one had eyes for anything but the two bodies of white-robed men approaching them from right and left, the third being hidden by the forest patch where the troops had bivouacked, and for which the enemy had made as soon as it was evacuated, evidently to cover their movements prior to a rush upon the rear.

The Colonel, upon seeing this, made a slight alteration in his plans, halting Captain Roberts's company with orders to close in and follow the rear of the column, thus bringing the impedimenta and servants more into the centre, the movement being performed without the slightest check to the advance, though the appearance of the bodies several hundred strong, to right and left, was very suggestive of an immediate attack.

This was delivered, evidently by an agreed-upon signal; for suddenly a tremendous burst of yelling arose, and the two unorganised crowds came rushing down upon the column, which halted, faced outward, and the next moment, while the enemy on either hand was about a couple of hundred yards off, there was a rolling volley nearly all along the line, and the white smoke began to rise, showing the two bodies of the enemy scattering and every man running for his life back towards the hills, but leaving the flowery grass dotted with patches of white, others dropping fast as they grew more distant and the wounds received began to take effect.

There was a little disorder in the centre among the servants, and mules and camels were restive as the shouting hill-men came rushing on, with their swords flashing in the sunshine, and the rattle of the musketry threatened to produce a panic; but the native servants behaved well, and were quieting their animals, when there was another suggestion of panic, as Captain Roberts suddenly exclaimed:

"Here they come, Bracy!"

For the sergeants and men thrown out in the rear a couple of hundred yards suddenly turned and fired and came running in to take their places, as the two rear companies were halted, swung out right and left in line, fixed bayonets, with the peculiar ringing, tinkling sound of metal against metal, and waited the coming of the third body of the enemy, as strong as the two which had attacked in front.

They came out from the shelter of the cedar forest with a rush, yelling furiously, each man waving his long jezail in his left hand, while a long curved tulwar, keen as a razor, flashed in his right—big, stalwart, long-bearded, dark-eyed men, with gleaming teeth and a fierce look of determination to slay painted in every feature.

It was enough to cow the stoutest-hearted, for in numbers they were enough to envelop and wipe out of existence the handful of slight-looking lads ranged shoulder to shoulder across their way.

But not a boy amongst them flinched; he only drew his breath hard as if trying to inflate his chest to the utmost with courage, and then at the word every other lad fired low, sending a hail of bullets to meet the rushing force when it was about a couple of hundred yards distant.

The men were staggered for the moment, but for the moment only, and they dashed on again, leaping over or darting aside to avoid those of their companions who staggered and fell. Then, as they reduced the distance by about one-half, the yelling grew fiercer, and the enemy came running and leaping on with increased speed.

"Fire!"

Some fifty rifles delivered their deadly contents with a roar as if only one had been discharged.

The effect was magical.

The yelling ceased, and as the cloud of soft grey smoke arose it was to show the crowded-together enemy halted in front, while those behind were pushing and struggling to get within reach to strike at the hedge of glittering bayonets, from which a third volley flashed out.

That was enough. As the smoke rose and the lads stood in double line now, ready to receive the charge upon their glittering points, the enemy was seen to be in full flight.

"Stand fast!" roared Roberts.

"Back, back!" shouted Bracy; and, sword in hand, the officers rushed along in front of their men, literally driving some of the most eager back, to re-form the line; for the sight of the flying enemy was too much for some of the younger, least-trained lads, who were in the very act of dashing forward with levelled bayonet in pursuit.

"Well done; very well done, my lads!" cried a familiar voice as the Colonel galloped back to them. "Steady, there; steady!" he shouted as he rode right along the little line and reined up his horse, to sit gazing after the flying enemy, frowning the while as he saw how many white cotton robes dotted the soil before the uninjured disappeared again in the cedar grove, from which they had delivered their attack.

"Capital, gentlemen!" he said a minute or so later; "but I did not like that unsteadiness. You must keep your men well in hand."

The next minute the orders were given, and the column resumed its march, for it was no time to think of prisoners or attending to the enemy's wounded. In fact, before the regiment was half a mile away their friends were back from the hills seeing to their dead and wounded, and gathering up their arms, greatly to the annoyance of the rear-guard lads, who one and all were troubled with longings for some of the keen tulwars to take back to England as trophies of their fight.

But the stern order "Forward!" rang in the lads' ears, and the expectation of being attacked at any time by one or other of the bodies of the enemy hovering on the hill-slopes on either side, or of a fresh dash being made upon the rear in the hope of cutting off the baggage, kept every one on the alert.

Chapter Six.

Up the Gorge.

"Yes," said Colonel Graves, as the morning glided by without incident and midday approached, with the men beginning to show traces of their hot, rapid march. "Pass the word on, for we cannot halt yet. It will cheer the lads, and have a good effect upon the enemy."

The next minute, just as many of the lads were straining their eyes forward in search of the place likely to be chosen for their midday halt, and making frequent use of their water-bottles, there were the preliminary taps on the big bass, a few vigorous rolls on the kettledrums, and the fifes began to shrill out their sharp notes in a merry air, which brightened every face at once. Some of the lads began to whistle the tune as they stepped out more briskly, and Judkins, of Captain Roberts's rear company, burst out with:

"Poor old Bill; that 'll do him good. Pity he ain't with us. Wonder how he is."

"Getting on, my lad," said Bracy, who overheard the remark; "and I don't think he'll be many days before he's back in the ranks."

Just then a cheer was given right in front, to be taken up and run right along the column, sounding as if it had been started by the men in thankfulness for Bracy's good news about Gedge, though it was only the effect produced by the band; while as soon as the air came to an end, and there was silence for a minute, another hearty cheer was given for that which was to come, the men knowing well the meaning of the silence, which was broken directly after by half-a-dozen beats of the drum, and then with a sonorous clash the brass instruments of the excellent band burst forth in a grand march, the clarion-like triumphant notes echoing softly from the hills on their right, where clusters of the enemy could be seen staring at them as if in wonder.

"Hear that, you black-muzzled old women? You in white night-gowns?" shouted Judkins. "That's better than your wheezy old squealing pipes, made to imitate our Highlanders'. I say, lads, how come they to have pipes like our fellows? Wish some one would ask Mr Bracy. I dessay he knows."

"Why don't you ask me yourself, Judkins?" said Bracy, who was close; at hand.

"Oh! Beg pardon, sir. I didn't know you could hear me."

"Don't be a sham, Judkins. You know I was just behind you."

The lad coloured like a girl, and his comrades laughed; but Bracy took no notice, and said quietly:

"I don't profess to understand these things; but the use of bagpipes for music seems to be a custom with the ancient tribes that migrated from the north of Asia and spread right away through Europe till they were stopped by the sea."

"Hullo, Bracy!" said Roberts, coming up. "Giving the men a lecture? You don't mean that the Scotch and Irish pipes had their origin out here?"

"I have read so. These hill-men have theirs right away east, and you pick up tribes of people with them at intervals till you get to Italy, where the mountaineers play them. Then it is not a very long jump to the Highlands and Ireland, where they use bellows instead of blowing into the bag."

"A discourse on wind," said Roberts quietly. "I want something more solid. How soon are we going to halt for a feed and rest?"

The bugle rang out soon after, for they readied a broad stream of bright clear water, and in a loop of this, which offered itself as a capital protection for two-thirds of the distance round their temporary camp, the regiment was halted, and with strong videttes thrown out along the unprotected portion, the men fell out, when a hasty meal was eaten, and the men ordered to lie down for half-an-hour, with their arms ready, so that they could spring to their places at the first alarm.

When the bugle rang out it was at the end of the hour's rest, and, thoroughly refreshed, the march was recommenced, the men stepping out to the merry strains of a favourite song, which was repeated in chorus as the band ceased playing; and the birds that had been hovering near were the only objects visible when the halting-place was vacated, though the thick woods on the hill-slopes on either side were felt to be lull of the enemy.

"Haven't given them all they wanted, have we?" said Roberts as they tramped towards where through the clear air the sides of the valley could be seen closing in and growing higher and more jagged of outline.

"No," said Bracy thoughtfully. "It will take something more than a brush like that to beat them off. We shall have our work ready for us yonder where the Colonel said the track rose again to continue like a shelf right away to Ghittah."

"I suppose so. Well, good luck to us, and may we have no more casualties."

"Amen," said Bracy. "I wish, though, if we are to have a sharp encounter, we could have it now we're fresh, instead of just at the end of a heavy day's march."

"Soldiers have to fight when the time comes, and they can't pick and choose, I suppose. But never mind; the lads won't be done up, for this is easy marching. It is not too hot, and we have plenty of good water. I say, I suppose we shall follow this stream right away now?"

"No doubt. It must come down from the snow-mountains, and through that gorge yonder."

"Yes, the one that seems so near, and does not get a bit nearer. It's capital, our having this river on our right flank, for it would be a nice job for the enemy if they tried to ford it."

Roberts was right, for every mile of their forward journey made the river a greater protection, the torrent growing fiercer and the banks rocky in the extreme, and for the most part nearly perpendicular, till at last it was a good fifty feet down to the water's level, so that it ceased to be of use for refreshment to the men.

At last the sides of the valley began to close in more rapidly, and their track became steeper, till all at once they were brought up short by what seemed to be the mighty gates of the gorge, up which they could see but a short distance, for it turned off to the right. But there, plainly enough in the western sunshine, crossing the end in a steep slope, was a part of the terrace-like path they were to follow, while on their left was its commencement, one heavy stone-strewn track, which in places rose like a series of gigantic steps.

Here a halt was called, and the men lay down for a brief rest, while the perilous-looking path in front was reconnoitred first by the officers with their glasses, the eminence above the track being carefully searched for hidden bodies of the enemy ready to commence their attack as before by thrusting off the stones which hung aloft ready to fall, almost at a touch.

But there was no sign of danger apparent. A great eagle was gliding here and there in the mouth of the wild ravine, out of which came the deep roar of the river in a series of foaming cascades; while no sign was visible of the enemy in the rear, and the officers soon came to the conclusion that there was nothing to fear from their left unless there was some pass known to their foes by which the mountains high above the shelf-like track could be reached.

"We're to form the rear-guard again, lads," said Roberts, who had just received his orders. "Did it so well before, the Colonel says," he added a little bitterly.

"Well, if we want more fighting we ought to have been sent in advance," replied Bracy, "for I feel convinced that there's something unpleasant waiting for us as soon as we enter that black rift."

"Most likely," said Roberts. "The Major leads again, but they're going to send half a company on first scouting. Yes," he said impatiently, "there must be something bad ready for us. The enemy would never be such fools as to let us go through there. Why, Bracy, give us our company, and twenty-four hours to prepare, and we could hold that place against a thousand."

"Yes, I suppose we could."

"Well, what are we waiting for?" cried Roberts impatiently. "It doesn't want above two hours to sunset, and to be caught there with the night coming on— Ugh!"

"There they go!" cried Bracy excitedly, as the active lads selected as scouts began to ascend the track in the lightest order; and their progress was watched with the keenest anxiety as they rose more and more into the full view of the regiment, apparently meeting with no obstacles to their progress, and showing the track to be followed by the waiting party below.

Just then the Colonel rode back to where the young officers were standing.

"This track is so narrow, Roberts," he said, "that your company will be ample to protect the rear; so I shall trust entirely to you. If we are to be attacked it will be in front; of that I am convinced, though probably the attacking will be on our part, for sooner or later we shall find a rough hill-fort, strongly held."

"Hope we shan't fall into some trap, sir," said Roberts earnestly.

"I hope not," said the Colonel, turning his horse and moving forward, but only to turn his head again.

"It will be stiff work for the train," he said; "but they must do it. You will help to keep the baggage-men well up to their work, for I mean to get through this pass to-night."

"Nice job," said Roberts bitterly. "We shall have the enemy behind us, stirring us up, and we shan't be able to get on without pricking up the mules and camels."

"No firing yet," said Bracy, without heeding the foreboding remarks of his companion. "They're getting well on. Ah! there goes the advance."

For a bugle rang out, its notes being repeated again and again with wondrous clearness from the faces of the black-looking barren rocks on high, and the scene became an animated picture to the men of the rear-guard, who lay on their arms, resting, while the regiment filed up the track, two abreast, giving life to the gloomy gorge, which grew and grew till the baggage animals added their quota to the scene.

"At last!" cried Roberts, as their own turn came, and after a long and careful search backward from a point of vantage with his glass, he gave the word, and his rested lads began to mount eagerly, but with every one keeping an eye aloft for the blocks of stone they expected to come crashing down, but which never came any more than did the sharp echoing rifle-fire announcing the attack upon some rough breastwork across the shelf.

It was a toilsome, incessant climb for an hour, and then the highest point was gained, the men cheering loudly as they clustered on the shelf, nowhere more than a dozen feet wide, while the rock fell perpendicularly below them for over a thousand feet to where the river foamed and roared, one terrible race of leaping cascades.

There had not been a single casualty with the mules, and the track, in spite of its roughness, was better for the camels in its freedom from loose stones than the former one they had traversed.

And now their way was fairly level for a time, and the descent of the path gentle when it did begin going down towards the river, which from the slope seemed to rise. But they could see only a little way forward, from the winding nature of the gorge, which now grew more and more narrow.

"Not so far to fall," said Bracy coolly, "if we do come to a fight."

"Deep enough to break our necks," grumbled Roberts. "Here, I say, it will be dark soon; look how black it looks below. I wish those fellows had not cheered; it was like telling the enemy we were coming on, for they must be round the corner yonder. There—look!"

As he spoke one of the men in front suddenly turned and pointed to where the gorge was at its narrowest.

"Yes, we can see them, my lad. Keep a sharp lookout to the rear," he shouted to the men behind. "We shall be hearing from them now, Bracy, for, take my word for it, they're flocking along the path. Well, we shall have to fight in the dark, old man, like rats, in this confounded trap."

"Very well," said Bracy between his teeth, as he took out and examined the chambers of his revolver, before he replaced it in its leather holster; "if the dogs do come on I mean to bite."

Chapter Seven.

Boots for Booty.

"Well, you needn't bite this time, old fellow," cried Roberts, with a sigh of relief, as a burst of cheers arose faintly from the front once more, to be taken up and run down the column, even the native mule and camel drivers joining in, till it reached the company which formed the rear-guard. "What does this mean?" cried Bracy excitedly. "That we're too far back to know what is going on in the front. Those are not enemies, but friends."

"What! people from the station come to meet us?"

"That's the right nail, struck well on the head, old chap; and I'm jolly glad of it, for I feel more like feeding than fighting, I can tell you."

"Roberts, old fellow, this seems too good to be true," cried Bracy joyfully.

"But for once in a way it is true. Push on, my lads; there'll be something better than bullets for a welcome to-night."

Roberts was right, for upon the last of the weary beasts bearing the baggage reaching the end of the defile, the young officers found themselves face to face with a couple of companies of their fellow-countrymen, bronzed, toil-worn looking men, many of them bearing the marks of hardly-healed sword-cuts, and looking overstrained and thin as if from anxiety and overwork, but one and all with their faces lit up by the warmth of the welcome they were ready to give the regiment which had come to their help.

The bandsmen played their best as they led the way across the lovely amphitheatre into which the gorge had opened out, towards where, high up along the northern side, and upon the rocky bank, stood the station and town of Ghittah. The river, which here flowed smooth and deep, seemed as if of ruddy golden metal, as it glistened in the rays of the sun dipping down behind the snow-mountains which shut them in. And every now and then the cheery echoing strains of the band were pretty well drowned by the cheers and counter-cheers of the relievers and the relieved.

Bracy felt his breast swell with pleasure at the warmth of the welcome, for the fraternisation was complete, the war-worn veterans seeming as if they could not make enough of the raw striplings marching by their sides towards where the British colours could be seen floating over the grim castle-like place that had been the home of one of the old hill-chiefs till the district was added to the British dominions. But look which way he would, the young officer could see no trace of the enemy.

Birds of a feather flock together naturally, and before half a mile had been covered a tall, thin, boyish-looking officer, with a star of merit in the shape of a series of strips of diachylon upon his brow, gravitated towards the rear-guard and suddenly joined their ranks, holding out and shaking hands with the new-comers.

"How are you?" he cried. "How are you? I say, don't look at a fellow like that. I'm an awful scarecrow, I know; but I'm Drummond—Tom Drummond of ours."

"Oh, you look right enough," cried Bracy merrily. "Only a bit of the polish rubbed off."

"And a bit chipped," said Roberts, laughing.

"Eh? Oh, this!" cried their new friend. "Getting better, though, now. Doesn't improve a fellow."

"Doesn't it?" cried Bracy. "I should be proud of such an order."

"It's very good of you to say so," said the young subaltern, with his eyes glistening.

"How did you get it?" asked Roberts.

"Oh, in a scrimmage with those treacherous beasts. They'd got me and about a dozen of the lads in a corner among the rocks, and it was either stand still and be cut up or make a dash with the bayonet. There were about fifty of 'em."

"So you made a dash?"

"Yes, but only six of us got through, and all damaged. One big fellow was nourishing a sharp tulwar, and he was in the act of cutting down one of my fellows, and I went at him to try and save the poor lad, but I was too late. The great brute cut him down and rushed at me."

"Well?" said Bracy, for the thin, boyish-looking officer stopped, and looked red.

"Oh, I gave point, and got well home. I put all my strength into it, and it brought me so close that instead of having my head split by his blade I had the hilt on my forehead here. It struck in a nasty place, but being, as my old Latin coach said, awfully thick-skulled, the pommel of the tulwar didn't break through. I say, though—never mind that—have either of you fellows a spare pair of boots? I can swap a lot of loot with you—fancy swords and guns and a chief's helmet—for them. Look;

47

I've come down to this."

He laughed and held up one leg, the lower part of which was bound in puttees, while the foot was covered with a bandaged rawhide sandal.

"Not smart on parade," said Bracy, laughing, "but good to keep off corns."

"Yes," said the subaltern; "but I'm blest if they keep out chilblains. Oh, crumpets, how my feet do itch of a night by the fire."

"Well, I should say my boots are about your size. Roberts's wouldn't lit. He has such big, ugly feet."

"Come, I like that, Bracy. Hang it all! my trotters look liliputian beside his."

"Now," said Bracy mockingly; "but wait till you can see Drummond's feet. Look here," he added, turning to the subaltern; "you have a pair of Roberts's too; they'll do for goloshes."

"I don't care how old they are, so long as they are boots."

"All right, old fellow; we'll set you up with anything we've got," said Bracy.

"Bless you, my children!" cried the young officer. "Bless you! Never mind the dramatic business. Oh, I say, we are all glad you've come."

"You've been in a tight corner, then?"

"Tight? We've lost a third of our number, and were beginning to think the Government was going to let us be quite wiped off the slate. Here, I feel like a schoolboy again, and want to cheer."

"All right; cheer, then," cried Bracy, smiling, and clapping the speaker on the shoulder as if he had known him for years.

"No; hoarse as a crow now, and I want my breath to talk. I say, we have been sharp set. We began to feel like the talking parrot who was plucked by the monkey, ready to say, 'Oh, we have been having such a time!' Those Dwats are beggars to fight."

"We've found that out—that is, when they can take you at a disadvantage," said Roberts.

"Ah, that's their idea of manoeuvring," said Drummond. "They can tight, though. We must have killed hundreds, but they come on all the same. There were thousands of them all about the hills here yesterday."

"But where are they now?" asked Bracy.

"They melted away like snow last night and this morning, just when we were expecting an assault on the old fort yonder, which we thought would be final."

"Final?"

"Yes; we were getting dead beat. That's what makes us all so fond of you."

"I see," said Bracy, who noticed a hysterical vibration in the youth's voice.

"That was the first inkling we got of your coming."

"What! Didn't you hear from our messengers?" said Roberts.

"Didn't they get through?" cried Bracy.

"Get through? No. They wouldn't let any messengers get through. Never mind. You've all come, and if we don't have a jollification to-night my name's something else."

"Then you're all right for provisions?"

"Oh yes, for some time to come. Ammunition was his weak point. We've blazed away till the men's barrels have been hot."

"It seems as if the men of your regiment are beggars to fight too," said Bracy dryly, "judging by the appearance of some of you."

"Fight? Obliged to," said the subaltern, laughing. "Talk about practising the art of war; we ought to pass any examination. But, joking apart, it has been an awful time for the poor women and children."

"Ah!" cried Bracy. "You have women and children yonder?"

"Yes, any number, bless 'em! The ladies and the men's wives have worked like slaves—hospital work, you know. As to our doctor, he'll be mad with joy to meet yours to share the work with him. Ah! there they go."

For just then a burst of cheering came from the grim walls of the old fort, which were lined by its occupants; and mingled with the enthusiastic cries came the strains of music.

"You have your band, then?" said Roberts.

"Bits of it," said the subaltern dryly. "The brass instruments are battered horribly; and as for the wood, they are all cracked and bandaged like wounded men; while the drums are nearly all as tubby as tom-toms, through the men having mended them with badly-cured goat-skins. I say, though, talk about goat-skins, I ought to have added sheep."

"Why?" said Bracy.

"Are you fellows fond of shooting?"

"Yes," said Bracy eagerly. "Is it good up here?"

"Grand, when there's a chance of the shooting being all on your side."

"The beggars try to stalk you, then, sometimes?" said Roberts.

"Sometimes? Nearly always."

"But what have you got here—tiger?"

"Never saw one. Plenty of bear."

"All! that will do."

"Chamois-like deer, goats, and splendid mountain sheep. Pheasants too. Ah! I can give you some glorious pheasant shooting. Here they come. Oh, I say, what a pity for the old man to march our poor ragged Jacks out to see you! They'll look—"

"Glorious," cried Bracy. "I should be proud of being one of your regiment. By George; what shrimps our lads seem beside them!"

"Your lads look perfection," cried the subaltern enthusiastically. "Don't you run them down. If you'd been looking despairingly for help for a whole month you'd feel as I do. Here, I must trot back to my chiefs. Just fancy; my captain and lieutenant are both down, *non com*, and I'm in command of my company. Isn't it disgusting for the poor fellows? But they behave very well. So glad to have met you, dear boys. Ta-ta for the present. We've got a splendid feed ready for you all, and we shall meet then.—Don't forget about the boots, old chap. You shall have these to present to the British Museum. Label 'em 'Officer's Foot-gear. End of Nineteenth Century. Rare.'"

The subaltern trotted off, and with the regiment going half-mad and cheering wildly in response to the cries of welcome which greeted them, the boyish ranks marched on, solid and stiff, for a time, their rifles sloped regularly, and step kept in a way which made even Sergeant Gee smile with satisfaction. But directly after, as caps and helmets, mingled with women's handkerchiefs, began to wave from the walls, the strong discipline of the corps was quite forgotten, helmets came out of their proper places and were mounted on the ends of rifles, to be carried steadily at the slope, to be held up on high at arm's-length, and even danced up and down, in the wild joy felt by the whole body, from the Colonel down to the meanest bugle-boy, that they had arrived in time to succour the brave and devoted men, marched out of the dark gateway and formed up in two lines for their friends to pass in between them. Hardly a dark face, lined, stern, and careworn, was without something to show in the shape of injury; while nearer the gate there was a body of about two-score badly wounded and bandaged men who had hobbled or been carried out, ready to add their faint share of cheering to that of their comrades.

As Roberts and Bracy led their company towards the gate, and the young officers caught sight of the ladies standing in a group ready to greet them with outstretched hands, one of them—never mind which —perhaps it was Bracy—felt half-suffocated, while the thin, careworn faces, many of them wet with the coursing tears, looked dim and distorted as if seen through bad spectacles on a wet day; and when, after having his hand shaken a score of times and listening to fervent greetings and blessings, he got through the gateway to the great inner court, where the baggage and pack-mules, camels, and the rest were packed together in company with the native servants, the said one—as aforesaid, never mind which—said to himself:

"Thank goodness that's over! If it had lasted much longer I should have made a fool of myself. I never felt anything like it in my life."

"Bracy, old chap," said Roberts just then, "we mustn't forget about that fellow's boots. I've a pair, too, as soon as I can get at my traps. I say, I know you've got a mother, but have you any sisters?"

"Yes; two."

"I've three. Now, can you explain to me why it was that as soon as I was marching by those poor women yonder I could think of nothing but my people at home?"

"For the same reason that I did," replied Bracy rather huskily. "Human nature; but thank Heaven, old man, that they're not here."

"Oh, I don't know," said Roberts thoughtfully. "It would be very nice to see them, and I know my dear old mother would have been very proud to see us march in. My word, this has been a day!"

"Yes, and here we are. Shall we ever get away?"

"Of course we shall. But, hullo! what does that mean?"

Bracy turned at the same moment, for rather faintly, but in a pleasant tenor voice, there came out of a long box-like ambulance gharry, borne on two mules in long shafts at either end:

"When Johnny comes marching home again—Hurrah!"

And from another voice a repetition of the cheer:

"Hurrah! Hurrah! When Johnny comes marching home again, Hurrah! Hurrah!"

"Ah, Mr Bracy, sir, just having a bit of a sing-song together."

"Why, Gedge, my lad, how are you—how are you getting on?"

"I don't look in, sir, and I'll tell yer. Doctor says it's all right, but my blessed head keeps on swelling still. I don't believe I shall ever get my 'elmet on agen. My mate here, though, is getting on swimming."

"That's right. You'll lie up in hospital for a hit and soon be well."

"Orspital, sir? Yes; but it's longing to be back in barracks, tents, or the ranks as worries me. But never say die, sir. We've got here.—How do, Captain? Thank ye for asking. Yes, sir; getting on, sir. We've got here with on'y us two knocked over. Now then, sir, what next?"

"Yes, Gedge," said the young officer thoughtfully; "what next?"

"I'll tell you," said Roberts cheerily; "find our traps and that fellow's hoots."

Chapter Eight.

In Quarters.

There was rest and refreshment in the old fort of Ghittah that night such as the regiment had not enjoyed since their march up-country; and to have seen the occupants of the stronghold, no one could have imagined that a few hours before the beleaguered were in a state of despair.

But they had cause for rejoicing, since, after a month's brave resistance, with heavy losses, they were now strengthened by the presence of nearly a thousand light, active young fellows, perfectly new to warfare, but well officered, in a high state of discipline, and eager to prove themselves against the enemy, whatever the odds.

There was plenty of room for the new-comers, for the stronghold was a little town in itself, and the regiment shook itself down into its new quarters as quickly as it would have formed camp out in the upon, so that the men paraded the next morning fresh and ready for anything; the senior Colonel inspecting the grand addition to his force, while his own men, after busy efforts, showed up in very different guise to that of the previous day, the thin and gaunt seeming to have plumped out during the night, while the officers' ladies showed that they had not quite forgotten how to dress.

Over the mess breakfast, which was had in common with the officers of the garrison, the new-comers had been made well acquainted with the enemy's tactics, and warned of the suddenness of the attacks made and attempts at surprise, so that they might be well prepared. They had already heard the result of the council of war held by the seniors of the two regiments, and were prepared to take over nearly all the duty, so as to give the harassed, worn-out regiment a rest.

Then the parade was held in due form, the lads of the new regiment mounted guard, and their officers made a tour of inspection afterwards with their new friends, who pointed out the strength and feebleness of the old fort.

The latter predominated, especially on the side of the river, and there were plenty of weak spots where Colonel Graves saw at a glance how easily an active body of mountaineers might scale the lower rocks of the mighty clump upon which the fort was built and mount to the ramparts, and unless the defence was strong there the place must fall.

"It tells well for the brave efforts you have made," said Colonel Graves to his brother in rank. "I should propose throwing up an additional wall at two of these spots—walls well loopholed for musketry."

"I have proposed it, and intended to do it," said Colonel Wrayford; "but it has been impossible. The enemy has kept us too thoroughly upon the *qui vive*."

"Well, there will be an opportunity now," said Colonel Graves as he stepped up on to an open place on the wall and began to sweep the mountain-slopes with his glass.

"See anything of them?" asked Colonel Wrayford.

"Nothing. Are they well in hiding?"

"Possibly. I do not understand our not having had a visit from them before now. We generally have their white-coats streaming down those ravines in two parties. It looks as if your coming had scared them away."

"That's too good to expect," said Colonel Graves, laughing. "They'll come, sure enough, and when least expected, no doubt. So much the better, so that we can give them a good lesson to teach them to behave with respect towards Her Majesty's forces, for this place is to be held at all hazard."

"Yes; of course," said Colonel Wrayford rather bitterly. "Well, it has been held."

"And bravely," said Colonel Graves, bowing, with a show of deference, towards his senior.

"Thank you," said the latter simply. "We have done our best."

He turned away, to begin using his glass, sweeping the different ravines—dark, savage-looking gorges which disembogued upon the smiling, garden-like expanse on both sides of the river, and seeming strangely in contrast, with their stony sides, to the tree-besprinkled verdure and lovely groves of the little plain not more than a mile long by half that space wide.

"Hah! I thought the visit would not be long deferred," said Colonel Wrayford, lowering the glass and pointing to a thin line of white figures slowly coming into sight and winding down a zigzag path on one side of the gorge, through which the river came down from the mountains beyond.

"I see," said Colonel Graves; "but I was watching those ravines to right and left."

"Yes; the enemy is changing his tactics to-day. You see, he does not mean us to have much rest."

The bugles rang out at the first appearance of the enemy, and the walls were manned with a strength to which they had been foreign; and as the two Colonels walked round and supervised the arrangements, the senior asked whether the new-comers could shoot.

"Admirably," said Colonel Graves, and then, with a smile—"at the target; they have to prove what they can really do now."

"They will have every opportunity, and from behind strong walls."

Meanwhile the white-robed enemy came streaming down to the plain in the most fearless manner, till they were well within shot, and still they came on.

"This seems strange," said Colonel Wrayford; "they have generally begun firing before this."

"They look more like friends than enemies," observed Colonel Graves.

"They may look so," replied the other as he scanned the advancing force, "but we have no friends among these tribes. They are all deeply imbued with the Mussulman's deadly hatred of the Christian, and only when firmly held down by force do they submit to the stronger power. Unfortunately they have broken out, and we have had enough to do to hold our own, while the very fact of one tribe boldly shutting us in has made half-a-dozen others forget their own enmity among themselves and come to their aid."

Meanwhile Captain Roberts's company occupied a strong position along a curtain defending the great gate, and the lads were all in a state of eager expectation of the order to fire.

"It's our turn now, Sergeant," said one of the youngest-looking. "I could pick off that chap in front before he knew where he was."

"Silence, sir!" said the Sergeant shortly; and then looking to right and left, he gave a general admonition:

"Less talking in the ranks."

"Yah!" whispered the lad who had been snubbed. "Why don't they make him curnel?"

"See Drummond just now?" said Bracy, where he and his companion stood together.

"Just a glance," replied Roberts.

"Why, he came close by you."

"Yes; but my attention was taken up by his boots—yours, I mean. I never saw a fellow look so conscious and proud of being well shod before."

"Hullo! What does this mean?" said Bracy. "Not an attack, surely? My word! that's brave; one, three—six of them. Why, Roberts, the cheek of it! They're coming to order us to surrender."

"Well, it will be exercise for them, for we shan't. We'll let them give up if they like."

"I say, look!" continued Bracy, as half-a-dozen of the well-built fellows came on alone, making for the gates. The officers scanned them with their glasses, and noted that their thickly-quilted cotton robes were of the whitest, and of line texture, while each wore about his waist a fine cashmere shawl stuck full of knives and supporting a curved tulwar in a handsome scabbard. "I say," cried Bracy, "what dandies! These must be chiefs."

Whatever they were, they made straight for the gates, and the two Colonels walked down to meet them.

"Keep a sharp lookout up there, Captain Roberts. You command the approach. Are these men quite alone?"

"Quite, sir, as far as I can see."

"Can you make out any strong body stealthily approaching, Mr Bracy?"

"No, sir; they seem to be quite alone."

"Be on the alert for a rush, and fire at once if you see anything.— You will have the gates opened, I presume?" continued Colonel Graves.

"Oh yes; it is an embassage, and they will expect to enter the place. Send for the two interpreters."

A couple of lithe-looking, dark-eyed hill-men came forward at once, the gates were thrown open, and the party of six stepped in, looking smiling and proud, ready to salute the two officers, who stood forward a little in advance of half a company of men with fixed bayonets.

Salutes were exchanged, and in a brief colloquy the eldest of the party, a smiling fellow with an enormous black beard, announced through one of the interpreters that he was the chief of the Red Dwats, come with his men to meet the English Captain and tell him that he and his people wore the most staunch friends the famous white Queen had, from there to the sources of the great river, the Indus.

Colonel Wrayford replied that he was glad to hear it, and if the chief and his people were faithful to Her Majesty's sway they would always be protected.

The chief said that he was and always would be faithful, and that he hoped the great white Queen would remember that and send them plenty of the guns which loaded at the bottoms instead of the tops, and boxes of powder and bullets to load them with. Then he would be able to fight for Her Majesty against the other chiefs who hated her, because they were all dogs and sons of Shaitan.

"Roberts, old fellow," whispered Bracy, high up on the wall, "I could swear I saw one of those fellows leading the attack made upon us from the cedar grove."

"Shouldn't be a bit surprised, dear boy. Perhaps he has repented and has come to say he is good now and will never do so any more. Can you understand any of his lingo?"

"Not a word. It doesn't seem a bit like Hindustani. What's that?"

"The Colonel asked what was the meaning of the attack made upon us yesterday."

"Ah, then he knows that fellow?" whispered Bracy.

"No doubt. The old man's pretty keen, and if that chap means treachery, I'm afraid he didn't get up early enough this morning if he has come to take in old Graves."

"I'm sure that's one of them. I had him at the end of my binocular, and I know him by that scar on his cheek."

"They all seem to have a good deal of cheek," said Roberts coolly.

"Look here; I'd better warn the Colonel."

"No need, old fellow. He knows what he's about. These niggers are precious cunning, but it's generally little child's deceit, and that's as transparent as a bit of glass. Don't be alarmed. Old Graves can see through any tricks of that kind, and Wrayford hasn't been on this station a twelvemonth without picking up a few native wrinkles."

"Pst! Listen to what they're saying."

"Can't: it's rude," said Roberts.

"Not at a time like this, when perhaps men's and women's lives are at stake."

"All right; let's listen, then. What's the boss saying?"

"I don't like it, Wrayford. These are part of the tribe that tried to destroy us as we came up yesterday, and now they find we have escaped them they want to make friends."

"Well, we want the tribes to be friendly."

"Yes, but not with sham friendliness, to lull us into security, and then, after waiting their time, to join their fellows in a general massacre."

"I am afraid you are misjudging our visitors here," said Colonel Wrayford quietly.

"I am sure I am not. I swear I saw that dark fellow with the cut on his cheek leading a charge."

"There; what did I tell you?" whispered Bracy.

"And what did I tell you about the old man seeing as far into a millstone as is necessary for being on the safe side?"

"Yes; and I am glad his observation was so keen."

"He's all right, old fellow; but hist! what is it? Ah, that's right.

58

Wrayford is glad to hear that the chief of the Red Dwats is so friendly to the Queen, and his request for arms and ammunition shall be sent to the proper quarter. Now, then, what does he say to that?"

One of the interpreters spoke to say that the great chief of the Red Dwats would camp in the valley above, so as to be close at hand if any of the sons of Shaitan who had been molesting the fort before should dare to approach again. They were all gone back now to their own valleys in fear, through his approach, and now the two great English Generals and their men might sleep in peace.

"Thank you. Bravo! Encore, Sambo!" said Roberts softly. "Going? Pray remember me to all at home."

"Ugh!" raged out Bracy below his breath; "if ever treachery was plainly marked upon a smiling, handsome face, it is there in that scoundrel's. Roberts, we must never trust these men within our guard."

"Most certainly not, old fellow; but I suppose we must let them go back in safety, like the noble ambassadors they are."

"What is going on now?" said Bracy. "Why, they're shaking hands with Colonel Wrayford, English fashion. Surely he is not going to trust them?"

"Seems as if he is," replied Roberts softly as the young men stood gazing down at the party below. "Perhaps he knows the native character better than we do, and thinks it's all right."

"Well, I don't," said Bracy shortly, "young as I am. Those fellows have come as spies, and I'm more and more convinced that they are the set who harassed us as we came."

"I begin to think you are right, old man," said Roberts.

"Well, of all—That scoundrel is going to offer to shake hands with Graves!"

"No, he isn't," replied Roberts softly. "Doesn't like the look of the old man's eyes. Made a sort of shy at him. Now they're off, after picking up all that they could about our strength and position. Well, it isn't right, perhaps, for us to pull our superior's actions to pieces; but I don't think Wrayford is right."

"And Graves seems to think as you do," said Bracy thoughtfully as he watched the departure of the chiefs. "Look! those fellows are not missing much with their rolling eyes. I wonder what they think of our lads. The poor fellows don't show up very well against these stout hill-men."

"They showed up well enough yesterday," said Roberts tartly. "Pooh! What has size got to do with it? Well, I'm glad they've gone; but I should like to know what they are saying to one another."

"Talking about the strength of the gates, you may depend, and whether this would be a good place to make their first attack when they come to put the garrison to the sword," said Bracy slowly.

"Well, you are a cheerful sort of a fellow for a companion," said Roberts, laughing.

"That's what they came for, cheerful or not."

"Perhaps so; but coming to do a thing and doing it are two different matters. Well, the show is over, and we may come down. Let's go and see about getting our new quarters a little more ship-shape. I want to see what the men are doing."

"Not yet," said Bracy. "I want to watch these fellows back to their own men, to see what they are about."

"You can't tell from this distance."

"Not much; but my glass is very powerful, and I want to try and judge from their actions what is going on yonder."

"All right; I'll stop with you."

Two-thirds of the guards mounted were dismissed, and soon after, the walls and towers were pretty well deserted. The two young officers remained, however, Captain Roberts dreamily watching the wondrous panorama of snowy mountains spreading out to the north as far as the eye could reach, while Bracy sat with his double glass carefully focussed and resting upon the stone parapet, watching the departing chiefs, who strode away looking proud and haughty, and apparently without holding any communication with one another till they were well on their way, when Bracy noted that they suddenly began to talk with a good deal of animation.

Bracy kept up his watch till they reached their followers, who closed round them in a very excited way.

It was just then that Roberts roused himself from his reverie.

"Hullo, there!" he cried; "'most done? Can't make out anything, can you?"

"Yes; there's a regular mob of fighting-men crowding round those fellows, and they're holding a regular meeting."

"Good little glass. I say, old man, I'll swop with you. Mine's a bigger and better-looking binoc. than yours. Anything else?"

"One of the party—I think it's the one with the scar on his face, but I can't be sure—"

"Can't you tell him?"

"Not at this distance."

"Then I won't swop. It's not such a good glass as I thought. Well, what next?"

"He's telling his experiences, and the beggars are lancing about, roaring with laughter."

"Can you see that?"

"Yes, quite plainly."

"Then I think I will swop, after all. Can't hear what they say, I suppose?"

"Hardly."

"Humph! Not so good a glass, then, as Pat's, that brought the church so near that he could hear the singing. Go on."

"He's gesticulating. Now he's marching up and down stiffly like Graves did while the conference was going on."

"Well, of all the impudence! But no flam: can you really make out all that?"

"Perfectly. Now he is taking off his puggree and pretending to take a handkerchief out and mopping his bald head."

"Like Wrayford does. Why, the scoundrel stood as stiff as a poker when he was here and let the others do the talking."

"Yes, while he was studying his part. Now they're laughing again and stamping about and holding their sides. He is going through everything he noted for their amusement, and telling them what absurd-looking people the English are."

"Oh yes," said Roberts; "we're a very humorous lot, we British— very amusing indeed, but best at a distance, for we're rather prickly, and easily induced to make use of our knives. What next?"

"The show's over; and look—you can see that?"

"What! that flashing in the sunshine?"

"Yes; every man has drawn his sword and is waving it in the air. He must have said something which excited them."

"Made 'em all draw and swear that they'd cut us to pieces and fling us in the river, I dare say."

"Oh, there you are!" cried a familiar voice, and the tall, thin subaltern hurried to their side. "I say, what do you think of that for a fit?" he cried, stopping, and then holding out one foot. "Just as if they had been made for me."

"If you say any more about them I'll take them away again," said Bracy, smiling.

"Then mum it is, for I wouldn't be so cruel to my poor plantigrades. They haven't been so happy and comfortable for months. Watching those Dwats?"

"I've been doing so," said Bracy, closing his glass and returning it to its case. "What do you think of them?"

"Think they're a set of humbugs. They've come here hunting for information and pretending to be friends; and the worst of it is, old Wrayford believes in them."

"Nonsense! He couldn't be so weak," cried Roberts.

"Oh, couldn't he? But he could. He hasn't been the same man since he was cut down about a month ago. Poor old man! he's as brave as a lion still, but he has done several weak things lately which none of us like. What do you think that thick-lipped, black-bearded ruffian proposed?"

"I don't know," said Bracy eagerly.

"To send on a couple of hundred of his cut-throats to help to defend the fort against the enemy."

"He proposed that?" cried Roberts.

"To be sure he did."

"But Colonel Wrayford," said Bracy, "he declined, of course—at once?"

"No, he didn't. He hesitated, and told your old man that an ally would be so valuable, and that it would not do, hemmed in as we are, to offend a powerful chief who desired to be friendly."

"But that's absurd," cried Roberts.

"Of course it is," replied Drummond. "The only way to deal with these fellows is to make 'em afraid of you, for they're as treacherous as they are proud. But there, it's all right."

"All right, when the senior Colonel here temporises with the enemy!"

"It was only one of his weak moments. He won't do anything of that kind. He'll talk it over with your old man and think better of it. Besides, we shouldn't let him."

"Oh, come, that's a comfort," said Roberts, glancing at Bracy, with a twinkle in his eye.

"Yes, I see," said Drummond, "you're chaffing because I bounced a bit; but I'm blessed if you don't have to bounce up here in the mountains if you want to hold your own. I should be nowhere amongst these hill-niggers if I didn't act as if I thought I was the biggest pot under the sun. That's one reason why I was so anxious about my boots. Why, if it hadn't been for you two I couldn't have shown my face before that party this morning. I wouldn't have had them see me with my feet bandaged up like they were for anything. It would have been lowering the dignity of Her Majesty's service in the eyes of the heathen."

"Of course," said Bracy, smiling; "but never mind that. You don't believe in these fellows, then?"

"Oh yes, I do."

"But just now you said—"

"What I say now, that they're a set of impostors, pretending to be friendly so as to see what your regiment was like and how the defences looked."

"There, Roberts!"

"All right, dear boy. Well, when they come again we must show them our boy-regiment, and how they've improved with the excellent practice we can make in firing."

"That's the way," said Drummond cheerily. "They'll soon come again with two or three other tribes, for they've all made up their minds to have us out of this old fort, palace, or whatever they call it."

"And we shan't go—eh?" said Bracy, with a quaint look in his eyes.

"Most decidedly not," replied Drummond. "Now then, you're not on duty. Come and have a look round. Hullo! this is your doctor, isn't it?"

"Yes," said Bracy.

"Don't like the cut of him," said Drummond. "He's doing it again."

"Doing what?"

"Same as he did first time we met—last night at the mess— looking me up and down as if thinking about the time when he'll have me to cut up and mend."

"Well, my dear boys," said the Doctor, coming up, rubbing his hands. "Ah! Mr Drummond, I think? Met you last night. Glad to know you. Come, all of you, and have a look at my hospital quarters. Splendid place for the lads. Light, airy, and cool. They can't help getting well."

"But I thought you had no patients, sir," said Drummond.

"Oh yes, two that we brought with us; and if Colonel Wrayford is willing, I propose that your wounded should be brought across, for it's a far better place than where they are. Come on, and I'll show you."

"Thanks, Doctor; I'm just going to see the Colonel," said Roberts.

"That's a pity. You must come without him, then, Bracy."

"I really can't, Doctor; not now. I am going with Roberts."

"Humph! that's unfortunate. Mr Drummond would like to see, perhaps, how we arrange for our men who are down?"

"Most happy, Doctor—"

"Hah!"

"But I am going with my friends here."

"Standing on ceremony—eh, gentlemen?" said the Doctor, smiling quickly and taking a pinch of snuff. "Well, we'll wait a bit. I dare say you will neither of you be so much occupied when you are once brought in to me. I thought perhaps you would like to go over the place first."

Bracy turned and took hold of the Doctor's arm.

"All right, Doctor," he said, laughing. "You had us there on the hip. I'll come."

"What, and keep the Colonel waiting?"

"We can go there afterwards," said Bracy quietly. "Come, Roberts, you can't hold back now."

"Not going to, old fellow. There, Doctor, I beg your pardon. I'll come."

"Granted, my dear boy," said the Doctor quietly. "There, Mr Drummond, you'll have to go alone."

"Not I," said the subaltern, smiling. "I'll come and take my dose with them."

"Good boy!" said the Doctor, smiling.

"I suppose you have not had your two patients taken to the hospital yet?" said Bracy.

"Then you supposed wrongly, sir. There they are, and as comfortable as can be."

"That's capital," cried Bracy, "for I wanted to come and see that poor fellow Gedge."

"That fits," said the Doctor, "for he was asking if you were likely to come to the hospital; but I told him no, for you would be on duty. This way, gentlemen, to my drawing-room, where I am at home night and day, ready to receive my visitors. Now, which of you, I wonder, will be the first to give me a call?"

"Look here, Doctor," said Roberts, "if you're going to keep on in this strain I'm off."

"No, no; don't go. You must see the place. I've a long room, with a small one close by, which I mean to reserve for my better-class patients.—Here, you two," he said to the injured privates lying upon a couple of charpoys, "I've brought you some visitors."

Sergeant Gee's wife, whose services had been enlisted as first nurse, rose from her chair, where she was busy with her needle, to curtsey to the visitors; and Gedge uttered a low groan as he caught up the light cotton coverlet and threw it over his head.

"Look at him," said the Doctor merrily, and he snatched the coverlet back. "Why, you vain peacock of a fellow, who do you think is going to notice the size of your head?"

"I, for one," said Bracy, smiling. "Why, Gedge, it is nothing like so big as it was."

The lad looked at him as if he doubted his words.

"Ain't it, sir? Ain't it really?"

"Certainly not."

"Hoo-roar, then! who cares? If it isn't so big now it's getting better, 'cos it was getting bigger and bigger last night—warn't it, sir?"

"Yes," said the Doctor; "but the night's rest and the long sleep gave the swelling time to subside."

"The which, please, sir."

"The long sleep," said the Doctor tartly.

"Please, sir, I didn't get no long sleep."

"Nonsense, man!"

"Well, you ask him, sir. I never went to sleep—did I, pardner?"

"No," said his wounded companion. "We was talking all night when we wasn't saying *Hff!* or *Oh!* or *Oh dear!* or *That's a stinger!*— wasn't we, Gedge, mate?"

"That's right, pardner. But it don't matter, sir—do it?—not a bit, as the swelling's going down?"

"Not a bit," said Bracy, to whom this question was addressed. "There, we are not going to stay. Make haste, my lad, and get well. I'm glad you are in such good quarters."

"Thank ye, sir, thank ye. Quarters is all right, sir; but I'd rather be in the ranks. So would he—wouldn't you, pardner?"

His fellow-sufferer, who looked doubtful at Gedge's free-and-easy way of talking, glancing the while at the Doctor to see how he would take it, nodded his head and delivered himself of a grunt, as the little party filed out of the long, whitewashed, barn-like room.

"A couple of wonderful escapes," said the Doctor, "and quite a treat. I've had nothing to see to but cases of fever, and lads sick through eating or drinking what they ought not to. But I dare say I shall be busy now."

"Thanks, Doctor," said Roberts as they returned to the great court of the large building. "Glad you've got such good quarters for your patients."

"Thanks to you for coming," replied the Doctor; and the parties separated, Drummond leading his new friends off to introduce them to some of the anxious, careworn ladies who had accompanied their husbands in the regiment, and of the Civil Service, who had come up to Ghittah at a time when a rising of the hill-tribes was not for a moment expected. On his way he turned with a look of disgust to Bracy.

"I say," he said, "does your Doctor always talk shop like that?"

"Well, not quite, but pretty frequently—eh, Roberts?"

The latter smiled grimly.

"He's a bit of an enthusiast in his profession, Drummond," he said. "Very clever man."

"Oh, is he? Well, I should like him better if he wasn't quite so much so. Did you see how he looked at me?"

"No."

"I did. Just as if he was turning me inside out, and I felt as if he were going all over me with one of those penny trumpet things doctors use to listen to you with. I know he came to the conclusion that I was too thin, and that he ought to put me through a course of medicine."

"Nonsense."

"Oh, but he did. Thank goodness, though, I don't belong to your regiment."

The young men were very warmly welcomed in the officers' quarters; and it seemed that morning as if their coming had brought sunshine into the dreary place, every worn face beginning to take a more hopeful look.

Drummond took this view at once, as he led the way back into the great court.

"Glad I took you in there," he said; "they don't look the same as they did yesterday. Just fancy, you know, the poor things sitting in there all day so as to be out of the reach of flying shots, and wondering whether their husbands will escape unhurt for another day, and whether that will be the last they'll ever see."

"Terrible!" said Bracy.

"Yes, isn't it? Don't think I shall ever get married, as I'm a soldier; for it doesn't seem right to bring a poor, tender lady out to such places as this. It gives me the shivers sometimes; but these poor things, they don't know what it will all be when they marry and come out."

"And if they did they would come all the same," said Roberts bluffly.

"Well, it's quite right," said Bracy thoughtfully. "It's splendidly English and plucky for a girl to be willing to share all the troubles her husband goes through."

"So it is," said Drummond. "I've always admired it when I've read of such things; and it makes you feel that heroines are much greater than heroes."

"It doesn't seem as if heroes were made nowadays," said Bracy, laughing. "Hullo! where are you taking us?"

"Right up to the top of the highest tower to pay your respects to the British Raj. I helped the colour-sergeant to fix it up there. We put up a new pole twice as high as the old one, so as to make the enemy waxy, and show him that we meant to stay."

"All right; we may as well see every place while we're about it."

"You can get a splendid lookout over the enemy's camping-ground, too, from up here."

"Then you still think that these are enemies?"

"Certain," said Drummond; and words were spared for breathing purposes till the flag-pole was reached, and the young subaltern passed his arm round it and stood waiting while his companions took a good long panoramic look.

"There you are," he then said. "See that green patch with the snow-pyramid rising out of it?"

"Yes; not big, is it?"

"Awful, and steep. That mountain's as big as Mont Blanc; and from that deodar forest right up the slope is the place to go for bear."

"Where are the pheasants?" asked Roberts, taking out his glass.

"Oh, in the woods down behind the hills there," said Drummond, pointing. "Splendid fellows; some of reddish-brown with white spots, and bare heads all blue and with sort of horns. Then you come upon some great fellows, the young ones and the hens about coloured like ours, but with short, broad tails. But you should see the cock-birds. Splendid. They have grand, greeny-gold crests, ruby-and-purple necks, a white patch on their back and the feathers all about it steely-blue and green, while their broad, short tails are cinnamon-colour."

"You seem to know all about them," said Bracy, laughing.

"Shot lots. They're thumpers, and a treat for the poor ladies, when I get any; but it has been getting worse and worse lately. Couldn't have a day's shooting without the beggars taking pop-shots at you from the hills. I don't know where we should have been if their guns shot straight."

"Well, we shall have to drive the scoundrels farther off," said Roberts, "for I want some shooting."

"Bring your gun?" cried Drummond, eagerly.

"Regular battery. So did he; didn't you, Bracy?"

There was no reply.

"Bracy, are you deaf?"

"No, no," said the young man hurriedly, as he stood in one corner of the square tower, resting his binocular upon the parapet, and gazing through it intently.

"See a bear on one of the hills?" said Drummond sharply.

"No; I was watching that fir-wood right away there in the hollow. Are they patches of snow I can see in there among the trees?"

"Where—where?" cried Drummond excitedly.

"Come and look. The glass is set right, and you can see the exact

69

spot without touching it."

Bracy made way, and Roberts stepped to the other side of the tower and looked over the wide interval to where their visitors of the morning were forming a kind of camp, as if they meant to stay.

"Phee-ew!"

Drummond gave a long, low whistle.

"Snow?" said Bracy.

"No snow there; at this time of year. That's where some of the enemy are, then—some of those who disappeared so suddenly yesterday. Those are their white gowns you can see, and there's a tremendous nest of them."

"Enemies of our visitors this morning?"

"They said so," replied Drummond, with a mocking laugh; "but it seems rather rum for them to come and camp so near one another, and neither party to know. Doesn't it to you?"

"Exactly," cried Bracy. "They would be sure to be aware, of course."

"Yes, of course. What idiots they must think us! I'd bet a penny that if we sent out scouts they'd find some more of the beauties creeping down the valleys. Well, it's a great comfort to know that this lot on the slope here are friends."

"Which you mean to be sarcastic?" said Bracy.

"Which I just do. I say, I'm glad I brought you up here, and that you spied out that party yonder. Come away down, and let's tell the Colonel. He'll alter his opinion then."

"And send out a few scouts?" said Bracy.

Drummond shook his head.

"Doesn't do to send out scouts here."

"Why?"

"They don't come back again."

"Get picked off?"

"Yes—by the beggars who lie about among the stones. We have

70

to make sallies in force when we go from behind these walls. But, I say, you two haven't had much fighting, I suppose?"

"None, till the bit of a brush as we came here."

"Like it?"

"Don't know," said Bracy. "It's very exciting."

"Oh, yes, it's exciting enough. We've had it pretty warm here, I can tell you. I begin to like it now."

"You do?"

"Yes; when I get warm. Not at first, because one's always thinking about whether the next bullet will hit you—'specially when the poor fellows get dropping about you; but you soon get warm. It makes you savage to see men you know going down without being able to get a shot in return. Then you're all right. You like it then."

"Humph!" ejaculated Bracy, and his brow wrinkled. "But had we not better go down and give the alarm?"

"Plenty of time. No need to hurry. They're not going to attack; only lying up waiting to see if those beggars who came this morning can do anything by scheming. I fancy they're getting a bit short of lead, for we've had all kinds of rubbish shot into the fort here—bits of iron, nails, stones, and broken bits of pot. We've seen them, too, hunting about among the rocks for our spent bullets. You'll find them very nice sort of fellows, ready to shoot at you with something from a distance to give you a wound that won't heal, and cut at you when they can come to close quarters with tulwars and knives that are sharp as razors. They will heal, for, as our doctor says, they are beautiful clean cuts that close well. Never saw the beauty of them, though. He's almost as bad as your old chap for that."

"But we had better go down and give the alarm," said Bracy anxiously.

"None to give," said Drummond coolly. "It's only a bit of news, and that's how it will be taken. Nothing to be done, but perhaps double the sentries in the weak places. Not that they're very weak, or we shouldn't have been hen; when you came."

"Well, I shall feel more comfortable when my Colonel knows—eh, Roberts?"

"Yes," said the latter, who had stood frowning and listening; "and I don't think he will be for sitting down so quietly as your old man."

"Not yet. Be for turning some of them out."

"Of course."

"Very spirited and nice; but it means losing men, and the beggars come back again. We used to do a lot of that sort of thing, but of late the policy has been to do nothing unless they attacked, and then to give them all we knew. Pays best."

"I don't know," said Roberts as they were descending fast; "it can't make any impression upon the enemy."

"Shows them that the English have come to stay," interposed Bracy.

"Yes, perhaps; but they may read it that we are afraid of them on seeing us keep behind walls."

A minute or two later the news was borne to headquarters, where the two Colonels were in eager conference, and upon hearing it Colonel Graves leaped up and turned to his senior as if expecting immediate orders for action; but his colleague's face wrinkled a little more, and he said quietly:

"Then that visit was a mere *ruse* to put us off our guard and give them an opportunity for meeting the fresh odds with which they have to contend."

"Of course it was," said Colonel Graves firmly.

"Well, there is nothing to be alarmed about; they will do nothing till they have waited to see whether we accept the offer of admitting as friends a couple of hundred Ghazees within the gates.—Thank you, gentlemen, for your information. There is no cause for alarm."

The young officers left their two seniors together, and as soon as they were alone Drummond frowned.

"Poor old Colonel!" he said sadly; "he has been getting weaker for days past, and your coming has finished him up. Don't you see?"

"No," said Bracy sharply. "What do you mean?"

"He has Colonel Graves to lean on now, and trust to save the ladies and the place. I shouldn't be surprised to see him give up

72

altogether and put himself in the doctor's hands. Well, you fellows will help us to do the work?"

"Yes," said Bracy quickly, "come what may."

"We're going to learn the art of war in earnest now, old chap," said Roberts as soon as they were alone again.

"Seems like it."

"Yes. I wonder whether we shall take it as coolly as this young Drummond."

"I wonder," said Bracy; "he's an oddfish."

"But I think I like him," said Roberts.

"Like him?" replied Bracy. "I'm sure I do."

Chapter Nine.

Warm Corners and Cold.

It was a glorious day, with the air so bright, elastic, and inspiriting that the young officers of the garrison felt their position irksome in the extreme. For the Colonel's orders were stringent. The limits allowed to officer or man outside the walls were very narrow, and all the time hill, mountain, forest, and valley were wooing them to come and investigate their depths.

It was afternoon when Roberts, Bracy, and Drummond, being off duty, had strolled for a short distance along the farther side of the main stream, and paused at last in a lovely spot where a side gorge came down from the hills, to end suddenly some hundred feet above their heads; and from the scarped rock the stream it brought down made a sudden leap, spread out at first into drops, which broke again into fine ruin, and reached the bottom like a thick veil of mist spanned by a lovely rainbow. The walls of rock, bedewed by the ever-falling water, were a series of the most brilliant greens supplied by the luxuriant ferns and mosses, while here and there, where their seeds had found nourishment in cleft and chasm, huge cedars, perfect in their pyramidal symmetry, rose spiring up to arrow-like points a hundred, two hundred feet in the pure air. Flowers dotted the grassy bottom; birds flitted here and there, and sang. There was the delicious lemony odour emitted by the deodars, and a dreamy feeling of its being good to live there always amidst so much beauty; for other music beside that of birds added to the enhancement—music supplied by the falling waters, sweet, silvery, tinkling, rising and falling, mingling with the deep bass of a low, humming roar.

The three young men had wandered on and on along a steep track, more than once sending the half-wild, goat-like sheep bounding away, and a feeling of annoyance was strong upon them, which state of feeling found vent in words, Drummond being the chief speaker.

"I don't care," he said; "it's just jolly rot of your old man. Wrayford was bad enough, but old Graves is a tyrant. He has no business to tie us down so."

"There's the enemy still in the hills," said Roberts.

"Yes, but whacked, and all the other tribes ready to follow the example of those fellows who have come down to make peace and fight against the rest who hold out. They're not fools."

"Not a bit of it," said Bracy. "They're as keen as men can be; but I shouldn't like to trust them."

"Nor I," said Roberts. "They're too keen."

"There you are," said Drummond petulantly. "That's the Englishman all over. You fellows keep the poor beggars at a distance, and that makes them wild when they want to be friends. If every one had acted in that spirit, where should we have been all through India?"

"Same place as we are now," said Bracy, laughing.

"Right, old fellow," said Roberts. "We've conquered the nation, and the people feel that they're a conquered race, and will never feel quite reconciled to our rule."

"Well, I don't know," said Bracy. "I'm not very well up in these matters, but I think there are hundreds of thousands in India who do like our rule; for it is firm and just, and keeps down the constant fighting of the past."

"Bother!" cried Drummond pettishly: "there's no arguing against you two beggars. You're so pig-headed. Never mind all that. These thingamy Dwats have come down to make peace—haven't they?"

"You thought otherwise," said Bracy, laughing. "But, by the way, if we two are pig-headed, aren't you rather hoggish—hedge-hoggish? I never met such a spiky young Scot before."

"Scotland for ever!" cried Drummond, tossing his pith helmet in the air and catching it again.

"By all means," said Bracy. "Scotland for ever! and if the snow-peaks were out of sight wouldn't this be just like a Scottish glen?"

"Just," said Roberts, and Drummond looked pleased.

"Here, how am I to speak if you boys keep on interrupting?" he said.

"Speak on, my son," said Bracy.

"Well, I was going to say these fellows have come down like a deputation to see if we will be friends; and if we show that we will, I think now that all the rest will follow in the course of a few weeks, and there will be peace."

"And plenty?" said Bracy.

"Of course."

"No, my boy; you're too sanguine, and don't understand the hill-man's character."

"Seen more of it than you have," said Drummond.

"Possibly; but I think you're wrong."

"Oh, very well, then, we'll say I'm wrong. But never mind that. We've done the fighting; the niggers are whopped, and here we are with the streams whispering to us to come and fish, the hills to go and shoot, and the forests and mountains begging us to up and bag deer, bear, and leopard. I shouldn't be at all surprised even if we came upon a tiger. They say there is one here and there."

"It is tempting," said Bracy. "I long for a day or two's try at something."

"Even if it's only a bit of a climb up the ice and snow," put in Roberts.

"All in turn," said Drummond. "Well, then, when we go back to mess this evening, let's get some of the other fellows to back us up and petition Graves to give us leave."

"No good," said Roberts; "I know him too well. I have asked him."

"And what did he say?" cried Drummond eagerly.

"As soon as ever I can feel that it is safe," said Bracy. "I was there."

"Oh!" cried Drummond.

"He's right," said Roberts. "I don't believe that we can count upon these people yet."

"Then let's have a thoroughly good fight, and whack them into their senses. We're sent up here to pacify these tribes, and I want to see it done."

"So do we," said Bracy; "but it must take time."

"Don't believe that any one else thinks as you do," said Drummond sulkily; and they toiled on in silence till they came near the side of the falling water, whose rush was loud enough to drown their approach; and here they all seated themselves on the edge of the mere shelf of rock, trampled by many generations of sheep, dangled their legs over the perpendicular side, and listened to the music of the waters, as they let their eyes wander over the lovely landscape of tree, rock, and fall.

The scene was so peaceful that it was hard to believe that they were in the valley through whose rugged mazes the warlike tribes had streamed to besiege the fort; and Bracy was just bending forward to pick a lovely alpine primula, when he sniffed softly and turned to whisper to his companions.

"Do you smell that?" he said.

"Eh? Oh, yes; it's the effect of the warm sunshine on the fir-trees."

"'Tisn't," said Drummond, laughing. "It's bad, strong tobacco.
There!" he said as the loud scratch of a match on a piece of stone rose from just beneath their feet, as if to endorse his words, and the odour grew more pronounced and the smoke visible, rising from a tuft of young seedling pines some twenty feet below.

"Here, wake up, pardners," cried a familiar voice. "You're both asleep."

"I wasn't," said a voice.

"Nor I," said another; "only thinking."

"Think with your eyes open, then. I say, any more of these niggers coming in to make peace?"

"S'pose so. The Colonel's going to let a lot of 'em come in and help do duty in the place—isn't he?"

"Ho, yus! Certainly. Of course! and hope you may get it. When old Graves has any of these white-cotton-gowny-diers doing sentry-go in Ghittah, just you come and tell me. Wake me up, you know, for I shall have been asleep for about twenty years."

"He will. You see if he don't."

"Yah! Never-come-never," cried Gedge. "Can't yer see it's all a dodge to get in the fort. They can't do it fair fighting, so they're beginning to scheme. Let 'em in? Ho, yus! Didn't you see the Colonel put his tongue in his cheek and say, 'Likely'?"

"No," said one of Gedge's companions, "nor you neither."

"Can't say I did see; but he must have done."

The officers had softly drawn up their legs and moved away so as not to play eavesdropper, but they could not help hearing the men's conversation thus far; and as soon as they had climbed out of earshot so as to get on a level with the top of the fall, where they meant to try and cross the stream, descend on the other side, and work their way back, after recrossing it at its exit into the river, Bracy took up the conversation again.

"There," he said to Drummond, "you heard that?"

"Oh yes, I heard: but what do these fellows know about it?"

"They think," said Bracy, "and—I say," he whispered; "look!"

He pointed upward, and his companions caught sight of that which had taken his attention.

"What are those two fellows doing there?" whispered Roberts.

"Scouting, evidently," said Bracy. "I saw their arms."

"So did I," replied Roberts. "Let's get back at once, and pick up those lads as we go. One never knows what may come next. There may be mischief afloat instead of peace."

At that moment Drummond gave Bracy a sharp nudge, and jerked his head in another direction.

"More of them," said Bracy gravely; "yes, and more higher up. Well, this doesn't look friendly."

"No," said Roberts. "Look sharp; they haven't seen us. Let's get back and take in the news."

It was a difficult task for the three young Englishmen to compete with men trained as mountaineers from childhood; but the living game of chess had to be played on the Dwats' own ground; and for a short time the party of officers carefully stole from rock to rock and from patch of trees to patch of trees till Roberts stopped short.

"No good," he said softly. "I feel sure that the beggars are watching us."

"Yes," said Bracy; "they have the advantage of us from being on the high ground. Let's go on openly and as if in perfect ignorance of their being near."

By this time the young officers were on the farther side of the stream, below the falls, with it between them and the men they wished to turn back and take with them to the fort.

"What do you propose doing now?" asked Drummond.

"I'll show you," replied Roberts, and, parting the underwood, he threaded his way till he was close to the deep gully down which the water from the falls raced; and then selecting the most open spot he could, he placed his whistle to his lips and blew. The rallying whistle rose up the mountain-slope towards the falls, like the note of some wild bird startled from its lair among the moist depths of the gully.

To their great delight, the call had instant effect; for, unwittingly, they had made their way to where they halted just level with the party of their men who were not forty yards away. Consequently, before the note had died away the voice of Gedge was plainly heard.

"I say, boys," he cried, "that's a whistle."

"Nobody said it was a bugle," was the laughing reply.

"But it means cease firing," said Gedge.

"That it don't, stoopid, for no one's shooting. Get out! Only some kind o' foreign bird."

"I don't care; it is," cried Gedge. "Way ho! Any one there?"

"Yes, my lads," cried Roberts; "make for the fort at once. Follow the stream down to the river, and join us there. Quick! Danger!"

There was a sharp rustling sound as of men forcing their way downward on each side of the gully, and the next minute, as the place grew lighter, consequent upon the trees being absent for a space of about, a dozen yards, there was the sharp whiz as of some great beetle darting across, followed by the report of a gun, which was magnified by echoes which died away into the distance.

"Forward!" cried Roberts. "Steady! don't make a stampede of it. Keep to all the cover you can."

Necessary advice, for the whiz of a second roughly-made bullet, seeking but not finding its billet, was heard, followed by a smothered report.

"I say, this is nice," said Drummond: "and you two seem to be right. I don't like it at all."

"Well, it's not pleasant," said Roberts, smiling.

"Pleasant? No. These people may not mean war, but only sport. They're beating this part of the valley."

"And routing us up," said Drummond, "as if we were pheasants. I say; I wonder whether pheasants feel the same as I do when they're beginning to be driven to the end of a spinney?"

"Don't know," said Roberts shortly; "but I'm glad we came."

"Oh! are you?" said Drummond. "Well, I'm not. A little of this sniping goes a very long way with me."

"Ditto," said Roberts shortly. Then, aloud, "How are you getting on there, my lads?"

"Oh, fairly, sir, and—phew! that was close!"

For a bullet whizzed by the speaker's ear.

"Keep under cover. Steady!" said the Captain; and then the cautious descent of the steep slope—more of a passage by hands as well as feet than a steady walk down—was kept up, and diversified in the most unpleasant way by shots, till the rocky shallow where the stream dashed into the main river was reached.

Here the deep gully, down which the stream ran, had grown shallower till it debouched, with the valley on either side reduced to a dead level and the banks only a foot or so above the surface of the rushing water, which only reached to the officers' knees when they stepped in. But, unfortunately, the last of the cover had been passed, and a couple of shots reminded the party of the danger they ran.

"Here y'are, sir," cried Gedge, reaching out his hand to Bracy and helping him out. "Oh! why ain't I got my rifle?"

"Don't talk," cried Bracy as his companions leaped, dripping, out of the stream.

"No; open out and follow, my lads," cried Roberts. "Forward! double!"

"Ugh!" grunted Gedge to his nearest comrade; "and they'll think we're running away."

"So we are, mate."

"Yah! only our legs. I ain't running. Think I'd cut away from one o' them black-looking, bed-gown biddies? Yah! go back and send yer clothes to the wash."

The retiring party had separated well, so as not to present too good a mark for the enemy, whose practice was far from bad. For the stones were struck close to them again and again, and leaves and twigs were cut from the low growth which here fringed the bank of the river, always in close proximity to where the party ran, and teaching them that not only were the hill-men who fired good shots, but many in number, the high, precipitous ascent to the left being evidently lined with concealed scouts.

"Forward there!" shouted Bracy suddenly, for Gedge began to slacken and hang back.

"Beg pardon, sir," puffed the lad; "wouldn't you rayther lead?"

"Forward, you scoundrel!" cried Roberts angrily; and Gedge darted back into the position in which he had been running before, with his two companions, the officers having kept behind.

"Getting pumped, pardner?" said his comrade on the left.

"Pumped! Me pumped!" said Gedge derisively. "Hor, hor! Why, I feel as if I'd on'y jus' begun to stretch my legs. Go on like this for a week to git a happy-tight. But orsifers ought to lead."

"Advancing, matey," said the man on the right. "Fust inter action; last out, you know."

"Ho, yus; I know," grumbled Gedge; "but 'tain't fair: they get all the best o' everything. Here, I say, look out, laddies. We're getting among the wild bees, ain't us? Hear 'em buzz?"

"Yes; and we shall have one of 'em a-stinging on us directly. There goes another."

For bullet after bullet came buzzing by the flying party's ears, but still without effect.

"I say," cried Gedge; "keep shying a hye back now and then to see if the gents is all right."

"No need," said the man on his left. "We should know fast enough."

Meanwhile the three officers had settled down behind to a steady double, and kept on their conversation as if in contemptuous disregard of the enemy hidden high among the patches of wood to their left.

"Thought they were better shots," said Bracy. "Nothing has come near us yet."

"Quite near enough," growled Roberts.

"Don't you holloa till you're out of the wood," said Drummond; "they can make splendid practice at a mark not moving; but it's not easy work to hit a running man."

"So it seems," said Bracy coolly.

"Here, I've been thinking that we must have passed a lot of these fellows as we came along," said Roberts.

"Not a doubt of it," said Bracy; "fresh ones keep taking up the firing. We're regularly running the gauntlet. Surely they'll soon hear this firing at, the fort."

"Hope so," said Roberts. "We ought to have known that, the beggars had advanced like this."

"Well, we have found out now," cried Drummond. "I say, you two; this means that the war has broken out in real earnest. But I say,"—He stopped suddenly.

"Say on," said Bracy merrily; "we can't stay to listen to your speech."

"What a fellow you are!" cried the subaltern. "I can't cut jokes at a time like this. I was going to say—phee-ew—that was close! I felt the wind of that bullet as it passed my face."

"Miss is as good as a mile," said Bracy cheerily. "We shall be having men out on the opposite bank before long, ready to cover us; and they will not have running objects to aim at. They'll soon crush out this sniping."

"Hope so," said Drummond; "but I say—"

"Well, let's have it this time," cried Roberts.

"All right," panted Drummond; "if I go down, don't stop for a moment, but get on. The relief can come and pick me up. I shall creep into cover, if I can."

"Yes," said Roberts coolly—"if you can. Now, just look here, my lad; you want all your breath to keep your machinery going; you've none to spare to teach us our duty."

"Well said, Rob," cried Bracy. "Just as if it's likely. But you'd better go down! I should like to see you!"

Crash! in the midst of some bushes, as a single shot succeeded a spattering fire, and one of the privates went down just ahead.

"Almost got your wish, Bracy. Wrong man down."

As Roberts spoke he and Bracy dashed to where two of the privates had pulled up to aid their comrade, who had pitched head first into the clump of growth ahead of where he was running.

"Don't say you've got it badly, Gedge," cried Bracy huskily, helping the men as they raised the lad, who stared from one to the other in a half-dazed way.

"*Habet*," muttered Roberts, with his face contracting.

"Eh?" panted the lad at last, as he tried to pull himself together.

"Here—where is it?" cried Drummond excitedly. "Where are you hurt?"

"Oh, my toe!" cried the lad. "Ketched it on a stone outer sight, sir. My! I did go down a rum un."

"Not wounded?" cried Bracy joyfully.

"Not me, sir! Yah! they can't shoot. Here, I say, mateys, where's my bay'net? There it is."

Gedge limped to where it lay with the hilt just visible amongst the shrubs, and he made a dart to get it, but overrated his powers. He seized the bayonet from where it had been jerked by his fall, but went down upon his face in the act, and when raised again he looked round with a painful grin upon his lips.

"Got a stone in my foot, p'raps, gen'lemen," he said.

"Carry him!" said Roberts briefly; and the men were lowering their arms to take the poor fellow between them, but he protested loudly.

"No, no; I can walk, sir," he cried. "One o' them just give me an arm for a bit. Leg's a bit numbed, that's all. Look out, mates. Bees is swarming fast."

For the enemy had stationary marks for their bullets now, and they were falling very closely around.

"In amongst the trees there," cried Roberts; and the shelter ahead was gained, Gedge walking by the help of one of his comrades, and then crouching with the rest.

But the shelter was too slight, and it became evident that they were seen from the shelves and niches occupied by the enemy, for the bullets began to come thickly, sending leaves and twigs pattering down upon the halting party's heads.

"We must get on," said Roberts after an anxious look out ahead.

"All right," said Bracy. "We may leave the scoundrels behind."

"Behind, sir? Yus, sir," cried Gedge, who had caught the last word. "You go on, sir, and I'll lie down here till you sends some of the lads to fetch me in."

"What's left of him," thought Bracy, "after the brutes have been at him with their knives."

"Can you walk at all?" said Roberts quietly.

Gedge rose quickly.

"Yus, sir," he cried. "There, it aren't half so bad now. Felt as if I hadn't got no foot at all for a time. Hurts a bit, sir. Here, I'm all right."

Roberts looked at him keenly without speaking. Then he cried:

"Rise quickly at the word; take two paces to the right, and drop into cover again. Make ready. Attention!"

The little manoeuvre was performed, and it had the expected result. A scattered volley of twenty or thirty shots made the twigs about them fly, the fire of the enemy being drawn—the fire of old-fashioned, long-barrelled matchlocks, which took time to reload and prime.

"Forward!" cried Roberts again, and at a walk the retreat was continued, the Captain keeping close beside Gedge, who marched in step with his comrades, though with a marked limp, which he tried hard to conceal.

After a brief pause the firing started again, but fortunately the growth upon the river-bank began to get thicker, hiding them from their foes; though, on the other hand, it grew unmistakably plain that more and more of the enemy were lying in wait, so that the position grew worse, for the rushing river curved in towards the occupied eminences on the retiring party's left.

"Beg pardon, sir," cried Gedge suddenly; "I can double now."

"Silence, my lad! Keep on steadily."

"But I can, sir," cried the man. "I will."

"Try him," whispered Bracy.

"Double!" cried Roberts; and the retreat went on, Gedge trotting with the rest, but in the most unmilitary style, for he threw his head back, doubled his fists in close to his sides, and, squaring his elbows, went on as if engaged in a race.

"Looks as if he were running for a wager," said Drummond.

"He is," said Bracy coldly. "We all are—for our lives."

The way they were about to go had now so markedly come towards the face of a precipice, from which puffs of smoke kept appearing, that it was evident something fresh must be done, or the end would lie very near, no mercy being expected from the foe; and as they went on Bracy kept turning his eyes to the right, seeking in vain for a glimpse of the rushing river, now hidden from their sight by tree and rock, though its musical roar kept striking plainly upon their ears.

"Rob, old chap," he suddenly cried, "we must get down to the water, and try to cross."

"Yes," said Roberts abruptly. "I've been thinking so. It's our only chance, and I've been waiting for an opening."

"We must not wait," said Bracy. "It's chance, and we must chance it."

"Halt! Right face, forward!"

As Roberts spoke he sprang to the front in one of the densest parts, where a wilderness of bush and rock lay between them and the river, and led on, with his companions following in single file; while, as perforce they moved slowly, they had the opportunity to regain their breath, and listened with a feeling of satisfaction to the firing which was kept up by the enemy upon the portion of the bosky bank where they were supposed to be still running.

"Wish they'd use all their powder," said Drummond breathlessly.

"Why?" said Bracy.

"They've no bayonets."

"Only tulwars and those horrible knives—eh?" said Bracy harshly.

"Ugh!" ejaculated Drummond. "You're right; but if they came to close quarters we could take it out of some of the brutes before we were done for. It's horrible to be doing nothing but run till you're shot down."

"Not shot down yet, old fellow. There, don't talk; we may get across."

"May!" muttered Drummond. "But, my word! how they are firing yonder! They're beginning to think we're hiding, and are trying to start us running again."

"Will you leave off talking!" cried Bracy angrily. "Here, Gedge, how are you getting on?"

"Splendid, sir. I could do anything if the pavement warn't so rough."

"In much pain?"

"Pretty tidy, sir. Sort o' bad toothache like in my left ankle. Beg pardon, sir; are we going to wade the river?"

"Going to try, my lad."

"That's just what'll set me up again. Had a sprained ankle once afore, and I used to sit on a high stool with my foot in the back-kitchen sink under the tap."

"Cold water cure—eh, my lad?" said Drummond, smiling.

"That's right, sir."

"Steady there!" came from the front, where the leaders were hidden from those behind. "Steep rock-slope here."

A rush and the breaking of twigs.

"Some one down," cried Bracy excitedly. "Any one hurt?"

Splash! and the sound of a struggle in the water.

Bracy dashed forward, forcing his way past the two men, his heart beating wildly as he reached the spot from whence the sound came.

"All right," cried Roberts from below; and, peering down through a tangle of overhanging bushes, Bracy saw his leader standing breast-high in foaming water, holding on by a branch and looking up at him.

"I fell. Unprepared. You can all slide down. Lower yourselves as far as you can, and then let go."

The distance was about thirty feet, and the descent not perpendicular.

"You go next," said Bracy to one of the men. "You can't hurt, it's only into water."

"Let me, sir," cried Gedge.

"Silence," said Bracy sternly, and he watched

'Here comes my ship full sail, cock warning!'

F. U. !   PAGE 114.

anxiously as the man he had spoken to set his teeth, made his way to the edge of the rock, lowered himself by holding on to some of the bushes through which Roberts had suddenly fallen, and then let go.

Hush—splash! and Bracy saw him standing in the water opposite to his Captain.

"Next, Gedge," said Bracy.

Gedge sprang forward as if his leg were uninjured, lowered himself down till his head was out of sight of those behind, and then, muttering the words of the old school game, "Here comes my ship full sail, cock warning!" he let go, glided down, made his splash, and the next minute was standing beyond Roberts, holding on, for the pressure of the rushing water was great. The others followed rapidly, Bracy last, and feeling as if he had suddenly plunged into liquid ice, so intensely cold was the water, which reached nearly to his chin. He glanced outward to get a dim peep of the river they were about to try and cross, and another chill ran through him, for it was like standing face to face with death, the surface eastward being one race of swirling and rushing foam, dotted here and there by masses of rock. There was a few moments' anxious pause, and, above the hissing rush of the water, the echoing crack, crack, crack of the enemies' jezails reached their ears, but sounding smothered and far away. Then Roberts spoke:

"You can swim, Drummond?"

"Yes, in smooth water," was the reply. "I don't know about cascades."

"You've got to, my lad," said Roberts shortly. "What about your men? You can, I know, Gedge."

"Yes, sir."

"You others?"

"I can swim a few strokes, sir," said one.

"Never was no water, sir, where I was," replied the other.

"A few strokes!" cried Roberts fiercely. "No water! Shame on you, lads! No one who calls himself a man ought, to be in a position to say such a thing. Well, we'll do our best. Don't cling, or you'll drown us as well."

"I can get one on 'em across like a shot, sir," cried Gedge excitedly.

"Silence!" cried Roberts.

"But I done drowning-man resky, sir, in Victory Park lots o' times."

"Then rescue the drowning-man with the injured leg—yourself," said Roberts, smiling—"if it comes to the worst. Draw swords, gentlemen. I'll lead. You take hold of my sword, my lad, and take fast grip of Mr Drummond's hand. Drummond, hold out your sword to Gedge. Gedge, take Mr Bracy's hand. Bracy, you can extend your sword to the last. We may be able to wade. If not we must go with the stream, and trust to the rocks. Each man who reaches a shallow can help the rest. Ready? Forward!"

Chapter Ten.

A Nice Walk.

"Halt!" cried Roberts in a low tone of voice; for, as he gave the order to advance for the attempt to ford the river, a fresh burst of firing arose from what seemed to be nearer, and he hesitated to lead his companions out into the rushing flood and beyond the shelter of the overhanging trees.

"It is like exposing ourselves to being shot down while perfectly helpless, old fellow," he said, with his lips close to Bracy's ear.

"But we can't stay here: they'll track us to where you fell, and see the broken branches overhead. What then?" said Bracy.

"Right; we shall be easy marks for the brutes. Now, then, forward!"

Without hesitation this time, and with his following linked in accordance with his orders, Roberts began to wade, facing the rushing water and leaning towards it as it pressed against his breast, to divide it, forming a little wave which rushed by to right and left. Step followed step taken sidewise, and at the third he and the private following him stood out clear of the overhanging growth, so that he could see plainly the task that was before him.

It was enough to startle the strongest man, for there were about fifty yards of a rushing torrent to stem, as it swept icily cold along the river's rocky bed, and already the pressure seemed greater than he could bear, while he felt that if the water rose higher he would be perfectly helpless to sustain its force. But a sharp glance upward and downward showed him spots where the water foamed and leaped, and there he knew that the stream must be shallower; in fact, in two places he kept on catching sight of patches of black rock which were bared again and again. Setting his teeth hard, and making the first of these his goal, he stepped on cautiously, this choice of direction, being diagonally up-stream, necessarily increasing the distance to be traversed, but lessening the pressure upon the little linked-together line of men.

"We shall never do it," thought Bracy as, in his turn, he waded out into the open stream, his arms well extended and his companions on either side gazing up-stream with a peculiar strained look about their eyes. But there was no sign of flinching, no hesitation; every man was full of determination, the three privates feeling strengthened by being linked with and thus sharing the danger with their officers; while Roberts, as leader, felt, however oppressed by the sense of all that depended upon him, invigorated by the knowledge that he must reach that shallow place. Once he had his men there, they could pause for a few minutes' rest before making the next step.

On he pressed, left shoulder forward, against the rushing waters; feeling moment by moment that the slightest drag from the next man must make him lose his footing, to be swept downward, with the result that if the links of the chain were not broken asunder there would be pluck, pluck, pluck, one after the other, and they would be all swept down the torrent.

Had he allowed his imagination free way, he would have let it picture the result—so many ghastly figures, battered out of recognition, found somewhere, miles away perhaps, among the blocks of stone in the shallows of the defile. But the stern man within him kept the mastery; and he went on a few inches at a time, edging his way along, with the water deepening, so that he was ready to pause. But he felt that hesitation would be fatal; and, pressing on, his left foot went down lower than ever, making him withdraw it and try to take a longer stride.

"It's all over," he thought, in his desperation; but even as the thought flashed through his brain he found that he reached bottom again, having passed a narrow gully, and his next and next, strides were into shallower water; while, toiling hard, he was in a minute only waist-deep, dragging his companions after him, and aiding them, so that they all stood together a third of the way across, with the rushing stream only knee-deep.

"Five minutes for faking breath," he cried, "and then on again for that white patch where the water is foaming."

No one else spoke, but all stood panting and not gazing up-stream or at the farther shore, with its rocks, trees, and ample cover, but throwing the pressure of every nerve, as it were, into their hearing, and listening for sounds of the enemy only to be heard above the roar of the water. For the firing had ceased, and one and all felt that this meant an advance on the part of the hill-men, who would be sweeping the wooded valley right to the river-bank, ready at any moment to open fire again; while now it would be upon the unprotected group part of the way towards mid-stream.

"Forward!" cried Roberts; and, with their grip tightening, the little party followed their Captain as he once more edged off to the left, performing his former evolution, and, to his delight, finding that the stone-bestrewn polished bottom never once deepened after the first few steps, which took him waist-deep, and kept about the same level, the result being that the next halt was made where the river was roughest, tossing in waves churned up as it was by the masses of rock in its way, a group lying just below the surface, with the water deepening behind them, so that the party had once more to stand breast-high, but in an eddy, the rocks above taking off the pressure which in the shallows had threatened to sweep them away.

The water was numbing, and the leader felt that their pause before recommencing their efforts must be very short; but he was face to face with the most difficult part of their transit, for it was only too plain that this last portion ran swift and deep, the bold, steady rush suggesting a power which he knew instinctively that he would not be able to stem, and he looked downward now to see what was below in the only too probable event of their being swept away.

As he turned to gaze upward again he caught Bracy's eyes fixed upon him inquiringly; but he paid no heed, though he did not for the moment read them aright, the idea being that his brother officer was mutely asking him if he thought he could do it.

He grasped Bracy's meaning the next minute, for he heard that which had reached Bracy's ears. It was a shout from the woody bank they had left, as if one of the enemy had made a discovery, followed by answering cries, and all knew now that their foes were close upon their track, and that at any moment they might be discovered and fire be opened upon them.

"Forward!" cried Roberts, and once more he set off, to be again agreeably surprised, for the water did not deepen in the least as he moved from out of the eddy, being still about breast-deep, with very little variation, the bottom being swept clear of stones and literally ground smooth by the constant passage over it of the fragments borne down from the glaciers in the north. But before many steps had been taken, and the little chain was extended to its extreme limit, Roberts knew that disaster was imminent. For it was impossible to stand against the dense, heavy rush of water, bear against it as he would.

He shouted back to his companions to bear against the pressure, and strove his best, but all in vain. At one and the same moment the double calamity came: there was a shot from out of the patch of forest they had left, and the leader was lifted from his feet. Then pluck, pluck, pluck, as if mighty hands had seized them, the men in turn were snatched from their positions, and with a scattered fire opened upon them from among the trees, they were being swept rapidly downstream.

Roberts shouted an order or two, and discipline prevailed for a space, the links of the chain remaining unbroken; but even the greatest training could not hold it together for long at such a time, and the non-swimmers were the first to go under and quit their hold, rolling over with the tremendous rush of the stream, and rising again, to snatch wildly at the nearest object, and in two cases to hamper the unfortunate who was within reach.

"*Sauve qui peut,*" muttered Bracy a's he glided along, with his sword hanging from his wrist by the knot; but his actions contradicted his thoughts, for instead of trying to save himself he turned to the help of Drummond, to whom one of the men was clinging desperately, and the very next minute he felt a hand clutch at his collar and grip him fast.

The rattle of firing was in his ears, and then the thundering of the water, as he was forced below the surface into the darkness; but he did not lose his presence of mind. He let himself go under, and then, with a few vigorous strokes, rose to the surface, with the man clinging to him behind, and wrenched himself round in his effort to get free. He was only partially successful, though; and, panting heavily, he swam with his burden, just catching sight of Drummond in a similar position to himself, many yards lower down the stream.

"Let go," he shouted to the man. "Let go, and I'll save you."

But the man's nerve was gone, and he only clung the tighter and made a drowning-man's effort to throw his legs about his officer's.

"Help! help!" he gasped, and a desperate struggle ensued, during which both went beneath the surface again, only to rise with Bracy completely crippled, for the poor drowning wretch had been completely mastered by his intense desire for life, and arms and legs were now round his officer in the death-grip.

Bracy cast a wild, despairing look round as he was borne rapidly along, and all seemed over, when a head suddenly came into sight from behind them, an arm rose above the surface, and the swimmer to whom it belonged drove his fist with a dull smack right on the drowning-man's ear, and with strange effect.

It was as if the whole muscular power had been instantaneously discharged like so much electricity at the touch of a rod, the horrible clinging grasp ceased, and with a feeble effort Bracy shook himself free and began to swim.

"A jolly idgit!" panted a voice; "a-holding on to yer orficer like that! Want to drown him? Can you keep up, sir?"

"Yes, I think so," said Bracy weakly.

"That's right, sir. You'll do it. I'll give yer a 'and if yer can't. It's easy enough if yer swim with the stream."

"Can you keep him up?" said Bracy more vigorously.

"Oh yus, sir; I can manage to keep him on his back and his nose out o' the water. Knocked him silly."

"Where are the others?"

"There they are, sir, ever so far along. The Captain's got old Parry, and Mr Drummond's swimming to his side to help him. You'll *do* it now, sir. Slow strokes wins. Feel better?"

"Yes. I was half-strangled."

"Then it's all right, sir."

"But the enemy?" panted Bracy, trying to look round.

"Never you mind them, sir. They're far enough off now, and can only get a shot now and then. River windles so. We're going ever so much faster than they can get through the woods. Ain't this jolly, sir? Done my ankle a sight o' good. I allus did like the water, on'y sojers' togs ain't made to swim in."

"I can't see any one in pursuit," said Bracy at the end of a minute.

"Don't you keep trying to look, sir. You've got enough to do to swim."

"I'm getting right again now, Gedge, and I think I can help you."

"What! to keep him up, sir? I don't want no help while he's like this; but if he comes to again and begins his games you might ketch him one in the ear. Chaps as thinks they're drowning is the silliest old idgits there is. 'Stead o' keeping still and their pads under water, they shoves them right up to try and ketch hold o' the wind or anything else as is near. 'Spose they can't help it, though. Hullo! look yonder, sir. Rocks and shaller water. Think we could get right across now?"

For a shout now reached them from fifty yards or so lower down, where their three companions in misfortune were standing knee-deep in mid-stream, and a rugged mass of rocks rose to divide the river and towered up twenty or thirty feet, forming a little rugged island about twice as long. Bracy's spirits, which were very low, rose now at the sight of Roberts and Drummond helping the other private up into safety, and turning directly to offer them the same aid if they could manage to get within reach.

"Keep it up, sir," cried Gedge, who was swimming hard, "or we shall be swep' one way or t'other. It'll be nigh as a touch, for the water shoots off jolly swift."

Bracy had needed no telling, and he exerted all his strength to keep so that they might strike the shallows where the island was worn by the fierce torrent to a sharp edge, for to swim a foot or two to the left meant being carried towards the side of the enemy, while to the right was into swifter water rushing by the island with increased force.

"Stick to it, sir," cried Gedge. "Side-stroke, sir. No fear o' not keeping afloat. That's your sort. We shall do it. Ah!"

Gedge's last cry was one of rage and disappointment, for, in spite of their efforts, just as they seemed to be within a few feet of the point at which they aimed, they found themselves snatched as it were by the under-current, and, still holding to their half-drowned companion, they would have been carried past but for a brave effort made by Roberts, who was prepared for the emergency. By stepping out as far as he dared, holding by Drummond's long arm, and reaching low, he caught Gedge's extended hand.

The shock was sharp, and he went down upon his face in the water; but Drummond held on, the little knot of struggling men swung round to the side, and in another minute they were among the rocks, where they regained their feet, and drew the insensible private up on to dry land.

"That was near," said Roberts, who was breathless from exertion. "Hurt, Drummond?"

"Oh no, not at, all," was the laughing reply. "I never did lie on the rack, having my arms torn out of the sockets; but it must have been something like this."

"I'm very sorry," cried Roberts.

"Oh, I'm not, old man. How are you, Bracy—not hit?"

"No, no; I shall be all right directly. Thank you, old chaps, for saving us. Never mind me; try and see to this poor fellow. I'm afraid he's drowned."

"No, sir; he ain't, sir," cried Gedge; "he's coming round all right. It's more that crack in the ear I give him than the water. I hit him as hard as I could. There! look, gents; his eyes is winking."

It was as the lad said; the unfortunate non-swimmer's eyelids were quivering slightly, and at the end of a minute he opened them widely and stared vacantly at the sunny sky. The officers were bending over him, when they received a broad hint that their position was known, a couple of shots being fired from the farther bank, higher up-stream, one of which struck the rock above them and splintered off a few scraps, which fell pattering down.

"Quick!" cried Roberts. "We must get those two along here for a bit. The high part will shelter us then; but as soon as possible we must have another try for the shore."

The shelter was soon reached, and all crouched together in the sunshine, with the water streaming from them, the officers busily scanning the bank of the rushing river opposite, and calculating the possibility of reaching it. There was plenty of cover, and very little likelihood of the enemy crossing the river in its swollen state; but there was that mad nice some twenty yards wide to get over with two helpless men; and at last Roberts spoke in a low tone to his companions.

"I can't see how it's to be done, boys. I dare say we four could reach the bank somewhere; but we're heavily handicapped by those two who can't swim."

"And there isn't time to teach them now," said Drummond sardonically.

"And we can't leave them," said Bracy. "What's to be done?"

Gedge was eager to offer a suggestion upon the slightest encouragement, and this he obtained from Roberts, who turned to him.

"How's the sprain, my lad?"

"Bit stiff, sir; that's all," was the reply. "Water done it a lot o' good."

"Think you could drop down with the stream and land somewhere near the fort to tell them how we're pressed?"

"Dessay I could, sir; but don't send me, please."

"Why?" asked Roberts and Bracy in a breath.

Gedge gave them a comical look, and waved his hand in the direction of his comrades.

"We all come out together to have what we called a nice little walk, sir, and a look at that there waterfall, as turned out to be farther off than we reckoned on. I shouldn't like to cut off and leave 'em in the lurch, sir."

"Lurch? Nonsense, my lad," said Bracy. "You would be going on a very risky errand to try and save us all."

"Yes, sir; o' course, sir; but I could get one of 'em over that little bit if you three gents could manage t'other. They'll be all right in a few minutes."

"I don't like sending him," said Roberts. "It is very dangerous, and we must, try it together."

His companions gave; a short, sharp nod, and acquiesced.

"If we only knew what is below us!" said Bracy as he gazed downstream.

"Niggers," said Drummond shortly. "There'll be a dozen or two beyond these rocks waiting to pot us as soon as we are carried into sight by the stream."

"Well, there'll only be our heads to aim at," said Bracy; "and we must not go down in a cluster this time."

"No," said Roberts. "As soon as you feel ready, Bracy, we must start. It is madness to stay here. You and Gedge take that fellow between you; and Drummond and I will go as before."

"Hear that?" whispered Gedge to his comrade, who gave him a sulky nod. "That's right; and mind, I'm ready for yer this time. I shan't hit yer; but if yer moves hand or foot when I've turned yer over on yer back to float, we lets yer go, and yer can get across the blessed river by yerself."

"All right," said the man; "but I don't believe yer, Billy Gedge. I never learnt to swim, but if I could I shouldn't talk about leaving a pardner to shift for hisself."

"Er-r-er!" growled Gedge, whom these words seemed to mollify. "Well, keep them 'ands o' yours in the water, for as long as you holds 'em down you helps me to keep yer afloat, and as soon as yer begins to make windmills of 'em and waves 'em, or chucks 'em about as if you was trying to ketch flies, down you goes."

"All right," said the man, as they heard more bullets spattering on the rocks above them; "but, oh, how my hands does itch for a rifle and a chance to be taking shots at some of these beauties!"

"Yes," said Gedge; "and I hope it won't be long first. I hadn't any spite partickler agen 'em before, but I have now. Ha' they got any orspitals or doctors?"

"I dunno," said the other; "but if we gets outer this and in the ranks again, there's going to be some of the beds filled, and a bit o' work for their doctors to do."

"Well, my lads," said Roberts, stepping to where the three men crouched gazing at the deep, rushing water; "feel strong enough to start?"

"Yes, sir," came in chorus.

"And we shan't get in a tangle this time, sir, I hope," said Gedge.

"I hope not, my lad. Up with you, then."

There were no preparations to make; nothing to do but for the two officers to get their man face upward between them, and stand ready while Bracy and Gedge followed suit with theirs.

"Ready?" said Roberts. "Count ten after we've started, and then follow."

As soon as he had spoken he gave Drummond a nod, and they stepped among the rocks to the swift water, bent down, and, as they lowered themselves in, the strong current seized them, as it were, their helpless companion was drawn out, and away they went as fast as a horse could have trotted, down what was a veritable water-slide.

"Now, my lad," cried Bracy as Gedge, at a signal, went on counting the ten slowly. "Keep a good heart. We won't leave you."

"All right, sir;" said the man, drawing a deep breath.

"Nine—ten!" counted Gedge.

"Off!" cried Bracy, but checked himself for a moment, startled by the noise of the ragged volley which was fired from the enemy's bank as soon as they caught sight of the three heads gliding down the stream.

"If they are hit!" mentally exclaimed Bracy; and then, making a sign to Gedge, they followed out the precedent shown them, and the water seized and bore them along, with the private floating between them, their steady subsidence into the water and slow strokes keeping them well upon the surface.

So swiftly did they pass along that only a few moments had passed before the crackling of the firing from the far bank came plainly, and bullets ricochetted from the water to strike the other bank, but without effect, the rate at which they were descending making the aim taken with the long, clumsy matchlocks of no effect. Not a word was littered; and with their friends far ahead, their heads just seen, the fugitives glided along the straight course below them, free as it was from rocks. But they were evidently in full view of fresh parties of the enemy, and shot after shot splashed the water.

"Now for the bank, Gedge," cried Bracy suddenly.

"Yes, sir; all right, sir; but it's of no use."

"It is," cried Bracy angrily. "They are making for it now."

"Yes, sir: and they're swept by it. Can't you see it's like a smooth wall, with the water running by it like a railway train?"

Gedge was right; and there was nothing for it but to go with the stream towards the rocks which now rose right in their way, the long race ending in a wide chaos of foaming water, which leaped and sparkled in the afternoon sun.

"We shall be torn to pieces there," thought Bracy; and he strained his eyes to try and make out an opening; but his attention was taken up the next moment by the cracking of matchlocks and the puffs of smoke rising to his left, as fire was opened upon their leaders, who were running the gauntlet that it would be their fate to share in another minute, when Gedge suddenly uttered a hoarse cheer, and nearly lost his grip of his companion; for, quick, sharp, and loud, a genuine British volley rattled out, almost like a report from a piece of artillery, the bullets sending the leaves on the enemy's bank pattering down. Then another, and at regular intervals others; while the eyes of the swimmers were gladdened by the sight of friends making their way down among the rocks, towards which they were being rushed. Another volley rang out; there was a cheer, in which the two helpless privates joined; and directly after the fugitives were saved from being battered among the rocks by ready hands, whose efforts were covered by the rapid firing from the bank above.

Five minutes after, the dripping party were retiring with a company of their regiment, whose captain contented himself with giving the enemy a volley from time to time, as they doubled to reach their quarters, now not a quarter of a mile away, the young officers learning that the enemy was out once more and converging upon the fort, this unexpected news of the termination of the temporary peace having been brought in by scouts, and none too soon.

"Graves said that you must be brought in somehow," said the officer in charge of the company; "but I was not to cross the river where you did, but to come up this side, for you would turn back after crossing higher up."

"Yes; I remember telling the Colonel so," said Bracy eagerly.

"Well, it has turned out all right; but he needn't have told me, for we could not have crossed, as far as I can see."

"We did," said Drummond, laughing; "and brought in these three fellows, too."

"Yes; but I wouldn't holloa too soon," said the officer addressed. "We're not safe yet. Look yonder; they're swarming down that gorge, and we must race for it, or they'll cut us off. Forward, my lads."

Ten minutes later there was a halt and a clinking rattle, as the order was given to fix bayonets ready for a strong body of the hill-men, who had crossed the shallows lower down and were coming on to dispute their way.

"Why doesn't Graves send out another company to cover us?" panted Roberts. "We shall be cut off after all."

The words had hardly passed his lips when—crash!—there was a tremendous volley from their right front, which checked the enemy's advance, the white-coated hill-men hesitating. The officer in command seized the opportunity, and a volley was fired by the rescue company, the men cheering as they dashed on with bristling bayonets. That was enough: the enemy turned and fled, their speed increased by another volley from the covering company; and ten minutes later the fugitives were marching along coolly, protected by the fire from the walls of the fort, where they were directly after being heartily shaken by the hand, the sally-port clanging to in their rear.

"Quite enough for one day," said Drummond.

"Yes," said Bracy grimly; "that's having what Gedge called a nice long walk."

"Yes," said Roberts; "with a swim thrown in."

Chapter Eleven.

Which was Braver?

"Steady, there; steady, my lads. Not too fast. Seize upon every bit of shelter, and have a few steady shots at them. They're beaten, and we shall soon scatter them now."

The lads were as steady as the most exacting officer could desire; and though the two sides of the narrow, winding defile were lined with the enemy, who made good use of their clumsy jezails, of whose long range several of the Fusiliers had had bitter experience, the deadly fire which searched out every sheltering crag was too much for the Dwats, who were retiring as fast as the difficult nature of the ground would allow.

Bracy felt that, the enemy was beaten, and knew that the fierce tribes-men would be only too glad to escape as soon as they could:

but as the tight had gone against them, their supposed to be secure hiding-places were one by one growing untenable as the Fusiliers advanced; and consequently, as giving up was about the last thing they thought of doing, their action was that of rats at bay—fighting to the bitter end. The men of Roberts's company knew, too, what they must do—drive the enemy completely out of the defile, or they would return again; so, partly held back by their officers, they advanced by a series of rushes, taking possession of every bit of fallen rock for shelter, and driving their enemies on and on, farther into the mountains, fully expecting that in a short time they would completely take to flight.

But disappointment followed disappointment. No sooner was one niche high up on the rocky sides cleared than there was firing from one on the other, and the work had to be gone through over again. Still they advanced, and the enemy retired; while the officers knew that sooner or later, in spite of numbers, this must come to an end, for nothing could withstand the accurate fire of the young Englishmen whenever they obtained a chance. Men dropped from time to time; but they had to lie where they fell till the fight was at an end, some to rise no more; others, knowing as they did the nature of the enemy, managed to creep to the shelter of a rock, where they laid their cartridges ready, and sat back watching the faces of the defile in anticipation of some marksman opening fire.

The company was in full pursuit, under the belief that they had completely cleared the defile as far as they had gone, when, in the midst of a rush led by Roberts and Bracy, both making for a rough breastwork of rocks built a hundred feet up one side and held by two or three score of the enemy, the latter uttered a sharp ejaculation, stopped short, and then dropped upon his knees, his sword, as it fell from his hand to the full extent of the knot secured by the slide to his wrist, jingling loudly on the stones. Roberts was at his side in a moment, and leaned over him.

"Not badly hurt?"

"No, no," cried Bracy; "never mind me. On with

P. B.:   Page 134.

you, and lead the boys; they're close up to that breastwork. On—on!"

Roberts turned and rushed up the rock-strewn defile, reaching his men as they crowded together for a rush, and Bracy and the man hurrying to him saw them go over it as if they were engaged in an obstacle race. The next minute they disappeared round another bend in the jagged rift, in full pursuit of the late occupants of the murderous shelter.

"And me not with 'em, and me not with 'em!" groaned the private who had fallen back. "But I don't care. I ain't going to leave him."

Before he could double back to where Bracy knelt, the wounded officer sank over sidewise, with the rugged defile seeming to swim round before his eyes, and, for a few minutes, glory, the hot rage of pursuit, and the bitter disappointment of failure were as nothing. Then he opened his eyes upon the lad who was bending over him, holding a water-bottle to his lips.

"Try and drink a drop, sir, if it's ever so little."

The words seemed to come from a great distance off and to echo in Bracy's head, as he made an effort and swallowed a few drops of the lukewarm fluid.

"Gedge," he said at last with difficulty, staring hard at the lad, whose head seemed to have gone back to its old state after the blow from the falling rock, but only to swell now to a monstrous size.

"Yes, sir; it's me, sir. Ought to have gone on with the boys, but I couldn't leave you, sir, for fear of some of the rats coming down from the holes to cut you up."

"Rats? Holes?" said Bracy feebly. "What's the matter?"

"Not much, I hope, sir; on'y you've got hit. Whereabouts is it? Ah, needn't ask," he muttered as he saw a dark mark beginning to show on the left breast of the young officer's tunic, and spreading like a big blot on a writing-pad.

"Hit? Nonsense—ah!" Bracy uttered a low groan, and clapped his right hand across to cover the spot.

"Yes, sir. Jus' there," said Gedge; "but don't you mind. It's too high up to be dangerous, I know. Now, then. Amb'lance dooty. Must practice; I ain't forgot that."

Gedge gave a sharp look round and up and down the defile, before laying down his gun and taking out a bandage and some lint.

"Hold still, sir," he said, drawing his breath through his teeth afterwards with a hiss, as he rapidly stripped open his officer's jacket, and then tore away the shirt, to lay bare his white breast, where, just below the collar-bone, an ugly red patch showed itself.

"Sponge and cold water," muttered Gedge; "and I ain't got 'em." Then aloud: "That hurt yer, sir?" for he was examining the wound.

"Never mind that; go on," said Bracy faintly. "Plug the wound."

"Right, sir. Jus' going to.—One o' their ugly bits o' hiron," muttered the lad as he stopped the effusion of blood in a rough-and-ready way which must have been agonising to the sufferer, who, however, never winced.

"That's done it, sir; but I must turn you over to fasten the bandage."

103

"Go on," said Bracy in a faint whisper.—"Hah! the firing's getting more distant."

"Yes, sir; they're driving 'em right out of it this time, and we not in it, and—oh, a mussy me!" whispered the speaker now, as in his manipulations he became conscious of the fact that his task was only half-done, for there was the place where the ragged missile had passed out close to the spine, and the plugging and bandaging had to be continued there.

"That's good, sir," he said cheerily. "You won't have the doctor worriting you to get the bullet out, as he does with some of the lads. Now, then, a drop more water, and then I'm going to get you up yonder, more out of the sun, so as you'll be more comf'table till they come back."

"Yes!" sighed Bracy. "I can't help you, my lad. Listen! they're firing still."

"Oh yes, sir; they're doing the job proper this time. Shots is a good way off too. How they eckers, and— Hullo!" Gedge gave a sudden start, snatched at his rifle, and looked up the defile in the direction where his companions had passed, for there was a report from close at hand following upon the small stones close to his side being driven up, and he was watching a puff of smoke slowly rising high up the left precipitous side, finger on trigger, ready for a return shot, when—whiz —something like a swift beetle in full flight passed close to his ear, and he ducked down, simultaneously with an echoing report from the right side of the defile.

"Just like 'em!" he muttered. "Oh, you cowards! Only just show your muzzles, and I'll let yer see what British musketry practice is like."

But all Gedge saw was the gleam of a ramrod a hundred yards away, where one of the hill-men who had kept to his coign of vantage was rapidly reloading.

"No good to stop here," muttered Gedge; "they'd be hitting him 'fore long. Me too, p'raps. Well, here goes."

The lad rose upon his knees, took off his helmet and passed the strap of his rifle over his head and arm, slung it, replaced his helmet, and turned to Bracy.

"Won't hurt yer more than I can 'elp, sir; but we can't stop here."

"No; lie down, my lad. Get into cover, and wait till you can reply."

A sharp report from below them stopped Gedge from answering, and the bullet flattened against the rock a yard from where the lad knelt.

"Well, this is pleasant," he said, showing his teeth in a grin which looked as vicious as that of a hunted dog. "Urrrr!" he snarled, "if I only had you three down on the level with my bay'net fixed. Draw a big breath, sir. Up yer comes. Now, then, you hold fast with yer right. Hook it round my neck, and don't get the spike o' my 'elmet in your eye.— Now, then, my lad; right-about face—quick march!"

Gedge strode off with his load held in his arms as a nurse would carry a baby, and at the first step—bang! bang! and echo—echo—two shots came from behind, and directly after another from the front, but from the opposite side to the spot from whence the former shot had been fired.

"Well, if they can't hit me now they orter," muttered Gedge as he strode on with his heavy burden. "This is going to be walking the gauntlet if any more on 'em's left behind on the sneak. Oh dear! oh dear! if I only had a snug shelter and plenty o' cartridges I think I could stop that little game.—Hurt yer much, sir?" he continued aloud after a few dozen yards had been covered. "Fainted! Poor chap! Better, p'raps, for he won't know what's going on.—Go it!" he snarled as shot after shot was fired; while, though he managed to get out of the line of fire of the two first enemies, he had to pass closer to the two next, who fired again and again from their eyries far up the sides of the defile, these nooks, fortunately for Gedge and his burden, having been reached from above—the perpendicular walls precluding all descent into the dried-up torrent-bed.

The young fellow was right; he had to run the gauntlet, for to his dismay, as he tramped on with his load, he awoke to the fact that the Dwats, who had retired from the upper shelves as the Fusiliers rushed up the defile, were coming back to their hiding-places, and, warned by the firing of their companions, were ready to harass the retreat.

"I don't care," he muttered, "if I can only get him outer fire; but they must hit one of us before long. 'Tain't possible for 'em to keep on without."

Bang! and then bang! again, and the stones close by where the brave fellow trod were struck up, one of them giving Gedge a sharp blow on the knee.

"Talk about hitting a 'aystack!" he snarled. "Why, I could make better practice with a indyrubber cattypult and a bag o' marbles."

"Gedge—Gedge!" came from Bracy's lips in excited tones, for he had slowly revived to a knowledge of their position.

"Yes, sir; all right, sir. I know. I'd double, but the going is too bad."

"Of course, my lad; impossible. But are you mad?"

"Yes, sir; downright savage at the murderous brutes. This is their way o' treating the wounded."

"I didn't mean that, my man, but the way you're carrying me."

Shot after shot came whistling and buzzing by them from behind as he spoke, but still without effect.

"I'm carrying you all right, sir. Can't help hurting you a bit. It's easy this way."

"Nonsense, man. Set me down at once. I can stand. Then sling your rifle in front, and take me on your back."

"There they go, sir," said Gedge as another shot buzzed by, telling of its rough shape. "They never did no pigeon-shooting, sir, nor practised at sparrers from the trap."

"Did you hear what I said, sir?" cried Bracy angrily. "Set me down, and get me on your back. I can hold on with one hand and leave yours free."

"Couldn't use 'em if they was, sir."

"Halt! Take me on your back at once, sir," cried Bracy, panting with anger and pain.

"Can't, sir. Who's a-going to halt with them firing at us like that from behind? Ain't I 'bliged to keep ree-treating?"

"Obey my orders, sir. I tell you I shall be easier to carry on your back."

"Oh yes, sir, a deal easier to carry, and a nice deal easier to hit. Aintcher got it bad enough as it is?" said Gedge sulkily.

Bracy was silent for a few moments as he felt his suspicions realised. Gedge was carrying him in that awkward fashion so as to shelter him from any better-aimed bullet that might come. To make quite sure, though, he drew a deep breath and spoke again:

"I am wounded, sir, but I will be obeyed."

"All right, sir; soon as ever we get out o' shot."

"But you are hurting me horribly; and can't you see that, carrying me like this, you may receive the next bullet?"

"Oh yes, sir; I can see," said Gedge coolly; "but you be quiet, and I won't hurt you more'n I can help."

Bracy's voice had lost all its anger, and it was in no tone of command that he said:

"Set me down, my lad, and hold my arm. I'll try to walk beside you while you take a shot or two at those cowardly brutes."

"Ah, that's just what I'd like to do, sir; but it would on'y be waste o' time. They'd hit us, too, if we stood still for me to fire. It's our keeping moving that helps. 'Sides, I know it would only make your wounds break out worse, and shift the bandage. You keep quiet, for I ain't got no breath for talking."

Bracy was silent, and slowly and steadily Gedge trudged on, growing more and more exhausted, and looking to right and left for some cavernous hole in which he could take refuge so as to screen his burden and defend him so long as he had a cartridge left.

"And even then," he muttered softly, "there's the bay'net. Wonder how I could get on in fair fight against one of the niggers with his tullywar. Too much for him, I fancy, for I am good at that game. Urrrr!" he snarled again, for half-a-dozen shots were fired at them almost together, but this time from lower down the defile in front, where the enemies who had fled were gathering again in force.

"That was a near un, sir," said Gedge as a bullet whizzed just over his head. "Well sir, I beg pardon, sir, and hope you won't report me for disobeying my sooperior orficer. I was a bit waxy and warm with a-carrying of yer; for you are a bit heavy, sir. Now, sir, please, I'm a-going to set you down gently and take you up on my back."

Bracy paid no heed, but gazed down the narrow gorge, from whose sides more shots were fired.

"D'yer hear, sir? You're most a-choking o' me with that there arm."

"Forward!" said Bracy between his teeth. "Mind, there's a great rift there. Don't stumble."

"I'm a-going to shift you first, sir. Once you're on my back I can straddle that easy."

"Yes, Gedge, I know," said Bracy as firmly as he could; "but don't insult me any more."

"Insult yer, sir? I wouldn't do it. How!"

"By thinking your officers want to shelter themselves behind their men. Forward, my lad, unless you find a place where we can shelter till our comrades come back."

"There aren't no shelter, sir, and there aren't no more mercy for them Dwats if we gets clear of this, which I don't think we shall. There, sir! It's all over, I suppose. Ain't hit, are yer?"

"No. But that volley."

"Yes, sir, there's any number waiting for us. Here, we must walk the gauntlet back again now. We may meet our chaps coming."

The firing was going on along the sides of the gorge, but just then there was another crash, a regular volley, and Gedge uttered a hoarse yell of excitement.

"It's hoo-roar, sir," he panted, "on'y I can't shout. That's our reserves coming up, and firing to keep the beggars' fire down. See, they've stopped now. Oh, if my rifle wasn't slung! Look at 'em. One—two—three of the cowardly beggars scuffling up yonder like great white rabbits, and on hands and feet, too."

Crash! again. A sharp volley from much nearer, and Gedge stopped short to gaze with his companion at the three hill-men away in front, a couple or three hundred feet above the level where Bracy's bearer stood forgetting his dangerous wound and his pangs as he felt horror-stricken at the terrible sight to his left.

There were, as Gedge said, three hill-men, crawling rapidly up a long shelf to reach a cluster of stones for shelter—a shelter they had left to get better aim at the struggling pair down below. And as the climbing Dwats were watched directly after the last volley, one who was last started up into a standing position, threw up his arms, and his long jezail fell from them down into the defile, while he balanced himself for a few moments and then dropped, turning over once, and disappearing from the watchers' eyes. The next moment the top one came to a stand by a great stone, and rolled over and over till he reached the steep precipice, down which he plunged, the horrible thud with which he struck the stones coming plainly to Bracy's ears.

There was still another white figure crawling up the narrow shelf, but he had stopped short; and as Bracy and his companion gazed, the poor wretch seemed to collapse and lie closer down to the rock. Just then another shot rang out, and the body gave a jerk, but did not move again.

"Hah!" ejaculated Gedge. "It's very horrid, sir, but it was their turn, and our lads can shoot. Come on, sir. I think we shall do it now."

He started off towards the body of their friends, who were coming rapidly on, but before they had gone a score of yards the firing from the enemy recommenced, and—spat! spat!—the bullets struck the stones close at hand.

"Oh, I say, sir, this is too bad!" groaned Gedge. "I did think we should do it now. Never mind. Britons never shall be slaves, and I will do it after all."

There was a rattling fire opened at once on the sides of the gorge, completely crushing that of the hill-men; and a few minutes after, as Gedge tramped on with his load, it was to be met by a burst of cheers, and a score of his comrades came racing on to his help. It was just then that a final shot came from somewhere behind, and poor Gedge started violently, staggered forward, and the next moment he would have gone down heavily with his burden but for the ready help of a dozen willing hands.

Directly after a distant cheering was heard. Roberts and his company were coming back.

Chapter Twelve.

Wounds.

The enemy had been driven off with heavy loss, but the little victory had been dearly-won. Several men had been wounded, and most serious to all seemed to be the fact that among them was the gallant young officer who was liked by every man in the regiment. So it was that the march back to the great fort was made in silence; and when a few of the enemy, encouraged by what they looked upon as a retreat, hung about the rear and harassed the retiring column with shots from the heights, they paid dearly for being so venturesome. For Captain Roberts, leaving a little party in hiding to wait till the enemy showed in their pursuit, listened with a grim smile upon his lip till there was a sudden outburst of firing, and then tramped on with the remainder of his company, keeping as much as he could by the mule ambulance which was bearing his friend back to the fort.

Within half-an-hour the little firing-party overtook the rear of the column, and Roberts halted till they came up to him.

"Well, Sergeant?" he said.

"All right now, sir," said Gee, who looked what the men called ugly. "I think we've brought 'em all down."

"You're not sure, of course?"

"Well, pretty nigh, sir. There ain't been a shot since."

"Good. Be on the lookout. I hate for our poor fellows to be harassed like this."

"It's horrid, sir; but, begging your pardon, sir, how's Mr Bracy?"

"Bad, Gee, bad. I'm afraid he is shot through the lungs."

Sergeant Gee's brow went into a mass of puckers and frowns, and there was the peculiar sound of one grinding his teeth together, as the man tramped on behind his officer for a few minutes before speaking again.

"Beg pardon, sir; there's that Bill Gedge. Is he much hurt?"

"Very gravely, I'm afraid. Dr Morton can't tell yet from the hasty examination he made, but he shook his head."

"Poor lad!" said the Sergeant. "We were always bad friends, sir; he was so full of his Cockney monkey-tricks, and he hated me, but we couldn't spare him. What a soldier he would have made!"

"Hah!" ejaculated Roberts; "as full of pluck as a lad could be. Mr Bracy's been telling me how he carried him through the fire, and sheltered him with his own body. That's how it was he had his wound."

There was another pause, with the silence only broken by the echoing tramp, tramp of the men.

"Won't die—will he, sir?" whispered Sergeant Gee.

"I pray Heaven no," said the Captain.

"That sounds bad, sir," said the Sergeant huskily. "I should like to shake hands with him afore he goes; and if he gets better I won't be so hard on him again."

"I suppose you have only done your duty by him."

"I hope so, sir."

"Double on to the ambulance, and see how he is. Corporal Green, take the Sergeant's place."

Roberts halted to let his men pass him, keenly watching every one in his company, and a man limping caught his eye.

"Here, Bracy, what's the matter?" he said.

"Oh, nothing much, sir. Spent shot glanced off the rock and hit me in the ankle."

"Give him your arm, Sergeant, and get him on one of the mules."

"Beg pardon, sir; I can walk back."

"You're making your leg worse at every step, sir," cried Roberts angrily. "Get on and ride."

The words were spoken sharply, the young Captain being in no very amiable mood, for he was cooling down after tremendous exertion and the reaction from the wild excitement of the fight. But he spoke in the man's interest and with the desire to save him from after-suffering.

Then the weary tramp went on almost in silence, but no one flagged, and at the end of a couple of hours they obtained a glimpse of the flag at the top of the staff. The silence in the column was broken by a hearty cheer, the men's spirits rising again after what had been a depressing march back; and when the gates were reached they were cheered by the men on the walls, and the hills around softly echoed back the replies to the hearty welcome they had received.

The Colonel, with the officers left behind, stood at the gate waiting, and the answer to his inquiry regarding the enemy brought forth a fresh cheer.

"Splendidly done!" said the Colonel; and then sharply, "What casualties?"

"Mr Bracy severely wounded. Privates Down and Gedge had bullet-wounds. Other hurts slight."

The Doctor hurried away to his operating-room, and his assistants went to the door to help in the three patients, who were attended to in turn.

The first man who had fallen had to have a bullet extracted from his leg, half-way to the hip, where it was deeply embedded in the muscle.

"Now, my dear Bracy," said the Doctor, "let's look at you."

"No, I can wait," was the reply. "My bandages is quite firm, and the bleeding has ceased."

The Doctor frowned, and was about to say something regarding interference; but he checked himself, glanced at the bandage, and nodded.

"Very well," he said; "the other man."

Poor Gedge was very white and remarkably quiet, but his eyes were full of motion; and he watched the Doctor's face and every action of his hands.

"Why, Gedge, my lad," said the Doctor cheerily after a certain amount of busy manipulation, "this isn't fair. I didn't want to have you in hospital again."

"Same to you, sir," said the sufferer, with a ghastly attempt at a smile, as he screwed his head round to look at the Doctor.

"Hold still, sir. Look the other way."

"Yes, sir," said Gedge faintly. "'Tain't my head this time, sir."

"No, my lad; it's not your head this time."

"Sorry it's my back, sir; but I warn't a-running away."

"Bah! of course you were not; our lads don't know how."

"No, sir; course not, sir."

"Got it carrying Mr Bracy out of the fire—eh?"

"Well, yes, sir, I s'pose so, sir. Shall I—shall I—"

The poor fellow stopped short.

"Shall you what?" said the Doctor kindly; "try to move?"

"No, sir," said the poor fellow feebly; "I didn't mean that. It was, shall I be a goner?"

"Oh, nonsense—nonsense! Humph! poor fellow! he has fainted."

"Is his wound serious, Doctor?" said Bracy huskily.

"Never you mind. You lie still and wait. Well, there. Yes, the hurt is a very bad one. I don't think he'll die; but the bullet is in a dangerous place, and I dare not try to extract it to-day."

A short time after poor Gedge was lying in a state of stupor upon the bed he had previously occupied, and the Doctor was examining the young officer's wounds.

"Very bad, Doctor?" asked Bracy.

"Bad enough, sir. I don't like this exit so close to the vertebrae.— That hurt?"

"No; it feels dull and cold just there."

"Raise that hand a little."

"Can't, Doctor; I'm so tightly bandaged."

"Humph! Yes, you are pretty well tied up. That poor fellow Gedge did wonderfully well for you, considering. He attended to his ambulance lessons. First help's a grand thing when a man's bleeding to death."

"Was I bleeding to death?" said Bracy rather faintly.

"Of course you were; or perhaps not. The bleeding might have stopped of itself, but I shouldn't have liked to trust it. There; shan't do any more to you to-day. We'll have you to bed and asleep. That's the first step towards getting well again. Sorry to have you down so soon, Bracy, my dear boy. There, keep a good heart, and I'll soon get you right again."

The Colonel was at the hospital door soon after, along with Major Graham, both anxious to hear about Bracy's hurt.

"Bad," said the Doctor shortly as he put on his coat. "Don't ask to see the poor boy; he's just dropping off to sleep."

"Bad?" said the Colonel anxiously.

"Yes, bad, sir. A young fellow can't have a hole drilled right through him by a piece of ragged iron without being in a very serious condition."

"But the wound is not fatal?"

"H'm! no, not fatal. He's young, strong, and healthy; but the exit of the missile was in close proximity to the spine, and there's no knowing what mischief may have been done."

"What do you mean?" said the Colonel anxiously.

"Injury to the nerve centre there. I can't say. Possibly nothing may follow, but I am obliged to say the wound is bad, and there is danger of his being crippled—permanently injured in a way which would render him unfit for service."

"But look here," said the Major excitedly, "you have a bad habit of making the worst of things, Morton. Come, explain yourself. Are there any symptoms suggestive of what you hint at?"

"My dear Graham, I never come and interfere with your work; don't you meddle with mine."

"I don't want to, sir," said the Major tartly. "I only want for the Colonel and yours obediently not to be left in the dark."

"Graham is quite right," said the Colonel gravely. "We should like to know a little more."

"Very good," said the Doctor, "but I can only say this: there is a peculiar absence of sensation in the lower extremities, and especially in the poor fellow's left arm. This may be temporary, and due to the terrible shock of the wound; but it also may be consequent upon injury to the nerves in connection with the spine. I can say no more. Time only will show."

The two officers left the hospital-room, looking terribly depressed.

"Poor lad! poor lad!" the Major kept on saying. "Such a brave, unassuming fellow. It's wonderful how little we realise how we like our fellow-men, Colonel, till they are badly hurt. Hah! I am sorry—more sorry than I can express."

The Colonel said nothing, but turned and held out his hand, which the Major took and pressed warmly.

"Thank you, Graves," he said, taking out a showy silk handkerchief and blowing his nose very hard, making it give forth sounds like those made by a boy beginning to learn the bugle. "Hah!" he said; "one never knows. Here to-day and gone to-morrow, Graves. May be our turn next."

"Yes," said the Colonel quietly: "but if it is in the way of duty, I don't see that we need mind."

"Humph! Well, I don't know about that. I should like to live to a hundred, if only for the sake of finding out what it feels like. Some people do."

"Yes," said the Colonel, smiling; "and over a hundred; but then they die."

"Yes, of course; but from old ago."

"And other things too, as the old epitaph says."

"What old epitaph?"

"On the venerable lady. The lines run something like this:—

"She lived strong and well to a hundred and ten,
And died by a fall from a cherry-tree then."

"Bah! don't talk about dying, Graves. Poor Bracy! Oh, the Doctor must set him all right again. But this sort of thing does make one feel a bit serious."

"It is very, very sad," said the Colonel.

"Yes, very. By the way, though, have you noticed how splendidly our lads are behaving?"

"Magnificently, for such mere boys," said the Colonel meaningly.

"For such mere boys?" said the Major sharply. "I never saw men in any regiment behave better. Why, sir, it was magnificent to-day. I didn't say anything to Roberts about it, because I don't want the lads to hear and get puffed up by pride. But, really, sir, I'm very proud of our regiment."

"And so am I. But you have changed your ideas a little."

"Bah! Pooh! Nonsense! Don't jump on a man because he spoke out a bit. You'll grant yourself that they are a very boyish-looking lot."

"Yes; but I do not judge them by appearances. I look at their discipline and acts."

"So do I," said the Major, "and I recant all I said about them before. There, sir, will that satisfy you?"

"Quite, Graham," said the Colonel. "There, we must be hopeful. I couldn't bear for poor Bracy to become a wreck."

Chapter Thirteen.

A Bit Queer.

"Tell us all about it," said Bracy as he lay partially dressed outside his simple charpoy bed in the small room Doctor Morton had annexed for his officer patients.

"All about what?" said Roberts, who had come in, according to his daily custom, to sit for a while and cheer up his suffering friend.

"All about what? All about everything that has been going on—is going on."

"And is going to go on!" said Roberts, laughing. "That's a large order, old chap."

"You may laugh," said Bracy dolefully; "but you don't know what it is to be lying here staring at the sky."

"And mountains."

"Pah! Well, at the mountains too, day after day, in this wearisome way. I hear the bugle and the firing, and sometimes a shout or two, and then I lie wondering what everything means—whether we're driving them away or being beaten, and no one to tell me anything but that dreadful woman; for old Morton thinks of nothing but sword-cuts and bullet-wounds, and will only talk of one's temperature or one's tongue. I tell you it's maddening when one wants to be up and doing something."

"Patience, patience, old man. You're getting better fast."

"How do you know?" cried Bracy petulantly.

"Morton ways so."

"Morton's an old—old—old woman," cried Bracy angrily. "I'm sick of him. I'm sick of that other disagreeable woman. I'm sick of physic—sick of everything."

"Poor old chap!" said Roberts, laying his cool hand upon his friend's burning forehead. "Come, you'll feel better after that."

"Don't—don't talk that way—and take away your hand. You make me feel as if I must hit you."

"I wish you would, old man, if it would make you feel better."

"Better! Pah! It's horrible. Morton only talks. Says I'm better when I'm worse."

"Oh, come now, that won't do, you know. You are stronger."

"Pah! How can I be stronger when I am as weak as a baby, unable to move hand or foot? There; I beg pardon for being so disagreeable."

"Oh, nonsense! Who thinks you disagreeable?"

"You do, Rob; only you're such a good old chap that you won't notice my sick man's whims."

"Love 'em," said Roberts coolly. "More you go it the better I like it, because it's all a sign of the spirit in you kicking against your weakness. I know how you feel—want to come and have another go in at the Dwats?"

"Yes," said Bracy in a sharp whisper through his closed teeth. "I do long to help give them an awful thrashing."

"Of course you do, my boy; and you shall soon. Now, if, instead of kicking against hospital routine, you took to it in a mean, spiritless sort of way, and lay there waiting to be roused up to speak, I should feel uncomfortable about you, for I should know it was a bad sign.—You'll be all right soon."

Bracy was silent for a few minutes, and lay gazing wistfully through the window at the dazzling snow-peaks flashing miles away in the bright sunshine. Then he shook his head slowly from side to side.

"It's of no use to be self-deceiving," he said at last. "I know as well as can be, Rob, what's wrong. I'm not going to die."

"Die? Ha, ha! I should think not. Take more than a bullet-hole to kill you."

Bracy smiled, and looked sadly in his friend's eyes.

"It's precious hard, old fellow," he said; "for as I lie here I feel that I'm almost a boy still, and it comes so soon."

"What comes so soon?"

"My big trouble, old fellow. Morton won't say a word about it; but I know."

"Come now; what do you know? You lie awake imagining all sorts of things."

"But I don't imagine that. You can see it for yourself. I'm strong enough in mind, but the weakness of body is terrible."

"Of course it is. You have had a hole right through you, made by a rough piece of iron fired from a gun; but it's healing up fast."

"Yes," said Bracy, with a sigh, "the wound is healing up fast."

"Then, what more do you want?"

"My old manly strength," cried the sufferer with energy. "This horrible, helpless weakness!"

"Dull! What an unreasonable patient you are!" cried Roberts. "How can you expect the strength to come till the wound is healed?"

"I don't expect it," sighed the poor fellow. "Roberts, old man, it will never come back. My spine was injured by that bullet."

"Yes; we know that."

"And it has affected the nerves so that I am going to be helpless for the rest of my life—a poor invalid, whose fate is to be carried about or wheeled everywhere."

"Don't believe it," said Roberts shortly. "Who told you that stuff?"

"My own instinct. You know I cannot move hand or foot."

"Not yet. Nature has bound you down so that your wound may not be disturbed till it is well."

"There, don't talk about it," said Bracy quickly. "I want to know how things are going on. I don't hear half enough."

"All right, old man," cried Roberts cheerfully. "You shall have it in brief. This is a hole—we're in a hole—the Dwats, bless 'em! are like the sand upon the seashore, and they come sliding into the hole. Then we shovel 'em out, and just like sand they come trickling down again upon us. Now it's down one of the gullies, now it's down another; and the more we kill the more seem to come on."

"Yes—yes—yes," sighed Bracy; "just as it has been from the first. We ought to have reinforcements."

"That's right, and I dare say some have been sent; but the tribes south and east have all risen, and are holding them in check, so we've got to do the work here ourselves."

"How are the supplies?"

"Tidy—tidy; and we keep on fretting a little game, only it's risky work; and I never feel as if I should get back again when I'm out shooting. Had some narrow escapes."

"What about ammunition?"

"That's all right. Enough for a couple of months yet, fire as hard as we like."

"Why didn't Drummond come to see me yesterday? Ah, I know; he has been wounded."

"Just scratched; that's all. I dare say he'll come in some time to-day."

"Poor fellow! I am sorry."

"He isn't—he's delighted. Goes about with his arm in a sling, showing it to everybody, and telling them about the fight he had with a big Dwat. Says he should have cut him down, only one of our lads was so precious handy with his bayonet and ran him through."

"Ah!" cried Bracy, flushing slightly, as he mentally pictured the scene. "How bravely our lads do stand by their officers!"

"They do. Good fellows; brave boys. I like the way, too, in which that chap Gedge waits on you."

"Yes," said Bracy, with a sigh; "and the poor fellow is not fit to be about. Morton owned to it; but he will wait on me hand and foot, to that horrible woman's disgust."

"What! Mrs Gee?"

Bracy nodded.

"Well, she is a disagreeable, tyrannical sort of female Jack-in-office; but she has her good points."

"Yes; but they're such sharp points, and they prick dreadfully."

"Ha, ha!" laughed Roberts. "A joke; and you say you're not getting better.—I say, what were we talking about? Oh, Gedge. I wish he wasn't such an awful East-end Cockney in his ways, for he's a splendid fellow inside. Times and times he has brightened the poor fellows up out yonder, singing and telling stories and playing some of his india-rubber games, bad as his own wounds are. I believe he'd pretend to laugh even if he were dying."

"I can never be grateful enough to him," sighed Bracy.

"Oh yes, you can. We must all petition for him to get his stripes as soon as we can, only it will make old Gee mad with jealousy."

"Yes," said Bracy thoughtfully; and then: "How long have I been lying here?"

"Three weeks, old man."

"And you are no further with the Dwats?"

"Not a bit. That thrashing we gave them together when you went down ought to have settled 'em and made 'em sue for peace; but they began sniping at us the very next day."

"It seems to be their nature to be always fighting," sighed Bracy.

"Yes. I don't believe they could live without it. They must fight something or somebody, and regularly enjoy a good skirmish."

"You haven't said anything about Colonel Wrayford the last day or two."

"No, poor fellow! he's in a very low state. Between ourselves, boy, we only came just, in time."

"What, do you mean?"

"To save Ghittah. Those fellows would have done their best; but they would have been overmatched, and without their Colonel they'd have given way at last, and the people at home would have been reading of a terrible reverse in the Dwat district. Massacre of the British force."

"Not so bad as that surely."

"I don't know. Poor Wrayford had worked till he was utterly exhausted, body and mind, and as soon as Graves began to relieve him of part of the strain it was just as if something snapped, and he curled up at once. Morton says it was all from overstrain after his wound, and that he'll want a twelvemonth at home to get back his strength."

"I beg pardon, sir," said a hard, acid voice; "it is quite time Mr Bracy had his lunch."

Roberts turned quickly upon the stern, frowning, youngish woman who had entered silently in a pair of home-made list slippers, and stood in the doorway gazing at him fixedly.

"That's right, Mrs Gee," said Roberts; "bring it in, and feed him up well, for he wants it, poor fellow!"

"Mr Bracy has everything, sir," said the woman coldly, "and given him to the minute when there's no one here."

"Oh, I'm nobody," said Roberts good-humouredly.

"No, sir."

"Eh? Oh, all right; bring in his lunch.—Hang the woman! I didn't mean that," he said to himself.

"No, sir; not while you are here," replied the woman in the most uncompromising way. "Mr Bracy can't lift his arms yet, and I have to give him his meals, and it troubles him for any one to see him fed."

"Yes, yes, of course. I ought to have known, Mrs Gee. Where is the lunch?"

"Being kept hot for him, sir."

"Go and fetch it, then, and I'll be off the moment you come."

Mrs Gee said nothing, but turned silently and disappeared, while Roberts rose and leaned over the bed.

"The tyrant of the sickroom, old boy. Never mind; she's a capital nurse, and sympathetic under her hard shell. But I say, old fellow, can you imagine it to be possible that Gee fell in love with that female dragon?"

"No," said Bracy, smiling. "It seems impossible. One can't understand these things. I don't mind her so much now, but I do wish she wouldn't be quite so hard on poor Gedge."

"Poor lad; no. What's that, though?—the click of crockery. Only fancy the willow-pattern plate out here in the hills!"

"Not so far out of place," said Bracy, smiling. "Chinese pattern, and we are very near to China."

"Good-bye, old man," said Roberts hastily. "Here she comes. Never mind about shaking hands yet. Do it in a look. Good-bye. See you to-morrow—if I don't get knocked over first," he added to himself; and, bonding low, as there was a short, hard cough outside, evidently meant for a signal to him to depart, he laid one hand upon Bracy's shoulder, the other on his brow, and gave him a very brotherly look and smile.

"You'll be all right soon, my helpless old cockalorum," he cried cheerily. "There, pitch into your corn well, and grow strong. Ta, ta!"

He turned quickly to cross the room, and then made a bound a yard away in his astonishment, for he received a tremendous blow across the loins, which made him turn sharply to gaze in wonder at his helpless friend, who was looking at him wildly.

"What the dickens did you do that for?" he asked.

"I beg pardon, sir. I thought you said—"

"Yes, yes, all right, Mrs Gee, I'm off," he cried; and he hurried away and out into the great court, where he passed one hand behind him to begin softly rubbing his spine.

"Is the poor fellow off his head?" he muttered in his wonderment and confusion. "Helpless and weak? Why, it was enough to break a fellow's back. Has he got a club in the bed?"

Roberts stopped short, as if about, to turn back.

"Ought I to go and warn that woman of his antics? No; she could summon help directly, and—"

"Morning, sir. Find Mr Bracy better, sir?"

Roberts looked up sharply, to find Gedge, with his face looking very thin and more angular than ever, leaning as far as he could out of a narrow window.

"Yes—no—well, getting on, Gedge."

"Oh yus, sir; he's getting on. Pecks better now."

"I'm glad of it. You're better too, my lad."

"Me, sir. Oh, I'm getting a reg'lar impostor, sir. Ought to be back in the ranks, only I don't want to leave Mr Bracy, sir."

"Certainly not. Keep with him, and do all you can."

"Right, sir. Do a lot more if old Gee's wife wasn't there, sir."

"Humph!" ejaculated Roberts, with his hand involuntarily busy rubbing his back. "By the way, Gedge, have you noticed anything particular about Mr Bracy when you've been with him?"

"No, sir. Oh yus, sir; I know what you mean."

"Ha!" cried Roberts. "You have noticed it?"

"Oh yus. You mean those fits o' the blue dumps as he has."

"Well—er—yes," said Roberts.

"Yus, sir; he has them bad. Gets a sort o' idee in his head as he'll never be all right again."

"Yes, yes; all weakness."

"Jest what I told him, sir. 'Look ye here, sir,' I says; 'see how you bled that day 'fore I could stop it. Yer can't expect to be strong as you was till you gets filled up again.'"

"Of course not," assented Roberts.

"That's it, sir. And I says to him, I says, 'Look at me, sir. Just afore I got my blue pill—leastwise it warn't a blue pill, but a bit o' iron—I was good for a five-and-twenty mile march on the level or a climb from eight hay-hem to eight pee-hem, while now four goes up and down the orspital ward and I'm used up.' He's getting on though, sir. You can see it when you cheers him up."

"Yes; I noticed that," said Roberts.

"Specially if you talks about paying them roughs out for shooting at us that day as they did."

"Ha! cowardly in the extreme."

"Warn't it, sir? When we're up and at it, we lads, we're not very nice; but fire at a poor beggar carrying his wounded orficer—why, I wouldn't think one of ours 'd do such a thing—let alone believe it."

"Of course they would not, my lad," said Roberts. "There, I'm glad to hear about how well you attend to Mr Bracy."

He nodded, and went on to his quarters, wondering to himself over what had taken place at Bracy's bedside.

"It was very queer," he thought; "but it shows one thing—the poor fellow's a good deal off his head at times, or he wouldn't have hit out at me like that; and it shows, too, that all his ideas about being so weak are fancy. That crack on the back didn't come from a weak arm. But it's all due to the wound, and it would be better not to say anything to him about it."

Chapter Fourteen.

The Uncomfortable Symptoms.

Captain Roberts intended to go and sit with his friend for an hour or two next day, but he was called off on duty, and Drummond seized the opportunity to pay a visit. He was met at the door by Mrs Gee, who looked at him sourly as he passed, for she had just been summoned by one of Doctor Morton's ambulance men to go and attend to one of the men who had been taken worse.

"How do, nurse?" said Drummond. "Just going in to see your patient."

"Then you must not stay long, sir. Ten minutes will be plenty of time. Mr Bracy can't get well if he is so bothered with visitors."

"Oh, I won't bother him, nurse; only cheer him up a bit."

The woman frowned and hurried away, leaving the course open, and Drummond went straight on, thinking aloud.

"Glad my arm's not worse," he said, as he nursed it gently, "for I shouldn't like to be under her ladyship's thumb. She ought to be called to order. Talk about a hen that can crow; she's nothing to my lady here. I wonder Bracy stands it. Hullo! what's the matter?"

Loud voices came from the door of Bracy's room—those of the latter and Gedge; and upon hurrying in the young subaltern was astounded to find, as it seemed to him, Private Gedge with one knee upon the edge of the charpoy, bending over the patient, holding him down by the arm, which was pressed across his chest close up to the throat.

"Here! Hi! Hullo here!" cried Drummond. "What's the meaning of this, sir?"

The words acted like magic. Gedge slipped back, drawing Bracy's arm from where it lay, and he then carefully laid it down beside him.

"It's all right, sir, now, sir; ain't it, Mr Bracy?"

"Yes, yes," said the latter faintly, and looking up at his visitor in a weary, dazed way.

"This fellow has not been assaulting you, has he?" cried Drummond.

"Me? 'Saulting him, sir?" cried Gedge. "Well, come now, I do like that!"

"Oh no; oh no," sighed Bracy.

"It was like this here," continued Gedge; "I was a-hanging about waiting to see if he wanted me to give him a drink or fetch him anything."

Bracy's lips moved, and an anxious expression came over his face; but he said nothing, only looked wildly from one to the other.

"Then all at once I hears him calling, and I went in. 'Here, Gedge, my lad,' he says—just like that, sir, all wild-like—'take this here arm away; it's trying to strangle me.'

"'What! yer own arm, sir?' I says, laughing. 'That won't do.'—'Yes, it will,' he says, just in that squeezy, buzzy way, sir; 'I can't bear it. Take it off, or it'll choke me!'"

"Well?" said Drummond anxiously; "did you?"

"Yes, sir, of course I did; for he spoke just as if it was so; and I got hold of it and tried to pull it away, but he wouldn't let me. He kep' it tight down close to his throat, and looked quite bad in the face."

"You should have used force," said Drummond.

"I did, sir; lots o' force; but he'd got it crooked, and it was just as if the joint had gone fast, so that I was afraid that if I pulled too hard I might break something; and it was just while I was hanging fire like that you came, and he let it come then quite easy. Didn't you, sir?"

"Yes, yes," said Bracy hurriedly. "It had gone to sleep, I suppose, and was as heavy and as cold as marble."

"Oh, I see," said Drummond, smiling; "been lying in an awkward position, I suppose?"

Bracy nodded, but there was a curious look in his eyes that his visitor did not see.

"Come to take a look at you and have a chat.—I say. You heard about me getting in for it?"

"Yes, I heard," said Bracy sadly. "You were wounded."

"Bit of a chop from a tulwar," replied Drummond, touching his bandaged arm lightly. "Nothing much, but I am off duty for a bit. Precious nuisance, isn't it?"

Bracy looked at him so piteously that the young fellow coloured.

"Of course," he said hurriedly; "I understand. Precious stupid of me to talk like that and make a fuss about being off duty for a few days, when you're in for it for weeks. But I say, you know, you are a lot better. Old Morton said you only wanted time."

"He told you that?" cried Bracy eagerly.

"Yes, last night when I met him and he asked me about my scratch. Said he was proud of your case, for with some surgeons you would have died. Ha, ha! He looked at my arm the while, with his face screwed up as if he pitied me for not being under his hands. I say, he's a rum chap, isn't he?"

"He has been very good and patient with me," sighed Bracy; "and I'm afraid I have been very ungrateful."

"Tchah! Not you, old fellow. We're all disagreeable and grumble when we're knocked over. That's only natural. Children are cross when they're unwell, and I suppose we're only big children. I say, heard the news?"

"News? No; I hear nothing here."

"Poor old man! Well, the scouts have brought in news that two more tribes have been bitten with the idea that they want their ranks thinned a bit, and so they've joined the Dwats; so I suppose we shall have some warm work."

"And I am lying here as helpless as a lump of lead. No; I did not hear."

"Why, sir, I told you all that only this morning," broke out Gedge.

"Eh? Did you, my lad?"

"Yes, sir; d'reckly after breakfast."

"So you did. I went to sleep afterwards, and it passed out of my memory. I'm getting weaker, I suppose."

"Not you," cried Drummond. "Here, I say, as I'm a cripple too, I shall come on more. What do you say to a game or two every day? Chess?"

Bracy shook his head.

"Of course not; chess is hard work. Well, then, draughts?"

Bracy shook his head again.

"Right; not much of a game. What do you say to dominoes? We've got a set of double doubles; regular big ones. Shall I bring 'em on?"

"No," said Bracy decisively; "bring your field-glass, and come and sit at that window. You can command a good deal of the valley there."

"What! and tell you all the movements I can make out? To be sure, dear boy. Now, I never thought of that. So I will. I'll come on this afternoon, and you and I will criticise them all and see if we could have planned the beggars' attack better. There, I promised your she-dragon of a nurse not to stay long, so off I go. Bye, bye, old chap; you're beginning to look blooming. We'll do some Von Moltke, and—ah! would you? I say, you are getting better. Larks—eh? But I was too quick for you."

The young officer smiled and nodded merrily, and then went out of the room, Gedge opening the door for him, and slipping out after.

"Well, what is it?" said Drummond, as Gedge stood looking at him anxiously, and as if waiting for him to speak.

"Thought you was going to say something to me, sir, 'bout Mr Bracy there. Don't speak so loud, or he'll hear you."

"Don't matter if he does, my lad. We're not conspiring against him. What did you expect me to say?"

"Something about that arm of his'n, sir, and about him trying to kick you just now."

"Oh, pooh! nonsense! His arm had gone dead; and as for his kicking at me—well, we're getting old friends now, and it was for a bit

128

of fun."

"Think so, sir?"

"Of course."

"Then you wouldn't tell the Doctor about it?"

"About that? Absurd! Here, you're not up to the mark yourself, my lad."

"Well, no, sir; can't quite reach it yet; but I'm a deal better."

"Full of fancies, that's all. What! were you thinking that your master was a bit off his head?"

"Something o' that sort, sir."

"Then don't think so any more. He's fanciful enough without you beginning."

"Then you don't think it's anything to mind?"

"No, of course not. I'm glad to see him getting so much stronger."

Drummond nodded, and being in a good deal of pain, began to nurse his arm again, and tried whether whistling would soothe the sharp, gnawing ache which seemed to run from his wrist up to his shoulder.

Gedge waited till his footsteps died out, and then turned to go back to Bracy's room.

"His is only a clean cut of a tullywor," he muttered, "and'll soon grow together. Different thing to a ragged bullet-wound right through the chest and back, or one like mine, right in the back. I don't like the looks o' all this, though; but he must know better than me, after seeing a lot o' poor fellows cut down and shot; but I think I ought to tell the Doctor."

He opened the door softly and went in, to find that Bracy had been watching for him anxiously.

"Here, Gedge!" saluted him.

"Yes, sir. Get yer a drink, sir?"

"No, no; I want to speak to you. I think I can trust you, Gedge?"

"Yes, sir; of course, sir. What yer want me to do?"

"Hold your tongue, my lad."

"Yes, sir."

"Don't tell the Doctor or Mrs Gee that I hit Captain Roberts on the back yesterday."

"How could I, sir? Did yer?"

"Yes, yes," said Bracy hurriedly. "Nor yet about my arm doing what it did."

"No, sir, cert'n'y not; but I say, sir, you know, your arm didn't do nothing but go to sleep."

"Nor yet about my trying to kick Mr Drummond," said Bracy, without heeding his fellow—sufferer's words.

"Oh no; I shan't say nothing to nobody, sir, unless you tell me to."

"That's right," said Bracy, with a sigh of relief. "That will do. Go now; I want to sleep till Mr Drummond comes back."

"Right, sir," said Gedge, and he went to the bed's head and gently raised the sufferer, while he turned the pillow.

"Makes yer head a bit cooler, sir."

"Yes, thanks, Gedge," said Bracy drowsily; and by the time the lad was outside he was half-asleep.

"I don't like them games of the guvnor's," said Gedge to himself. —"Guvnor? Well, why not? I'm like being oficer's servant now. There's something queer about him, as if he was a bit off his head and it made him get up to larks; for he can't be— No, no, that's impossible, even if it looks like it. He ain't the sorter chap to be playing at sham Abram and make-believe because he was sick of fighting and didn't want to run no more risks."

Chapter Fifteen.

The Doctor In A Fantigue.

Drummond returned to the hospital with his glass, and, to Mrs Sergeant Gee's disgust, installed himself in the window and sat for a couple of hours lightening the painful monotony of Bracy's imprisonment by scanning the movements of the distant enemy hovering about in the hills, and making comments thereon.

"Ah," he said at last, "what we want here is a company of gunners, with light howitzers to throw shells a tremendous distance. If we could have that cleverly and accurately done, we could soon scatter the beggars; but as it is—"

"Yes, as it is," said Bracy peevishly, "we have no gunners and no howitzers; and if we had, how could they be dragged about among these hills?"

"It would be difficult," said Drummond. "There are some fellows crawling out of that west ravine now. Wait till I've focussed them, and —"

"No, no; don't do any more to-day," cried Bracy. "I can't bear it. You only make me fretful because I can't be about doing something again."

"Of course it does; but what is it, old fellow? Are you in pain?"

"Pain? I'm in agony, Drummond. I can't sit up, for I seem to have no power; and I can't lie still, because I feel as if there; was something red-hot burning through my spine."

"Poor old chap! I say—think the bullet is still there?"

"No, no; it passed right through."

"What does the Doctor say?"

"Always the same—always the same: 'You're getting better.'"

"That's right; so you are," said the Doctor, who had just come to the door.—"Ah, Mr Drummond, you here?"

"Yes, sir. Cheering poor old Bracy up a bit."

"That's right. How's your wound?"

"Horrible nuisance, sir."

"Hum! ha! I should like to have; a look at it, but I suppose it would not be etiquette. All the same, etiquette or no, if it does not begin to mend soon come to me."

"I will, sir. Good-afternoon. Ta, ta, Bracy, old man. Keep up your spirits."

"You needn't go, Mr Drummond," said the Doctor. "I can't stay many minutes, and you can talk to him after I'm gone. Well, Bracy, my lad, wounds easier?"

"No. Worse."

"That they are not, sir. You told me you felt a little numbness of the extremities."

"Yes, sir. Arm and leg go dead."

The Doctor nodded.

"That agonising pain in the back goes on too," continued Bracy. "Sometimes it is unbearable."

"Do you think the bullet is still there, sir?" ventured Drummond.

"You stick to your regimental manoeuvres, sir," said the Doctor gruffly. "What do you know about such things?"

"Not much, sir; only one of our fellows was very bad that way before you came, and it was through the bullet remaining in the wound."

The Doctor nodded slowly, and made an examination of his patient, promised to send him something to lull the pain, and then, after a few cheerful words, went away, sent a draught, and the sufferer dropped into a heavy sleep.

The days went on, with plenty of what Shakespeare called alarums and excursions in the neighbourhood of the great fort, the enemy being constantly making desultory attacks, but only to find Graves's boys and Wrayford's men, as they were laughingly called, always on the alert, so that the attacking party were beaten off with more or less loss, but only to come on again from some unexpected direction.

Bracy had plenty of visitors, and Mrs Gee told him that this was the cause of his want of progress; but the visitors dropped in all the same, and the patient made no advance towards convalescence. Now it would be the Colonel, who was kind and fatherly, and went away feeling uneasy at the peculiarity of his young officer's symptoms, for Bracy was fretful and nervous in the extreme; now an arm would jerk, then a leg, and his manner was so strange that when the Colonel went away he sent for Dr Morton, who bustled in, to meet the Colonel's eye searchingly.

"Doctor," said the latter, "I've just come from Bracy's bedside. He does not get on."

"Not a bit," said the Doctor gruffly.

"I have been watching his symptoms carefully."

"Very good of you," said the Doctor gruffly. "I've been watching your manoeuvres too."

This was meant for a sarcastic retort, but the Colonel paid no heed, and went on:

"That poor fellow has the bullet still in the wound."

"No, he has not," retorted the Doctor.

"Then there is something else?"

"Tell me something I don't know," said the Doctor gruffly.

"You think there is, then?"

"I know there is," replied the Doctor. "Do you think, sir, I don't understand my profession?"

"Don't be pettish, Morton. I don't wish to interfere; but I am extremely anxious about poor Bracy."

"Can't be more so than I am, sir."

"Tell me what you feel is wrong."

"Bit of iron, I expect, close up to the vertebrae. The abominable missile broke up, and part remained behind."

"Then, in the name of all that's sensible, why don't you extract it?"

"Because, in the name of all that's sensible, I don't want to see the poor fellow die of *tetanus*—lockjaw, as you call it."

"You dare not extract it?"

"That's it, sir. The piece—a mere scrap, I dare say—keeps his nerves in a horrible state of tension, but it is beyond my reach. Are you satisfied now?"

"Perfectly; but can nothing be done?"

"Nothing but leave it to Nature. She may do what I can't."

"Danger?"

"Of being a cripple; not of anything fatal."

"Poor fellow!" said the Colonel sadly.

"Yes, poor fellow!" said the Doctor. "I'm doing all I know, and must be off now, for you keep me very busy."

Roberts had been sitting with the patient that same afternoon, and towards evening the Major dropped in, glass in eye, and sat talking for a bit, with Bracy fighting hard to keep down his irritability, for the Major was a bad visitor in his way.

"You ought to be up and about, Bracy," he said.

"Yes; I long to be."

"Then why don't you try to brace yourself up—be bracy by nature as well as by name—eh? Ha, ha! Don't you see?"

"Because I am so weak, sir," replied the patient grimly.

"Ah, that's what you think, my dear boy," said the Major, yawning, and shooting his glass out of his eye. "That's what you think. Now, if you were to pull yourself together and make up your mind to get well you'd soon master that weakness."

"Do you think I'm shamming, then, sir?"

"Well, no, my dear boy," said the Major, stretching the string of his eyeglass as he picked it up, and then giving the latter a polish with his handkerchief before proceeding to stick it into its place; "I don't think you are shamming, but that you are in a weak state, and consequently have become hypochon—what you may call it. If you were to—"

Flick! and a sudden jump of the Major to his feet, as he turned sharply to look down at Bracy.

"Confound you, sir! What do you mean by that?"

"Mean by—mean by what?" stammered Bracy, who lay perfectly motionless, with his arms by his sides.

"Mean by what, sir? Why, by striking at my eyeglass and sending it flying."

"No, Major; no, I assure you I—"

"Don't prevaricate with me, sir. There's the string broken, and

134

there's the glass yonder. I—I can forgive a certain amount of irritability in a sick man; but this is impish mischief, sir—the action of a demented boy. How dare you, sir? What the dickens do you mean?"

"Major, I assure you I wouldn't do such a thing," cried Bracy wildly.

"Don't tell me," muttered the Major, striding across to where his glass lay, and picking it up. "Cracked, sir, cracked."

"Indeed, no, Major; I am sure I am quite—"

"I didn't say you were, sir: but my glass. The last I have, and not a chance of replacing it. How am I to go on duty? Why, you must be mad, sir. You might have struck me."

The Major's words were so loud and excited that they brought Mrs Gee to the door, to glance in and hurry away, with the result that directly after the Doctor appeared.

"What's the matter?" he cried. "Bracy worse?"

"Worse, sir?" cried the Major, who was now in a towering rage, the broken glass, a part of which had come out of the frame into his hand, having completely overset his equanimity. "Worse, sir? Look at that."

"Broken your eyeglass?" said the Doctor angrily, "and a good job too. You can see right enough, for we tested your eyes. Only a piece of confounded puppyism, of which you ought to be ashamed."

"Doctor Morton," cried the Major, puffing out his

'You are exaggerating, and—— Oh, my gracious!'
P. B. ?
PAGE 178.

cheeks, his red face growing mottled in his anger. "How dare you!"

"How dare I, sir?" cried the Doctor, who was quite as angry. "How dare you come here, disturbing my patients, and turning the place into a bear-garden just because you have dropped your idiotic eyeglass and broken it? Do you know I have poor fellows in the next room in a precarious state?"

"What! Dropped my eyeglass, sir? I tell you, this lunatic here struck at me, sir, and knocked the glass flying."

"What!" cried the Doctor. "Did you do that, Bracy?"

"No, no, Doctor," stammered the young man; "I assure you I—I—"

"I—I—I!" roared the Major. "How dare you deny it, sir! He did, Doctor. The fellow's stark staring mad, and ought to be in a strait-waistcoat. He isn't safe. He might have blinded me. I came in here quite out of sympathy, to sit with him a little while, and this is the

136

treatment I received. Suppose I had lost my sight."

"Look here, Major," said the Doctor, turning to him, after stepping to the bed and laying his hand upon Bracy's forehead; "the poor fellow is as weak as a babe, and could no more have done what you say than flown out of the window and across the valley. You are exaggerating, and—Oh, my gracious!"

The Major had just time to hop aside and avoid the Doctor's head, for all at once a tremendous kick was delivered from the bed, and the receiver was propelled as if from a catapult across the room, to bring himself up against the wall. Here he turned sharply, to see Bracy lying perfectly still upon the bed, staring at him wildly, and the Major holding his sides, his always prominent eyes threatening to start from his head, while his cheeks became purple as he choked with laughter and stamped about, trying hard to catch his breath.

"Ho, ho, ho! Ho, ho, ho!" he laughed hoarsely. "Oh Doctor! you'll be the death of me. This is too rich—this is too rich—this is too rich!"

"Too rich? Be the death of you? I wish it would," panted the Doctor, turning to the bed to shake his fist at Bracy, but keeping well out of reach of his leg, "You treacherous young scoundrel! How dare you play me such a trick as this?"

Bracy's lips moved, but no sound was heard, and his eyes looked wildly pathetic in their expression.

"I didn't give you credit for such monkey-tricks; but I've done with you now. You've been imposing upon me—you're shamming—malingering, so as to keep out of going on duty again. You might have injured me for life."

"Don't bully the poor fellow, Doctor," cried the Major, wiping his eyes, and picking up one piece of his glass which he had dropped. "I don't think he's shamming, he's off his head. Look how his eyes roll. Poor lad! Give him a dose of something to quiet him, for he's as mad as a March hare."

"Mad as a March hare!" snarled the Doctor, rubbing himself. "I told you it's all a trick."

"I—I—I—d-d-don't care what it is," stammered the Major; "but I wouldn't have missed it for a hundred eyeglasses. Ho, ho, ho! Ho, ho, ho! I can't stop myself. I never laughed so much in my life.—Ha!" he added as he sank into a chair and wiped his eyes; "I feel better now."

"Better!" cried the Doctor. "You may as well let me give you something, or you'll be disgracing yourself before the men."

That was enough. The Major sprang to his feet, to look threateningly at the Doctor.

"Disgrace myself, sir?" he cried furiously.

"Bah!" cried the Doctor, and he bounced out of the room, and, forgetting his patients in the ward near, banged the door.

"There, you've done it now, Bracy!" cried the Major, calming down, and going up to the bedside. "No more of those games, sir, or I shall hit out too. What's the matter with you? Are you shamming, or are you off your head?"

"Beg pardon, sir," said Gedge, entering the room; "the Doctor's sent me to keep watch by Mr Bracy, sir; and he has given me orders that no one is to be near him till he has decided what is to be done."

"What! Order me to go?" said the Major fiercely. "You go back to Doctor Morton, and tell him never to dare to send me such a message as that again."

"Yes, sir," said Gedge, saluting.

"No; stop. This is his own ground," said the Major. "Here, go on with your duty, my lad, and keep a sharp eye on Mr Bracy. He is… or—er—not quite so well to-day. You needn't tell the Doctor what I said."

"No, sir; cert'n'y not, sir," replied Gedge, and he held the door open, standing like a sentry till the Major had passed out, closed it, and I hen stood looking down at Bracy, who lay gazing at him despairingly for some moments before raising his hand cautiously and doubtingly towards his lips.

Chapter Sixteen.

Low Spirits.

"Drink o' water, sir? Yus, sir—there you are."

Gedge gently raised Bracy's head and, all the time on the watch, hit him drink with avidity: but lowered his burden quickly the next instant, for with a sudden jerk the remainder of the water in the brass cup presented was jerked over his face, and the lotah went flying with a bell-like ring.

"I was on the lookout for that, sir," said Gedge good-humouredly, "but you was too quick for me. I say, sir, don't you say you ain't getting better no more."

"Better, Gedge?" said Bracy pitifully. "I am horribly worse."

"Not you, sir, when you can play games like that."

"Oh, my lad—my lad, I could not help it!" Gedge grinned as he looked at him, and shook his head.

"You don't believe me," said Bracy sadly. "Well, you see, sir, I can't very well after that. I couldn't quite take it in when the Doctor told me what you'd done to him, and how you'd served the Major."

"What did he say?" asked Bracy eagerly.

"Said you'd broke out, sir, and was playing all kinds o' games; and that you had been cheating him and everybody else."

"Anything else?"

"Yus, sir; that it was a reg'lar case o' malingering, on'y I don't think he quite meant it. He was cross because he said you kicked him. Did you, sir?"

"Yes—no—my leg jerked out at him, suddenly, Gedge."

"Same thing, sir. Said you'd knocked the Major's eyeglass off and broke it. Did you do that, sir?"

"My arm jerked out and came in contact with his glass, Gedge."

"Same thing, sir, on'y we call it hitting out."

Bracy made a weary gesture with his head, and then, in despairing tones, asked for more water.

"All right, sir; but no larks this time."

"What?"

"Don't get chucking it in my face, sir, unless it does you a lot o' good. If it do I won't mind, for I should like to see you full o' fun again."

"Fun!" groaned Bracy. "Give me the water. It is no fun, but a horror that is upon me, my lad."

"Sorry to hear that, sir," said Gedge, filling the brass cup again from a tall metal bottle. "Still, it do seem rather comic. What makes you do it, sir?"

"I can't help it, my lad," groaned Bracy, who once more drank thirstily and emptied the cup; Gedge, who had been watching him sharply, ready to dodge the water if it were thrown, managing to get it away this time without receiving a drop.

"Now you'll be better, sir."

"Thank you, my lad. I wish I could think so."

"Well, do think so, sir. You ought to, for you must be an awful deal stronger."

"No, no; I am weaker than ever."

"Are yer, sir?"

"Yes, my lad. I was a little like this the other day."

"Yus, sir, I know."

"And it has been getting worst; and worse."

"Better and better, sir. It's a sign the nat'ral larkiness in yer's coming back."

"No, no, my lad. The Doctor noticed it when my arm twitched, and told me it was involuntary action of the nerves, caused by the injury from the bullet."

"Well, sir, he ought to know: and I dare say it's all right. But I say, sir—I don't, mind, and I won't say a word—you did it o' purpose."

"No, Gedge; indeed no."

"But really, sir, do you mean to tell me that when your arm was laid acrost your chest you couldn't get it away?"

"Yes, of course I do."

"And that you hit out and kick at people like that without being able to help it?"

"Yes; it is quite true, my lad, and it is horrible."

"Well, I dunno about being horrible, sir. Things like that can't last, no more than a fellow being off his head and talking all kinds o' stuff for a bit."

"You can't grasp it, Gedge," sighed Bracy.

"No, sir; wish I could."

"What!"

"Only wish you had my shot in the back, and I'd got yours."

"You don't know what you're talking about, my lad."

"Oh, don't I, sir? I just do. Voluntary action, don't you call it? I just seem to see myself lying in yonder with old Gee coming to see me, and with a leg and a arm ready to go off as yours seem to do. My word, the times I've felt like giving old Gee one, but dursen't, because it's striking your sooperior officer. Just think of it, sir; knocking him right over all innercent like, and not being able to help it. Why, I'd give anything to have your complaint."

"Nonsense, nonsense! You are talking folly."

"Can't help that, sir. It'd be worth months o' pain to see old Gee's face, and to hear him asking yer what yer meant by that."

"No, no; it's horrible—and it means, I'm afraid, becoming a hopeless cripple."

"There, you're getting down in the mouth again. Don't you get thinking that. But even if you did, we'd make the best of it."

"The best of it, man!" groaned Bracy.

"O' course, sir. You could get me my discharge, I dessay, and I'd come and carry yer or push yer in one o' them pramblater things as gents sets in and steers themselves. Then yer could ride o' horseback, or I could drive yer in a shay; and then there's boats as you could be rowed about in or have sails. It don't matter much about being a 'opeless cripple, so long as you're a gentleman and don't have to work for your living. Then, as to them two spring limbs, I could soon get used to them, sir, and learn to dodge 'em; and if I was too late sometimes, it wouldn't matter. All be in the day's work, sir. So don't you be down."

Bracy was silent for a few minutes; and seeing that he wished to think, Gedge moved silently about the room, sponging up the water, that had been spilled, taking down Bracy's sword and giving it a polish,

141

rearranging his clothes upon a stool, and whistling softly, though he was in a good deal of pain, till he began chuckling to himself, and Bracy turned his head.

"What are you laughing at?" he said.

"Only thinking about old Gee, sir. He 'listed just at the same time as me, sir; and then, all along of his bumptiousness and liking to bully everybody, while I was always easy-going and friends with every one, he gets first his corp'ral's stripes, and then his sergeant's, and begins to play Jack-in-office, till his uniform's always ready to crack at the seams. Just fancy, sir, being able to give him a floorer without helping it. Ho, my!"

Gedge had to wipe his eyes with the backs of his hands, so full of mirth seemed the thought of discomfiting the tyrant who had hectored over him so long; and Bracy lay looking at him till he calmed down again.

"You don't believe in all this being involuntary, Gedge?" he said at last.

"Didn't at first, sir. I thought it was your larks, or else you were off your head. But I believe it all now, every bit, and I can't get over it. Just to be able to hit your sooperior officer, and no court-martial. Then the Doctor. Just to be able to make him feel a bit, after what he has made us squirm over."

"Then you do believe me now?"

"Of course, sir. And I tell yer it's grand to have a complaint like that. I mean for such as me. No punishment-drill, no lines, no prison, no nothing at all, for bowling your sooperior officer over like a skittle."

Bracy turned his head wearily.

"Ah, Gedge, you can't realise what it all means, to be a hopeless cripple, always in pain."

"Wuth it, sir, every twinge; and as to being a hopeless cripple, what's that so long as there's plenty o' crutches to be had? Pst! Some un coming, sir."

Gedge was right, for directly after the Doctor entered the room, signed to Gedge to go, and then detained him.

"How has Mr Bracy been?" he said sharply.

"Bit low-sperrited, sir."

"Yes; but has he exhibited any of those peculiar phenomena?"

Gedge passed his hand over his chin and stared.

"Bah! Has he kicked at you, or struck you, or done anything of that kind?"

"No, sir; not a bit."

"That's right. Well, Bracy, you quite startled me, my lad; I was taken by surprise, and I looked at it from the commonplace point of view. I've had time to think of it now from the scientific side. Tell me, can you control yourself when those fits come on? I mean, this involuntary nerve and muscular action!"

"Do you think that I should let it go on if I could, Doctor?" said Bracy sadly.

"No, of course not, my dear fellow. Pardon me for asking you."

"Tell me, then: can you cure it? Can you stop these terrible contractions?"

"Yes, with Nature's help, my dear boy."

"Ha!" sighed Bracy: "then may it come. But why is it? I never heard of such a thing before."

"Naturally; and I never encountered such a case. It is all due to the irritation of the spinal nerves, and until we can get rid of the cause we cannot arrive at the cure."

"But, Doctor—"

"Patience, my dear boy—patience."

"Can you give me some?" said Bracy sadly.

"I hope so, for I am going to appeal to your manliness, your strength of mind. You must try to bear your sufferings, and I will help you by means of sedatives."

"Thanks, Doctor. If you could only get me to be strong enough to act in some way."

"Go out with the men and help them to shoot a few of the enemy —eh!"

"Yes," cried Bracy eagerly. "It would keep me from thinking so, and wearing myself out with dread of my helpless future."

"Well, listen to reason," said the Doctor cheerily. "Your helpless future, in which you see yourself a miserable cripple, old before your time, and utterly useless—"

"Yes, yes," cried Bracy eagerly; "it is all that which keeps me back."

"Of course; and what is all that but a kind of waking ill-dream, which you invent and build up for yourself? Come, you must own that."

"Yes," said Bracy, with a sigh; "but I am very bad, Doctor."

"Were."

"I am still; but I will and can fight harder—"

"No, no; not as you did this morning," said the Doctor, smiling.

"I say, I can fight harder if you tell me that I may recover from these terrible fits."

"I tell you, then, that you may and will. There, you've talked enough. Shake hands, and I'll go."

He held out his hand, but there was no response, for Bracy's right arm lay motionless by his side, and a look of misery crossed the poor fellow's face.

"Never mind," said the Doctor quietly; and he took Bracy's hand in his, when the fingers contracted over his in a tremendous pressure, which he had hard work to hear without wincing. But he stood smiling down at his patient till the contraction of the muscles ceased, and Bracy did not know till afterwards the pain that his grip had caused.

Chapter Seventeen.

On the Balance.

The enemy had been very quiet for some days. The weather had been bad. Heavy rains had changed the rills and streams which ran along the gullies and ravines into fierce torrents, which leaped and bounded downward, foaming and tearing at the rocks which blocked their way, till with a tremendous plunge they joined the river in the valley, which kept up one deep, thunder-like boom, echoing from the mountains round.

Before the rain came the sun had seemed to beat down with double force, and the valley had become intolerable during the day, the perpendicular rocks sending back the heat till the fort felt like an oven, and the poor fellows lying wounded under the doctor's care suffered terribly, panting in the great heat as they did, feeling the pangs of Tantalus, for there, always glittering before their eyes in the pure air, were the mountain-peaks draped in fold upon fold of the purest ice and snow.

"We should lose 'em all, poor fellows!" the Doctor said, "if it were not for these glorious evenings and perfect nights. It wouldn't matter so much if we could get a few mule-loads of the ice from up yonder. Can't be done, I suppose?"

"No," said Colonel Graves sadly. "Plenty of men would volunteer, but, much as every one is suffering—the ladies almost as bad as your wounded, Morton—I dare not send them, for they would never get back with their loads. Many of the brave fellows would straggle back, of course, but instead of bringing ice, Doctor, they would be bearing their wounded and dead comrades."

"Yes, that's what I feel," sighed the Doctor, "and, Heaven knows, we don't want any more patients. Must be content with what coolness we get at night."

"And that's glorious," said the Major, wiping his wet brow.

"Delightful," added Captain Roberts. "It's the making of poor old Bracy. He seems to hang his head and droop more and more every day, till the sun goes down, and to begin to pick up again with the first

145

breath that comes down from between the two big peaks there—what do they call them—Erpah and Brum?"

"Ha! wish it was coming now," said the Doctor; "iced and pure air, to sweep right down the valley and clear away all the hot air, while it cools the sides of the precipices."

"Why don't you let me go, Colonel!" said Drummond suddenly. "I want to get some ice badly for poor old Bracy. Six mules, six drivers, and a dozen of our boys. Oh, I could do it. Let me go, sir."

The Colonel shook his head, and every day at the hottest time Drummond proposed the same thing; till on the last day, after gradually growing weaker in his determination, urged as he was on all sides by the sufferers in hospital, the wan looks of the ladies, and the longings of the men, the Colonel said:

"Well, Mr Drummond, I'll sleep on it to-night, and if I come to a determination favourable to the proposition, you shall go; but not alone. One of my officers must go with you."

"Glad to have him, sir," cried the subaltern eagerly. "Whom will you send, sir?"

"I'll volunteer, sir," said Roberts quietly.

"Good," said the Colonel; "so it will be as well for you and Drummond here to quietly select your men and the mules with their drivers, plus tools for cutting out the ice-like compressed snow. If I decide against it there will be no harm done."

"Better make our plans, then, as to which way to go. Study it all by daylight with our glasses."

"Needn't do that," said Drummond eagerly. "I know. We'll go straight up the steep gully that I followed when I went after the bears, it's awfully rough, but it's the best way, for the niggers never camp there; it's too wet for them."

"Very well," said the Colonel; and the two young officers went straight through the scorching sunshine, which turned the great court of the fort into an oven, to where Bracy lay panting with the heat, with Gedge doing his best to make life bearable by applying freshly wrung-out towels to his aching brow.

"News for you, old chap," said Drummond in a whisper. "But send

146

that fellow of yours away."

"There is no need," said Bracy faintly. "I can't spare him, and he's better worth trusting than I am."

"Oh yes, we can trust Gedge," said Roberts in a low tone, while the lad was fetching a fresh bucket of water from the great well-like hole in the court, through which an underground duct from the river ran, always keeping it full of clear water fresh from the mountains, but in these days heated by the sun as it flamed down.

The news was imparted by Drummond, and Bracy shook his head.

"It would be glorious," he said; "but you ought not to go. Graves mustn't let a dozen men run such risks for the sake of us poor fellows. It would be madness. We must wait for the cool nights."

"He will let us go," said Drummond; "and we can do it."

"No," said Bracy, speaking with more energy, and he turned his head to Roberts. "I beg you will not think of such a thing, old lad," he said earnestly.

"Well, we shall see."

"Ready for another, sir?" said Gedge, coming in with the bucket.

"Yes, yes, as soon as you can," said Bracy. "This one feels boiling hot."

The fresh, cool, wet cloth was laid across his forehead; and, rousing up from the disappointment he felt at Bracy taking so decided a view against an expedition which the young subaltern had proposed to make almost solely in his friend's interest, and moved by the boyish spirit of mischief within him, Drummond suddenly exclaimed:

"Look out, Gedge, or he'll bowl you over!—Oh, I beg your pardon, Bracy, old chap. I didn't mean to hurt your feelings. Knock me over, Roberts. I deserve it."

For Bracy had winced sharply, and a look as of one suffering mental agony came into his eyes.

"It does not matter," he said, smiling faintly and holding out his hand, which Drummond caught in his.

"Ain't no fear, sir," said Gedge, who was soaking the hot cloth.

"The guv'nor ain't had a touch now for a week."

"Quiet!" whispered Roberts to the man.

"He is quite right, Roberts, old fellow," sighed Bracy; "I am certainly better. But if I could only get rid of that constant pain!"

"That must go soon," said Drummond cheerily. "I wish I could take your agony-duty for a few hours everyday. Honour bright, I would."

"I know you would, old chap," said Bracy, smiling at him; "but I shall beg Graves not to let you go."

"Nonsense! Don't say a word," cried Drummond. "If you do, hang me if ever I confide in you again!"

Bracy laughed softly.

"I am pretty free from scepticism," he said; "but I can't believe that. Now you fellows must go. The dragon will be here to start you if you stay any longer. Serve him right, though, Roberts, to let him go on this mad foray, for he'd get wounded, and be brought back and placed under Dame Gee's hands."

"Oh, hang it! no; I couldn't stand that," cried the young officer; and a few minutes later they left the room, for Drummond to begin grumbling.

"I don't care," he said. "If the Colonel gives us leave we must go. You won't back out, will you?"

"No; for it would be the saving of some of the poor fellows. But we shall see."

They did that very night, for, instead of the regular cool wind coming down the upper valley, a fierce hot gust roared from the other direction like a furnaces-blast from the plains; and at midnight down came the most furious storm the most travelled of the officers had ever encountered. The lightning flashed as if it were splintering the peaks which pierced the clouds, and the peals of thunder which followed sounded like the falling together of the shattered mountains, while amidst the intense darkness the sentries on the walls could hear the hiss and seething of the rain as it tore by on the rushing winds which swept through gorge and valley.

The next morning the storm broke dark and gloomy, with the rain falling heavily and the river rolling along thick and turbulent, while one of the first things the sentries had to report was the fact that one of the hostile camps—the one nearest to the fort—was being struck.

By night the tribe in another of the side valleys was withdrawn, and during the days which followed one by one the little camps of white-robed tribes-men melted away like the snow upon the lower hills, till not a man of the investing forces remained, and the long-harassed defenders looked in vain from the highest tower of the fort for their foes.

The falling rain had effected in a few days that which the brave; defenders had been unable; to compass in as many weeks; while the alteration from the insufferable heat to the soft, cool, moist air had a wonderful effect upon the wounded, and made Doctor Morton chuckle and rub his hands as he rejoiced over the change.

And still the rain went, on falling; the valley seemed surrounded by cascades, the streams rushed and thundered down, and the main river swept by the walls of the fort with a sullen roar; while, as if dejected and utterly out of heart, the British flag, which had flaunted out so bravely from the flagstaff, as if bidding defiance to the whole hill-country and all its swarthy tribes, hung down and clung and wrapped itself about the flagstaff, the halyard singing a dolefully weird strain in a minor key, while the wind whistled by it on its way down towards the plains.

Chapter Eighteen.

Uncooked Mutton.

Two days passed—two of about the wettest and most dismal days imaginable. There was no sign of the enemy, and the scouts sent out came back dripping, and always with the same news—that the hill-men had given up the siege in disgust, and were right away making for their homes in the valleys at the foot of the mountain-slopes.

There was no relaxation in the watchfulness of the garrison, however, the treacherous nature of the tribes being too well-known. Hence it was that the sentries in their heavy greatcoats stood in such shelter as they possessed, keeping watch and ward, with the valley stretched out dark and gloomy, and the booming and roaring river dimly-seen through the gloom of the night, as it foamed and tossed itself in spray against the various obstacles it encountered on its way towards the lower gorge whence Colonel Graves's regiment had made its appearance when it first came to the assistance of the beleaguered in Ghittah Fort.

The rain had ceased and given place to a thick mist, so peculiar in its appearance that one of two officers going the rounds, both nearly invisible in their long overcoats, said softly to the other:

"Might fancy we were at home after one of our muggy days."

"Yes; just like a London suburban fog, old fellow."

Then there was silence for a minute, as they walked on along the terraced wall, before the one who had just spoken said in a quick whisper:

"I say, Roberts, oughtn't there to be a sentry here?"

"I was just thinking so," was the reply. "I hope to goodness he isn't asleep, for I hate having to report a man for neglect."

He had hardly whispered the words when there was the click of a rifle, a voice challenged them, and they gave the customary response.

"This is not your place, my man," said Roberts then.

"No, sir; twenty yards farther that way. But there's something down below then; that I can't quite make out. It seemed to come past and on this way."

"What! up on the ramparts?" said Drummond quickly.

"No, no, sir; right down below the face of the wall, and I come on a bit so as to follow and look down. I didn't like to give the alarm."

"Why?" said Roberts sharply.

"Because it might be a false one, sir."

"Better give a dozen false alarms, my lad, than miss a real danger. Now, then, what did you see?"

"Well, sir, if we was at home I should say it was a drove o' sheep or a herd o' pigs; but these hill-niggers are so artful and ready to be down upon us that I fancied it might be men."

"Men haven't four legs," said Drummond, laughing softly.

"No, sir; but these Dwats don't think anything o' going down on all-fours."

"But there have been none about lately," said Drummond; "the rain seemed to be too much for them."

"Yes, sir; but ain't they the more likely to come down on us when they think we believe we're safe?—Change guard, sir."

For steps were heard, and a party of men came up smartly, were challenged, and the non-commissioned officer in charge answered.

"That you, Gee?" said Roberts.

"Yes, sir."

"Come here. The sentry thinks there are people below there. Come and have a look."

"The sentry I've just relieved thought the same, sir," replied Gee sharply, "and I had a good look. They're sheep driven down from the hills by the bad weather. I was going to report to the Colonel, sir, and ask whether he'd order a sally from the gate to drive them in. Be useful, sir."

"To be sure. You'd better do it. Let's have a look over first."

They stepped together to the embattled wall, and peered down into the darkness; but nothing was visible now, and Roberts was about to give the matter up as all a mistake, when, from where the mist was most dense, there was the pattering of hoofs in the wet mud, followed by the peculiarly human cough of one of the sheep of the district.

"No mistake about what they are, sir," said Sergeant Gee softly. "They've come down to the low grounds on account of the storm."

"Yes," said Roberts, "and because there are none of the Dwats to keep them back. Why, Gee, we're in luck. We must have the men out and the flock driven in."

"Not much room for them in the court, sir," said the Sergeant.

"No; but to-morrow we must have something in the way of hurdles to shut them in close under the wall, and they can be driven out to pasture every day by some of the men, with a guard to watch over them. You try and keep them under your eye now while I go and tell the Colonel."

The two young men peered down at where the pattering of hoofs could be heard through the mist twenty feet below them; though nothing was visible but a dimly-seen moving mass.

A few minutes later they announced the find to the Colonel.

"This is good news, gentlemen," he said; "such a store of fresh provisions will be a treasure. Order out your company, Roberts, and you had better get five-and-twenty or thirty of your men, Mr Drummond."

"Yes, sir," said the subaltern, smiling.

"What's that you're thinking—rather absurd to get out two companies to drive in a flock of sheep?"

"Well, sir, I was thinking something of the sort," said the young man, colouring.

"I want them to strengthen the guard," said the Colonel quietly. "A dozen of the native servants can be sent round the flock to head the sheep toward the open gates. There is nothing like being on your guard when dealing with a venturesome as well as a treacherous enemy."

"You think the enemy may make a rush, sir, as soon as the gates are open?"

"No, Roberts," said the Colonel, laying his hand on the young man's shoulder. "I think the enemy might make a rush if they were near; but, happily, I do not believe there are any of the hill-men for many miles round. The last reports are that they are heading homewards, and I begin to hope that the breaking-up of the weather has set us at liberty."

The arrangements were soon made, everything being done quietly and without any display of lights. The Fusiliers and the draft of Colonel Wrayford's regiment were stationed on either side of the gates, and about twenty of the native servants, under the guidance of a couple of the friendly hill-men, accustomed to look after the camp live-stock, were detailed with their orders to divide as soon as the gates were opened, and steal cautiously round to the far side of the flock before trying to head them in.

Strict orders had been given to keep the court still and dark, so that the sheep might not take fright upon reaching the gates; while the news spread very rapidly, and the men turned out of their rough quarters, seeking the walls, so as to try and see something of what was going on.

At last, all being ready, the Colonel gave the order for the guard occupying the two towers which commanded the gates to report the state of affairs. Sergeant Gee had taken his place there, and he came down to announce that the sheep were in a very large flock, apparently huddled together about a hundred yards from the gate. But they were quite invisible, and their position could only be made out by their fidgety movements.

"Sounds to me, sir, as if they'd got wolves hanging about them, or maybe a bear."

"Then they'll be all the more ready to come into shelter," said the Colonel, who then gave the word. The great leaves of the entrance were drawn inward, and, each party under his leader, the native servants slipped silently out in Indian file, turned to right and left, and disappeared in the darkness, the mist seeming to swallow them up after their third step.

"Quite a bit of sport, old fellow," whispered Drummond, who had charge of the men on one side, Roberts being on the other, while the regular guard manned the tower and adjacent wall in strength, so as to see the fun, as they dubbed it.

All was silent now, and the only lights visible were those of the windows in the officers' quarters, so that it was hard to imagine that many hundred men, for the most part unarmed, were listening eagerly for the first approach of the unsuspecting sheep.

The listeners were not kept in suspense as to whether plenty of roast mutton was to supersede the short commons of the past. There was what seemed to be a long period of silence and darkness, during which a cloud of dense mist floated in through the gateway to fill the court; and during this time of waiting the watchers, by other senses rather than sight, pictured the dark scouts playing the same part as falls to the lot of a collie dog at home, doubling round the great flock, whose restless trampling they could hear in the soft, wet soil. But at last there was the sound of many pattering feet, telling that the flock was in motion; and the suspense deepened, for the question was, "Would the men be able to head the sheep in, or would they dash off to right or left, avoiding the big opening through the gates as the mouth of a trap?"

"Will they—won't they?" muttered Drummond; and Roberts, like the men in the angle hidden by the tower on the side, held his breath.

The minutes seemed long drawn out now, as the pent-up excitement increased; and Gedge, who was at the open window of the hospital quarters, reached out as far as he could, his heart beating hard as he listened, hearing the pattering quite plainly, and reporting progress to his officer, stretched upon his pallet. For the news had penetrated to where they were. Gedge had heard it from an ambulance sergeant, and hurried in to Bracy.

"Hoo-roar, sir!" he said excitedly, panting hard the while. "Tell yer direckly. It's wonderful how soon I gets out o' breath since I had my last wound,"—the knock-down from the stone in the pass was always "my first wound."—"The boys have captured a flock o' sheep, sir, and it's going to be cuts out o' roast legs and hot mutton-chops for us every day."

Bracy sighed on hearing this.

"Ah, you go like that, sir," said Gedge; "but just you wait till you smell one o' them chops, frizzled as I'll do it, and peppered and salted —wonder whether there is a bit o' pepper to be got."

Gedge did not get the news till the arrangements were well in progress, and a pang of disappointment shot, through him, mingled with a longing to go and join in the fun. But he kept his thoughts to himself, and set to work to make his invalid participate as much as was possible by listening and reporting all he could hear.

"Just you hark, sir; can't hear a whisper, and it's as black as can be," he said softly. "Hope; those chaps as they've sent won't muff it and let the sheep get away to the mountains."

"They most likely will," sighed Bracy, who was more low-spirited than usual that night.

"That's what I'm afraid on, sir. Can't hear nothing, sir," he said mournfully. "Yes, I can; just a soft sort o' sound as is getting louder. It's pitter-patter o' little feet in the mud. Yes, that's it, sir. They're a-coming nigher and nigher. Oh! don't I wish I was out behind 'em with a couple of those grey dogs without any tails the drovers uses. I'd have 'em in through the gates in no time, without losing one."

"Are they going to drive the flock into the courtyard?" said Bracy wearily.

"Why, I told him they were just now," muttered Gedge; and then aloud, "Yes, sir, that's it; and here they come, and—I can't see, but I can hear—they're a-getting quite near. And of course, as soon as they're all in, bing-bang our chaps'll swing them great gates to and make 'em fast, and there, you are. What a glorious grab, and won't the niggers be wild! Say, Mr Bracy, sir."

"Yes."

"Don't you feel as if you want to shout?"

"No, Gedge, no."

"I do, sir. I say, sir, if I was you I'd give me orders to see the butchers, and buy four o' the sheepskins. I could dress 'em, and you could have 'em made up into a rug, or let the tailor line your greatcoat with 'em. For if we're going to be shut up here all the winter, every one of them skins 'll be better for you than two ton o' coals."

"Buy six for me, my lad," said Bracy, "and have three to line your own coat."

"Oh, thank ye, sir; but—"

"No, no; three will do, my lad, for I shall be lying asleep under the turf before the winter comes."

"Mr Bracy, sir!" cried Gedge in a husky voice. "Oh, sir, plee, sir, don't go and talk like that, sir! Oh, blow the sheep, and the mutton, and the skins!" he muttered; "what do I care about 'em now?"

He was turning away, when, regretting what he had said, Bracy raised himself a little on one elbow, and said softly, and with his voice sounding stronger:

"Why don't you go on telling me, my lad! Is the flock coming nearer?"

Gedge thrust his head out again, and then partly withdrew it.

"Yes, sir—close in, sir. You can hear 'em now; they must be coming in at the gates. Oh, do be careful!" he whispered to nobody, once more full of excitement, and imagining everything in the darkness. "Steady, steady! Mind, you nigger to the left. Yah! don't get waving your arms like that; you'll scare one o' them old rams. Can't you see him tossing his head about? He'll bolt directly, and if he does the whole flock 'll be after him and off and away to the hills."

"Can you see them, Gedge?" said Bracy, beginning to take interest in the capture now for his lad's sake, for deep down in his breast there was a well-spring of gratitude for all the poor, rough, coarse fellow had done.

"See 'em, sir? No; it's as black as the inside of a tar-barrel: but I can hear and fancy it all, and I've helped drive many a flock out Whitechapel way when I was a small boy. Here they come, though, patter, patter, and the chaps have done it splendid; they haven't made a sound. Here they come; they must be half in by now. There's some on 'em close under the winder, sir. Hear 'em puffing and breathing?"

"Yes, yes; I can hear them there quite plainly, Gedge. I hope they will secure them now, for every one's sake."

"So do I, sir; but they're not caught till they're all in and the gates is shut. Our sheep in London's wild enough when they take fright, while these things is more like goats, and you know how they can run up among the rocks. Oh, steady, steady, out there; look sharp and shut those gates," whispered the listener. "Oh, do mind! If I sees all them legs o' mutton cutting their sticks off to the mountains I shall go mad."

"What's that?" cried Bracy, as in the wild flush of excitement that flashed through his brain it seemed as if he had received a galvanic shock, and he sat right up in his bed, to keep in that position, gazing wildly towards the darkened window.

Gedge doubtless replied, but his voice was drowned by the wild, warlike yell of triumph which rose from the court—a yell which told its own tale of the success of a *ruse*. The sheep had been driven into the court through the mist and darkness—a great flock; but with them fully a hundred tulwar and knife armed Dwats in their winter sheepskin-coats, who had crept in with the quiet sheep on all-fours, the placid animals having doubtless been accustomed to the manoeuvre, thought out and practised for weeks past, with a so far perfectly successful result.

The yell was answered by the Colonel's voice shouting clearly the order for the gates to be shut; but the massacre had begun, the mad

Mussulman fanatics who had undertaken the forlorn hope being ready to do or die; and, as the rattle of the moving gates began, an answering war-cry came from not far away, the rush of a large body of men making for the opening being plainly heard.

"Taken by surprise!" shouted Bracy wildly as he realised the horror. "Gedge, it means the slaughter of the poor women and our wounded comrades in the ward. Here, quick, my sword! my revolver! Quick! get one yourself."

"I've got yours, sir, here," cried Gedge excitedly as he snatched them from where they hung. "Don't—don't move, sir; you're too weak and bad, and I'll keep the window and the door, sir. They shan't come near yer while I'm alive. After that—here, ketch hold, sir—your pistol, sir—after that you must lie still and shoot."

The light had been extinguished, so that the sheep should not be scared by a glare from the window; and in the darkness, amidst the howls, yells, and shouts in the courtyard, Gedge felt for the bed so as to thrust the loaded revolver into Bracy's hand. But, to his astonishment, a strong hand was laid upon his shoulder, and the sword was snatched from his grasp, while Bracy cried in a voice the lad hardly knew:

"Keep the pistol, close that door and window, and come on. Gedge, lad, we must try and keep the ward, before these savages get in."

Chapter Nineteen.

Ghazis and Cunning.

As Bracy, closely followed by Gedge, made for the door, the noise and confusion in the darkness were horrible. There were nearly a score of sick and wounded in the two rows of beds, some of whom were groaning and appealing for help; but the majority were making brave efforts to get on some clothes, and one man was shouting for the nurse to go to the armoury and bring as many rifles and bayonets as she could carry. But there was no answer to their appeals, as Bracy, tottering at first, but growing stronger as he passed between the two rows of beds, struggled for the door at the end, and passed through into a little lobby, from which another door led at once into the court, a mere slit of a window at the side admitting a few faint rays of light.

"Ha!" ejaculated Bracy in a tone of thankfulness. "The door's fast, Gedge, lad, and we must defend it to the last. We can do no good outside."

"Who's this?" cried a harsh, sharp voice. "Bracy, my dear boy, you here?" cried the Doctor almost simultaneously.

"Nurse!—Doctor!" panted the young officer.

"Yes, here we are, my boy, on duty; and bless this woman! she's as plucky as half-a-dozen men."

"Nonsense!" said Mrs Gee harshly. "You don't suppose I was going to stand still and let the wretches massycree my patients—do you, Doctor?"

"No, my dear, I don't think anything of the kind, and certainly I won't. Have you got plenty of cartridges?"

"A dozen packets, and there's four rifles with fixed bayonets behind the door."

"I'll have one, my lass. I was afraid I should have to take to my surgical instruments. But, look here, Bracy, my boy, you can do no good, so go back to bed and send that scoundrel Gedge here. He's hiding under one of the beds. He could load for nurse, here, and me, while we fired."

"If you warn't like one o' my sooperior officers," snarled Gedge, "I'd say something nasty to you, Doctor. Give us one of them rifles, old lady; I'm better with them and a bay'net than with this popgun. You take your pistol, Mr Bracy, sir."

"No, no—yes, yes," said the Doctor hurriedly. "You may want it, my boy. Now, then, go back to your bed. You'll be in the way here."

"In the way of some of these yelling fiends, I hope, Doctor," said Bracy, thrusting the revolver into the waistband of his hurriedly dragged on trousers. "Now, then, where will they try to break in?"

"The first window they can reach, when they fail at this door. You, Gedge, watch that window. No one can get in, but some one is sure to try."

The keen point of a bayonet was held within a few inches of the opening the next moment, and then the little party, awaiting the attack, stood listening to the terrible sounds from without. It was hard work to distinguish one from the other, for the confusion was now dreadful; but, from time to time, Bracy, as he stood quivering there as if a strange thrill of reserved force was running through every vein, nerve, and muscle, made out something of what was going on, and primarily he grasped the fact, from the loud clanging, that the great gates had been closed and barred against the entrance of those who were rushing forward to the support of the fanatical Ghazis who had been so successful in their *ruse*.

Then came other sounds which sent a ray of hope through the confusion; first one or two shots rang out, then there was a ragged volley, and a more or less steady fire was being kept up from the towers and walls. But this was doubtless outward, begun by the sentries, and aided by the two companies that rapidly mounted to their side by the orders of their officers, who felt that it would be madness to begin firing in the dark upon the Ghazis raging about the court, for fear of hitting their unarmed friends.

It was some minutes before the Colonel could reach the guard-room, which was held by the relief, and he had a couple of narrow escapes from cuts aimed at him; but he reached the place at last, in company with about a dozen unarmed men, and in a few minutes there was one nucleus here ready with fixed bayonets to follow his orders. Other men made a rush for their quarters from the walls where they had flocked, unarmed, to be spectators of the capture; but to reach them and their rifles and ammunition they had to cross the court, which was now one tossing chaos of cutting and slashing fiends in human form, rushing here and there, and stumbling over the frightened sheep, which plunged and leaped wildly, adding greatly to the din by their piteous bleating, many to fall, wounded, dying, and struggling madly, beneath the sword-cuts intended for the garrison. These were flying unarmed seeking for refuge, and often finding none, but turning in their despair upon their assailants, many of whom went down, to be trampled under foot by those whom they sought to slay.

The firing now began to rapidly increase, the flashings of the rifles seeming to cut through the dense mist, now growing thicker with the smoke, which, instead of rising, hung in a heavy cloud, mingling with the fog, and making the efforts of the defenders more difficult as it increased. For some time every one seemed to have lost his head, as, in spite of the efforts of the officers, the panic was on the increase, and the Ghazis had everything their own way. Colonel Graves, as soon as he had got his little force together, gave the word for a rush with the bayonet, and led the way, his men following bravely, but the difficulties they encountered were intense. It was almost impossible to form in line, and when at last this was roughly achieved in the darkness, and the order to advance was given, it was upon a mass of struggling sheep mingled with the yelling fiends; and, to the horror of the line of sturdy men, they found that to fire, or advance with the bayonet, would be to the destruction of friend as well as foe.

To add to the horror, the wild and piteous shrieks of women arose now from the portion of the fort containing the officers' quarters; and at this Roberts, who was firing with his men down into the seething mass of fresh assailants swarming at the gates and striving, so far vainly, to mount the walls, gave a sharp order.

"Here, cease firing, my lads," he yelled. "Drummond—Drummond! Where's Mr Drummond?"

"Gone, sir," came from one of the men.

"What! down?" cried Roberts.

"No, sir; he said something about go on firing, and hooked it off along the ramp."

An angry groan arose, and Roberts muttered something about his friend before shouting again.

"Sergeant," he cried, "take the command of your men, and keep these dogs from mounting the gate. I am going to lead my company to the officers' quarters. Ready, my lads? No firing. The bayonet. We must save those women, or die."

A loud, sharp, snapping hurrah rang out, seeming to cut through the mist, and then at Roberts's "Forward!" they dashed after him at the double, to reach the next descent into the court, which meant right among the yelling Ghazis, but at the opposite end to that where Colonel Graves and the Major—who had reached them now with a couple of dozen men, mostly armed with the Indians' tulwars—had managed to struggle into line.

Very few minutes elapsed before the shouting of Captain Roberts's men, as they dashed down, two abreast, cutting into the mass below, added to the wild confusion, and for a time it seemed as if the struggle would become hopeless, as the brave fellows' strength began to yield to exhaustion, for the power to combine seemed gone, and the *mêlée* grew more a hand-to-hand fight, in which the savage Ghazis had the advantage with their keen swords, their adversaries

'Fire—fire!' shouted a voice, and a yell of triumph rose from the Ghazis.
Page 212.

F. R.!

wanting room to use their bayonets after a few fierce and telling thrusts.

"This is useless, Graham," panted the Colonel at last; "these sheep hamper every movement. We can do nothing in this horrible darkness. I am going to give the order for every man to make for the walls, where we must defend ourselves with the bayonet as the fellows attack us. We must wait for morning, and then shoot them down."

"And by then they will have slaughtered every woman and non-combatant in the fort," growled the Major savagely.

"No; we must each lead a company or two for the quarters. You take as many as you can collect straight for the ladies' rooms."

"Roberts has gone ten minutes ago, and is fighting his way across."

"Go round by the walls on the other side and get in behind. I am going to rush for the hospital. Bracy and all those poor fellows must be saved."

"Too late," said the Major bitterly. "Two of the men here left a score of the hounds fighting their way into the ward. Oh, if we only had a light!"

Strange things occur when least expected, and there are times when, as if by a miracle, the asked-for gift is bestowed.

"God bless you, Graves!" whispered the Major; "if we don't meet again, I'll do all that man can do."

"I know it, Graham. You'll save the women, I'm sure. Ah! what's that?"

"Fire—fire!" shouted a voice, and a yell of triumph rose from the Ghazis, to be echoed by the seething mob of fanatics outside the gates, who burst forth with their war-cry of "Allah! Allah—uh!"

"We're done, Graves," said the Major in an awestricken, whisper. "It's the fodder-store, and it will attack our quarters soon. It's all of wood."

"If it does we shall see how to die fighting," said the Colonel hoarsely, as a wreath of flame and sparks rolled out of a two-story building at the far end of the court, lighting up the whole place and revealing all the horrors of the scene.

Chapter Twenty.

Non-Combatants.

Meanwhile, completely cut off by the enemy from the rest of the garrison, the occupants of the hospital made such preparations as they could to strengthen their defences. Little enough they were, consisting as they did of three or four pieces of wood placed like stays from the floor to the cross-pieces of the roughly-made door; and when it was done the Doctor said sadly:

"It's of no use. If they come with a rush they will drive that in as if it were so much cardboard."

"Let them," said Bracy. "They will find three bayonets and a sword-point ready for them to fall upon."

"Yes; and then?" said the Doctor bitterly. "There will be four bodies lying in front of us between our breasts and the men who come on, and so again and again till we have made a rampart of the wretched bodies."

"Very well in theory, my good patient," said the Doctor sadly; "but I'm afraid we shall have made part of the breastwork ourselves. These Ghazis not only know how to fight, but they do fight as if there were no such thing as fear."

"There's not much of that in British soldiers when they are at bay," said Bracy proudly. "But it's of no use to talk, Doctor; we must defend this door to the last, and then retreat into the ward, barricading that next."

"And after that?"

"There are my quarters: but we must carry the helpless in there first."

"And lastly?"

"Never mind that," said Bracy coldly; "let us get through firstly and secondly; a dozen things may happen before then."

"Hist!" whispered Mrs Gee. "Some one is coming."

All listened, and heard a swift movement like a hand being passed over the rough door as if feeling for the fastening. Then there were several hard thrusts, and directly after a quick whispering, a scratching as of feet against the wall, and then a slight change in the appearance of the window, the darkness growing a little deeper. In an instant there was the loud rattle of a rifle being thrown out to the full extent of its holder's arms, the bayonet darting through the narrow slit; there was a savage yell, the dull thud of some one falling, and with a fierce shout of rage two or three of the enemy flung themselves at the door, repeating the act again and again, but without result.

"Can't some of us come and help, sir?" said a feeble voice.

"Yes; there's six of us, sir," said another; "and we've all got rifles."

"Back to your beds directly," cried the Doctor. "What's the use of me trying to save your lives, and— Well, it's very good of you, my lads," he said, breaking off suddenly. "Fix bayonets, and stand outside the ward ready to help if we, the first line, are driven in."

There was a sharp crackety-crack as the metal sockets of the bayonets rattled on the muzzles of the rifles, and the six invalids took their places on either side of the ward-door, where the rest of the sufferers lay in silence listening to the yelling outside and the firing now going vigorously on.

There was another crash against the outer door, but still it did not yield, though it sounded as if it was being dashed from its fastenings, and then a shuffling, scraping sound told that another attempt was being made by one of the mad fanatics to get in by the slit of a window. But again there was the peculiar rattling sound of a thrust being made with a rifle thrown right forward and grazing the sides of the opening. A wild shriek followed, and Gedge withdrew his piece, panting heavily and trembling from weakness.

"Did you get home?" whispered the Doctor.

"Yes, sir, clean," whispered back Gedge; "and oh, if that only was the chap as shot Mr Bracy that day!"

There was a crash at the door now, as if a mass of stone had been hurled at it; a couple of boards were driven out, and a strange animal odour floated in, with a yell of triumph, heard above the piteous bleating of sheep and the sharp rattle of the rifles.

"Give me room, Doctor; I can do it. My man taught me," said the nurse, standing with Gedge, friendly for the first time in their lives; and they delivered rapidly thrust after thrust with their full strength, one of the savage Ghazis going down at each.

It was too dark to do much, and Bracy felt his helplessness, after trying to parry a cut or two delivered by one of the enemy; so, drawing his revolver, he fired slowly shot after shot as the enemy reached in to cut at the defenders, their blows mostly falling upon the sides of the broken door.

"It's of no use to try and hold this place longer, Doctor," he said, bringing now to bear his military knowledge. "We have to bear the full rush of these men."

"But it's like giving up to them," panted the Doctor.

"Never mind; let's retire into the ward. You see, the door is at right-angles to this, and when they press in they can only fill this little place, and we shall have to contend with four or five instead of fifty."

"That's good talk," said the Doctor. "I'm not a soldier. Very well, then, back in, and I'll cover you."

"No; you retire with the nurse and Gedge, and I will hold them at bay till you get in. Make the men present their bayonets as soon as we are in. Just give the word, and they will know. It will check the wretches while we try to get the door closed."

"No," cried the Sergeant's wife through her teeth. "Bill Gedge and I will keep them off till you are in and tell us to fall back."

"Right," said the Doctor; "don't stop to parley, Bracy, my lad. Ah, what does that mean?" he cried sharply, for Mrs Gee and Gedge both thrust and then thrust again.

"Means a roosh, gentlemen," said Gedge hoarsely. "In with you; we can't hold 'em back any longer."

"Back in," said Bracy hoarsely. "We must do it, Doctor; they're mad for our blood."

The Doctor stepped through the inner door, and Bracy followed.

"Right and left," he said sharply; "cover the advance as they fall back."

A low hissing sound accompanied a quick movement, and then, after delivering a couple more thrusts, Gedge whispered:

"In with you, nurse."

"You first, boy," she answered, as she thrust fiercely again, a sharp cry following her delivery.

"I don't go afore a woman," said Gedge bluntly, as he delivered point once more.

"Nor I before my patient," said Mrs Gee, following his example, and feeling the bayonet strike flesh.

"Back, you two, at once," cried Bracy sternly; and as the strangely assorted couple took a step or two back and darted into the ward, a hedge of bayonets dropped down breast-high, in time to meet the rush of Ghazis who dashed forward with upraised swords.

Then, to the surprise of all, there was the crackle of a little volley, and the faces of the fierce warriors were for a moment illumined, efforts being made to strengthen the position by dragging a charpoy across, planting a second upon the first, and heaping thereon everything that could be seized upon in the darkness. There was a fresh burst of yelling, the Ghazis raging in their disappointment and at the losses that had befallen them, just, too, when they believed that an entry had been made.

The Doctor took advantage of the pause in the attack to order every invalid who could move by his own efforts to seek refuge in the officers' ward, and with groans and sighs they obeyed, one helping the other, and in many instances having to be helped in turn, while several by slow degrees managed to crawl. A pause in the attack did not give time for all this, the enemy coming fiercely on again before the ward was half clear; but the bristling array of bayonets presented at the narrow doorway kept them from gaining an entrance, each stroke of their tulwars being received on the rifle-barrels, and several going down as deadly thrusts were made.

It was evident enough to Bracy and the Doctor that their defence could not last, much longer. A party of able-bodied men, dividing and taking their duty in turn, might have kept the whole body of the hill-men at bay for an indefinite time; but the efforts of Gedge and Mrs Gee were growing weaker, and at last it was all that the invalids could do to keep their bayonets from being beaten down.

"We must make for our last refuge, Doctor," said Bracy at last.

"Yes, and none too soon," was his reply; "but first of all let's have as much of the bedding as we can get taken to the other room to form a breastwork. Half you men retire and carry mattresses and blankets till you are ordered to cease."

This was done, and then the order was given, just as the enemy was making one of its most savage attacks, the men pressing on with all their might, till a volley was fired which made them recoil. It was only to recover themselves and pour fiercely in through the dense smoke, to begin yelling with rage as they found by degrees that the long ward was empty, and a fresh barrier of bayonets bristling ready for them at the farther door, where a couple of charpoys had been hastily thrown across one upon the other, and piled on the top was all the bedding, principally rough straw mattresses and blankets—a slight enough breastwork, but impervious to sword-cuts, while to reach over in order to make a blow was to expose whoever struck to a deadly bayonet-thrust. Here the defence was gallantly maintained again, the attack as fiercely made, till the floor became wet with blood, and several of the carnage-seeking enemy slipped and fell, either to crawl or be dragged away by their companions.

"It's getting to be a matter of minutes now," said the Doctor in a whisper to Bracy. "This is the last of it."

"The window," said Bracy, calmly enough now. "Take Mrs Gee and help her out. Then you and Gedge climb out, and drop down; you may make your escape in the darkness. You hear, Mrs Gee?"

"Yes, sir, I hear," said the woman in her sourest tones; "but my man told me I was to stick to my patients, no matter what happened."

"And I order you to escape."

"Yes, sir; but I'm not one of your men," said the woman, with a triumphant masterful ring in her words, "and under your orders; but you are my patient and under mine. So you go and get as many of the poor boys away with you as you can. Off with you, Gedge; you're as bad as any of them, in spite of your brag. Then you others follow, one at a time; me and the Doctor can't leave, the rest, and we're going to stay."

"Go!" said Gedge sharply. "Go and leave my comrades and my orficer as can't help theirselves. Not me!"

There was a low murmur at this, and then a cessation of all words in the desperate defence forced upon the little party; for, as if maddened by the long resistance, and utterly reckless of the losses they had suffered, the Ghazis came on, howling and bounding to the door, leaping up and reaching in to strike downward with all their force, and generally paying the penalty of death; for even with their swords extended to the full extent of the holders' arms, not once was a damaging cut inflicted.

The result of this last rush was that, horrible to relate, the breastwork was raised by the bodies of three fatally wounded Ghazis, who in their dying moments sought to revenue their deaths by cutting savagely at their foes as they lay.

"I can't bay'net chaps who are down," muttered Gedge, shrinking back; while at the same moment Mrs Gee uttered a wild cry, for one of the dying men had inflicted a horrible upward cut, which, as she was leaning forward, took effect upon her chin.

This movement on the part, of two of the strongest of the defenders seemed to be fatal. A weak place in their defence was displayed, and with a fierce yell the enemy crowded on in a final attack. This would have been fatal but for the bravery of the tottering invalids, who met the rush with a sharp volley from half-a-dozen pieces, and the flash and smoke were followed by a sudden burst of light, which flooded the ward, showing the enemy retiring a little, startled by the unexpected volley and wondering at the glare. This gave time for reloading, and another volley was fired as the enemy came on again.

This volley was followed by the commencement of a rolling fire outside, mingled with yells of rage, imprecations, loud orders, and the hoarse commands of officers. For the light given by the burning building was the opportunity required; and minute by minute the firing increased from the walls, as the scattered soldiery, many of whom had remained unarmed, found their way into their quarters to obtain rifles and bayonets, and joined their companions on the wall, able, and willing too, to take aim down into the seething mob of savages in the court, without risking destruction to a comrade or friend.

Three times over Colonel Graves summoned the enemy to surrender, and twice over native attendants were dragged forth to yell down to the Ghazis that their lives would be spared. All was in vain; the announcements were received with shouts of defiance, yells of hatred at the Christian dogs, and savage rushes were made at the steps leading up to the ramparts, in each case for the venturers to be partly shot down, the residue being hurled back from the point of the bayonet.

"It's of no use, Graves—Roberts," cried the Major; "it's their lives or ours. Fire, my lads, fire!"

And by the increasing light of the flaming building, whose ruddy rays illumined the horrible scene of carnage, the fight went on, till the courtyard was dotted with the bodies of the wounded and slain, the survivors of the great flock of sheep cowering together close to the main gate, while others lay trampled down amongst the fallen, their thick fleeces having protected many from the cuts of the Ghazis' swords.

Chapter Twenty One.

A Pause.

The moment the court could be crossed, a rush was made for the hospital, where the fight was still going on; but the mingled company of excited men were checked twice over by wounded and shamming Ghazis springing up to foot or knee to deliver one final blow at their hated Christian conquerors, and several of the soldiers were badly wounded by the deadly razor-edged tulwars before the wielder was borne to the earth by bayonets, struggling fiercely still, though riddled with wounds.

Then the entrance to the hospital was reached, and the wild cheer of a dozen men sent a reviving thrill of hope through the fast-falling defenders, and they held their *chevaux-de-frise* of bayonets once more now, though with trembling, unnerved hands.

A minute before it seemed to them that their last blow had been struck, and that there was nothing else to do but die with their face to the dead and living enemy. But that wild British cheer sent a thrill through them; the massacre of the wounded was after all to be stayed, and they stood firmly there in the brightly illumined room, witnesses of the bayoneting, till the last savage lay dying on the floor.

Roberts had headed his party, and was the first to return to try and save his friend and comrade; and it was into his arms Bracy fell and was carried out, while the men crowded in now to bear out Mrs Gee, the Doctor, Gedge, and the rest, those outside cheering madly as first one and then another bloodstained, ghastly object was borne into the light; while, in the interval between two of the outbursts, poor Gedge, who was being cheered by his comrades, seemed drunk with excitement, as he contrived with failing arm to wave his rifle above his head and shout:

"Three cheers for Mr Bracy; three cheers for the Doctor and old Mother Gee! Three cheers for us all!"

There was a tremendous roar at this, heard loudly above the crackling fire kept up on the enemy still striving to force a way in from beyond the walls.

"Three more," cried Gedge. "Cripples, all on us, but we held our own, and hip—hip—hip—hoo—"

Gedge did not finish his cheer, for half-way through the last word he fell forward, utterly exhausted, fainting dead away.

It was just then that an officer with blackened face and sword in hand suddenly made his appearance high up in the golden light of the fire, and the moment he appeared a howl of execration was raised, which ran through the crowd of soldiery, while the officers scowled and turned away.

The tall, thin figure stopped short in front of the burning building, to gaze down wonderingly.

"Drummond—Scotch coward!" roared a voice, and a yell of execration burst forth.

Just at that moment, from behind an angle of the building, four of the Ghazis, who had lain hidden there and escaped the deadly fire, rushed forth yelling and waving their swords as they made for the figure standing apparently beyond the reach of help.

"Quick, some one—fire, fire!" shouted Roberts.

The figure heard the cry, and turned just in time to face his enemies, two of whom reached him together, cutting at him with all their might. But, active as a cat, the tall, lithe youth avoided one of his foes by leaping aside, ran the other man through, and swinging round, with a tremendous cut severed the wrist of the wretch he had avoided, when coming at him for a second blow.

The other two did not reach him, for half-a-dozen shots rang out, and the true firing of the boy-regiment was again proved, the two Ghazis leaping high in the air, and falling backward on to the bayonets of the men below. There was another cheer at this, but it was dominated directly after by a renewal of the howl of execration which had broken out before.

The hearer looked for a moment or two puzzled, and hesitated to advance; but the next minute he turned half-face, doubled along the rampart to the steps, and descended to the court, passing coolly among the men where Colonel Graves was standing giving orders.

"Mr Drummond," he said, "I am told that you left your men in a way that disgraces a British officer."

171

"That I didn't," cried the young man indignantly. "I heard you say that if we only had light we could see to fire, or something of that sort."

"Yes, sir, I did," said the Colonel sternly.

"Well, sir, I ran along the ramp and climbed up three times before I could get to the store, and then set fire to the fodder; but it was ever so long before I could get it to burn, and then I couldn't get out."

"You did that?" cried the Colonel.

"To be sure I did, sir. Wasn't it right? Oh, I see now; the men thought I went and hid to get out of the light."

"My dear boy," cried the Colonel; "of course."

"Oh," cried Drummond, "what jolly fools the lads can be! But I say, sir, who's hurt? and was old Bracy safe?"

A minute later the men cheered even louder than before, as they watched Drummond—a hero now in their midst—place a bag of powder to blow down the burning building and save the place from risk of the fire spreading.

That was soon done. It was a risky task, but bravely set about; and, as the place went up in a rush of flames and sparks, the assault from outside ceased, the enemy drawing off under cover of the mist; and an hour later silence fell upon the horrible scene of carnage, not even a bleat arising from the sheep.

But the fort was safe, the dim morning light showing the British flag, wet and clinging, but still hanging in its place upon the flagstaff; while by that time all save the doubled sentries upon the walls and the suffering wounded lay plunged in a heavy sleep wherever a place could be found roomy enough for the poor fellows' aching limbs.

Chapter Twenty Two.

Bracy's Nurse.

"Bracy, my dear old man!"

"My dear old chap!" These were the salutations of Drummond and Roberts later on in the morning, when they sought him out, to find him with Gedge in a portion of the soldiers' quarters which had been temporarily turned into a hospital.

"Ah, Roberts," sighed Bracy drowsily as he raised himself on one arm. "Not hurt, I hope?"

"Not a scratch. But you—you? Morton tells me you fought like a lion all through that horrible attack."

"Like a very weak lion," said Bracy, smiling faintly.

"But how are you?"

"Oh, so much better," said the young officer, with a sigh. "I feel so restful, and as if I could do nothing but sleep."

"Thank Heaven! But what a change in you!"

"And you, Drummond? But your face—blackened. Were you in that explosion I heard?"

"Yes; I helped to pop off the powder."

"Helped!" cried Roberts. "Why, you placed the powder-bag and fired the fuse."

"Well, what of that? Some one had to do it. I wasn't hurt there, though, old man. It was in setting fire to the store and coaxing it into a blaze, for the blessed wood refused to burn. Spoiled my lovely looks a bit—eh? But I say—it's harder work than you would think for to burn a — I say! Bracy, old chap!—Why, he's asleep!"

"Fast," said Roberts, looking wonderingly at their friend, who had sunk back on his rough pillow, formed of a doubled-up greatcoat, and was breathing deeply, with his face looking peaceful and calm.

"Here, I say, you, Bill Gedge," cried Drummond; "this can't be right. Go and fetch the Doctor."

"No, sir; it's all right, sir. The Doctor was here half-an-hour ago. He was fast as a top then; but he heard the Doctor speaking to me, and roused up while he had his wounds looked at. What d'yer think o' that, sir?"

He drew a small, ragged scrap of something from his pocket, and held it out before the two officers.

"Nothing," said Roberts shortly; "but I don't like Mr Bracy's looks. This can't be right."

"Doctor says it is, sir, and that it's exhorschon. He's to sleep as much as he can. You see, he had a horful night of it, sir, just when he wasn't fit."

"But how in the world could he fight like the Doctor says he did?"

"I dunno, sir," replied Gedge, grinning. "Doctor says it was the excitement set him going, and then he couldn't stop hisself. You know how he was a bit ago, gentlemen, when he hit out and kicked, and couldn't help it."

Roberts nodded.

"And he did fight wonderful, and never got a scratch. That's what the Doctor said it was, and when he zamined his bandages he found this here under his back."

"That! What is it?" said Drummond, now taking the object and examining it curiously.

"His complaint, sir, that kept him bad so long. The bit of iron the Doctor said he dursen't try to get out. It worked out last night in the fight. He's going to get well now."

It was Roberts's turn now to examine the little ragged scrap of discoloured iron.

"Seems wonderful," he said, "that so trifling a thing as that should cause so much agony, and bring a man so low."

"Oh, I dunno, sir," said Gedge respectfully. "I had a horful toe once as got bigger and bigger and sorer till I couldn't get a boot on, only the sole; and when my leg got as big as a Dan'l Lambert's, some un says, 'Why don't you go to the orspital?' he says, sir; and so I did, and as soon as I got there I began to wish I hadn't gone, for there was a lot o' doctors looked at it, and they said my leg must come off half-way up my thigh, but they'd wait a day or two first, and they did; but only the next morning one of 'em has another good look, and he gets out something—just a teeny bit of a nail as had gone into my toe out of my boot."

"Humph!" said Roberts rather contemptuously.

"Lor' bless yer, gentlemen, I was 'nother sort o' feller that night, and was just like Mr Bracy here; hadn't had no proper sleep for weeks, and there I was at it like one o'clock, going to sleep as you may say all over the place. Shouldn't ha' been here if it hadn't been for that there doctor. Wouldn't have had a one-legged un in the ridgiment, sir—would yer?"

"No," said Roberts, who was leaning over and gazing at his sleeping comrade curiously. "Yes, he is sleeping as peacefully as a child. And what about you, Gedge?"

"Me, sir? Oh, I'm all right, sir. Bit stiff in the arms with all that bay'net exercise, and got the skin off one elber with ketching it agen the wall. Yer see, we'd no room."

"We've been there this morning," said Roberts, with a slight shudder. "The woodwork is chipped and cut into splinters, and the sight is horrible."

"Well, yus, I s'pose so, sir. It was horrible work, but we was obliged to do it; they'd have cut us all to pieces. Reg'lar butchers—that they are—and deserved it. Coming on like that at a lot o' poor cripples and a woman, besides the nong-combytant. Savages they are to try and cut down a doctor who's ready to 'tend to everybody, either side, and tie or sew them up."

"You're right, Gedge, my lad; they are savages," said Drummond, patting the speaker on the shoulder.

"Hff! gently, please, sir," said Gedge, flinching.

"I beg your pardon. Are you hurt there?" cried Drummond hastily.

"Oh, all right, sir," said the lad, grinning; "but you said, 'Hurt there.' Why, it's all over, sir. There aren't a place as I've found yet where you could put a finger on without making me squirm. Doctor made me yell like a great calf. But there's nothing broke or cracked, and no fresh holes nowhere."

"That's a comfort," said Drummond.

"Yus; but it aren't very comf'table yet, sir. He says I shall soon be better, though."

"Yes, Gedge, you must regularly lie up till the pain has gone."

"I mean to, sir, all the time that I can get from tending Mr Bracy here. I must tend him."

"You can stay with him; but someone else ought to be sent in."

"No, sir, please; I can manage. It wouldn't be fair, sir, for some un else to come in now the gov'nor's getting better. Doctor says I've saved his life so fur, and I wants to go on and save his life so further. See?"

"Yes, of course," said Roberts, smiling. "It would not be fair for you to be robbed of the credit of what you have done."

"Thank ye, sir. That does a chap good, sir. But I beg your pardon, Captain: you see, I'm noo to sojering and fighting. I thought we'd had it tidy 'ot in the coming up along o' the stone-throwing. Then it was a bit warm when Mr Bracy was shot down and I got my bullet. But that was all like playing skretch-cradle to our set-to last night in the dark. Shall we have it much worse by-and-by?"

"Worse? No," cried the Captain sharply. "Nothing could be worse than last night's work."

"Oh, come, I'm glad o' that, sir; for arterward, when I begun to cool down, it seemed to me that if it could be much worse I should begin to think as sojering might get to be a little bit too strong."

It was just then that Doctor Morton came in, and for the moment he frowned; but the angry look passed off after a glance at Bracy.

"I was afraid you would disturb him," he said; "but there is no need to mind; he will sleep a great deal for days, till this state of exhaustion has passed off. My dear boys, what a night we had! I wonder that any of us are alive."

"There were some narrow escapes, Doctor," said Roberts.

"Awful, awful; and what a morning for me! I feel as if I could do as Bracy is doing—sleep for days; but here I am with a terrible load of fresh cases on my hands, and my chief nurse turned into a patient— Gee's wife. What a woman! what a woman! She must have descended from the Amazons of old. But there, I must go; I only wanted to see that poor Bracy was all right."

"And you do think he is, Doctor?" said Roberts.

"Sure of it, sir. He'll be back with his company before long."

He nodded sharply, and after a word or two with Gedge, who looked ten years older for his night's work, the room was left for sleep, and the young officers hurried off to their several duties. For there was ample work for every one of the defenders, whose loss had, however, been wonderfully small, the Ghazis having been comparatively helpless after their successful entry, their attacks being repulsed by the bayonet, and the soldiery for the most part having the advantage of the walls, while their fanatical foes were raging about the court, repulsed at every attempt to get on close quarters with the infidels they sought to destroy.

As the morning wore on, and the horrible traces of the deadly fray were rapidly removed by the fatigue-parties set to work, a soft breeze from the mountains waited away the heavy clouds of mist, the sun came out, and with it the horrors of the night faded away so rapidly that, had it not been for the blackened ruins of the fodder-store, it would have been hard to realise the fact that such a night had been passed.

Scouting parties went, out in different directions, and returned all with the same report—that the enemy had disappeared, not a trace of them being visible, not even one of the dead or wounded, though their losses must have been considerable. That evening a time of perfect rest seemed to have descended upon Ghittah, which, by the light of the sinking sun, looked, with its magnificent surroundings of dazzling snow-peak, verdant hill, forest, and falling water, orange, golden, and sparkling in the reflections from the glorified sky.

"Yes, lovely, lovely," said Colonel Graves sadly, "if one could only feel that we might lie down and sleep in peace."

"Well, can't we?" said one of the younger officers. "Surely, sir, this has been such a lesson as the enemy will not forget."

"Quite right," said the Colonel; "they will not forget it, nor rest till they have had revenge."

"But look at their losses last night," said the Major.

"I do," replied the Colonel; "but men are plentiful up here in the hills, and they all belong to a fighting race. If they were not fighting with us they would be among themselves, and it is the education of their boys: being taught to fight."

"Then you think they'll renew their attacks, sir?" said Roberts.

"I feel sure of it, and they must find us more upon the *qui vive* next time. I feel ashamed for allowing myself to be such an easy victim to their cunning *ruse*."

"Never mind now," said the Major; "it has furnished us with a fine supply of fresh meat."

"Yes," said the Colonel sadly; "but at a heavy cost of wounded men."

Chapter Twenty Three.

After a Rest.

The Colonel was right; there were plenty of men in the hills, and they all belonged to fighting tribes-men who, whether Moslem or of the various sects which inhabited the vast tracts of mountainous countries, looked upon it as a religious duty to cut off every one who believed differently, as an infidel or a dog. Many days, then, had not elapsed before there was another gathering of the fierce tribes, whose object was to secure the fort, with its wealth of arms and ammunition. But during the week of respite Colonel Graves and his officers were busy enough. The country round was foraged for stores; and, partly in fear, but as much for the sake of cheating good customers and making everything possible out of the people whom they might be helping to slaughter the very next day, a couple of the tribes brought in grain, fodder, and other necessaries largely.

So the loss incurred by the burning of the store was soon made up, and the fort was better provisioned than ever, even to being prepared to stand the stern winter when it should leave the hills and descend to the valleys and plains.

No despatches had reached the fort for some time past; but the last, in answer to the Colonel's report of his having relieved the fort, where all was well, and that he had no doubt of being able to hold it as long as was necessary, bade him go on holding it at any cost, and wait for further orders. But if he found reinforcements necessary to give the tribes a severe lesson, he was to communicate with the station in the Ghil Valley, whence a Ghoorkha regiment would be immediately despatched to his help.

A little council of war was held, in which Colonel Wrayford managed to take part; and, after due consideration, it was decided that the help was not required, for the unanimous opinion was that the Ghittah force could hold its own, and that they did not need any regiment to come in and carry off part of the laurels they wished to keep for themselves.

Doctor Morton had probably been the busiest man at the station; for, after the repulse of the night attack, every hospital-bed had been occupied, and an additional ward provided; but he had hardly a loss, and he went about, as Gedge said, "looking as proud as a two-tailed peacock in a 'logical garden."

Certainly he chuckled and rubbed his hands a great deal over his patients; and one evening at the mess dinner, when the topic had arisen of the number of men he had sent back to duty cured, and all were rejoicing in the fact, that Bracy—looking thin and careworn, but now wonderfully well—was back in his place, the Doctor, who was pleased and flattered, became exceedingly confidential, and talked more freely than was his wont.

"There, dear boys," he said: "I won't be a sham. I've worked hard among my cripples, of course, and I'm proud of what I've done. If you want an example of the powers of surgery, there you are—look at Bracy. He's a better man than ever now. Look at his condition—hard as a nail. Got rid of all that superfluous fat."

"Here, gently, Doctor," cried Bracy, flushing. "What superfluous fat?"

"All that you got rid of, sir."

"Why, I've always been thin."

"You leave me to judge best what you have always been, sir. I know. Come, you'll own that you're well as ever now?"

"Certainly."

"Be satisfied, then. Well, as I was saying, my dear boys, I'll be quite open with you all. I've been wonderfully successful with all my cases—have I not?"

"Wonderfully," came in a chorus.

"And frightfully modest," whispered Drummond.

"Eh! what is that, Mr Drummond?" cried the Doctor. "I heard what you said. Don't you offend me, for you may come under my care some day. Now, then, all of you—wonderfully successful. Yes, Mr Drummond, and modest too, as you'll own if you'll let me finish my remarks before you stick yourself up as a judge. For I'm going to let the cat out of the bag."

"Let's have her, Doctor," cried the younger men merrily.

"Here she is, then," said the Doctor. "My colleague. She has done ten times as much for the wounded as I have."

"He means Mrs Gee," said Bracy quietly. "Well, she is a splendid nurse."

"Ha! what a woman!" said the Colonel. "She is quite well now, Doctor—is she not?"

"Always is," said the Doctor. "Absolutely perfect."

"I don't understand you, Doctor. The poor woman suffered a great deal in her daring defence of her patients."

"Hah! we're playing at cross purposes," said the Doctor importantly. "You're talking about Mrs Gee."

"Of course. Weren't you?"

"Pish! Poo! Bah! No. I meant my great help and patroness Dame Nature."

"Oh!" ran round the table, in disappointed tones.

"Yes, gentlemen," repeated the Doctor; "Dame Nature. She has set all my wounded right again, and put it to my credit. Why, if the poor fellows had been in stuffy barracks down in the hot plains they'd have died like flies. But up here, in this wonderfully pure mountain air, all I have to do is to see that the wounds are carefully bandaged, and cuts and bullet-holes grow up and together again in no time. As for the hill-men, their surgeon seems to be the next man, who operates with a bit of rag."

"And kills or cures at once," said Roberts, smiling.

"Exactly," said the Doctor good-humouredly; "but really it's wonderful how Nature does nearly all the work. Well, any news, Colonel?"

"About the enemy?"

"Yes; you've been doing nothing lately, and my last bed was vacated to-day."

"I am very sorry that you should be in so low a condition, Doctor," said the Colonel coldly; "but you must understand that I shall do my best to keep you so."

"Why, of course," cried the Doctor. "You don't suppose I want to have the poor fellows cut or shot down to keep me busy—do you?"

"You spoke as if you did?"

"Then I spoke clumsily," cried the Doctor. "But tell me—the Dwats are collecting again—are they not?"

"Yes; they mean to give us no rest."

"So much the better for the men. Keep 'em active. You boys had any sport to-day?"

"Yes; we got six mountain sheep," said Roberts.

"Safe into camp?" said the Doctor eagerly.

"Oh yes. It was hard work, though; for three of them fell right down into one of the deepest gorges from the snow-slope on which we shot them—splendid shots Drummond made after our stalk, he killed with right and left barrels. My one dropped at the first shot, but sprang up and was going off again till my second barrel stopped him."

"Had an awful job to get them out of the gorge and home; but the hunters fetched them out, and we got all safe into quarters."

"Ha!" cried the Doctor; "I'm glad of that. Splendid gamy meat, that mountain mutton. Glorious stuff for convalescents. It gives me the heartache when I hear of you leaving lost ones to the wolves and vultures."

"I quite agree with the Doctor about the quality of the mutton," said the Colonel gravely; "but I'm getting anxious about these shooting-trips, gentlemen. Your guides belong to one or other of the tribes."

"Yes, I suppose they do, sir," said Roberts carelessly.

"Well, what is to prevent them from leading you some day into a trap, and, instead of the news coming into mess of there being an extra supply for the larder, I hear that I am minus two or three of my best officers?"

"I don't know about best officers, sir," said Roberts, laughing; "but I don't think there is anything to fear. These hill-shikarees are very genuine fellows, and their intense love of the sport will keep them honest and true to us. You cannot think how proud they are of leading us to the quarry if we are successful."

"I grant all that," said the Colonel, "knowing as I do what a freemasonry there is in sport, and how clever hunters have a feeling of fellowship for men of their own tastes, whatever their religion; but you must not forget that the hill-tribes are completely under the thumb of their Mullahs, and that the will of these priests is the law which they must obey. Supposing one of these Mullahs to give them orders in the interest of their tribe, they would lead you into an ambush for a certainty."

"Oh, Colonel Graves," cried Drummond, "this is spoiling the only pleasure we have!"

"I hope not," said the Colonel, smiling gravely. "Set it down to interest in my officers' welfare. I only ask you to be careful—well on your guard—and not to do anything rash."

"Just as if it was likely that we should do anything rash," said Drummond pettishly later on. "I'm sure I'm always as careful as can be."

"Always!" said Roberts, laughing, and giving Bracy a peculiar look.

"Here, I say—what does that mean? You two are chaffing me again."

"Oh dear, no," said Bracy. "Our consciences are smiting us for being so reckless, and we're making up our minds to be more careful in future."

"Yes, as the Colonel suggests," chimed in Roberts, "and take friend Drummond o' that ilk for our example."

"Here! Yes, you are chaffing me," cried Drummond anxiously. "I say, old chaps, though—you don't think I am rash, do you?"

"Rather," said Roberts.

"Bosh with your rather! Chaff, because I'm so tall and thin. Bracy, you're not half such a boy as the Captain. You don't think I'm wild and harum-scarum, do you—regularly rash?"

"Well, to speak frankly,"—began Bracy.

"Of course I want you to be frank," cried Drummond hastily. "That's why I like you chaps."

"Well, then, my dear boy," said Bracy, "I do think you are about the most rash fellow I ever met."

"Oh!" cried Drummond, with a look of distrust.

"You do things that no thoughtful fellow would ever think of doing."

"I? Come now; when?"

"Over those sheep, then, to-day. I felt quite sick to see you walk along that shelf of snow, when the slightest slip would have sent you down headlong a thousand feet on to the jagged rocks below."

"Yes, it was horrible," said Roberts.

Drummond exploded into a tremendous burst of laughter, and sat at last wiping his eyes.

"Oh, I say, come. That is good. I like that. Dangerous—made one of you feel sick and the other think it was horrible!"

"Well, it's the truth," said Bracy.

"And you both came along it afterwards, and we got that magnificent sport."

"I came along it after you had set the example," said Bracy quietly.

"But you are a couple of years older than I am, and ought to know better."

"I was not going to show the white feather after what you had done."

"Same here," said Roberts sharply.

"Oh, that was it—eh? I was a boy to you, and you wouldn't let me think you daren't."

"Something of that kind," said Bracy.

"Humph!" said Drummond thoughtfully. "I suppose it was dangerous."

"Of course it was," replied Bracy. "You saw that the guide wouldn't venture."

"Yes; but that made me determined to do it. We can't afford to let

183

those chaps think we're afraid to go anywhere. Come now—didn't you two think something of that kind too?"

"Probably," said Bracy.

"But it didn't seem dangerous when I was doing it," cried Drummond. "I never thought about toppling down, only about getting right across and after those moufflons."

"Same here," said Roberts.

"Well, I did look down once and think of what might happen," said Bracy.

"Ah, that's where you were wrong. Never do that, lad. Keep perfectly cool, and you can get almost anywhere up yonder in the snow. I've got to be quite a climber since I've been here."

"Well, I gave myself the credit of being pretty good on ice and snow to-day," said Bracy, smiling. "I mean pretty well for a cripple. I wish I had done as well over the shooting. That was a miserable show of mine. Thanks for not exposing me at the mess."

"Rubbish!" said Drummond. "Who's going to tell tales out of school? I say, though, that ice-climbing in the mountains is splendid— isn't it? The more one does the easier it seems. It feels quite cool and comfortable."

"Which one can't help feeling on the ice," said Bracy, laughing. "But seriously, we are getting pretty good at it up yonder in the snow."

"Regular climbers," said Drummond; "and I vote that we do as much of it as we can while our shoes are good. There, don't look at a fellow like that—your shoes, then, that you gave me. But I didn't mean shoes literally. I mean before the old man puts a stop to our hunting and climbing."

"He soon will, you may depend upon that," said Roberts. "He's getting nervous about us all."

"Because we are such splendid officers," put in Bracy merrily.

"Well, we are what he has; and, judging from the way we are shut in and left by the authorities, he is not likely to get a fresh supply if he loses us."

"What about the messengers he has sent, Bracy? Think they get through with the despatches? I feel sure they do not. Either they are killed or so scared by the dangers they run that they destroy their despatches and dare not show their faces again."

"Well, I hope that's not the case," said Bracy. "I don't want to give the poor fellows the credit of being treacherous."

"Like enough it is that, treacherous as we deem it; but they are so much accustomed to the tricks and cunning amongst which they have been brought up that they look upon such a thing as being very venial —a kind of cleverness by which we, their conquerors are bested."

"Here, I say, don't get into a dissertation upon the moral character of the natives," cried Drummond, "because there is no end to that. Here, I say—"

"Say away," said the others.

"I've been thinking about what old Graves said as to the shikarees selling us to the enemy. They won't."

"I hope not," said Bracy, laying his hand upon his chest.

"Hullo! What's the matter? Wound hurt?"

"Gives me a stab like that sometimes when the weather is going to change. We shall have rain, I think."

"Ha! and that means snow higher up. Hoo-roar! as the lads say. A nice light coating of fresh snow, and every bear footprint showing clearly. We mustn't miss one. Bear ham is good, and then there are the skins. We shall want 'em in the winter for warm rugs."

"You mean to stay the winter, then?" said Bracy, laughing.

"We shall have to; see if we don't."

"We shall get no bearskins," said Roberts. "The Colonel will stop our going on account of his uneasiness. I heard him say that we should be running upon some prowling body of the enemy one of these times, and never be heard of any more."

"He doesn't know what he's talking about. Just as if it were likely. They sneak along in the lowest valleys; they never go up among the snowfields. No one does but the hunters. It's the same as it was in Switzerland; you never caught the people climbing the mountains till the English taught them, and bribed them to come as carriers. They'd never have made the ascent of any of their mountains. I tell you that in our shooting-trips up yonder we're as safe as we are here. Safer, for the beggars keep away from there, while here they're lying up in every hole and corner all around."

"He's about right," said Roberts thoughtfully; "and, now you're strong enough again, I don't like to lose our trips. We don't get much pleasure up here. Let's make our hay while the sun shines."

"Even if it is in the snow," said Bracy. "Very well; I'm glad enough to go, for the mountain air seems to send fresh vigour through me every time I climb."

The result of this was that whenever the way up into the mountains was clear, and the Dwats who acted as guides to the different hills came in with news, the young officers had their excursions, and generally returned with their men pretty well laden, while the three friends became masters of the district among the heights in a way that suggested years of active residence in that silver land.

There were plenty of alarms, plenty of little encounters with the parties who were always on the lookout to harass the occupants of the fort; but a little extra work for the Doctor and excitement for the men, to keep off the stagnation which threatened them, was all that ensued.

In the interim the Colonel sent off five more messengers with despatches, in the hope that they would get through the enemy and bring back letters; but they were seen no more; and the Colonel's face grew more serious day by day.

"Thinks the tribes mean to starve us out," said Roberts one evening when the Colonel went away from the table looking more depressed and anxious than usual.

"And they won't," said Drummond. "Why, there are mountain sheep enough up yonder to keep us for years."

"They get more difficult to shoot, though," said Bracy.

"Pooh! not they. A few close by are a bit shy; but, look here, when we get right up on the shoulder of that left-hand peak and look north what do we see?"

"Mountains," replied Bracy.

"And when we were right up on that farthest peak last week, and looked north, what did we see then?"

"More mountains."

"That's it; and you might go on and on for a month, and it would be the same—more mountains."

Bracy nodded and looked thoughtful.

"Yes," he said at last; "the world's a long way from being played out yet. We can see hundreds of peaks, and the soft blue valleys between them, which I suppose have never been traversed by man."

"That's right enough, and that's where the wild sheep and goats are just as they always have been, perfectly undisturbed. Thousands —perhaps millions, without counting the goats and yaks, which look as if they were a vain brood of beast who try to grow tails like a horse."

"I suppose you're correct, Drummond," said Bracy.

"Of course I am; and if we shoot down all the sheep near at hand one month, more will come down from the north next month."

"Just the same as when you catch a big trout out of a hole at home, another is sure to come within a day or two to take his empty house."

"Why, they do up here, and the little seer in the river too," cried Drummond. "I say, I wish this was a bigger and deeper stream, so that it held the big forty and fifty pound fish."

"Quite deep and swift enough for us," said Bracy merrily.

"Ah, yes," said Drummond slowly; "I haven't forgotten our going for that nice long walk."

"No," said Roberts; "that was a close shave for all of us. How many more times are we going to run the gauntlet and not get hit?"

"Hundreds, I hope," replied Drummond; and Bracy, who was very quiet, thought, by no means for the first time, of his escapes, and of how it would be at home if a letter reached them some day reporting that one of the lieutenants had been checked once for all in his career.

Chapter Twenty Four.

Peril in a Poshtin.

Another fortnight passed, during which the officers had a day's shooting as often as they could be spared; and, though the Colonel's face grew more and more serious he made no further objection to these excursions so long as they were sensibly carried out, for he had realised how thoroughly the enemy avoided the higher portions of the mountains, the snow-line being rarely crossed; and when they did break through their rule, it was only in crossing from one valley to another, and it was necessitated by the pass which linked the two being more than usually high.

It was a bright, sunny morning, and glasses had been busy in the fort, for certain well-known signs suggested that the day would not pass without their hearing from the enemy, of whom glances were obtained, first in one well-known locality, then in another, which they seemed to affect as a matter of course, showing very little disposition to break out of their regular routine, while one tribe followed in the steps of another so closely that it was generally possible to prognosticate where the attack would be made, and make arrangements to foil it.

The officers were chatting together; and in the group where Drummond stood with his friends he started a good grumbling discourse, something after this fashion:

"It's always the case. So sure as I overlook my tackle, and have a good clean up of the rifles ready for a long day amongst the muttons, some of these beggars come and plant themselves just in the way we mean to go."

"Mr Bracy," said an orderly, coming up and saluting, "the Colonel wishes to see you."

"Ha, ha!" laughed Drummond; "it's to tell you that we are not to attempt a shoot to-day. Tell him, Bracy, that we had given it up."

Bracy nodded, and went straight to the Colonel's room, to find him busily writing.

He just glanced up and nodded.

"Sit down, Bracy," he said, and he went on writing, his table being a couple of bullock-trunks, with a scarlet blanket by way of cover.

"Enemy are out pretty strong this morning."

"Yes, sir."

"Ha! yes."

There was a pause, filled up by a good deal of scratching of the pen, before the stern-looking officer began again.

"You are quite strong now, Bracy?" he said at last, without looking up.

"Never felt better in my life, sir."

"I said strong, Bracy."

"Nor stronger, sir."

"That's right," said the Colonel, reading over his despatch and crossing i's and dotting i's here and there.

"Wound trouble you much still?"

"Gives me a sharp sting, sir, at times, back and front; but I always find that it is when we are going to have a change of weather."

The Colonel paid no heed, and Bracy added:

"I dare say it will soon pass off, though."

"It will not," said the Colonel quietly, and to the young man's dismay. "You will feel it more or less all your life. Yes," he added, looking up and smiling, "a twinge to remind you that you were once a brave officer of the Queen."

Bracy coughed, for he felt a little husky, and as if he were standing near a fire.

"Now, Bracy, business. I cannot go on sending despatch after despatch, none of which reach their destination. Either going or coming, my messengers have come to a bad end or been unfaithful."

Bracy made no reply, for none was expected; and the Colonel now looked up, and, with his hands resting upon the table, gazed full in the young man's eyes.

"I want a messenger whom I can trust," he said, "a man who will undertake the task of delivering my despatch as a duty to his country. There are plenty of good, trusty lads in the regiment. Whom would you select—the best you know?"

Bracy was silent for a few moments before speaking.

"I should be sorry to see him go upon so dangerous a mission, sir;

but if I had to select a lad in whom I should have perfect confidence, I should choose Private Gedge."

"A very good selection, Bracy; but I want an officer."

The young man stalled, and drew his breath hard.

"There is Andrews, or Elder, or Morrison," continued the Colonel, "or Drummond, of Wrayford's; but he is too volatile. Roberts would be a splendid fellow for the task, for, like Drummond, he is strong amongst ice and snow, and my messenger will have to take to the snow nearly all the way to save being stopped."

"A wise plan, sir," said Bracy eagerly; "one that should succeed."

"I think it will; but my messenger will be face to face with death from the hour he starts, doubly facing it—from nature as well as man. But I cannot spare Roberts. Do you understand me?"

"Yes, sir; you wish me to volunteer."

"Yes, Bracy," said the Colonel, holding out his hand, which Bracy caught in both his. "God bless and protect you, my dear boy! I do."

"Yes, sir," said the young man firmly. "I'll go."

"Not alone. Take that man Gedge with you; he has had little to do amongst the snow, but—"

"Yes, sir; he'll learn anything. When am I to start?"

"As soon as you can be ready. Then, I will clear the way for you by making a feint, so that you can make at once for the upper ground."

"Not by the mountains above the Gor Pass, sir?"

"No; the other direction entirely. You are to make for the Ghil Valley, and bring back the Ghoorkas, Bracy. It is time that we took the offensive; the enemy must be driven back before the autumn closes in. No; you are going upon an extremely dangerous mission, Bracy; I tell you so frankly. I will be quite open with you. I am sending you upon this horribly risky journey; but it is as a soldier to risk your life to save ours."

"To save yours, sir?" said Bracy wonderingly.

"Surely the fort is quite safe if you act on the defensive."

"It would be, my dear boy, if we had an ample supply of

ammunition."

Bracy started, and gazed wide-eyed at his Colonel, who had leaned across the table and said these last words almost in a whisper.

"I am speaking quite openly to you, Bracy—telling you what must be a secret between us two; and I tell you because it is just to one sent upon such a perilous enterprise that he should feel satisfied as to the urgency of the need."

Bracy made a gesture, but the Colonel checked him.

"Yes; I know what you would say," he continued: "that dangerous or no, you would do your duty. I know you would. I have perfect faith in my officers; but this is a matter of conscience on my side. Bracy, I find that our ammunition will not last a month. Once that is gone, we are no longer the superiors of the enemy. The bayonet is a splendid weapon; but these hill-tribes are magnificent swordsmen, and when, many times outnumbering us as they do, they come on to a hand-to-hand fight, adding their reckless religious fervour to their natural bravery, they must master us in the end; and that means taking the fort, and— you know what would follow."

Bracy bowed his head; he could not speak.

"An indiscriminate massacres a horrible death to every man and woman in the place."

"Horrible, sir," cried Bracy excitedly. "Oh, Colonel Graves, surely things are not so bad as you think!"

The Colonel smiled.

"You ought to know me by this time, Bracy," he said quietly. "I don't think I am a man likely to raise bugbears."

"No, no, sir! I beg your pardon."

"That will do," said the Colonel quietly. "When you leave me, be prepared to start. You must not confide in your nearest friend; go about your work cheerfully, and as if only to bear a despatch, but conscious the while that our lives here depend upon your success. You understand?"

"Yes," said Bracy gravely, "I understand; and if I do not bring the help, sir, it is because—"

"You have died trying to do your duty to your friends. I know.

191

There, we need no more words, Bracy. Look here."

He took the despatch from the table and tore it up into bits.

"Your appearance before the Ghoorka Colonel will be sufficient, and you will have no alarming announcement upon you if you are taken prisoner. Certainly it would be by people similar to those who are besieging us; but one never knows what soldiers of fortune may be among them, ready to be summoned by a chief to interpret the message."

"I understand, sir."

"Once you are well on the road you must make your companion fully understand the importance of the mission, so that if you go down there may still be the chance left to us of this man carrying on the news of our urgent need."

Bracy nodded shortly and drew a deep breath, waiting for the Colonel to speak again.

"As to preparations," said Colonel Graves at last, "go as you are; but you will each need a *poshtin* (long sheepskin coat) to cover your Kharkee uniforms, for concealment and warmth. You will be a great deal among the snow and rocks, and nothing can be less likely to attract attention. You will take sword, revolver, rifle, and bayonet. See that Gedge carries the same weapons. In addition, take as much simple provisions and ammunition as you can carry."

"And rob you all at such a time of need, sir?"

"The amount you two can carry away in cartridges will not be missed if it comes to the worst, Bracy," said the Colonel, smiling. "Once more, are you quite satisfied that you have selected the right lad?"

"A man who will carry his wounded officer, with the enemy firing down at him from both sides of a rocky defile, cannot be bettered, sir," said the young officer quietly.

"Right, Bracy," cried the Colonel. "He is the man. Ha! here comes Roberts to announce the advance of the enemy. I could hear the war-cries.—Yes, Roberts—the rascals worrying us again?"

"Yes, sir; coming down the right gully in strong numbers. Will you come and look?"

The Colonel picked up his glass and held out his hand.

"I shall lead the men to-day, Bracy," he said, "for a change. Major Graham will be in command here. I shall tell him of your mission. Within an hour I shall depend upon you making your start."

"Within an hour, sir," said Bracy, as Roberts looked on in wonder.

"I have been thinking that a mule would help your journey at the first. What do you think?"

"I think not, sir," said Bracy quietly. "We should be better free to climb anywhere. A baggage animal would tie us down to tracks."

"Quite right. Go as we arranged.—Roberts," he continued, turning to the Captain, "Bracy is going to take a despatch for me. He starts directly."

"Directly, sir?" said Roberts, looking aghast.

"Yes; he has his instructions. You can have half-an-hour with him before he starts; but you will ask no questions, only help him in any way you can to start without delay, while I am keeping the enemy well employed at this end of the valley."

"Yes, sir."

"After Bracy has started you can bring your company along the upper track to act as a reserve, and cover us if it is necessary when we retire. That will do."

The two officers left the Colonel's quarters and hurried out.

"My dear boy," cried Roberts excitedly, "this is horribly sudden. Had you any idea of it before this morning?"

"Not the slightest," said Bracy gravely.

"Glad of it, for I should have been hurt if you had not told me."

"But you will not be hurt now? You heard what Graves said."

"I was not to question you? Yes. Still, you have some confidences to make?"

"Not one, old fellow."

"But surely—it is such a risky thing. Oh! it is preposterous; he ought not to have sent you. It is like sending a good man and true to his death."

"The Colonel thinks it best, and I agree with him. As to the risk—is it not risk enough to stay?"

"But Bracy, old fellow, if—"

"If," said the young man calmly. "Soldiers should not talk to one another about the 'if.' Let that be."

"Tell me this, though: are you satisfied to go?"

"Quite. Help me to get off—"

"I will; but—"

"By being silent, and then putting everything in one good grip of the hand."

"I see," he said, accompanying Bracy to his quarters. "Now, what can I do?"

"Send for Gedge."

"What for? Surely you have not chosen him for your companion?"

"I have. The Colonel said he could not spare you."

"Ha! That's better, old fellow. I was beginning to feel horribly set aside."

"I was to have one of the men for my companion. Can you suggest a better?"

"No," said Roberts, and he hurried out to seek the lad, who was standing in line with his fellows of the company, looking gloomy and discontented, for the sally-party to follow the Colonel, who was to lead them himself, did not include "Roberts's lot," as they were termed.

"Fall out, Private Gedge," said Roberts sharply.

"Didn't hear what I said, did he?" muttered the lad, with an anxious look, for he had been growling at what he called the favouritism served out to some of the companies in choosing them to go out and have the first chance of being shot; and this, he told himself, was mutinous.

But he pulled himself together and stood as erect as a ramrod, waiting for the next order, which came directly:

"Right face; march!"

And he marched after his Captain, with heart beating heavily, and then sinking deeper and deeper, as he found himself led to the officers' quarters.

"It's court-martial for a threep'ny-bit," he muttered. "Next thing 'll be 'Disarm!' and all because I wanted to go and fight. Oh! they are jolly 'ard on us chaps in the ranks."

"Come in, my lad," said Roberts, stooping to enter the low door, and Gedge's heart went down to its lowest point as he found himself face to face with Bracy.

"Them two to drop on me!" he thought. "Wouldn't ha' keared if it had been the Major."

The next moment poor Gedge's heavily plumping heart jumped, as he afterwards expressed it from his boots right up to his throat.

"Gedge," said Bracy coldly and quietly, "I am going on a very dangerous mission."

"Oh, sir, please don't go without me!"

"I have sent for you to say that I have selected you for my companion."

"Hoo—beg pardon, sir," cried the lad, turning scarlet.

"No cheering, no nonsense, no boy's tricks, my lad. This is desperate men's work. I have chosen you to go with me on a journey of many days, during which we shall suffer terrible hardships."

"That's right, sir; used to it ever since I was—"

"Silence, man!" said Bracy sternly. "We shall go with our lives in our hands, and probably never get to our journey's end; but we shall have to try. Now then, if you feel the slightest qualm, speak out honestly, and I will choose some one else."

"Don't do that, sir, please; but I will speak out honest. I must, when you axes me to."

"Ah!" cried Bracy.

"I'm strong as a horse again, sir; but sometimes I do get a sorter dig in the back, just as if a red-hot iron rod were touching up my wound when the bit o' iron—"

"No, no, man," cried Bracy, laughing. "I mean qualm of dread, or shrinking about running the risk."

195

"Oh, that, sir? Not me. Ain't I just as likely to be shot if I stop quiet here? They're allus trying to do it. I gets more sniping than any chap in the company."

"Then you will go with me?"

"I just will, sir. Anywheres."

"Thank you, Gedge. I'll say no more, for I know that you will stick to me like a man."

"Ha!" ejaculated Gedge, exhaling an enormous amount of pent-up emotion, and drawing his arm across his thickly perspiring brow, while a pleasant, contented smile lit up his plain features, as he drew himself up more stiffly to attention, waiting for orders.

"Well done, Gedge!" said Roberts softly.—"You've picked the right lad, Bracy."

Gedge did not move a muscle, but stood as upright as the rifle at his side, and looking as inanimate, but quite as dangerous, while his two officers said a few words in a low tone. The next moment Roberts went out of the room, and Bracy turned to the lad.

"We have to carry everything ourselves, and we must take all we can without overloading, my lad, for we shall have to climb a great deal amongst the snow. Now, mind this: we have just three-quarters of an hour for preparation. Then we must pass out of the gate."

Gedge did not move, but stood as if carved out of a block of hardened putty by the hand of an artistic drill-sergeant; listening, though, with his ears, which looked preternaturally large from the closeness of the regimental barber's efforts, and seeming to gape. Then he left his rifle in a corner, and was off.

The result was that, with five minutes to spare, officer and man, strangely transformed by their thick, woolly overcoats, stood ready in that room. Haversacks of provisions hung from their broad leather bands; revolvers balanced dagger-bay'nets from their belts; as much ammunition as they could carry was in their pockets, and necessary odds and ends were bestowed in satchels.

"All ready?" said Roberts at last.

"All ready. Nothing forgotten that I can think of."

"Then you will start at once. I have warned the men that you are to be allowed to slip out quietly, or they would have cheered you."

"Thanks," said Bracy.—"You hear that, Gedge?"

"Yes, sir."

"You will follow me without a word."

Gedge's face now looked as if if had been carved in oil-stone, it was so hard, and he made no reply. But mentally he was discoursing vigorously in his wild state of excitement, for he could judge of his own appearance by that of his officer.

"Just like a couple o' second-hand Robinson Crusoes out of a pantymime, and bound for the North Pole. Talk about a lark. Oh, don't I wish my poor old mother could see her bee-u-tiful boy!—Poor old chaps! Poor old pardners! Won't they be waxy when they knows I'm gone! Here, blessed if I can get, at my clean pocket-'ankychy, and I wants to shed a purlin' tear for poor old Sergeant Gee."

"Ready!" came to check the flow of Gedge's thoughts, and, picking up his rifle, the fellow to that placed ready for Bracy, he stepped out into the court, to find all the men left in the fort gathered to see them start, for the news was every one's property now; and as they marched towards the gates there was a low murmur, but no man stirred.

It was different, though, with the women; though here, too, all was done in silence. Officers' wives stepped forward to press Bracy's hands, with the tears standing in their eyes, and many a "God-speed!" was murmured in the ears of both.

"But no one shakes a hand with me," said Gedge sadly to himself; and then, "Well, I'm blessed!"

For Sergeant Gee was on one side of him to lay a hand upon his shoulder.

"Good-bye, Gedge," he said in his harsh, uncompromising way; "you'll stick to your officer like a brave lad, I know."

"Thank ye, Sergeant; and same to you," growled Gedge; and then the tears stood in his eyes, for Mrs Gee had hold of his unoccupied hand, to press it hard, with a grip, in fact, like a man's.

"Here," she said, taking a small, flat, black packet from her breast, and Gedge saw that it was envelope-shaped, but home-made in oilskin, and instead of being adhesive; there was a neat button and buttonhole. "Put that in your breast-pocket, my boy," she said, "and never part with it. Bandages, oiled silk, needles and thread, and a pair o' scissors. And mind this: plug a bullet-hole directly; and whatever you do, clean water, and lots of it, for all wounds."

"Thank ye, missus."

"For you and Mr Bracy too. There, Bill Gedge, you're a brave lad, and I'll kiss you for your mother's sake, in case you don't come back; and if ever I return to England I'll write and tell the Queen how her brave boys are always ready to do or die, though I know she won't get my letter if I do."

The men nearly disobeyed orders when Mrs Gee took hold of Gedge by his woolly *poshtin* and gave him a sounding kiss first on one cheek and then on the other, but they forbore; and the brave lad's eyes very nearly brimmed over the next moment, for, leaving Bracy, now on his way to the gate, the officers' ladies crowded round Gedge and shook hands, two dying to thrust upon him packages of what would have been luxuries to them in nights to come; but he was obliged to shake his head, for he was already laden to the fullest extent.

"Now, Gedge!" came from the gate, and the next minute it had been opened and closed after two bulky, stooping figures, who, with rifles at the trail, started off in Indian file along the track by the river-side, making for the upper portion of the valley, but without uttering a word.

Their ears were listening, though, to the sounds of firing in the distance, the reports of many pieces coming reverberating out of the chasm-like rift leading south. Their eyes, too, were as much upon the alert as those of some timid animal whose life depends upon its watchfulness from day to day, existing, as it does, in the midst of numberless enemies, who look upon it as their natural prey.

But though their rolling eyes scanned every spot familiar, from long experience, as the lurking-place; of an enemy, there was not a glimpse of a white coat nor the gleam of a polished weapon to be seen. At the same time, careful watch was kept upon the track they traversed every time it opened out sufficiently for a forward glance of any extent, and the heavy, matter-of-fact, hill-country-looking pair had nearly reached a spot from whence a good view of the fort could be obtained before a word was spoken.

Then the silence was broken by Bracy, who said abruptly:

"Don't look back, my lad."

"No, sir," came promptly from the front.

"Our lookout is forward from this hour till the time we bring back help to those we leave behind."

Gedge was silent, and kept on the watch, as, with rounded shoulders and camelled back, he planted his puttee-bandaged legs in the safest parts of the rugged track.

"Well, don't you want to know where we're going?"

"Yus, sir; 'orrid."

"Over the mountains to bring back a Ghoorka regiment, my lad."

"Right, sir."

"And by the hardest way we can find."

"Something like them ways over the snow, like you goes for the bears and sheep, sir?"

"Yes: and harder ways still, Gedge: for to meet any of the people may mean—"

Bracy paused, and Gedge waited for him to end his sentence. But he waited in vain, till he was tired, and then finished it to himself, and in the way he liked best.

"May mean," he said, and then paused—"having to put bullets through some o' these savage savages, for I'm blest if I'm going to let 'em have the first shot at us. Yes," he added, "savages; that's what's about their size. I never see such beasts. Yes, that's what they are— wild beasts. I don't call such things men. The best of it is, they thinks they're so precious religious, and sticks theirselves up to pray every morning and every night, I'm blest!—praying!—and often as not with their knives and swords! Ugh! and phew! My word! it's warm walking in these here coats. Wish I hadn't got mine."

Is thought electric, or magnetic, or telepathic, or scientific, some way or another, that so often it is communicated from one person to another free of cost, and without a form, or boy to leave it, and wait for an answer? Certainly it was in that, clear mountain air, which blew softly among the cedars in the valley, coming off the clear ice and dazzling snow from one side, getting warmed in hot sunshine, and then rising up the mighty slopes on the other side, to grow from pure transparency, in its vast distance and extent, to be of a wonderfully delicious amethystine blue.

Anyhow, Gedge had no sooner given himself his opinions about the heat engendered by walking in a thick, sheepskin coat than Bracy said:

"Find the *poshtin* hot, Gedge?"

"'Ot ain't the word for it, sir," was the reply. "I ain't quite sure whether it's me, or whether they didn't scrape the fat off proper when they tanned the skin, sir; but something's running."

"Steady down, then. It is very warm here among the cedars; but they hide us from the enemy, my lad. As soon as we begin to climb we shall be getting out of summer into winter; and by the time it's dark, and we lie down to sleep, we shall think it would be pleasanter if we had two apiece."

"Shall us, sir? Well, you know, sir; but all this caps me. Here we are, as you say, in summer, and we've on'y got to climb up one o' them mountains and there we are in winter. They say it freezes there every night."

"Quite right, Gedge."

"But all the snow melts away some time in the year?"

"Never, my lad. Up there before you, where the sun shines on those glorious peaks, it is eternal winter, only that there is so much melting in the hottest parts of the day."

"To make the rivers, sir?"

"Of course!"

"And the rain helps when they're all in the clouds up there, I suppose, sir?"

"Rain!" said Bracy, laughing; "there is no rain there, my lad; when the clouds discharge their burden it is in the form of snow. But now, silence once more. The less we talk the better till we are among the snow, for at any moment we may be walking into a trap."

"Like we did, sir, when you three gentlemen come and whistled us from the side o' them falls?"

"Yes."

"Well, we don't want none o' that sort o' thing, sir, or we shall never be bringing that ridgement back."

"Right. Now you see the necessity for taking to the snow where the hill-men rarely climb."

"Yus, sir, going; but what about coming back?"

"The same, or a nearer way."

"But with a ridgement, sir?"

"Oh yes; the Ghoorkhas will go anywhere if they are told."

"So'll us," said Gedge to himself; and then, with a word or two at times from behind, he trudged on and on towards the mighty snowfields, but ever with his eyes on the lookout for the danger—keen knife, tulwar, matchlock, ball, or spear—invisible so far, but which at any moment might be so near.

Chapter Twenty Five.

First Checks.

The last echoes of the distant firing had quite died out; the windings of the river valley had long enough hidden away the mountainous hills which surrounded the fort; and far below where they slowly toiled along the faintly-marked track, worn where there was pasture by the feet of the mountain sheep, the river rushed, torrent-like, along in a greatly narrowed bed, whose perpendicular shrub and fern decked sides hid its leaping and tearing waters from the travellers' gaze. At rare intervals the river made a plunge over some mighty rock and flashed into sight, though its position was often revealed by a cloud of spray, which rose like steam into the sunshine, to become brilliant with an iris which, rainbow-like, spanned the falls.

The ascent had been gradual but marked, for, though trees were in abundance, rising in clumps of spires, their tops were well below the adventurers, while, where they trod, the forest was dwarfed and scrub-like, but thick enough to greatly hinder their advance.

Hardly a word had been spoken for hours, during which the watchfulness observed had been painful, especially when they had crept along under cover by three lateral valleys, familiar to both as the roads by which the enemy had approached for their attacks, one to the east being that made unenviable by the terrible adventure when they had received their wounds.

The passing of the mouths of these gorges was a crucial task, from its being almost a certainty that part of one or the other of the tribes would be, stationed there. But the slow approaches and all the caution exercised, as far as Bracy could judge, were waste of energy: not an enemy was seen, and when, twice over, rifles were brought to the ready, and their bearers stood prepared to fire at the foe rustling along among the low growth and tangle, it was to find, to their great relief, that the alarm was caused in the first instance by goat-like sheep, and in the other by a bear, which had been feasting upon the berries growing low down the cliff towards the hidden torrent.

The sun was long past the meridian, and, in spite, of the height, their shut-in position made the breathless valley seem hotter than ever, while the thorny nature of the low growth hindered them so much that at last Bracy had hard work to force his way through a tangled mass, whose thorny hooks clung to the *poshtin* he was wearing, and kept on robbing it of its wool. This brought them to a standstill, and Gedge, who had just freed himself from similar hindrances, stepped back, with his dagger-like bayonet in his hand, with which he delivered a few sharp cuts, and Bracy struggled out.

"Ha!" he said; "that's better."

"Yus, sir; these are handier tools than the old-fashioned bay'nets; but what we ought to have had was a couple o' those pretty, bill-hooky blades the Ghoorkha boys use. They'd make short work of briars and brambles and things. Toothpicks, our lads calls 'em; and the little fellows the Toothpick Brigade.—Tired, sir?"

"Terribly!" said Bracy. "This is awful going; but we shall be out of the wood before many hours have passed. We might have avoided this by striking up to the left, but I felt that it was not safe. Better be slow and sure. Look, my lad, it is more open yonder, and seems like a way down to the torrent. We've earned a rest, and we must have one. Let's get down to where we can reach water, and lighten our load by making a meal."

Gedge's eyes sparkled, and he led on at once, reaching at the end of some hundred paces a sharp slope, which showed traces of the moss and ferns having been trampled down, while twigs were broken here and there, some being left hanging, and others snapped sharp off!

"People been along here, Gedge," said Bracy, taking suspicious notice of the signs around.

"No, sir, I think not," said the lad, whose keen eyes were busy. "I should say it was only goats. Pst!"

Gedge had been speaking in a low tone, but the "Pst!" was sharply distinct, and had its effect. For in an instant there was a rush, and something brown came into sight, making the adventurers present their rifles in the full belief that they were about to be face to face with an enemy. But the next moment the object rose up to peer over the bushes and all around, proving to be a great brown bear, whose little, pig-like eyes flashed and glistened as it scanned the place, looking wonderfully human in its actions as it balanced itself upon its hind-legs, its fore-legs hanging half raised on either side, till it caught sight of the disturbers of its solitude, when it uttered a growling grunt, dropped down on all-fours again, and dashed up the slope towards the mountains.

"Might easily have shot him, sir," said Gedge as the sounds of the breaking twigs died out.

"Easily," said Bracy; "but we have as much as we can carry now, and— Hark!"

Gedge was already listening, for, from up in the direction taken by the bear—which, unfortunately, was the continuation of their route— the report of a gun rang out, followed by another and another. Then there was a burst of exultant shouts, and the pair drew back more into shelter.

"They've hit him, whoever they are, sir," whispered Gedge excitedly: "and they'll be along here direckly. Which way will you go, sir? We can't go that."

"Away towards the water, my lad," said Bracy, quickly. "They're coming down to reach the fort."

He led the way himself now, following the easier portions of the slope, and when close to where the now narrow river came thundering down, he plunged in amongst a chaos of creeper and fern hung rocks, down in a hollow of which they sank into a kneeling position, crouching low and waiting.

"Well hidden, are we not, Gedge?" whispered Bracy.

"Splendid, sir. Couldn't see us 'less they was close to, and if we kept our heads down they'd take us then for sheep."

"And fire at us."

"They'd better not!" growled Gedge. "But, say, sir, as we're resting mightn't we just as well have a bite?"

"Could you eat now?" whispered Bracy.

"Could I eat now, sir?" said the lad wonderingly. "It's couldn't I eat! My! If you only knew what I've been feeling ever since dinner-time you wouldn't ask that."

"Go on, then," said Bracy, and as he listened he saw his companion take a packet of bread and meat from his haversack and begin to munch, when the sight of the food so woke him up to the state of his own appetite that he opened his wallet, drew out some hastily-cut mutton and bread-cake sandwiches, and went on eating till there was the sound of voices close at hand, followed by the rustling of leaf and twig, with the dull tramp of soft feet telling that a large body of men were passing in Indian file, talking loudly; but the hidden pair were well concealed and satisfied that they were perfectly safe, till all at once a voice was raised, and they heard the word "Water" uttered in the Dwat dialect.

There was an eager buzz of voices at this, and instead of continuing their course the party clustered together, and, to Bracy's horror, began to descend the sharp slope as if coming right upon their hiding-place, but turning off by one of the bigger rocks, and rapidly crushing through the thin shrubs and ferns so close that Bracy, as he lay there, could have touched one man by stretching out the barrel of his rifle.

For the next ten minutes the position was agonising, the men coming and going, and even the noise they made in drinking just below was plainly heard; while Bracy, as he cowered down among the ferns, felt that it was impossible for them to escape the observation of the keen-eyed mountaineers.

But still the discovery was deferred; and, as the drinking went on, a gleam or two of hope illumined the position, but only to be damped again, and Bracy held his revolver ready, for there was a sudden movement on the part of one of the men, whose sword and shield seemed to be of a superior type, like his cotton clothes and the turban he wore.

It was as if this man had just caught sight of them, and, his curiosity being excited, he came straight on, drawing his keen tulwar and striking with if to right and left so as to clear the way towards the rocks, his eyes seeming to be fixed upon those of Bracy, who slightly raised the muzzle of his revolver, his finger resting upon the trigger.

Probably never was man nearer to his death, for the slightest additional pressure of the young officer's finger would have sent a bullet crashing through the man's breast, as he came on till almost within touch, when he suddenly turned round, and seated himself upon a mossy rock just in front, his broad back, in its loose while cotton garb, effectually hiding the fugitives from the men going up and down.

Bracy felt as if he would have given anything to have been able to utter a low "Hah!" of relief, as he breathed long and heavily, instead of crouching there nearly suffocated by holding it back; for he knew that the slightest movement, the faintest sound, must result in the man, evidently the leader, turning sharply, sword in hand, to discover the pair lying so close.

"I should have a bullet through him 'fore he could lift his sword," said Gedge to himself; "but what's the good o' that? Twenty or thirty would be upon us before we could get away, and a nice condition we're in for that! Why, I feel like a fat sheep at Christmas. Couldn't run if I wanted to, and I don't, 'less he runs fust, and he won't, I know. Know him too well."

Bracy's thoughts were many as he crouched there. He wanted to feel decisive; but the weary walk, heavily-laden as he was, had dulled his brain a little, and he could not come to a conclusion as to whether it would not be best to take the initiative and attack at once, trusting to their sudden appearance and the shots they could be creating a panic; for it was not likely that the enemy would imagine such an attack would be made unless by a force at least equal to their own.

The idea was tempting; but, on the other hand, it seemed madness to make so wild a venture; and he was giving it up, when they were both startled by half-a-dozen of the party who were going and coming stopping short just in front of their leader, to begin taking out some blackish-looking cakes. Then others beginning to join them, they looked round, and a couple of the party pointed to the rocks behind which Bracy and Gedge were hidden.

That was fatal, and from the movement which followed it was evident that they were about to make this their resting-place.

At the same moment Gedge's hand stole forward and touched his leader's arm, when Bracy softly turned his head, to see his follower holding his revolver in his right hand, signing as if asking should he use it.

Bracy did not delay his silent reply, for, quick as lightning, he had realised that in another few moments they would be forced to fight in defence, and that it was far better to take the initiative and make the enemy believe that they had fallen into an ambuscade.

At the word 'Fire!' the chief had made a sudden bound, . . . and rushed
at his men, who turned and fled at full speed.

F. II. ?   PAGE 273.

He gave a short nod, raised his own revolver, glanced at Gedge to see that he was ready, and then roared at the top of his voice:

"Fire!"

Gedge's shot followed his sharply, and then in rapid succession they fired again and again till a dozen bullets had gone hurtling over their sheltering rock amongst the trees, and then, springing up, they fixed bayonets with a rattle, and stood ready to fire again; but not an enemy was visible to charge or be shot down.

For at the word "Fire!" the chief had made a sudden bound from the stone, upon which he had sat, and rushed at his men, who turned and fled at full speed away in the direction from which our adventurers had come: and for the next few minutes Bracy and Gedge stood listening as they recharged their revolvers, hearing the distant crackling and rustling of leaf and twig till all was still.

"Think they'll rally, Gedge?" said Bracy at last.

"Not them, sir: it was too much of a scare, and so sudden. It's hard work to start these beggars running, but once you do get 'em on the move it's twice as hard to stop 'em."

"You are right," said Bracy quietly.

"They'll go on till they come upon the next lot o' their pardners, and then they'll tell 'em they were attacked by two whole ridgements, and show their wounds, if they've got any. Don't think I hit one, sir. Did you?"

"I did not even try to," said Bracy. "I only thought of firing as quickly as I could. Now, then, a drink of water apiece, and forward. We can't stop to rest, but must eat as we go."

They hurried down in turn to where the tribes-men had refreshed themselves, each watching while the other drank hastily, and remounted to the track; after which, food in hand, they were about to recommence their journey, when Gedge started.

"What is it?" said Bracy quickly.

"One on 'em down, sir. Didn't think we had hit any of 'em, but yonder's one lying among the bushes."

"Yes," said Bracy; "perfectly still. I saw and covered him while you were drinking, and was going to see if he is dead as we went by, in case he might be only wounded, and dangerous."

"Pouf!"

"What is it?" said Bracy wonderingly, for Gedge had broken into a quiet little laugh.

"It's the bear they shot, sir, and brought into camp with 'em. Won't come back to fetch it—will they?"

"We will not stop to see," said Bracy quietly. "Now, forward once more."

Their path took them by the dead bear, whose paws were bound together with twigs, and a freshly-cut pole was thrust through, showing how the trophy had been borne so far. The next minute the pair were steadily climbing again, and finding by degrees that, though the slope increased, the way was less cumbered with dense growth, so that the advance was easier; while as the sun sank lower a gentle breeze sprang up to refresh them, making Gedge stretch out and increase the pace, in spite of the path growing more steep.

"Don't think they're after us—do you, sir?" said the lad at last, as they trudged on, watching the gradual ascent of a shadow on one of the hills in front.

"No; I think we succeeded in our scare."

"Because it makes a lot o' difference, sir."

"I don't understand you," said Bracy.

"We've a lot to do to-morrow, sir; and while it's dark I s'pose you'll bivvywack."

"I shall keep on till it's too dark to see, my lad," said Bracy, "and then we must sleep till it is light enough to see, and go on again. I want to get twenty-four hours' walking between us and the fort."

"Exactly, sir. Be safer then."

"Perhaps," said Bracy, smiling grimly.

"O' course, sir," said Gedge sharply; "but I was thinking about to-night. Is it to be watch and watch, sir—one on dooty, t'other off."

"No; our work will be too hard for that, Gedge," replied Bracy. "We must have as many hours' heavy sleep as we can, or we shall never get to the Ghil Valley. The work to-day has been play to some of the climbing we shall have."

"Yus, sir; I s'pose so," said Gedge cheerily; "lot o' uphill, o' course."

"Up mountain, my lad."

"Yus, sir; only got in the way o' calling all these snow-pynts hills; but it'll be very fine; and after getting up one there must be some downhill on the other side. Do you know, sir, I've been reg'lar longing, like, ever since we come here, to go up a mountain—a reg'lar big one; but I didn't think I should ever have the chance, and here it is come."

Instead of rapidly growing darker a glorious sunset lit up cloud and mountain, till the peaks literally blazed and flashed with the colours of the various precious stones, wondrously magnified, till the ever-changing scene rose higher, fading rapidly, and only a few points burned as before. Then, in a minute, all was grey, and a peculiar sense of cold tempered the climbers' brows.

"We shall just have time to reach that great patch of firs, Gedge," said Bracy; "yonder, this side of the snow."

"Right, sir, I see; but it's a good two mile away."

"Surely not," said Bracy sceptically.

"'Tis, sir," persisted the man. "Distances is precious deceiving."

They kept on, with the gloom darkening rapidly now in the valleys, and the peaks in the distance standing up of a ghastly grey; while Gedge shook his head and said to himself:

"Gov'nor ought to know; but it 'll be dark 'fore we get there."

The next minute Gedge was looking in wonder at the peculiar rosy glow which suddenly began to suffuse the great mountain. The chilly grey died out and the ruddy glow grew richer and brighter for a time, while the sky in the west seemed to be blazing and as if the glow were being dragged backward, to aid the weary messengers till they could reach the fir-tree forest that was to form their camp.

"Think there's a tremenjus fire somewhere, sir?" said Gedge at last.

"No; it is only what people call the Alpenglow," said Bracy softly, for the wondrous beauty of the scene impressed him. "It will soon die out again, but it will help us on our way: for you were right, Gedge; that patch of trees was fully two miles from where we stood, and we have all our work cut out to reach it before dark. If we cannot we must shelter beneath the first wind-screen of rock we can find. What about your sheepskin coat? Is it too hot?"

"Not a bit, sir; I'm cooling down fast; and, I say, there goes the last of the light. Shall we get to the wood?"

"I'm afraid not," said Bracy. "Look to the left, and I'll look to the right. We'll stop at the most likely spot we see."

"Don't, sir. I can keep my eye on that tall tree that goes up like a spike, and hit it if it gets twice as dark. Wind feels cool now; by-and-by it'll be like ice up here. Hadn't we better get right, into shelter?"

"Go on, then, my lad. I was thinking of you."

"Then don't, please, sir; I can keep on as long as you."

The next minute—it seemed so close—the stars were shining brightly out of the deep purple sky, and it was as if their coming brought on a cooler breath of wind, which Gedge suggested had a sniff of frost in it. But they had no time for conversation; and, making a final effort to overcome their weariness, they pressed on till it had grown so dark that they felt that it would be hopeless to persevere, for the forest could not be readied. The next minute the darkness was profound; they were no longer stumbling along a stony way, but passing silently over a thick carpet of fir-needles; the sky was blotted out as if by a dense black cloud; and there was a strange humming overhead as of the sea upon the shore. For they had unwittingly reached and plunged into the forest when giving it up in despair.

"Mind the trees, sir," said Gedge warningly. "I've just ketched myself an awful rap."

"Feel your way with your rifle," said Bracy hoarsely. "We need only go a little farther, so as to be well in shelter."

So, after cautiously advancing about a hundred yards, feeling their way from trunk to trunk, they stopped short beneath one of the largest trees, and sank down amongst the fir-needles.

"Shall I make a fire, sir?" said Gedge; "here's heaps of wood as 'll burn like hoorrah."

"Fire! Are you mad?" cried Bracy.

"No, sir; but I was feared you'd be cold."

"No fire, and no watch, my lad," said Bracy. "It would be impossible for any one to find us here. Make the best meal you can in the dark; then take out your revolver, and lie down with it in your hand, as I shall. You must sleep as hard as you like till daybreak. Think you can?"

Gedge said something indistinctly, for he had begun eating, but ten minutes later his voice sounded clear again.

"Likely to be any bears, sir?" he said.

"Very likely," replied Bracy. "If one comes supper-hunting he'll wake us by pawing us about and sniffing. Use your revolver then, only make sure of his head. Good-night, my lad."

"Good-night, sir," said Gedge, snuggling himself as close as he could, and nestling among the fir-needles. "Here," he muttered; "and I was grumbling because I had to carry this here coat. Why, it's a patent feather-bed, wool mattress, and blankets, all in one. Scrumptious!— How my trotters aches!—And if one comes supper-hunting he'll wake us by pawing us about and sniffing. 'Use your revolver then, only make sure of his head,' he says. Just as if I was going to fire at his tail! I say, though, have bears got tails? I never see one at the 'Logical Gardens as had—and it don't matter now. Well, this here is a change, and—and —"

The next muttered word somehow stretched itself out thin, and into a long deep-sighing breath, which seemed to be the echo of another close at hand, and to have nothing to do with the cool breeze which rushed through the pines, making that soft peculiar sound as of the sea breaking upon a sandy shore; for the two adventurers, relieved of their loads, and tightly buttoned up in their *poshtins*, were sleeping the sleep of the weary through that long night, undisturbed by enemy, wild beast, or dream.

Chapter Twenty Six.

Human Stalking.

"Eh? Yes, sir. All right, sir? I'm awake. Didn't know it was my turn to-night."

"It is morning, Gedge," said Bracy as he bent over his companion, whose face was just visible in the faint grey light which seemed to be creeping in beneath the fir-boughs.

"My word, sir, so it is! I thought I was being called for sentry-go. Nights seems precious short up here in the hills." Bracy laughed.

"Oh no," he said; "we've had a good long rest. Now, then. We must have our wash at the first stream we come to. Let's get on at once."

"Ready in a jiffy, sir. Seems a pity, though, not to have our breakfast, first."

"Why?" said Bracy sharply as he slung on his haversack.

"Such a nice lot o' dry wood to make a fire, sir."

"To make tea or coffee, or to boil eggs, my lad?" said Bracy.

"Think o' that, now! I forgot, sir. Seemed to come nat'ral for me to get your breakfast ready, sir. Think o' that."

In two minutes Gedge was as ready as his officer, and he finished off by shaking and beating the fir-needles off his *poshtin*, and stroking his very short hair down first with one hand and then with the other, so as to look as respectable and smart as he could when going on what he called parade.

"Forward!" said Bracy suddenly. "We'll halt at the edge of the forest, and have a good reconnoitre, though it is not light enough for us to see far."

Bracy was quite right; for as they cautiously advanced to the open they could see very little but the tall pyramidal peaks here and there, one of which stood out more clearly than the others, and served as a familiar landmark by which to steer for that day's journey, another which Bracy had noted on the previous evening being set down as to be somewhere about the end of their second day's march; but it was not visible yet, a pile of clouds in its direction being all that could be seen.

"Right. Forward!" said Bracy as he finished his careful look round. "Two hours' good walk in this cool air, and then breakfast. To-morrow we must begin to look out for anything that will serve for our future meals, and use our rifles."

"Not try at any of the villages?"

"Villages!" said Bracy, smiling. "By that time we shall be far above any villages, and up amongst the snow."

"Right, sir; all the same to me. I love a bit o' sport, though I never got no farther at home than rats."

"Talk lower," said Bracy. "Sound travels far when everything is so still."

Striking to the right now, and keeping near the deep gully along which the river ran, Bracy sought for a spot where they could cross to the far side, and before long they came upon a rock-strewn part opposite to where another of the several streams joined it from the east. Here, with a little careful balancing and stepping from stone to stone, they had not much difficulty in crossing to the other side; where, the minor affluent being also crossed, their course was directed up its right bank to the north and east. The side of the little ravine being surmounted, a far wider scope of view was obtained, the mountain before hidden in clouds now showing its crest in the coming sun; and, satisfied as to the course he was to take, and marking it down by the little pocket-compass he carried, Bracy pointed to a sheltered spot amongst some scrub pine, and a halt was made for a short time for the promised breakfast.

Nothing could have been more simple, nothing more delicious. For the glorious mountain air gave a wonderful zest to everything; and in about a quarter of an hour they were ready to resume their journey, refreshed, in high spirits, and with their task in the bright morning sunshine, which glorified the wondrous panorama of snow-peaks, seeming to assume the aspect of a holiday trip.

"I'll take one look round first," said Bracy, "in case our friends of yesterday are anywhere upon our track;" and, before exposing himself, he drew out the little glass he had brought, and swept the sides of the valley they had ascended, then slowly turned his glass upon the ridge they had gained, following it to where it joined the main valley, and afterwards turned from the varied panorama of grassy upland forest and rock, over the boundary-line to where to his right all was snow—pure white snow, which looked deliciously soft, and sparked with a million rays.

"All seems clear, Gedge," he said at last. "So let us start. That is to be our resting-place to-night, or as near to it as we can get."

"That mountain with a big point and a little un, sir?"

"Yes."

"Don't seem half a day's journey, sir. Everything's so clear that things look close to yer. But I know better now. Ready, sir?"

"We'll keep a little to the left, so as to get nearer to the snow, and where it seems easy walking we'll take to it; but for the most part I shall keep to the division-line between the snow and the scrubby growth. It will be rough travelling; but we shall not have to cut our way through briars. I'll lead now. Forward!"

They started at once, and soon found the journeying far more rough than either could have imagined, for what had looked in the distance a pebbly track was a slope burdened with blocks of shaley rock, which yielded to their tread, and slipped and rattled to such an extent that Bracy was glad to strike off higher still, towards the snow, which ran up in a beautiful curve towards one of the nearest mountains, round whose shoulder they could make a cut which would bring them out miles nearer their goal.

At the end of a couple of miles the bottom of the snow-slope was reached, and the line of demarcation was boldly marked, the flattened, broken stones ending at once, so that the leader stepped directly upon the dazzling crystals, which filled in all the little rifts and hollows, and treacherously promised smooth, easy going for miles. But Bracy was undeceived at the first step, for he plunged his leg to the knee in granular snow, as yielding and incoherent as so much sand. Withdrawing it, he walked on a few steps and tried again, to find the frozen particles just as yielding; while Gedge had the same experience.

"Not much chance o' sliding and skating over this stuff, sir," he cried.

"No. It is impossible. We should be done up at the end of a mile. We must keep to the rocks and stones."

Bracy was looking wistfully at the soft, tempting-looking expanse, when a quick movement on Gedge's part took his attention.

"What is it?" he asked.

"Didn't you say we must soon be thinking of shooting something for rations?"

"Yes. But it is too soon yet. We don't want anything more to carry. But what can you see?"

"Looks like a drove o' somethings, sir—goats, I think—right across the snow yonder, where there's a dark mark like rocks. I can't quite make 'em out; for I dessay it's a couple o' miles away; but it's moving."

"Wait a moment," said Bracy; and he got out his glass, set the butt of his rifle on a stone, and rested the glass on the muzzle, so as to get a steady look.

"I see nothing," he said—"nothing but field after field of snow, with a few rocky ridges; and beyond them, rocks again, a long slope, and— Yes, I see now. Why, Gedge, man, there must be a couple of hundred."

"Well, sir, we don't want 'em," said Gedge, on the fox and grapes principle; "and goat's meat's awful strong, no matter how you cook it."

"Goats? Nonsense! Armed men, Gedge, for I could see the flashing of the sunshine off their weapons."

"Phee-ew!" whistled Gedge. "See us, sir?"

"I hope not. But they are going in a direction which will take them right across our road just at the same time as we reach the spot."

"That's awk'ard, sir. But I thought we'd been getting high up here because there'd be no people to hinder us."

"So I thought, my lad; but this is an exception. These people are crossing the mountain-passes, possibly to join the tribes besieging the fort."

"And what about them yonder?" said Gedge, nodding to the right.

"What! You don't mean to say that you can see more in that direction?"

As Bracy spoke he snatched out the glass he was replacing, and held it half-way to his eyes, for he did not need it. The object seen was too plain against the sky-line, where a few tiny figures could be seen, and trailing down a slope from them towards the east was a long, white, irregular line, which the glass directly after proved to be a strong body of followers.

"Same sort, sir?" said Gedge coolly.

"Yes; going as if to cut us off. Gedge, we must start back into the little valley, and follow it up, so as to get into another. It means miles more to tramp; but we can do nothing in this direction."

"Right, sir. When you're ready."

"But we can't walk right away, for these last would see us. We must crawl for a few yards to those rocks below there."

The next minute they were on all-fours, crawling from stone to stone—a laborious task, laden as they were; but, short as the distance was, they had not half-covered it before Bracy whispered sharply:

"Flat down. Perhaps they have not seen us."

"Not they, sir. They were too far off."

"Hush! Don't you see—right in front, four or five hundred yards away—those four men stalking us? Why, Gedge, they see our coats as we crawl, and are taking us for sheep."

"Ah-h!" ejaculated Gedge, as for the first time he realised the fresh danger threatening them, in the shape of a little party, evidently coming from the direction of their last night's resting-place. As he saw that one of them had thrown himself down, and, dragging his gun after him, was making for a heap of stones, from whence he evidently intended to fire, Gedge prepared to meet the shot in military fashion.

"Trying to stalk us, sir. You're right; that's it. Give me the word, and I'll open fire. He'll think he never stalked such a sheep as me before."

"It was my fancy, Gedge," said Bracy. "They belong to the party whom we scattered yesterday, and they've been following on our track. Quick! we must have first fire."

The last words had not quitted his lips when Gedge's rifle cracked, and the danger was averted, for the man's long gun dropped from his hands as he sprang up, crawling though he was, into a curious position on all-fours, rolled over on to his side, and them back again, to spring to his feet, and run as hard as he could after his companions, who had already taken to their heels.

"That's a bad shot, and no mistake, sir," said Gedge.

"The best you ever made, Gedge," cried Bracy; "for it has done all we required."

"Took him in the arm, sir, and spoiled his shooting for a month, I know. As good as killing him, I s'pose."

"Better," said Bracy. "We don't want the poor wretch's life; only to save our own. Now, what next? We'd better lie still for a bit to see if they rally and come on again."

"Yes, sir," said Gedge, watching the retreating party, and fiddling with the sighting of his rifle—"five hundred yards—six—eight,"—and last of all "thousand. I think I could send a bullet among their legs, sir. Shall I? Let 'em see that they'd better keep their distance."

"Try and scatter the stones close to them," replied Bracy. And as he lay upon his chest, with his feet raised and legs crossed, Gedge took a long and careful aim, pressed the trigger gently, and the next moment the retreating party bounded apart, scattering, and running swiftly on.

"Another good shot," said Bracy; "though I could not see where it struck; it is evident that it did strike close to their feet."

The glass was in the young officer's hand, and he followed the enemy's movements with it, seeing the little party close up again, and then make for a ridge in the distance—one which threatened to conceal them as soon as it was passed; but there was something else to see, for all at once the solitude of the elevation was broken by a figure springing into sight, to be followed by a large group, who began to descend slowly to meet the retreating four; and of their movements Bracy kept his companion aware with a word or two at intervals, without changing his position or removing his glass from his eye.

"They're close together now—the last man has joined them—they're looking in this direction—they've turned round, and are going up the slope again. Ha! the last man has passed over—gone."

"Would you mind having a look at the other two lots now, sir, to see what they're doing?" said Gedge quietly.

The little glass was slowed round on the instant, and Bracy examined the party to the right, and then, turning to the left, made a long examination of the danger there, before closing the glass again.

"They are keeping steadily on along those slopes, Gedge, as if to converge some miles farther on."

"Hadn't we better play the same game, sir?" said Gedge quietly.

"What do you mean?"

"Do a bit o' converging, sir, whatever it is."

"I don't set; how we can at present," replied Bracy, laughing sadly. "No. It seems as if the only thing left for us to do is to lie still here till the coast is clear—I mean, the enemy out of sight; then keep on cautiously, and trust to getting beyond them in the darkness. It is terribly unfortunate, Gedge."

"'Tis, sir, and wastes so much time. Think they have seen us?"

"No."

"Nor those chaps as was stalking us?"

"The distance is too great unless they have powerful glasses."

"That's good, sir. Then all we've got to mind is those chaps we've been skirmishing with. They'll be like the rest of 'em, I expect— hanging after us till they can get a shot."

"Yes; and I'm afraid that they will descend into yon little side valley to try and get ahead of us, so as to lie in wait, farther on."

"Like as not, sir. Just the sort of mean thing they would do, never stopping to think as we could easily have shot their chief in the back when we were in ambush, just as I could have dropped that chap in his tracks just now. I don't want to brag, sir; but I could."

"It is not boasting, my lad," said Bracy. "You have your marks for good shooting. But we must countermarch those fellows. We have nearly a mile the start of them, and I don't suppose those two bodies of men are likely to take any notice of such a pair of rough-looking objects as we are; so come along."

"Which way, sir?"

"Straight for our mountain yonder. What we want is a deep gully into which we could plunge, and then we could walk fast or run part of the way."

"And hide again, sir? Well, it'll be strange if in all this great mountainy place we can't puzzle those fellows behind."

"We can, Gedge," said Bracy, "if once we get out of their sight."

"So we are now, sir."

"We don't know that. Several pairs of keen eyes may be watching our movements, for I dare say as soon as we stand up our figures will show plainly against the snow. But we must risk all that. There, we must chance it now, so let's get on our way."

Bracy took another good look round with his glass from where he lay upon his chest among the stones; and though the enemy looked distant, the mountain he had marked down seemed to have doubled its remoteness, and the snowy passes and peaks which moved slowly across the field of his glass raised themselves up like so many terrible impediments to the mission he had set himself to carry through. Only a brief inspection, but there was time enough for a rush of thoughts to sweep to his brain, all of which looked dim and confused in the cloud of doubt which arose as to the possibility of reaching the Ghil Valley.

It was horrible, for he could see in imagination the scene at the fort, where all were gathered to see him off, and every eye was brightened with the hope its owner felt; each countenance looked full of trust in one who, they felt sure, would bring back success, and save the fort in its terrible time of need. While now a cold chill seemed to be stealing through him, and failure was staring him in the face.

A quick mental and bodily effort, a blush of shame suffusing his face, and he was himself again—the young soldier ready for any emergency; and the next minute he was biting his lip with vexation at his momentary weakness. For there was Gedge watching him patiently, his follower who looked up to him for help and guidance—his man ready to obey him to the death, but, on the other hand, who looked for the payment of being cared for and protected, and not having his services misused by the cowardly action of a superior.

"It is just as I felt that day when I was swimming a mile from shore," he said to himself. "I felt that same chill, and thought that there was nothing for me to do but give up and drown. Then the same feeling of shame at my cowardice attacked me, and I struck out quietly, and went on and on to land. The fort is my land this time, and I'm going to reach it again by being cool. Oh, what a brain and power of self-control a General must possess to master all his awful responsibilities! but he does, and leads his men to victory against tremendous odds; while here I have but my one man to lead, and am staggered at a difficulty that may dissolve like a mist. Gedge!"

"Sir?"

"Forward for that patch of rocks a quarter of a mile away in front, without hesitation or turning to look back."

"Yes, sir."

"Once there, I'll bring the glass to bear again on our rear. Make a bee-line for it, as if you were going to take up new ground for your company. Once there, we can make for another and another, and if we are pursued each clump of rocks will make us breastworks or rifle-pits. Up! Forward!"

Gedge started on the instant, talking to himself, as he felt that he ought still to maintain a soldierly silence.

"Quarter of a mile—eh? That's a good half, or I've failed in judging distance, after all, and turned out a reg'lar duller. Cheeky, though, to think I know better than my orficer. Dunno, though; I've done twice as much of it as he have.—Wonder whether them beggars have begun stalking us again. Dessay they have. Sure to. My! how I should like to look back! That's the worst o' being a swaddy on dooty. Your soul even don't seem to be your own. Never mind; orders is orders, and I'm straight for them rocks; but natur's natur', even if it's in a savage nigger with a firework-spark gun and a long knife. If those chaps don't come sneaking after us for a shot as soon as they've seen us on the move, I'm a Dutchman."

Bill Gedge was not a Dutchman, but East London to the backbone, and quite right; for, before he and the officer were a hundred yards on their way to take up new ground, first one and then another white-clothed figure came cautiously into the wide field of view, quite a mile away, but plainly seen in that wonderfully clear air, and came on in a half-stooping way, suggesting hungry wolves slinking steadily and surely along after their prey.

Chapter Twenty Seven.

A Question of Helmets.

Bracy felt quite sure that they were being tracked, but he did not look round till they were well within the shelter of the rocks for which they aimed. Then, as soon as he could feel that he was certain of being unobserved, he raised his head above one of the blocks, and took his glass to read more fully their position. For, in a long line, at intervals of some ten yards or so, the enemy was coming on, without a sign of haste, but in the quiet, determined way of those who know that they are following an absolute certainty, and that it is only a matter of time before their prey drops down at their mercy.

The day was gloriously bright, and the vast landscape of rock, forest, and gleaming water to their left, and the dazzling stretch of peak, snowfield, and glacier, with its many gradations of silver and delicious blue, on their right, presented a scene which the mind might have revelled in for hours. But Bracy saw nothing of Nature's beauties, for his attention was centred in the long line of tribes-men coming slowly on, their movements being so full of suggestion and offering themselves for easy reading.

Bracy closed his glass, and turned with wrinkled brow to Gedge, who took this as an invitation to give his opinion; and he went on at once, as if in answer to a few remarks from his officer.

"Yes, sir," he said; "it is a nice game, and no mistake. The cowards! Look at 'em, sir. That's what they mean to do—come sneaking along after us, waiting for a chance to rush in and take a stroke, and then slipping off again before we can get a shot at 'em. That's what they think; but they're making the biggest mistake they over made in their lives. They don't know yet what one of our rifles can do."

"You think they mean to follow us up, Gedge?"

"That's it, sir. They'll hang about for a chance. These niggers haven't got anything to do; so, when they see a chance of doing a bit of a job so as to get something, they give theirselves up to it and go on, spending days and weeks to get hold of what they could have got honestly in half the time. But, look here, sir."

"Yes," said Bracy, nodding, as his companion tapped his rifle. "We could keep them off by good shooting, Gedge, while it is light; but what about the darkness?"

"Yes; that's what bothers me, sir. They don't try the shooting then, but sets their guns on one side, and lakes to those long, sharp knives."

Bracy nodded again, and Gedge drew back, and began to make quick points with his rifle, acting as if the bayonet were fixed.

"That'll be it after dark, sir. Bay'net's more than a match for any knife in the dark."

"Yes," said Bracy; "but it means one of us to be always awake, and in such a journey as ours this will be distressing."

"Never mind, sir. We'll take double allowance of sleep first chance afterwards. Yes; I see, sir; that patch o' stones, one of which lies over o' one side—to the left."

"Forward!" said Bracy; and the spot indicated was reached, the short halt made, and they went on again, after noting that the enemy was slowly following on their track.

That seemed a day of days to Bracy, and interminably long and wearisome. They kept along as near the edge of the snow as they could, and watched the two bodies of men to right and left till they were hidden by the inequalities of the ground; but they came into sight again and again. About midday the two parties were seen to meet, and then come to a halt, about a mile from where Bracy and his companion crouched, as usual, in among some loose rocks, in the unenviable position of being between two fires, the enemy in the rear halting too, and making no effort to come to close quarters after the lesson they had learned about the long, thin, pencil-like bullets sent whistling from Gedge's rifle.

"Can you make out what they are doing, sir?" asked Gedge.

"Sitting together, and I think eating."

"That's what you said the others were doing, sir."

"Yes."

"Then wouldn't it be a good time for us to be having a refresher, sir?"

"Very good time indeed, Gedge, if you can eat," said Bracy meaningly.

"If I can eat, sir?" said Gedge, turning over his officer's words. "Why, sir, I feel famished. Don't you?"

"No," said Bracy sadly. "I suppose the anxiety has taken away my appetite."

"But you must eat, sir. Make your load lighter, too. There are times when I feel as if I should like to eat all I want, and then chuck all the rest away. One don't seem to want anything but cartridges; but then, you see, sir, one does, or else the works won't go. I'm wonderful like a watch, I am—I want winding up reg'lar, and then I go very tidy; but if I'm not wound up to time I runs down and turns faint and queer, and about the biggest coward as ever shouldered a rifle. I'm just no use at all, not even to run away, for I ain't got no strength. Yes, sir, that's how it is: I must be wound up as much as a Waterbury watch, and wittles is the key."

"Go on, then," said Bracy, smiling; "wind yourself up, Gedge, and I'll do the same."

"Thank ye, sir; that's done me no end o' good," cried the lad, brightening up. "You've give me a reg'lar good appetite now."

Gedge proceeded to prove this fact at once, and his words and the example set him had the effect of making his leader begin to eat a few mouthfuls, these leading to more; and at the end of a minute or two both were heartily enjoying their repast, although the prospect before them seemed to promise that this would be the last meal of which they would partake.

As they watched the enemy in front and rear they could only come to the conclusion that it was as impossible to continue their journey as it was to retreat. There was the open north to the left of their intended course, but as far as they could make out it was impassable. By stern endeavour they felt that they might in time wade through the deep snow and reach the mountains; but, as far as they could judge, farther progress in the way of striking through them, and then turning round to their right, was not possible without the aid of ice-axe and rope. And again, there was the less mountainous part of the country across the side valley they had traversed, and where they might climb the ridge and make a circuit to the left; but that course would probably lead them more amongst the encampments of the enemy besieging the fort; and they had hardly begun discussing this course when Gedge exclaimed:

"Take your spy-glass, sir. There's game or something on the move over yonder to the south."

"A strong body of men, Gedge," said Bracy decisively. "The country's alive with the wretches, and these are evidently going to join those in our valley."

"Hard lines for the two Colonels and our poor lads, sir," said Gedge, with his face puckering up. "If it wasn't for orders I wouldn't mind them beggars behind; we'd get through them somehow, for it would be far better to go at 'em sharp and have it out, so that it might end one way or t'other, than keep creeping on here, never knowing when they may make a rush."

"I feel the same, Gedge," said Bracy firmly; "but we have our orders, and that mountain we must reach by night."

"Right, sir; I'm not grumbling; we're a-going to do it; but don't it seem rum? Only the other day the place was empty everywhere, and it was just as if the enemy had all been shot and buried theirselves, while when you gents went out shooting, and the Colonel sent out little parties to scout and cover you coming back, in case the niggers showed, we went about over and over again, and never see a soul. And now, just because you've got to take word to the Ghoorkha Colonel that we want help, all of 'em have turned out so as to send us back to our quarters."

Bracy let his companion chatter on; but he was actively busy the while with his glass, which gave him a clear picture in miniature of every movement of their pursuers, at the same time convincing him that neither the enemy in front, nor those, perfectly plain now on the ridge across the little valley, were aware of their presence.

"We must be getting on, Gedge," he said at last; "the enemy behind is on the move, and they are opening out to the left."

"That means getting down to the hollow yonder, sir, to come upon our flank or cut us off. Oh! don't I wish you could detach a party skirmishing, ready to counter upon them and send 'em back; but the force aren't strong enough, sir. You see, you want me to form the reserve."

Bracy smiled, and once more they stepped out, making for patch after patch of rocks, the more boldly now that they saw the enemy in front was crossing their intended track as if to get to the ridge on the other side of the valley, and form a junction with the men there.

"Double!" said Bracy suddenly; and they trotted now wherever the ground would allow of such a way of progressing, and in the hope of getting well forward; but, to their disgust, it was to find that their indefatigable pursuers imitated every movement, running when they ran, and settling down again to a walk as soon as they slowed.

And so the afternoon wore on, with the position in the rear unchanged, but the front clearing as the sun sank lower in the west.

"There's a more hopeful lookout yonder, Gedge," said Bracy, "but these scoundrels seem more determined than ever."

"That's right, sir; and the worst of it is they won't come, within shot. They're waiting for the dark. That's their game. Couldn't we steal a march on 'em somehow, sir? for this is getting a bit stupid."

"We can steal the march as soon as it's dark," replied Bracy. "I have been thinking of that; but then there is the difficulty of getting along in this rough place, and we may be getting out of the frying-pan into the fire."

"Well, I don't know as if would be any hotter, sir. Don't you think we'd better lie down behind some of the stones and pick a few of 'em off as they come up?"

"It might cheek them, if we could do it; but if you look through the glass you will see that they keep sending a couple of men up all the high places, who keep watch, and they'd signal to their companions that we were in ambush."

"I was afraid so, sir," said Gedge grimly; "that's always the way with my plans. There's always a hole in the bottom o' the tub I make 'em in, and they run out like sand."

"How would this do?" said Bracy. "Suppose we pick out a good place just as it is getting dark, and settle ourselves down to watch."

"That sounds right, sir," said Gedge encouragingly. "Then, as soon as they have got used to seeing us there looking over the stones, suppose we slip off our 'elmets, and leave them on the rocks, and creep away for some distance before we rise, and then go on as fast as we can so as the 'elmets may keep 'em off for a bit, sir."

"Yes; I see what you mean, but the trick is too old. Remember how the men put their helmets or caps above the breastworks to tempt them to fire. Depend upon it they would suspect."

"May be, sir, may be not; but we're in a fix, and we must do something."

"But the thing is what?"

"If we wanted to go back, sir—to retreat," began Gedge.

"Which we do not," said Bracy coldly.

"Of course not right away, sir; but to make a fresh start, that dodge would do."

"What do you mean?"

"Why, this, sir; suppose we put our 'elmets on the tops o' two stones just as it's getting dark."

"Well, go on," said Bracy impatiently.

"Then we keep our eyes upon our gentlemen to see whether they come in nigh enough first so as to give us a shot, and if they don't we wait till it's dark enough."

"And then go on as fast as we can, and without our helmets, to be exposed to the sun by day, the cold wind and snow by night, if we were not overtaken and finished. Bah, my lad! that will not do."

"No, sir; but that ain't the way my story goes," said Gedge, grinning.

"Let's have your way, then," said Bracy impatiently, as he scanned the enemy in the distance with his glass.

"I mean this, sir. We puts our 'elmets as 'fore-said on the rocks, watches till it's quite dark, and then, instead o' doubling off on our journey, we just creeps away to right or left, say a hundred yards, and then lies down."

"Yes?"

"Bimeby, one by one, my gentlemen comes creeping up with their long knives, ready to cut us up in the dark, supposing that we're there on the watch. Dessay dozen of 'em would come, front, right, left, and rear; and then, after they've surrounded our 'elmets, they goes right in for us, and slashes them instead of us. Next minute there's a reg'lar hoo-roar, and most likely, if we're lucky, they've chopped one; another awful. But whether they have or not, they've found out we're not there, and that they've been done; and on they goes in a passion right away, hoping to catch up to us again in the morning to carry on the same game of following us and giving us no rest till we're quite done, and the job to finish us is as easy as that."

He kissed his hand by way of illustrating the simplicity of the business.

"Yes; we should get rid of their hideous, heart-wearing pursuit," said Bracy thoughtfully, "and then be able to make a fresh start, of course. But what about covering for our heads?"

"Oh, don't you worry about that, sir. I'm on'y a thin un, and there's plenty o' spare stuff in this skin coat to spare for a couple o' woolly busbies as 'll suit us for this journey far better than 'elmets. The niggers at a distance would take us for the real article then. Now the spikes on our heads says English to every one as sees 'em."

"Yes," said Bracy thoughtfully; "that might be done if we could make the wool hats."

"Don't you worry yourself about that, sir. It's on'y like cutting two big long squares to measure, and doubling 'em over sidewise, and sewing two edges together. Then you sews the top edges, turns the thing inside out, and—"

"Well, and what?" said Bracy, for the lad stopped short and grinned.

"Puts 'em on, sir. That's all."

"And we have scissors and needles and thread and thimbles, of course," said Bracy mockingly.

"That's right, sir. In my pocket. Didn't Mother Gee give me 'em all ready for sewing up bandages and seeing to wounds? I'd a deal rather make caps with 'em; wouldn't you?"

"Of course, of course, Gedge," Bracy hastened to say. "Here, it's time we began to put our plan in action."

"Time to get on a bit farther first, sir. But do you really think that dodge would do?"

"I think enough of it to make me say that we'll try it, Gedge; and, if it succeeds, I tell you what, hard as it may be, we'll try the snow."

"That's the place to hide in, sir, when we creep away."

"Of course. Capital!"

"Might roll ourselves over in it, and it would stick to our coats, and they'd never find us. But I don't know about going on that way, sir."

"We must; I see no other."

"But what about footmarks afterwards, sir? It's like putting down a lot o' holes to show 'em the way we've gone."

"Holes that the sun would soon till in, or fresh snow fall to hide. But we need not study that. The enemy would go on and never think of coming back to make a fresh start. Even if they did, they would never find the place again that they went to in the dark."

"Not by the 'elmets, sir?"

"No; they'd make sure of them—carry them off as trophies. But I see a terrible difficulty."

"Do yer, sir? I'm very sorry."

"Suppose, while we're lying in the snow, one or two of the ruffians

228

come and stumble right over us?"

"I hope they won't, sir," said Gedge, with a grim look in his eyes, as he drew his dagger-like bayonet out and touched the point with his thumb. "That's pretty sharp, sir, and we should be on the lookout, and holding 'em in our hands, as what Sergeant Gee calls a shiver-de-freexe. They might tumble on them."

"Gedge, my lad, you're full of resources," said Bracy eagerly. "We'll try your plan, exactly as you propose."

"Thank ye, sir," said the lad uneasily; "but I don't want you to think I'm cocky and knowing, and like to be thought double cunning."

"That will do," said Bracy, smiling. "Let's think of the task we have in hand. It is no time to discuss trifles. This is all part of fighting for our lives."

Chapter Twenty Eight.

In the Snow.

In the tramp which followed, with the hill-men creeping on after them in the same slow, untiring way, Gedge had his eyes about him, and drew forth a sharp order from his officer when he began to deviate a little from the straight course towards a dwarf clump of pines, the highest of which was not above six feet.

"What are you going there for?"

"Want 'em, sir, for rifles," was the reply. Bracy nodded; and upon reaching the clump, a few sharp strokes from the lad's bayonet cut down and trimmed what formed a couple of longish walking-sticks, one of which he handed over to his officer, who used his in the latter capacity, Gedge soon following suit.

"That's what I want them to think, sir," said Gedge, digging his down at every second pace. "Now, sir, what do you say? Don't you think we might edge in more towards the snow?"

"Soon," said Bracy, pointing. "There's just the spot we want;" and, raising his glass, he stopped to examine a group of blocks of stone some fifty yards from the edge of the snowfield, which here sent down a few sharp points, giving it the appearance at a distance of a huge, vandyked piece of white lace.

"Couldn't find a better place if we tried, sir," said Gedge; "but we ain't left ourselves time enough. If we had thought of it sooner, I could have cut out and made the busbies."

"We shall have plenty of time for that to-morrow," said Bracy. "We must manage by tying on handkerchiefs for to-night, and pulling up the great collars as if they were hoods."

A short time after, each with his handkerchief over his head, the pair crouched behind two stones, upon which their helmets had been placed; and beside them the two sticks were planted, so that at a short distance any one would have been deceived and made to believe that a couple of men were on the watch for danger.

Two men were on the watch for danger, but in a different way, both lying prone, Bracy, with his glass to his eyes, carefully sweeping the distance, and keeping it fixed upon the enemy, who looked strangely quiet, as they grouped together and seemed to be feasting.

"Looks as if they meant to settle there, then, for the night, sir," said Gedge, as Bracy reported to him everything he noted.

"Yes; it looks so."

"But we don't trust 'em, bless yer, sir. That's their artfulness; foxing —that's what they're doing. Won't be able to see 'em much longer— will you, sir?"

"No; it's getting dark very fast; but I can make them out, I dare say, till they begin to move."

"Hope you will, sir," said Gedge softly, and lying with his knees bent, kicking his feet about in the air, after the fashion of a boy in a field on a sunny day, and looking quite unconscious of the fact that this night might be one of the most terrible they had ever been called upon to pass.

Some minutes elapsed now in perfect silence, during which a fiery look on the topmost peak of one of the mountains died out slowly into cherry red, and finally became invisible, a few stars twinkling out as the red light died.

"Gedge," said Bracy in a quick whisper, such as he might have uttered had the enemy been close upon them, and about to spring, instead of many hundred yards away.

"Sir?"

"They are on the move."

"Can't see 'em, sir."

"No; and they cannot see us, but I can dimly make them out with the glass. They are separating from their centre, and coming on. Ha! gone. I can see no more."

He put away the glass in the darkness, which now seemed to roll down upon them like a cloud from the mountains, giving the snowfield a ghastly look which made Bracy hesitate.

"I'm afraid it would be better to go off to the left among the stones."

"Don't, sir, pray," said Gedge earnestly.

"But our dark bodies will show against the snow."

"Not they, sir. We'll roll in it, and it'll be darker in half-an-hour. They'll be all that before they get here—won't they?"

"Quite. They are sure to come on very slowly, and allow time for part of them to get right into our rear."

"Yes, sir; that's right."

"Now, then, are you ready?"

"Yes, sir."

There was again silence, and, but for the ghostly glare of the snow, all was very dark.

"We seem to be going into the most dangerous place," whispered Bracy, with his breath coming thickly.

"And that's the very place they'll never think we should hide in, sir, if they were likely to think we were going to hide. No, sir: their keen eyes 'll just make out them two 'elmets, and they'll think o' nothing else but driving their long knives into them as wears 'em, from behind. I do hope we shall hear 'em blunting the points against, the stones."

"Have you everything?"

"Yes, sir."

"Then, forward! Go fifty paces slowly over the snow. I shall follow close behind you in your steps."

The snow yielded, so that they were knee-deep, but it was still loose and so sand-like in its grains that as each foot was withdrawn the icy particles flowed together again into each freshly-made hole.

Five minutes later the adventurous pair lay softly down, and rolled over and over a few times, before lying prone upon their chests, each with his head towards the invisible helmets, and near enough to whisper or touch one another with the hand. Their rifles lay by their sides, with the cartouche-boxes handy: and, in case of a close attack, their revolvers were in the right sides of their belts, half dragged round to the back, while each held his dagger-like bayonet in his band.

"Do you feel the cold, Gedge?" whispered Bracy.

"Cold, sir? Why, I'm as hot as hot. This work's too warm for a fellow to feel the cold. Do you, sir?"

"No; my face burns as if with fever, and every nerve tingles with excitement. There, we must not even whisper again."

"Right, sir."

"The first moment you hear a sound of any one approaching, touch my left arm."

"Right, sir; but hadn't I better lie t'other side of you? They'll come that way."

"They'll come from all round at once, my lad. There, don't be afraid. If we are going to have trouble, I dare say you will get your full share. Now, silence; and when they come you must hardly breathe."

Then silence ensued, and seemed to Bracy the most oppressive that he had ever encountered in facing danger. For the solemnity of the night in the great mountains was brooding over them, out of which at any moment death, in the shape of a keen knife, might descend. There was not a breath of air, but an icy chill dropped down from above, making the snow crystals turn sharp and crisp, crackling softly at the slightest movement. But the frosty air had no effect upon them, save to make their blood tingle in their veins and a peculiar, pricking sensation play about their nostrils as they drew their breath, tiny needles of ice twining as they respired, and making a hoar-frost upon Bracy's moustache.

The time went on as if the movement of the earth had been checked by the frost; but, listen as they would, the silence was profound, and a full hour seemed to have passed, though it was not a fourth part of that time.

"They will not come," thought Bracy, as his eyes were turned in every direction he could force them to sweep, and the change appeared very striking from the black atmosphere in front, and right and left to the faint light suggestive of electricity or phosphorescence which made the snow dimly visible.

But the enemy made no sign: and, with that horrible stillness as of death reigning and seeming to crush them into the snow, they lay waiting and longing for some sound—for the coming of the enemy; for the wild excitement of an encounter would, Bracy felt, be far preferable

233

to that maddening suspense.

As he lay there and thought, his ever-active brain was full of suggestions regarding what would take place. The enemy would not dare to come, and a night's sleep would have been lost—they would come, see them with their penetrating eyes, pounce upon them, there would be a few savage unexpected strokes, and all would be over; while poor Colonel Graves would watch and wait, looking ever for the succour that did not come.

"But he will not lose faith in his messengers," Bracy thought, with a thrill of satisfaction running through him. "He will know that I strove to do my best."

Then his thoughts took another direction. Why should not—after the careful preparations made—the *ruse* be successful, the enemy be deceived, and go in pursuit according to their ideas, leaving the two adventurers free to make their fresh departure? But that, the most natural outcome of the plan, Bracy, in his excitement, set aside as being the least likely to occur, and he lay in agony, straining every nerve to condense his faculties into the one great sense of hearing, till it seemed to him that his companion's breathing sounded preternaturally loud.

"Why, he's asleep! The miserable, careless scoundrel!" thought Bracy. "Those men have no thought beyond the present. How can one trust them? How easily we might be surprised if he were the watch!"

A flush of shame made the thinker's cheeks burn the next moment, he had, in his annoyance, stretched out his left hand to reach dodge's shoulder and give him a violent shake. But half-way he checked the progress of his hand; for, sotting aside the danger of waking a sleeper and making him start and utter some ejaculation, which might betray them to a lurking enemy, he recalled the fact that a touch was to be the signal to announce the coming of the enemy.

The next moment, as his hand lay upon the snow where he had let it fall, another hand was laid upon it, and his fingers were gripped by a set of fingers which held it fast and gave it a firm, steady pressure, to which he warmly responded, his heart beating fast, and a genial glow of satisfaction running through him in his penitence for misjudging his faithful companion.

Then the hand that grasped his was snatched away, and he lay listening and gazing in every direction that he could command for the danger just signalled to him by Gedge. Nothing to right or left, and he dared not stir to look back over the snow. Nothing in front, not a sign of any one near; and in his excitement he began to wonder whether his companion had made a mistake in his over-eagerness, for the silence was more oppressive than ever.

"What was that?"

A spasm shot through the listener, making every nerve and muscle tense as steel; his breath came thick and fast, and the dull, heavy throb, throb of his heart sounded loudly in his brain—so loudly that he held his breath and would have checked the pulsations if he could.

There was no doubt now: the enemy was close at hand, and Bracy's fingers closed over the hilt of his bayonet with a tremendous grip, for he felt that his revolver would be useless in that terrible darkness, and he shrank from wasting a shot.

He could see nothing, but there was the danger just in front in the snow of those thirty yards which lay between them and the rocks. That danger was represented to the listeners in imagination by the figure— two figures—of the white-coated enemy, crawling slowly as huge worms might, have progressed over the snow. At times they were perfectly still, but ever and again there was the extremely gentle, crackling sound of the icy grains rubbing together with a soft, rustling sound, no more than a snake would have made passing along a dusty track.

Bracy strained his eyes, but he could see nothing. He could not tell whether the two enemies were a yard or ten or twenty away from where he lay; but his straining ears told him that they were there, passing him from right to left, and he felt convinced that others must be moving slowly from all directions towards that one point, where the helmets were placed upon the pieces of stone.

So far, then, all was right; but he felt that at any moment he might hear others coming along behind, and those might strike the very spot where they two were lying.

Thought after thought of this kind flashed through Bracy's brain, as he tightened his hold of the bayonet, and held it point upward ready for use against his first assailant, while the strange crepitation of the frozen snow went on for what seemed like a long period, so greatly was everything magnified by the excitement through which it was mentally viewed.

By degrees, though, the creeping sound, which had seemed to stop more than once, ceased entirely, and the listeners waited quite half-an-hour, fancying twice over that they heard the faint click of stone against stone; but they could not be sure, and they dared not communicate otherwise than by a pressure of the hand, for there was still the possibility of the enemy being close in front. Though as the minutes crawled slowly by, and no fresh sound was heard, the feeling grew stronger and stronger that they had attributed the creeping noise to the enemy, when it was probably some inoffensive wild creature seeking for food, while the enemy had passed the spot in the dark, and were by now far away.

Bracy had just come to this conclusion, and had begun to think of the wisdom of crawling off the snow, which was beginning to melt beneath him from the warmth of his body, when his heart gave a leap as if some nerve had received a sudden twitch. For there came low and clear from a short distance away a peculiar sound such as might be produced by a night-bird on the wing. Then all was still once more.

"Was that a signal?" thought Bracy; "or have we been deceived?"

He thought earnestly, and felt that, after all, the enemy would under the circumstances act just as they were acting. There seemed to be an excess of caution, but none too much, approaching as they would be to surprise whoever was on the watch, and going with their lives literally in their hands.

"Phit!"

The same low, peculiar sound again, making Bracy start into a wild fit of excitement. Then there was a quick running as of many feet towards the central spot, followed by clink, clink, clink—the striking of steel on stone, and then a momentary silence, followed by a peculiar rumbling and a burst of voices.

"Gug!"

Bracy turned sharply, bayonet in hand, ready to strike, for the horrible thought struck him that Gedge had just received a tierce thrust which pinned him to the frozen snow; but as he leaned in his direction a hand touched his wrist and gave it a grip, holding it tightly, and making him draw a deep breath full of relief.

Meanwhile the voices increased, their owners talking fiercely, and though the tongue was almost unintelligible, a word was caught here and there, and they grasped the fact that every man seemed to want to talk at once, and to be making suggestions.

But the speakers did not keep to one place. As far as Bracy could make out, they had broken up into parties, which hurried here and there, one coming so near to where the listeners lay that they felt that their time for action had come at last, and, palpitating with excitement, they prepared to meet the first attack.

And now Bracy heard a sound as of some one breathing hard, and turned his head sharply to whisper a word of warning to his companion; but it was not uttered, for the sound came from beyond him, and with its repetition came the sound of laborious steps being taken through the snow, he who made them panting hard with the exertion as he came on to within a couple of yards of Gedge, and then suddenly turned off and made for the rocks.

He made so much noise now that he knew there was no need for concealment, that Gedge took advantage of the man getting more distant to reach over to his officer and whisper, with his lips close to Bracy's ear:

"That chap 'll never know how near he was to leaving off snoring like that, sir, for good."

"Hush!" whispered Bracy, and a fresh burst of talking arose as if to greet the man who had returned to the rocks from making a circuit round the trap.

And now it seemed as if the whole party were spreading out and coming towards where the couple lay, for the voices sounded louder and came nearer, making Bracy gently raise himself ready to hurry his follower away: but the sounds came no closer, the speakers pausing at the edge of the snow, where it sounded as if their plans were; being discussed.

Then all at once the talking ceased, and the beat of many feet, with the rattling of loose stones, fell on the listener's ears, telling that the enemy was in motion; and the sounds they made grew fainter and fainter, and then died out entirely.

"They seem to be gone," whispered Bracy, with his lips close to Gedge's ear.

"Oh yes, they're gone, sir, at last," was the reply.

"We must not be too sure. A few may be left behind to keep watch."

"Not them, sir. I can't see as it's likely."

Bracy was silent for a few moments, during which he listened intently for the faintest sound; but all was still.

"Get up," he said briefly, and then started at his own voice, it sounded so husky and strange.

Gedge uttered a sigh of relief as he shook the adhering snow from his woolly coat.

"Stiff, Gedge?" said Bracy.

"Horrid, sir. A good fight wouldn't come amiss. Hear me laugh, sir?"

"When you made that sound?"

"Yes, sir: that bit would come out, though I'd shut my mouth with my hand."

"What made you laugh at such a time?"

"To hear them cuttin' and stabbin' at the rocks, sir, and blunting their knives."

"Oh, I see!"

"Wonder whether they chopped our 'elmets, sir. Would you mind ordering me to see if there's any bits left?"

"The task is of no good," said Bracy. "But we'll walk back to the place and try if we can find them. Take out your revolver. No. Fix bayonets—we could use them better now."

There was a faint clicking, and then, with their rifles levelled, the pair marched laboriously off the snow, and then cautiously felt their way among the stones, Bracy's main object being to find out for certain that there were no sentries left. The noise they could not help making among the stones proved this directly, and they unwittingly, in spite of the darkness, went straight to the spot where they had set up the sticks and helmets, when Gedge uttered a low cry full of excitement.

"Why, they never come across 'em, sir. I've got 'em, standing here just as we left 'em. Well, I'm blessed! I know the difference by the feel. That's yours, sir, and this is mine. Talk about luck! Ha! I feel better now. Woolly busbies is all very well, but they don't look soldierly. I could have made some right enough, but we should ha' wanted to take 'em off before we got back to the fort."

"A splendid bit of luck, Gedge," said Bracy as he drew the strap of his helmet beneath his chin. "Now for our next step. What do you think?"

"Wittles, sir. Can't think o' nothing else just now. I should say, with what we've got to do, the next thing's to begin stoking before our fires go out."

Chapter Twenty Nine.

Awful Moments.

It was with serious feelings of compunction that Bracy set this example to his eager companion, by seating himself on one of the stones and beginning to combat the weary sensation of faintness which troubled him by partaking of a portion of his fast-shrinking store of provisions. For the fact was beginning to stare him in the face that, going on as they had begun, their little store could not by any possibility last, till they reached the Ghoorkha camp, and that in depending upon their rifles for a fresh supply they would be leaning upon a very rotten reed, since, surrounded as they seemed to be by enemies, it would be impossible to fire, while everything in the shape of game had so far been absent. But his spirits rose as he refreshed himself.

"I will not build imaginary mountains," he said mentally; "there are plenty about us at last."

"There, sir," said Gedge, breaking in upon his musings suddenly; "I'm ready for anything now. I should like to lie down and have a good sleep; but I s'pose we mustn't do that."

"Not till we have crossed that ridge up to the north, Gedge. It will be hard work, but it must be done."

"And get into the valley on the other side, sir, 'fore we go on east'ard?"

"Yes."

"S'pose there'll be a valley t'other side, sir?"

"No doubt about it."

"Then, when you're ready, sir, I am. If we've got it to do, let's begin and get this soft bit over, for we shan't get along very fast."

"No; the soft snow makes the travelling bad; but we go higher at every step, and by-and-by we may find it hard. Now then, I'll lead. The ridge must be right before us, as far as I can make out."

"Don't ask me, sir," said Gedge. "Wants a cat to see in the dark; but I think you must be right. Best way seems to me to keep on going uphill. That must be right, and when it's flat or going downhill it must be wrong."

Bracy made no reply, but, after judging the direction as well as he could, strode off, and found that his ideas were right, for at the end of a few minutes the snow was crackling under their feet.

"Now for it, Gedge. You'll have to lift your feet high at every step, while they sink so deeply. Hullo!"

There was a sharp crackling as he extended his left foot, bore down upon it, and with a good deal of resistance it went through a crust of ice, but only a short way above the ankle. Quickly bringing up the other foot, he stepped forward, and it crushed through the hardening surface, but only for a few inches. The next step was on the rugged surface of slippery ice, and as they progressed slowly for about a hundred yards, it was to find the surface grow firmer and less disposed to give beneath their weight.

"There's one difficulty mastered," said Bracy cheerily. "The surface is freezing hard, and we can get on like this till the sun beats upon it again."

"I call it grand, sir; but I hope it won't get to be more uphill."

"Why?"

"Because if we makes one slip we shall go skating down to the bottom of the slope again in double-quick time. I feel a'ready as if I ought to go to the blacksmith's to get roughed."

240

"Stamp your feet down if you are disposed to slip, my lad. I do not want to do this, but if the slope grows steeper we must fix bayonets and use them to steady us."

"Take the edge off on 'em, sir."

"Yes; but we must get across the ridge. Forward."

They toiled on, the task growing heavier as they progressed, for the gradient became steeper, and they halted from time to time for a rest, the plan of using the bayonets being kept for a last resource. But there were compensations to make up for the severity of the toil, one of which was expressed by the travellers at one of the halts.

"Makes one feel jolly comf'table and warm, sir."

"Yes; and takes away all doubt of our going in the right direction, for we must be right."

"I didn't think we was at first, sir. 'Tain't so dark neither."

"No: we are getting higher, and the snow and ice are all round us. Now then, forward!"

Crunch, squeak, crunch went the snow as they tramped steadily, with the surface curving slowly upward, till all at once there was a slip, a thud, and a scramble, Gedge was down, and he began to glide, but checked himself with the butt of his rifle.

"I'm all right, sir; but I was on the go," he said, panting.

"Hurt?" replied Bracy laconically.

"Not a bit, six. Knocked some o' the wind out o' me, but I'm all right again now."

"Forward!"

Bracy led on again, to find that the curve made by the snowfield rose more and more steeply, and the inclination to slip increased. But he stamped his feet down as he kept on, with his breathing growing quicker, and had the satisfaction of hearing his follower imitate his example, till he began to find that he must soon make another halt.

His spirits were rising, however, with an increasing hopeful feeling, for this was evidently the way to avoid pursuit or check. They were on the ice, and to this they must trust for the rest of their journey till they were well within reach of the Ghil Valley, to which they must descend.

Slip.

In an instant Bracy was down, starting on a rapid descent toward the place they had left; but at his first rush he heard beneath him a sharp blow delivered in the glazed surface, and he was suddenly brought up by the body of Gedge.

"Hold tight, sir! All right. I've got something to anchor us."

"Ha!" ejaculated Bracy breathlessly. "It was so sudden."

"Yes, sir; don't give you much time to think. You'd better do as I do."

"What's that?"

"Keep your bay'net in your hand ready to dig down into the ice. Stopped me d'reckly, and that stopped you."

"Yes, I'll do so. A minute's rest, and then we'll go on again."

"Make it two, sir. You sound as if you haven't got your wind back."

"I shall be all right directly, my lad. This is grand. I hope by daylight that we shall be in safety."

"That's right, sir. My! shouldn't I have liked this when I was a youngster! Think we shall come back this way?"

"Possibly," said Bracy.

"Be easy travelling, sir. Why, we could sit down on our heels and skim along on the nails of our boots, with nothing to do but steer."

"Don't talk, my lad," said Bracy. "Now, forward once more."

The journey was continued, and grew so laborious at last from the smoothness of the ice, which increased as the gradient grew heavier— the melted snow having run and made the surface more compact during the sunny noon; and at the end of another couple of hours the difficulty of getting on and up was so great that Bracy changed his course a little so as to lessen the ascent by taking it diagonally.

This made matters a little better, and tramp, tramp, they went on and on, rising more swiftly than they knew, and little incommoded now by the darkness, for the stars were shining out through the cloudy mist which hung over the slope, while their spirits seemed to rise with the ascent.

"Have we passed the rocks along which we saw that body of men moving?" said Bracy at last.

"I s'pose not, sir, or we must have felt 'em. They must have been a long way off when we saw 'em going along."

"Yes; the distances are very deceptive, and—Ah! stones, rocks. Here is the rough track at last."

They halted again, for by walking here and there they could make out that there was a rough track to right and left, comparatively free from snow, and if this were followed to the right there would be travelling which would necessitate their waiting for daylight, since it was all in and out among huge masses of stone.

"We couldn't get along here, sir, very fast," said Gedge after making a few essays.

"No, it is impossible now," replied Bracy. "It would be a dangerous way, too, for it must, as we saw, cut the valley when; the enemy will come out."

He stood looking back and around him, to see that the darkness was lightened by the strange faint glare from the ice and snow around him; then, turning, he crossed the ridge of broken rocks and tried what the slope seemed like upon the other side, to find that it was a continuation of that up which they had toiled, and apparently much the same, the gradual curve upward to the mountain being cut by this band of rocks.

"Forward again, Gedge," he cried. "This must be right, for we are getting a trifle nearer to our journey's end, and more out of reach of our pursuers."

"Then it is right, sir; but I suppose we shall get a bit o' downhill some time."

They tramped on for the next hour, but not without making several halts, three of which were involuntary, and caused by more or less sudden slips. These were saved from being serious by the quick action of driving dagger-like the bayonet each carried into the frozen snow; and after repetitions of this the falls seemed to lose; their risky character, the man who went down scrambling to his feet again the next instant and being ready to proceed. The still air was piercingly cold, but it only seemed to make their blood thrill in their veins, and a sense of exhilaration arose from the warm glow which pervaded them, and temptingly suggested the removal of their woollen *poshtins*. But the temptation was forced back, and the tramp continued hour after hour up what seemed to be an interminable slope, while fatigue was persistently ignored.

At last, though, Bracy was brought to a halt, and he stood panting.

"Anything wrong, sir?" whispered Gedge hoarsely.

"No; only that I can get no farther in this way. We must fix bayonets, and use our rifles as staves."

"Right, sir."

"Be careful not to force your barrel down too far, so as to get it plugged with the snow," said Bracy; and then, as soon as the keen-pointed weapons were fixed, he started onward again, the rifles answering this new purpose admirably, and giving a steadiness to the progress that had before been wanting.

Consequently far better progress was made for the next half-hour, with much less exertion, and Bracy made up his mind that the first patch of pines they came to on the lower ground should supply them with a couple of saplings whose poles should have the bayonets fixed or bound upon them, so as to take the place of the rifles.

"I'm longing for the daylight, Gedge," said Bracy suddenly, for they had plunged into a mist which obscured the stars, "so that we can see better in which direction to go, for we ought to be high enough now to be safe from— Ha!"

Then silence.

"Safe from what, sir?" said Gedge, stopping short.

There was no reply, and after waiting a few seconds, feeling alarmed, the lad spoke again.

"Didn't quite hear what you said, sir; safe from what?"

There was no reply, and Gedge suddenly turned frantic.

"Mr Bracy, sir," he said hoarsely, and then, raising his voice, he called his officer by name again and again; but the same terrible darkness and silence reigned together, and he grew maddened now.

"Oh Lor'!" he cried, "what's come to him?" and he went upon his hands and knees to crawl and feel about. "He's gone down in a fit, and slipped sudden right away; for he ain't here. He's half-way down the mountain by now, and I don't know which way to go and help him, and — Ah!" he shrieked wildly, and threw himself over backwards, to begin rolling and sliding swiftly back in the way he had come, his rifle escaping from his grasp.

Chapter Thirty.

A Prayer for Light.

Gedge glided rapidly down the icy slope for a good fifty yards in the darkness, with the pace increasing, before he was able to turn on his back and check himself by forcing his heels into the frozen snow.

"And my rifle gone—where I shall never find it again," was his first thought, as he forced back his helmet, which had been driven over his eyes: but, just as the thought was grasped, he was conscious of a scratching, scraping noise approaching, and he had just time to fling out his hands and catch his weapon, the effort, however, sending him gliding down again, this time to check himself by bringing the point of the bayonet to bear upon the snow. And now stopped, he lay motionless for a few moments.

"Mustn't be in a flurry," he panted, with his heart beating violently, "or I shan't find the gov'nor, and I must find him. I will find him, pore chap. Want to think it out cool like, and I'm as hot as if I'd been runnin' a mile. Now then; he's gone down, and he must ha' gone strite down here, so if I lets myself slither gently I'm sure to come upon him, for I shall be pulled up same as he'd be."

He lay panting, still, for a few minutes, and his thinking powers, which had been upset by the suddenness of the scare, began to settle themselves again. Then he listened as he went on, putting, as he mentally termed it, that and that together.

"Can't hear nothing of him," he said to himself. "He must have gone down with a rush 'stead o' falling in a fit as I thought fust; but it ain't like a fall. He wouldn't smash hisself, on'y rub some skin off, and he'll be hollering to me d'reckly from somewheres below. Oh dear! if it only warn't so precious dark I might see him: but there ain't no moon, and no stars now, and it's no use to light a match. I say, why don't he holler?—I could hear him a mile away—or use his whistle? He'd know that would bring me, and be safer than shouting. But I can't hear nothing on him. Here: I know."

Gedge rose to his feet and drove his bayonet into the snow to steady himself, without turning either to the right or the left.

"Mustn't change front," he said, "or I may go sliding down wrong and pass him," he thought. Then raising his hand, he thrust two fingers into his mouth and produced a long drawn whistle, which was a near imitation of that which would be blown by an officer to bring his men together to rally round him and form square.

"That ought to wake him up," he thought. "He'd hear that if he was miles away."

There was a faint reply which made his heart leap; and thrusting his fingers between his lips, he whistled again in a peculiar way, with the result that the sound came back as before, and Gedge's heart sank with something akin to despair.

"'Tain't him," he groaned. "It's them blessed eckers. I'll make sure, though."

He stood listening for some minutes, and then, with his heart feeling like lead, took off his helmet and wiped his dripping brow.

"Oh dear!" he groaned; "ain't it dark! Reg'lar fog, and cold as cold. Makes a chap shiver. I dunno how it is. When I'm along with him I feel as bold as a lion. I ain't afeared o' anything. I'd foller him anywheres, and face as many as he'd lead me agen. 'Tain't braggin', for I've done it; but I'm blessed now if I don't feel a reg'lar mouse—a poor, shiverin' wet mouse with his back up, and ready to die o' fright through being caught in a trap, just as the poor little beggars do, and turns it up without being hurt a bit. I can't help it; I'm a beastly coward; and I says it out aloud for any one to bear. That's it—a cussed coward, and I can't help it, 'cause I was born so. He's gone, and I shan't never find him agen, and there's nothing left for me to do but sneak back to the fort, and tell the Colonel as we did try, but luck was agen us.

"Nay, I won't," he muttered. "I'll never show my face there again, even if they call it desertion, unless I can get to the Ghoorkha Colonel and tell him to bring up his toothpick brigade.

"Oh, here, I say, Bill, old man," he said aloud after a pause, during which he listened in vain for some signal from his officer, "this here won't do. This ain't acting like a sojer o' the Queen. Standin' still here till yer get yerself froze inter a pillar o' salt. You've got to fetch your orficer just as much now as if if hailed bullets and bits o' rusty ragged iron. Here goes. Pull yourself together, old man! Yer wanted to have a slide, so now's your time."

Grasping his rifle, he squatted down on his heels, and laid the weapon across his knees preparatory to setting himself in motion, on the faint chance of gliding down to where Bracy would have gone before him.

"Would you have thought it so steep that he could have slithered away like that? But there it is," he muttered. "Now then, here goes." Letting himself go, he began to glide slowly upon his well-nailed shoes; then the speed increased, and he would the next minute have been rushing rapidly down the slope had he not driven in his heels and stopped himself.

"Well, one can put on the brake when one likes," he muttered; "but he couldn't ha' gone like this or I should have heard him making just the same sort o' noise. He had no time to sit down; he must ha' gone on his side or his back, heads up or heads down, and not so very fast. If I go down like this I shall be flying by him, and p'raps never stop till I get to the end of the snow. I know—I'll lie down."

Throwing himself over on his side, he gave a thrust with his hands and began to glide, but very slowly, and in a few seconds the wool of his *poshtin* adhered so firmly to the smooth surface that he was brought up and had to start himself again.

This took place twice, and he slowly rose to his feet.

"Wants a good start," he muttered, and he was about to throw himself down when a fresh thought crossed his brain.

"I don't care," he said aloud, as if addressing some one who had spoken; "think what yer like, I ain't afraid to pitch myself down and go skidding to the bottom, and get up with all the skin off! I sez he ain't down there. I never heerd him go, and there's something more than I knows on. It is a fit, and he's lying up yonder. Bill Gedge, lad, you're a-going wrong."

He stood trying to pierce the thickening mist, looking as nearly as he could judge straight upward in the course they had taken, and was about to start: but, not satisfied, he took out his match-box, struck a light, and, holding it down, sought for the marks made by the bayonets in the climb. But there was no sign where he stood, neither was there to his left; and, taking a few paces to the right, with the rapidly-burning match close to the snow, the flame was just reaching his fingers when he uttered a sigh of satisfaction: for, as the light had to be dropped, there, one after the other, he saw two marks in the freshly-chipped snow glistening in the faint light. Keeping their direction fresh in his mind, he stalled upward on his search.

"How far did I come down?" he said to himself. "I reckon 'bout a hundred yards. Say 'undred and twenty steps."

He went on taking the hundred and twenty paces, and then he stopped short.

"Must be close here somewhere," he muttered; and he paused to listen, but there was not a sound.

"Nobody couldn't hear me up here," he thought, and he called his companion by name, to rouse up strange echoes from close at hand; and when he changed to whistling, the echoes were sudden and startling in the extreme.

"It's rum," said Gedge. "He was just in front of me, one minute talking to me, and then 'Ha!' he says, and he was gone."

Gedge took off his helmet, and wiped his wet brow again before replacing it.

"Ugh, you idjit!" he muttered. "You were right at first. He dropped down in a sort o' fit from overdoing it—one as took him all at wunst, and he's lying somewheres about fast asleep, as people goes off in the snow and never wakes again. He's lying close by here somewheres, and you ought to have done fust what you're going to do last.

"Mustn't forget where I left you," he muttered as he gave a dig down with his rifle, driving the bayonet into the snow, and sending some scraps flying with a curious whispering noise which startled him.

"What does that mean?" he said, and he caught at the butt of his piece, now sticking upward in the snow, but dropped his hand again to his pocket and again took out his match-box.

"Sort o' fancy," he muttered; and, getting out a match, he struck it, after shutting the box with a snap, which again made him start, something like an echo rising from close at hand.

"Why, I'm as nervous as a great gal," he muttered, as the tiny match burst into a bright flame which formed a bit of a halo about itself, and, stooping to bring the tiny clear light burning so brightly close to the surface, he took two steps forward, the ground at the second giving way beneath him, and at the same moment he uttered a wild shriek of horror, dashed the match from him, and threw himself backward on to the snow. For the tiny light had in that one brief moment revealed a horror to him which was a full explanation of the trouble, and as he lay trembling in every limb, his shriek was repeated from a short distance away, and then again and again rapidly, till it took the form of a wild burst of laughter.

"Get up, you coward!" growled Gedge the next minute, as he made a brave effort to master the terrible shock he had sustained, for he felt that he had been within an inch of following his officer to a horrible death.

The self-delivered charge of cowardice brought him to himself directly, and he sprang to his feet. Then, with fingers wet with a cold perspiration, and trembling as if with palsy, he dragged out his match-box, took out one of the tiny tapers, and essayed to light it, but only produced streaks of phosphorescent light, for he had taken the match out by the end, and his wet fingers had quenched its lighting powers.

With the next attempt he was more successful; and, setting aside all fear of being seen, he held out the flaming light, which burned without motion in the still air, and, holding it before him, stepped towards the edge of the snow, which ended suddenly in a black gulf, over which he was in the act of leaning, when once more he sprang back and listened, for the snow where he stood had given way, and as he remained motionless for a few moments, there suddenly came up from far below, a dull thud, followed by a strange whispering series of echoes as if off the face of some rocks beyond.

"Oh!" he groaned. "That's it, then. It was down there he went; and he must be killed."

It was one of the young soldier's weak moments; but his life of late had taught him self-concentration and the necessity for action, and he recovered himself quickly. The trembling fit passed off, and he look out another match, lit it, stepped as near as he dared to the edge of the gulf, and then pitched the burning flame gently from him, seeing it go down out of sight; but nothing more, for the place was immense.

He lay down upon his breast now, and crawled in what seemed to be greater darkness, consequent upon the light he had burned having made his eyes contract, and worked himself so close that his hand was over the edge, a short distance to the left of where he had broken it away with his weight. Here he gathered up a handful of the frozen snow, threw it from him, and listened till a faint pattering sound came up.

His next act was to utter a shout, which came back at once, as if from a wall of rock, while other repetitions seemed to come from right and left. Then, raising his fingers to his mouth, he gave vent to a long, shrill whistle, which he repeated again and again, and then, with a strange stony sensation, he worked himself slowly back, feet foremost, at first very slowly, and then with frantic haste, as it suddenly dawned upon him that he was going uphill. For the snowy mass was sinking, and it was only just in time that he reached a firmer part, and lay quivering in the darkness, while he listened to a rushing sound, for his weight had started an immense cornice-like piece of the snow, which went down with a sullen roar.

"It's no use while it's like this," groaned Gedge. "I can't do nothing to help him till the day comes. I should on'y be chucking my own life away. I'd do it if it was any good; but it wouldn't be no use to try, and I might p'raps find him if I could only see."

He had risen to his knees now, and the position brought the words to his lips; the rough lad speaking, but with as perfect reverence as ever came from the lips of man:

"Oh, please, God, can't you make the light come soon, and end this dreadful night?"

Poor, rough, rude Bill Gedge had covered his eyes as he softly whispered his prayer; and when he opened them again, it was to look upon no marvel greater than that grand old miracle which we, with leaden eyes sealed up, allow to pass away unheeded, unseen. It was but the beginning of another of the many days seen in a wild mountain land; for the watchings and tramps of the two adventurers had pretty well used up the hours of darkness; and, black though the snow lay where Bill Gedge knelt, right beyond, straight away upon the mighty peak overhead, there was a tiny point of glowing orange light, looking like the tip of some huge spear that was heated red-hot.

For the supplicant was gazing heavenward, and between the sky and his eyes there towered up one of the huge peaks of the Karakoram range, receiving the first touch of the coming day.

Chapter Thirty One.

The Light that came.

Gedge knelt there gazing upward, unable to grasp the truth of that which he saw; for all around him seemed blacker than ever; but as he looked there was another glowing speck high up in the distance, and then another and another started into sight, while the first he had seen went on increasing in brightness; and, as he still kept his eyes fixed upon it, the fact came to him at last—the belief that it was indeed the sun lighting up the glittering peaks of the vast range—and he started to his feet with a cry of exultation.

"Why, it is to-morrow morning!" he shouted. "Ah! I can help him now."

But for a time he could only wait on patiently, and watch the bright glow extending, and stealing slowly downward, in a way which suggested that it would be hours before the spot where he stood would be lit up by the full light of day; and, hardly daring to move, he listened, and twice over gave one of his long, piercing whistles, which were echoed and re-echoed in a way which made him shudder and hesitate to raise the strange sounds again.

"It's o' no use," he said. "He's gone down there, and he's dead— he's dead; and I shall never see him again.—Yah! yer great snivelling idjit!" he cried the next moment, in his rage against himself. "The old woman was right when I 'listed. She said I wasn't fit for a sojer—no good for nothing but to stop at home, carry back the washing, and turn the mangle. I'm ashamed o' myself. My word, though, the fog's not so thick, but ain't it cold! If I don't do something I shall freeze hard, and not be able to help him when it gets light."

It was a fact; for, consequent upon standing still so long, a peculiar numbing sensation began to attack his extremities, and it was none too soon when he felt his way down the slope for a few yards, and then turned to climb again. A very short time longer, and he would have been unable to stir; as it was, he could hardly climb back to the place from which he started. But he strove hard to restore the failing circulation, keeping his body in active motion, till, by slow degrees, his natural activity returned, and, forgetting the weariness produced by such a night of exertion, he felt ready to do anything towards finding and rescuing his officer.

"There's no mistake about it," he muttered, "standing still up in these parts means hands and feet freezing hard. It's wonderful, though, how these sheepskins keep out the cold. I ought to feel worse than I do, though, at a time like this; but it's because I won't believe the gov'nor's dead. It ain't possible, like, for it's so much more sudden than being caught by a bullet through the heart. Oh he ain't dead—he can't be—I won't believe it. Tumbled down into the soft snow somewhere, and on'y wants me to go down and help him out."

He took another turn up and down to keep up the circulation, and by this time he could move about freely, and without having to climb the ascent in dread of going too far and reaching the perilous edge, with its treachery of snow.

"Getting lighter fast," he said, "and I shall be able to get to work soon. And that's it. I've got to think o' that. There's no help to be got. You've got to find all the help in yourself, old man. My! ain't it beautiful how the light's coming! It's just as if the angels was pouring glory on the tops o' the mountains, and it's running more and more down the sides, till these great holes and hollows are full, and it's day once more."

As the golden rays of sunshine came lower, the mountain in front grew dazzling in its beauty. Minute by minute the glaciers which combed its sides leaped into sight, shining with dazzling beauty, like rivers and falls of golden water; the dark rifts and chasms became purple, lightening into vivid blue; and the reflected light kept on flashing upon hollows and points, till, saving the lower portions, the vast mass of tumbled-together ice and snow shone with a glory that filled the ignorant common lad with a strange feeling of awe.

This passed off directly, however; and, as the darkness on a level with where he stood grew more and more transparent, Gedge's active mind was searching everything in the most practical way, in connection with the task he had in hand. He could see now dimly that the snow to right and left of him curved over the vast gulf in front—vast in length only; for, thirty or forty yards from where he stood, there was the huge blank face of the mountain going downward, as one vast perpendicular wall of grey rock, streaked with snow where there were ledges for it to cling. In fact, the snow from above hung hen; and there as if ready to fall into the black gulf, still full of darkness, and whose depths could not be plumbed until the light displaced the gloom, and a safe coign of vantage could be found from which the adventurer could look down.

In fact, the young soldier was on the edge of a stupendous *bergschrund*, as the phenomenon is termed by Swiss climbers—a deep chasm formed by the ice and snow shrinking or falling away from the side of a mountain, where the latter is too steep for it to cling. And then, after a little examination to right and left, Gedge, with beating heart, found the place where Bracy had stepped forward and instantaneously fallen. There was no doubt about it, for the searcher found the two spots where he himself had so nearly gone down, the snow showing great irregular patches, bitten off, as it were, leaving sharp, rugged, perpendicular edges; while where Bracy had fallen there were two footprints and a deep furrow, evidently formed by the rifle, to which he had clung, the furrow growing deeper as it neared the edge of the snow, through which it had been dragged.

Gedge's face flushed with excitement as he grasped all this and proved its truth, for, between where he stood and the footprints made through the crust of snow, there were his own marks, those made by his bayonet, and others where he had flung himself down, for the snow here was far softer than upon the slope.

In spite of the darkness still clinging to the depths, Gedge began at once searching for a safe place—one where he could crawl to the edge of the gulf, get his face over, and look down; but anywhere near where Bracy had gone down this was in vain, for the snow curved over like some huge volute of glittering whiteness, and several times over, when he ventured, it was to feel that his weight was sufficient to make the snow yield, sending him back with a shudder.

Baffled again and again, he looked to right and left, in search of some slope by whose means he could descend into the gulf; but he looked in vain—everywhere the snow hung over, and as the light increased he saw that the curve was far more than he had imagined.

"Oh, if I only knowed what to do!" he groaned. "I can't seem to help him; and I can't leave him to go for help. I must get down somehow; but I dursen't jump."

This last thought had hardly crossed his brain when a feeling of wild excitement rushed through him; for faintly heard from far away below, and to his left, there came the shrill chirruping note of an officer's whistle, and Gedge snatched at the spike of his helmet, plucked it off, and waved it frantically in the air.

"Hoorray!" he yelled. "Hoorray! and I don't care if any one hears me. Hoorray! He ain't dead a bit; he's down somewhere in the soft snow, and hoorray! I'm going to get him out."

At that moment the whistle chirruped faint and shrill again, the note being repeated from the vast wall.

"He's this side somewhere," cried Gedge. "Out o' sight under this curl-over o' snow. There he goes again, and I haven't answered. Of all the—"

The cramming of his fingers into his mouth checked the speech, and, blowing with all his might, the young soldier sent forth a shrill imitation of the officer's whistle, to echo from the mountain face; and then, unmistakably, and no echo, came another faint, shrill whistle from far to the left.

"All right, Mr Bracy, sir! Hoorray! and good luck to you! I'm a-coming."

He whistled again, and went off in the direction from which his summons seemed to have come, and again he was answered, and again and again, till, quite a quarter of a mile along the edge, the young soldier stopped, for the whistles had sounded nearer and nearer, till he felt convinced that he had reached a spot on the snow hanging just above his summoner's head.

As he stopped he whistled again, and the answer sounded shrill and near.

"Below there! Ahoy!" he yelled, and mingling with the echoes came his name, faintly heard, but in the familiar tones.

"Oh dear! What's a chap to do?" panted Gedge. "I want to holler and shout, and dance a 'ornpipe. Here, I feel as if I'm goin' as mad as a hatter. Hi! Oh, Mr Bracy—sir—ain't—half—dead—are—yer?" he shouted, as if he had punctuated his words with full stops.

"Not—much—hurt," came up distinctly.

"Then here goes!" muttered Gedge. "I must try and get a look at yer, to see where yer are."

The speaker threw himself on his faces once more, and began to crawl towards the edge of the cornice, to look down into the fairly-light chasm; but shrank back only just in time to save himself from going down with a great patch of snow; and he listened, shudderingly, to the dull rush it made, followed by a heavy pat and a series of whispering echoes. Then faintly heard came the words: "Keep back, or you'll send an avalanche down."

"What's a haverlarnsh?" muttered Gedge. Then aloud, "All right, sir. Can yer get out?"

"I don't know yet. I must rest a bit. Don't talk, or you'll be sending the snow down."

"All right, sir; but can't yer tell me what to do?"

"You can do nothing," came slowly back in distinct tones. "The snow curves over my head, and there is a tremendous depth. Keep still where you are, and don't come near."

"Oh, I can keep still now," said Gedge coolly. "It's like being another man to know that's he's all alive. Oh! can't be very much hurt, or he wouldn't call like he does. Poor chap! But what's he going to do? Climb up the side somehow? Well, I s'pose I must obey orders; but I should like to be doing something to help him out."

Gedge was of that type which cannot remain quiet; and, feeling irritated now by his enforced state of helplessness, he spent the time in looking down and around him for signs of danger.

The sun was now above the horizon, lighting up the diversified scene at the foot of the mountain, and away along the valleys spreading to right and left; but for some time he could make out nothing save a few specks in the far distance, which might have been men, or a flock of some creatures pasturing on the green valley-side, miles beyond the termination of the snow-slope up which they had climbed. He made out, too, the continuation of the stony track leading to the head of the valley, and along which the party of tribes-men had been seen to pass; but there was apparently nothing there, and Gedge drew a breath full of relief as he felt how safe they were, and beyond the reach of the enemy.

Then, turning to the gulf again, he went as near as he dared to the edge, and stood listening to a dull sound, which was frequently repeated, and was followed by a low rushing noise, which kept gathering in force till it was like a heavy rush, and then dying away.

"What's he doing?" muttered Gedge. "Sounds like digging. That's it; he's been buried alive; and he's hard at work trying to dig himself out of the snow with his bayonet stuck at the end of his rifle. Well, good luck to him. Wonder where he'll come up first."

Gedge watched the cornice-like edge of the snowfield as the sounds as of some one feebly digging went on; but he could gain no further hint of what was going on, and at last his excitement proved too much for him, and he once more began to creep towards the edge of the snow, getting so far without accident this time that he could form an idea of what must be the depth from seeing far down the grey face of the wall of rock, certainly four or five hundred feet, but no bottom.

"He couldn't have fallen all that way," he said to himself. "It must go down with a slope on this side."

A sharp crack warned him that he was in danger, and he forced himself back on to firm snow, receiving another warning of the peril to which he had exposed himself, for a portion many feet square went down with a hissing rush, to which he stood listening till all was still once more.

Suddenly he jumped back farther, for from somewhere higher up there was a heavy report as of a cannon, followed by a loud echoing roar, and, gazing upward over a shoulder of the mountain, he had a good view of what seemed to be a waterfall plunging over a rock, to disappear afterwards behind a buttress-like mass of rock and ice. This was followed by another roar, and another, before all was still again.

"Must be ice and snow," he said to himself; "can't be water."

Gedge was right; for he had been gazing up at an ice-fall, whose drops were blocks and masses of ice diminished into dust by the great distance, and probably being formed of thousands of tons.

"Bad to have been climbing up there," he muttered, and he shrank a little farther away from the edge of the great chasm. "It's precious horrid being all among this ice and snow. It sets me thinking, as it always does when I've nothing to do.—If I could only do something to help him, instead of standing here.—Oh, I say," he cried wildly, "look at that!"

He had been listening to the regular dull dig, dig, dig, going on below the cornice, and to the faint rushing sound, as of snow falling, thinking deeply of his own helplessness the while, wondering too, for the twentieth time, where Bracy would appear, when, to his intense astonishment, he saw a bayonet dart through the snow into daylight about twenty feet back from the edge of the great gulf.

The blade disappeared again directly, and reappeared rapidly two or three times as he ran towards the spot, and then hesitated, for it

Quick as a flash he caught hold of the barrel of the rifle.

Page 343.

F. B. !

was dangerous to approach

the hole growing in the snow, the direction of the thrusts made being various, and the risk was that the weapon might be darted into the looker-on. Gedge stood then as near as he dared go, watching the progress made by the miner, and seeing the hole rapidly increase in size as the surface crumbled in.

Then all at once Gedge's heart seemed to leap towards his mouth, for there was a sudden eddy of the loose snow, as if some one were struggling, the bayonet, followed by the rifle, was thrust out into daylight, held by a pair of hands which sought to force it crosswise over the mouth of the hole, and the next instant the watcher saw why. For the caked snow from the opening to the edge of the gulf, and for many yards on either side, was slowly sinking; while, starting from the hole in two opposite directions, and keeping parallel with the edge; of the cornice, a couple of cracks appeared, looking like dark jagged lines.

It was a matter of but a few moments. Gedge had had his lessons regarding the curving-over snow, and knew the danger, which gave him the apt promptitude necessary for action in the terrible peril.

Dropping his own rifle on the ice, he sprang forward, stooped, and, quick as a flash, caught hold of the barrel of the rifle lying on the surface just below the hilt of the bayonet. Then throwing himself back with all the force he could command, he literally jerked Bracy out from where he lay buried in the loose snow and drew him several yards rapidly over the smooth surface. The long lines were opening out and gaping the while, and he had hardly drawn his officer clear before there was a soft, dull report, and a rush, tons of the cornice having been undermined where it hung to the edge of the icefield, and now went downward with a hissing sound, which was followed by a dull roar.

"Ah-h-h!" groaned Gedge, and he dropped down upon his knees beside the prostrate snowy figure, jerked his hands towards his face, and then fell over sidewise, to lie motionless with his eyes fast closed.

When he opened them again it was to see Bracy kneeling by his side and bending over him, the young officer's countenance looking blue and swollen, while his voice when he spoke sounded husky and faint.

"Are you better now?" he said.

"Better!" replied Gedge hoarsely as he stared confusedly at the speaker. "Ain't been ill agen, have I! Here, what yer been doing to make my head ache like this here? I—I—I d' know. Something's buzzing, and my head's going round. Some one's been giving me— Oh, Mr Bracy, sir! I remember now. Do tell me, sir; are yer all right?"

"Yes, nearly," replied the young officer, with a weary smile. "Twisted my ankle badly, and I'm faint and sick. I can't talk."

"Course not, sir; but you're all right again now. You want something to eat. I say, sir, did you finish your rations?"

"No; they're here in my haversack. You can take a part if you want some."

"Me, sir? I've got plenty. Ain't had nothing since when we had our feed together. I ain't touched nothing."

"Eat, then; you must want food."

"Yes, I am a bit peckish, sir, I s'pose; but I can't eat 'less you do."

Bracy smiled faintly, and began to open his snow-covered haversack, taking from it a piece of hard cake, which he began to eat very slowly, looking hard and strange of manner, a fact which did not escape Gedge's eyes; but the latter said nothing, opened his canvas bag with trembling hands, and began to eat in a hurried, excited way, but soon left off.

"Don't feel like eating no more, sir," he said huskily. "Can't for thinking about how you got on. Don't say nothing till you feel well enough, sir. I can see that you're reg'lar upset. Ain't got froze, have you—hands or feet?"

"No, no," said Bracy slowly, speaking like one suffering from some terrible shock. "I did not feel the cold so much. There, I am coming round, my lad, and I can't quite grasp yet that I am sitting here alive in the sunshine. I'm stunned. It is as if I were still in that horrible dream-like time of being face to face with death. Ha! how good it is to feel the sun once more!"

"Yes, sir; capital, sir," said Gedge more cheerfully. "Quite puzzling to think its all ice and snow about us. Shines up quite warm; 'most as warm as it shines down."

"Ha!" sighed Bracy; "it sends life into me again."

He closed his eyes, and seemed to be drinking in the warm glow, which was increasing fast, giving colour to the magnificent view around. But after a few minutes, during which Gedge sat munching slowly and gazing anxiously in the strangely swollen and discoloured face, the eyes were reopened, to meet those of Gedge, who pretended to be looking another way.

The sun's warmth was working wonders, and shortly after Bracy's voice sounded stronger as he said quietly:

"It would have been hard if I had been carried back by the snow at the last, Gedge."

"Hard, sir? Horrid."

"It turned you sick afterwards—the narrow escape I had."

"Dreadful, sir. I was as bad as a gal. I'm a poor sort o' thing sometimes, sir. But don't you talk till you feel all right, sir."

"I am beginning to feel as if talking will do me good and spur me back into being more myself."

"Think so, sir? Well, you know best, sir."

"I think so," said Bracy quietly; "but I shall not be right till I have had a few hours' sleep."

"Look here, then, sir; you lie down in the sun here on my *poshtin*. I'll keep watch."

"No! no! Not till night. There, I am getting my strength back. I was completely stunned, Gedge, and I have been acting like a man walking in his sleep."

Gedge kept glancing at his officer furtively, and there was an anxious look in his eyes as he said to himself:

"He's like a fellow going to have a touch of fever. Bit wandering-like, poor chap! I know what's wrong. I'll ask him."

He did not ask at once, though, for he saw that Bracy was eating the piece of cake with better appetite, breaking off scraps more frequently; while the food, simple as it was, seemed to have a wonderfully reviving effect, and he turned at last to his companion.

"You are not eating, my lad," he said, smiling faintly. "Come, you know what you have said to me."

"Oh, I'm all right again now, sir; I'm only keeping time with you.

There. Dry bread-cake ain't bad, sir, up here in the mountains, when you're hungry. Hurt your head a bit—didn't you, sir?"

"No, no," said Bracy more firmly. "My right ankle; that is all. How horribly sudden it was!"

"Awful, sir; but don't you talk."

"I must now; it does me good, horrible as it all was; but, as I tell you, I was stunned mentally and bodily, to a great extent. I must have dropped a great distance into the soft snow upon a slope, and I was a long time before I could get rid of the feeling of being suffocated. I was quite buried, I suppose; but at last, in a misty way, I seemed to be breathing the cold air in great draughts as I lay on the snow, holding fast to my rifle, which somehow seemed to be the one hope I had of getting back to you."

"You did a lot of good with it, sir."

"Did I?"

"Course you did, sir. Digging through the snow."

"Oh yes, I remember now," said Bracy, with a sigh. "Yes, I remember having some idea that the snow hung above me like some enormous wave curling right over before it broke, and then becoming frozen hard. Then I remember feeling that I was like one of the rabbits in the sandhills at home, burrowing away to make a hole to get to the surface, and as fast as I got the sand down from above me I kept on kicking it out with my feet, and it slid away far below with a dull, hissing sound."

"Yes, sir, I heard it; but that was this morning. How did you get on in the night, after you began to breathe again? You couldn't ha' been buried long, or you'd ha' been quite smothered."

"Of course," said Bracy rather vacantly—"in the night?"

"Yes; didn't you hear me hollering?"

"No."

"When you were gone all in a moment I thought you'd slipped and gone sliding down like them chaps do the tobogganing, sir."

"You did call to me, then?"

"Call, sir? I expect that made me so hoarse this morning."

"I did not hear you till I whistled and you answered, not long ago."

"Why, I whistled too, sir, lots o' times, and nigh went mad with thinking about you."

"Thank you, Gedge," said Bracy quietly, and he held out his hand and gripped his companion's warmly. "I give you a great deal of trouble."

"Trouble, sir? Hark at you! That ain't trouble. But after you got out of the snow?"

"After I got out of the snow?"

"Yus, sir; you was there all night."

"Was I? Yes, I suppose so. I must have been. But I don't know much. It was all darkness and snow, and—oh yes, I remember now! I did not dare to move much, because whenever I did stir I began to glide down as if I were going on for ever."

"But don't you remember, sir, any more than that?"

"No," said Bracy, speaking with greater animation now. "As I told you, I must have been stunned by my terrible fall, and that saved me from a time of agony that would have driven me mad. As soon as it was light I must have begun moving in a mechanical way to try and escape from that terrible death-trap: but all that has been dream-like, and—and I feel as if I were still in a kind of nightmare. I am quite faint, too, and giddy with pain. Yes, I must lie down here in the sunshine for a bit. Don't let me sleep long if I drop off."

"No, sir; I won't, sir," replied Gedge, as Bracy sank to his elbow and then subsided with a restful sigh, lying prone upon the snow.

"He's fainted! No, he ain't; he's going right off to sleep. Not let him sleep long? Yes, I will; I must, poor chap! It's knocked half the sense out of him, just when he was done up, too. Not sleep? Why, that's the doctor as'll pull him round. All right, sir; you're going to have my sheepskin too, and you ain't going to be called till the sun's going down, and after that we shall see."

Ten minutes later Bracy was sleeping, carefully wrapped in Gedge's *poshtin*, while the latter was eating heartily of the remains of his rations.

"And he might ha' been dead, and me left alone!" said Gedge, speaking to himself. "My! how soon things change! Shall I have a bit more, or shan't I! Yes; I can't put my greatcoat on outside, so I must put some extra lining in."

Chapter Thirty Two.

Only Human.

As the sun gathered force in rising higher, a thin veil of snow was melted from off a broad patch of rock, which dried rapidly; and, after a little consideration, Gedge went to Bracy's shoulders, took fast hold of his *poshtin*, and drew him softly and quickly off the icy surface right on to the warm, dry rock, the young officer's eyes opening widely in transit, and then closing again without their owner becoming conscious, but, as his head was gently lowered down again upon its sheepskin pillow, the deep sleep of exhaustion went on.

"Needn't ha' been 'fraid o' waking you," said Gedge softly, and looking down at the sleeper as if proud of his work.—"There, you'll be dry and warm as a toast, and won't wake up lying in a pond o' water.— Now I'll just have a look round, and then sit down and wait till he wakes."

Gedge took his good look round, making use of Bracy's glass, and in two places made out bodies of white-coated men whose weapons glinted in the sun shine; but they were far away, and in hollows among the hills.

"That's all I can make out," said Gedge, closing the glass and replacing it softly in the case slung from Bracy's shoulders; "but there's holes and cracks and all sorts o' places where any number more may be. Blest if I don't think all the country must have heard that we're going for help, and turned out to stop us. My! how easy it all looked when we started! Just a long walk and a little dodging the niggers, and the job done. One never thought o' climbing up here and skating down, and have a launching in the snow."

Gedge yawned tremendously, and being now in excellent spirits and contentment with himself, he chuckled softly.

"That was a good one," he said. "What a mouth I've got! I say, though, my lad, mouths have to be filled, and there ain't much left. We were going, I thought, to shoot pheasants, and kill a sheep now and then, to make a fire and have roast bird one day, leg o' mutton the next, and cold meat when we was obliged; but seems to me that it was all cooking your roast chickens before they was hatched. Fancy lighting a fire anywhere! Why, it would bring a swarm of the beauties round to carve us up instead of the wittles; and as to prog, why, I ain't seen nothing but that one bear. Don't seem to hanker after bear," continued Gedge after a few minutes' musing, during which he made sure that Bracy was sleeping comfortably. "Bears outer the 'Logical Gardens, nicely fatted up on buns, might be nice, and there'd be plenty o' nice fresh bear's grease for one's 'air; but these here wild bears in the mountains must feed theirselves on young niggers and their mothers, and it'd be like being a sort o' second-hand cannibal to cook and eat one of the hairy brutes. No, thanky; not this time, sir. I'll wait for the pudden."

Human nature is human nature, which nobody can deny; and, uncultivated save in military matters, and rough as he was, Bill Gedge was as human as he could be. He had just had a tremendous tramp for a whole day, a sleepless night of terrible excitement and care, a sudden respite from anxiety, a meal, and the glow of a hot sun upon a patch of rock which sent a genial thrill of comfort through his whole frame. These were the difficulties which were weighing hard in one of the scales of the young private's constitution, while he was doing his best to weigh down the other scale with duty, principle, and a manly, honest feeling of liking for the officer whom he had set up from the first moment of being attached to the company as the model of what a soldier should be. It was hard work. Those yawns came again and again, increasing in violence.

"Well done, boa-constructor," he said. "Little more practice, and you'll be able to swallow something as big as yourself; but my! don't it stretch the corners of your mouth! I want a bit o' bear's grease ready to rub in, for they're safe to crack.

"My! how sleepy I am!" he muttered a little later. "I ain't been put on sentry-go, but it's just the same, and a chap as goes to sleep in the face of the enemy ought to be shot. Sarve him right, too, for not keeping a good lookout. Might mean all his mates being cut up. Oh! I say, this here won't do," he cried, springing up. "Let's have a hoky-poky penny ice, free, grashus, for nothing."

He went off on tiptoe, glancing at Bracy as he passed, and then stooped down over a patch of glittering snow, scraping up a handful and straightening himself in the sunshine, as he amused himself by addressing an imaginary personage.

"Say, gov'nor," he cried, "you've got a bigger stock than you'll get shut of to-day.—Eh? You don't expect to? Right you are, old man. Break yer barrer if yer tried to carry it away. Say; looks cleaner and nicer to-day without any o' that red or yeller paint mixed up with it. I like it best when it's white. Looks more icy.—What say? Spoon? No, thank ye. Your customers is too fond o' sucking the spoons, and I never see you wash 'em after.—Ha! this is prime. Beats Whitechapel all to fits; and it's real cold, too. I don't care about it when it's beginning to melt and got so much juist.—But I say! Come! Fair play's a jewel. One likes a man to make his profit and be 'conimycal with the sugar, but you ain't put none in this.

"Never mind," he added after a pause, during which the Italian ice-vendor faded out of his imagination; "it's reg'lar 'freshing when you're so sleepy. Wonder what made them Italians come to London and start selling that stuff o' theirs. Seems rum; ours don't seem a country for that sort o' thing. Baked taters seems so much more English, and does a chap so much more good."

He walked back to the warm patch of rock, looked at Bracy, and then placed both rifles and bayonets ready, sat down cross-legged, and after withdrawing the cartridges, set to work with an oily rag to remove all traces of rust, and gave each in turn a good polish, ending by carefully wiping the bayonets after unfixing them, and returning them to their sheaths, handling Bracy's most carefully, for fear of disturbing the sleeper. This done, he began to yawn again, and, as he expressed it, took another penny ice and nodding at vacancy, which he filled with a peripatetic vendor, he said:

"All right, gov'nor; got no small change. Pay next time I come this way."

Then he marked out a beat, and began marching up and down.

"Bah!" he cried; "that ice only makes you feel dry and thirsty.—My! how sleepy I am!—Here, steady!" he cried, as he yawned horribly; "you'll have your head right off, old man, if you do that.—Never was so sleepy in my life."

He marched up and down a little faster—ten paces and turn—ten paces and turn—up and down, up and down, in the warm sunshine; but it was as if some deadly stupor enveloped him, and as he kept up the steady regulation march, walking and turning like an automaton, he was suddenly fast asleep and dreaming for quite a minute, when he gave a violent start, waking himself, protesting loudly against a charge made against him, and all strangely mixed up the imaginary and the real.

"Swear I wasn't, Sergeant!" he cried angrily. "Look for yerself.—Didn't yer see, pardners? I was walking up and down like a clockwork himidge.—Sleep at my post? Me sleep at my post? Wish I may die if I do such a thing. It's the old game. Yer allus 'ated me, Sergeant, from the very first, and— Phew! Here! What's the matter? I've caught something, and it's got me in the nut. I'm going off my chump."

Poor Gedge stood with his hands clasped to his forehead, staring wildly before him.

"Blest if I wasn't dreaming!" he said wonderingly. "Ain't took bad, am I? Thought old Gee come and pounced upon me, and said I was sleepin' on duty. And it's a fack. It's as true as true; I was fast asleep; leastwise I was up'ards. Legs couldn't ha' been, because they'd ha' laid down. Oh! this here won't do. It was being on dooty without arms."

Drawing himself up, he snatched his bayonet from its scabbard, and resumed his march, going off last asleep again; but this time the cessation of consciousness descended as it were right below the waist-belt and began to steal down his legs, whose movements became slower and slower, hips, then knees, stiffening; and then, as the drowsy god's work attacked his ankles, his whole body became rigid, and he stood as if he had been gradually frozen stiff for quite a minute, when it seemed as if something touched him, and he sprang into wakefulness again, and went on with his march up and down.

"Oh, it's horrid!" he said piteously. "Of course. That'll do it."

He sheathed his bayonet, and catching up his rifle, went through the regular forms as if receiving orders: he grounded arms; then drew and fixed bayonet, shouldered arms, and began the march again.

"That's done it," he said. "Reg'larly woke up now. S'pose a fellow can't quite do without sleep, unless he got used to it, like the chap's 'oss, only he died when he'd got used to living upon one eat a day. Rum thing, sleep, though. I allus was a good un to sleep. Sleep anywhere; but I didn't know I was so clever as to sleep standing up. Wonder whether I could sleep on one leg. Might do it on my head. Often said I could do anything on my head. There, it's a-coming on again."

He stepped to the nearest snow and rubbed his temples with it before resuming his march; but the relief was merely temporary. He went to Bracy's side, to see that he was sleeping heavily, and an intense feeling of envy and longing to follow his officer's example and lie down and sleep for hours nearly mastered him.

"But I won't—I won't sleep," he said, grinding his teeth. "I'll die first. I'm going to keep awake and do my dooty like a soldier by my orficer. I'd do it for any orficer in the ridgement, so of course I would for the gov'nor, poor chap! He's watched over me before now.—Yes, I'm going to keep on. I shall be better soon. Ten minutes would set me right, and if there was a mate here to take my post I'd have a nap; but there ain't a pardner to share it, and I've got to do it on my head. Wonder whether I should feel better if I did stand on my head for a minute. Anyhow, I ain't goin' to try."

Gedge spent the next ten minutes in carefully examining his rifle; then he turned to Bracy, and soon after he took out the latter's glass and swept the country round, to find more groups of men in motion.

"Why, the place is getting alive with the beggars," he growled. "We shall be having some of 'em cocking an eye up and seeing us here. Don't know, though; they couldn't make us out, and even if they did we look like a couple o' sheep. I've got to look out sharp, though, to see as we're not surprised. Almost wish three or four would come now, so as I could have a set-to with 'em. That would wake me up, and no mistake. —Ah! it's wonderful what one can see with a bit or two o' glass set in a brown thing like this.—Ah! there it is again."

Gedge lowered the glass and started violently, for the feeling of sleep was now overmastering.

"Nearly dropped and smashed his glass," he said petulantly, and, laying down his rifle, he closed the little lorgnette slowly and carefully with half-numbed fingers, which fumbled about the instrument feebly.

"He'd ha'—he'd ha'—fine—tongue-thrashing when he woke— foun' glass—smashed."

Gedge sank upon his knees and bent over the sleeper, fumbling for the strap and case to replace the glass.

"Where ha' you got to?" he muttered. "What yer swinging about half a mile away for? Ah! that's got yer," he went on, aiming at the case with a strange fixity of expression. "Now then—the lid—the lid—and the strap through the buckle, and the buckle—done it—me go to sleep —on dooty, Sergeant? Not me!—I—I—ha-h-h!"

Poor Gedge was only human, and his drowsy head sank across Bracy's breast, so wrapped in sleep that the firing of a rifle by his ear would hardly have roused him up.

Chapter Thirty Three.

Like a Dying Dog.

The sun was rapidly going down towards the western peaks, which stood out dark and clear against the golden orange sky, when Gedge opened his eyes and began to stare in a vacant way at a little peculiarly shaded brown leather case which rose and fell in regular motion a few inches from his nose. He watched it for some minutes, feeling very comfortable the while, for his pillow was warm; though it seemed strange to him that it should move gently up and down. But he grew more wakeful a minute later, and told himself that he knew why it was. He and two London companions had made up their minds to tramp down into Kent for a holiday, and to go hop-picking, and they slept under haystacks, in barns, or in the shade of trees; and at such times as the nights were cool and they had no covering they huddled together to get warm, taking in turns that one of the party should lie crosswise and play pillow for the benefit of his two companions.

It was one of his comrades that time, and the sun was rising, so they ought to be stirring to see about, something for breakfast. But in his drowsy state he could not make out that this was six years ago, nor yet what this brown leather thing was which kept going up and down.

Then all at once he could. It was not six years ago, neither was it early morning, but close upon sunset; that movement was caused by Bracy's respirations, and the brown leather case contained the little field-glass; while the well-drilled soldier, and one of the smartest lads in Captain Roberts's company, had shamefully disgraced himself by going to sleep at his post.

Before he had half-thought this he was upon his feet, to stoop again and pick up his rifle, and then begin stamping up and down with rage.

"Oh!" he groaned; "I ought to be shot—I ought to be shot! Why, the niggers might ha' come and knifed Mr Bracy as he lay there helpless as a kid, and all through me. Slep'? Why, I must ha' slep' hours upon hours. What's the good o' saying you couldn't help it, sir? You ought to have helped it. Call yourself a soldier, and go to sleep at your post in the face of the enemy! That's what the Colonel will say. I can't never face no one agen. I shall desert; that's what I shall do—cut right away and jyne the rebels if they'll have me. Better go and jump down into that hole and bury myself in the snow; but I can't.

"How am I to go and leave the gov'nor when he wants me as he does? Oh dear, oh dear! This is the worst of all. And I was hoping that I should have my stripes when I got back to the fort. Yes, that's it— stripes. I shall get 'em, o' course, but on my back instead of my sleeve. There, I'm a marked man now, and it's about all over."

Gedge grew calmer as he went, on pacing up and down, for he stopped twice over by Bracy, to find that he was sleeping as quietly as a child, and he evidently had not stirred. The young soldier's next act was to get possession of the little field-glass again, and, to his dismay, he made out no less than three bodies of men in the valley far below, one of which was streaming along as if marching quickly, while the other two were stationary, close up to a little clump of pines or cedars, he could not make out which.

"T'others are going to ketch up to 'em and camp for the night, I bet. Yes, that they are," he added as a tiny cloud of grey smoke began to rise. "They're going to cook, so they must have something to roast, and I'm—oh, how hungry I do feel! Better not hold up this rifle, or they may see it in the sunshine, and come and cook us."

He had a good long look, swept the valley as far as he could see, and then laid down his rifle, to go down on one knee by Bracy and begin replacing the glass in its leather case.

"It's all right, sir; on'y me," cried Gedge, for, awakened by the light touch, Bracy seized one hand and made an effort to pull out his revolver.

"Ha!" he cried. "You startled me, Gedge. Want the glass?"

"Had it, sir, thank ye."

"See anything?"

"Yes, sir. There's three lots o' them Dwats down low there—six or seven hundred of 'em, I should say."

"Ah!" cried Bracy, rising quickly into a sitting position, but yielding to an agonising pain and letting himself sink back with a groan.

"Hurt yer, sir?" said Gedge commiseratingly.

"Horribly. But tell me; have I been asleep?"

"Hours and hours, sir. It's just sundown. I was in hopes you'd be better, sir."

"I am, Gedge. I was in a horrible state before. My brain seemed numbed."

"No wonder, sir, lying in the snow all night; but you talk quite straight now."

"Did I seem incoherent before?" said Bracy excitedly.

"Well, sir, I don't say you was ink-o—what you call it: but you was a bit touched in the upper story; and that was only nat'ral, sir."

"Tell me about the enemy down below. Have they made us out?"

"I think not, sir; but I must out with it, sir."

"Ah! there is danger?"

"Oh no, sir, I don't think so; but I can't give much of a report, for I had to do sentry-go while you slep', sir."

"Did you? Well, you're a good fellow, Gedge."

"Not a bit of it, sir. There, it must come to the top. I'd rather tell you than you should find it out, sir. I held up as long as I could, and kep' going to sleep walking or standing still; and at last, after getting out your glass, I knelt down to put it back, and down I went right off to sleep, just as if some one had hit me on the head with the butt of his piece."

"I'm glad of it, Gedge," said Bracy, smiling.

"Glad of it, sir?" said the lad, staring.

"Heartily. It was the only thing you could do after what you had gone through."

"Beg pardon, sir, but as a soldier—" began Gedge.

"Soldiers cannot do impossibilities, my lad. I have all the will and spirit to get on to the Ghil Valley, and yet here I am with my urgent message undelivered, and lying sleeping the greater part of a day."

"Oh, that's different, sir. You're sorter like being in hospital and wounded."

"If not wounded, Gedge," said Bracy sadly, "I am crippled."

"Don't say that, sir," cried the lad excitedly. "I thought you said there was nothing broke."

"I did not think so then, my lad, but there is something wrong with my right leg."

"Amb'lance dooty—first help," said Gedge quickly. "Let's look, sir."

Bracy bowed his head, and the young soldier ran his hand down the puttee bandage about his officer's leg, and drew in his breath sharply.

"Well," said Bracy faintly, "what do you make out?"

"Leg's not broke, sir, but there's something awfully wrong with the ankle. It's all puffed up as big as my 'elmet."

"I was afraid so. Here, help me to stand up."

"Better not, sir," protested Gedge.

"Obey orders, my lad," said Bracy softly, and with a smile at his attendant. "You're not the Doctor."

"No, sir, but—"

"Your hands."

Gedge extended his hands, and by their help Bracy rose, to stand on one leg, the other hanging perfectly helpless, with the toes touching the rock.

"Help—me—" said Bracy faintly, and he made a snatch at Gedge, who was on the alert and caught him round the waist, just in time to save him from a fall.

The next moment he had fainted dead away, to come-to in a few minutes and find his companion laying snow upon his temples.

"Ah!" he sighed; "that's refreshing, Gedge."

"Have a bit to suck, sir?"

"Yes."

Bracy lay for a few minutes letting the snow melt in his mouth; then calmly enough he went on:

"I've got a bad wrench, my lad. My ankle must have doubled under me when I fell. There's no help for it; we have had nothing but misfortunes from the start, but this is the culmination—the worst of all."

"Is it, sir? I'm glad o'that."

"Glad?"

"Yes, sir; 'cause, you see, when things comes to the worst they begins to mend. So will your leg if you let me get the puttee and boot off. If you don't I shall be 'bliged to cut it off before long."

"Go on; you're quite right, my lad," said Bracy calmly; and as the young soldier eagerly busied himself over the frightfully swollen place, unwinding the bandages, which cut down into the flesh, and unlacing the boot, he went on talking calmly:

"About this boot, sir; I've unlaced it as far as I can, and it's quite fast on. Shall I cut it or will you try and bear a wrench?"

"Don't cut it, my lad. Give a quiet, firm drag. I'll bear the pain as well as I can."

The next moment the boot was off, and Bracy lay with his eyes closed.

"Like some more ice, sir?" said Gedge eagerly.

"No, my lad; I'm not going to faint this time. Got some snow, and take my handkerchief to bind some round the ankle. But look first whether you can make out any movement amongst the enemy."

"It's getting dark down there, sir, though it's so bright up here, and the great long shadders of the mountain seems to have swallered 'em up. But they've got a whacking great fire, sir, so they must be going to camp there for the night."

"I don't think they could have made us out, Gedge.—Ha! that feels comforting. But now listen to me."

"Yus, sir. I may go on doing up your leg, though?"

"Oh yes; only attend."

"Of course, sir."

"You can tell the Ghoorkha Colonel—"

"Yes, sir?" said Gedge, for Bracy stopped short.—"He's going off his head again."

"And Colonel Graves, if you get back—"

"Yus, sir."

"That I did everything that man could do to reach the Ghil Valley."

"That I'll swear, sir."

"And that he must lose no time in hurrying to the fort. If he likes to detach half a company to try and pick me up, he will do so; but the fort is to be the first consideration. Do you hear?"

"Yus, sir.—Oh yus, I hears," said Gedge through his teeth as, with the help of Mrs Gee's pocket-book packet, he put some oil-silk over the snow, and then applied the broadest bandage he could find cleverly enough.

"That's right. I'm a bit of a coward, Gedge," continued the poor fellow, with a smile.

"Yes, sir, you are, sir," said Gedge; "an out-and-outer."

"And I want to have as little pain to bear as I can while you're gone."

"Course you do, sir. That's why I'm doing this."

"Make haste, while the light lasts. I want you then to take the rest of the food and put it in your own haversack."

"Yes, sir; not inside?"

"To use as sparingly as you can, so as to make it last till you reach the Ghil Valley. I have broken down, Gedge, but you must get there. Do you hear?—must."

"Yes, sir, I hear—must."

"It means salvation for the poor creatures yonder, holding out their hands to us for help."

"Yes, sir.—But a deal you can see that," muttered Gedge.

"And it means a sergeant's stripes for the brave lad who took the message in the terrible emergency."

"Sergeant, sir? As big a man as old Gee?"

"Yes; and as good a non-commissioned officer, and I hope a more popular man."

"Rigid, sir. That sounds good," cried Gedge cheerily. "But about you, sir? If you get the ridgement o' little chaps and saves the fort, it means your company, don't it—Captain?"

Bracy groaned.

"I was not striving for promotion, Gedge, but to save our fellow-countrymen and women yonder. But listen: in case I faint again—give me a scrap or two more snow, my lad."

He took and sucked the icy particles handed to him, and felt refreshed.

"Now, then," he said; "listen once more, and be quick. Just tie that bandage, and then put the food together. I am not going to load you with instructions which you may not be able to carry out, but look yonder—there is the top of the mountain you have to skirt, shining bright and hopefully in the distance."

"I can see it, sir."

"That is your guide. Once you compass that the way will be easier."

"Yes, sir. When ought I to start?"

"To-night, man, as soon as the sun is down; therefore, mark well where the bright peak lies, so as to take your bearings. The enemy's fire will enable you to avoid that danger. Quick; there is no time to spare; and remember—you must get there."

"Yes, sir; I won't forget."

"Leave me some cartridges to defend myself, if I can. It would be more like a soldier to die like that."

"Yes, sir, o' course; more English and plucky," said Gedge, giving the last bandage its final knot, and then opening his haversack to take out what it contained and divide it.

"What are you doing?" said Bracy sharply.

"Getting your supper ready, sir, and mine," said the lad coldly.

Bracy tried to raise himself up in the fit of anger which attacked him, but fell back with a groan. Fighting back the sensation of weakness, though, he spoke as firmly as he could.

"I want no food," he said quietly, "and you are wasting time. A good twenty-four hours have been lost. Go at once."

"But you must eat something, sir," said Gedge stubbornly. "There's the cold coming on awful now the sun's down, and it will keep it out."

"Those poor creatures at the fort are waiting and praying for help to come, while the hungry wolves of Dwats are crowding closer and closer in ready for the massacre."

"Yes, sir—the beasts!—it's precious hard, but let's hope—"

"There is no hope, Gedge. It was the last card the Colonel had to play in sending us, and we must not fail. You must go at once."

"But I aren't had nothing to-day, sir," pleaded Gedge, "and my inside's going mad. Wolves? Why, I feel just as if one was tearing me."

"Take all the provisions left, and eat as you go."

"And what about you, sir?"

"Never mind me. Go at once."

"But it'll be dark as pitch in 'alf-a-hour, sir. How am I to see my way?"

"I told you. The descent will be easy. You can almost slide down all the way, for the snow is getting glassy again, and you must guide yourself by leaving the enemy's fire on the right. Look! it is glowing brightly now."

"That's right, sir, till I get to the bottom. But what then?"

"Gedge, are you going to fail me in this terrible emergency?"

"Not me, sir," cried the lad excitedly. "I'll stick to you till we both goes under fighting to the last, for they don't want to make prisoners of us; their knives are too sharp."

"Then go."

"But I'm sure I couldn't find the way, sir. I should be taking the first turning to the left, or else to the right, or tumbling into another hole like this, or doing some stoopid thing. I'm no use, sir, without my orficer to tell me what to do."

Bracy drew a deep breath and pressed his lips together, as he fought hard to keep down his anger against his follower.

"I have told you what to do," he said at last quite calmly. "You must use your brains."

"Never had much, sir," replied Gedge bitterly; "and now they're about froze up with cold and hungriness and trouble. I ain't fit to send on such a job as this, sir. I'm sure to muff it."

"Do you want to find out some day, my lad, that those poor comrades of ours have been massacred to a man through your hanging back from doing what might have saved them?"

"I wish I may die if I do, sir!" cried Gedge passionately.

"Then go."

"But I'm cold and hungry, sir, and it's getting dark, and I don't know my way."

"Crush those feelings down like a hero, and go."

"Hero, sir? Me a hero!" cried Gedge bitterly. "Oh? there's none of that stuff in me."

There was just enough light reflected from the upper peaks to enable the couple to see each other's faces—the one frowning and angry, and belying the calm, stern fixedness into which it had been forced; the other wild, anxious, and with the nerves twitching sharply at the corners of the eyes and mouth, as if its owner were grimacing in mockery of the young officer's helplessness and suffering.

"Gedge," said Bracy suddenly, after making an effort as if to swallow down the rage and despair from which he suffered.

"Yes, sir, I know what you're going to say; but you're awful bad. Now, you have a bit to eat, and then go to sleep, and when you wake up let's see if I can't manage to get you on one of those flat bits o' slaty stone, and then I'll get a strap to it, and pull you down the slope—you'll quite slide like—and when we're off the snow I'll pig-a-back you to the first wood, and we'll hide there, and I'll keep helping you on a bit till we get to this here Jack-and-Jill Valley. You see, the job can't be done without you."

"This is all shuffling and scheming, Gedge, to escape doing your duty," said Bracy sternly.

"Is it, sir?" said the lad, with an assumption of innocence.

"You know it is, sir. You don't want to go?"

"Well, sir, I suppose that is about the size of it."

"Do you want me to look upon you as a contemptible cur?" said Bracy, flashing out into anger now.

"No, sir; o' course not."

"I see how it is. I've been believing you to be all that is manly and true, while all the time I've been labouring under a gross mistake, for now you are put to the test you are only base metal. Go; leave me. Gedge, you are a miserable, contemptible coward after all."

"Yes, sir; that's it, sir," said the lad bitterly; "bit o' common brass as got into the service, and you orficers and old Gee and the rest of you drilled up and polished and dressed up and put some gilt on; but when yer comes to rub it off, I'm on'y a bit o' brass after all."

"Yes, you know exactly—coward!—dog!"

"Don't, sir!" cried the poor fellow in a choking voice; "don't! It's like laying it on to a chap with a wire whip."

"Then do your duty. Go."

"I can't, sir; I can't," cried the lad, literally writhing, as if the blows were falling upon his back and sides. "I dessay I am a coward, but I'd follow you anywheres, sir, if the bullets was whistling round us, and them devils were waiting for us with their knives; but I can't go and leave you now, sir. You ain't fit to leave. It'd be like killing you—murdering of you, sir, with the cold and starvation."

"It is your duty to go."

"But you don't know how bad you are, sir," pleaded the lad, with the great sobs struggling to escape from his breast. "You don't know, sir; but I do, sir. You'd be frozen stiff before it was light again."

"Perhaps; but I should die knowing that an effort was being made to save those we have left behind."

"You've done all you can do, sir," pleaded Gedge passionately. "We can't do no more."

"I can't, but you can. I call upon you once more to go and do this thing. If you have any manhood in you, go."

"I can't, sir," groaned Gedge.

"You coward!—it's your duty to go."

"It ain't, sir; it can't be, to leave my orficer to die like this. I know it can't. Why, if I did, and got the help, and took the men back, and the Colonel got to know how, he'd think it warn't worth getting it at such a price. He'd call me a cowardly dog and a hound, and the lads would groan and spit at me. Why, they'd cob me when they got me alone, and I couldn't say a word, because I should feel, as I always should to the last day I lived, that I'd been a miserable sneak."

"I tell you it is your duty, my man," cried Bracy again.

"Don't send me, sir! I ain't afraid," pleaded Gedge once more. "It's leaving you to die in the cold and dark. I can't go!—I can't go!"

Bracy struggled up at this, supporting himself with his left hand, moved now as he was by his companion's devotion; but he choked down all he longed to say in the one supreme effort he was making to fulfil the mission he had failed in by another hand.

"I am your officer, sir. You are a soldier, sworn to serve your country and your Queen."

Gedge looked down at the speaker through the gloom, and saw him fumbling beneath his sheepskin coat with his right hand. The next minute he had drawn his revolver, and Gedge heard it click.

"You hear me, sir?" cried Bracy sternly.

"Yes, sir, I hear."

"Then obey your officer's orders."

"You ain't an officer now, sir; you're a patient waiting to be carried to the rear, after going down in front."

"How dare you!" cried Bracy fiercely. "Obey my orders."

"They ain't your orders, and it ain't my dooty to obey a poor fellow as has gone stick stark raving mad."

279

"Obey my orders, dog, or—"

"I won't!" cried Gedge passionately. "I'll be drummed out if I do."

"You dog!" roared Bracy, and the pistol clicked.

"Shoot me, then, for a dog," cried Gedge passionately, "and if I can I'll try to lick yer hand, but I won't leave you now."

The pistol fell with a dull sound as Bracy sank back, and in that terrible darkness and silence, amid the icy snow, a hoarse groan seemed to tear its way from the young officer's breast.

Chapter Thirty Four.

A Wild Idea.

How long that silence lasted neither could have afterwards said, but after a time Bracy felt a couple of hands busy drawing the spare *poshtin* more about him. Then a face was placed close to his, and a hand touched his forehead softly. "I'm not asleep, Gedge," he said.

"Ha!" sighed the lad, with a long drawn breath: "getting afraid, sir; you lay so still."

"It's all over, my man," said Bracy wearily.

"No, no; don't say that, sir," cried Gedge. "I was obliged to—"

"Hush! I don't mean that. I only feel now that I can sleep."

"Yes, sir; do, sir. Have a good try."

"I cannot while I know that I have your coat."

"Oh, I don't mind, sir; and I've got to be sentry."

"We want no sentry here, my lad. Take the coat from under me."

"But—"

"Come, obey me now," said Bracy quietly. "Get close to me, then, and cover it over us both."

"You mean that, sir?"

"Yes.—There, my lad, all men are equal at a time like this. I have striven to the last, but Fate has been against me from the first. I give up now."

"I didn't want to run against you, sir; but I was obliged."

"Yes, I suppose so."

"You wouldn't have gone and left me, sir?"

"I don't know," said Bracy slowly.

"I do, sir; I know you wouldn't."

"Let it rest, my lad, and we'll wait for day. God help the poor creatures at the fort, and God help us too!"

"Amen!" said Gedge to himself; and as the warmth began to steal through his half-frozen limbs he lay gazing at the distant glow of the enemy's fire far away below, till it grew more and more faint, and then seemed to die right out—seemed, for it was well replenished again and again through the night, and sent up flames and sparks as if to give a signal far away, for the supply of fir-branches was abundant, and the fire rose in spirals up into the frosty sky.

Bracy too lay watching the distant blaze till it grew dim to his half-closed eyes. A calmer feeling of despair had come over him, and the feeling that he had done all that man could do softened the mental agony from which he had suffered. This was to be the end, he felt; and, if ever their remains were found, those who knew them would deal gently with their memory. For the inevitable future stared him blankly in the face. Gedge would strive his utmost to obtain help, but he felt that the poor fellow's efforts would be in vain, and that, if they lived through the night, many hours would not elapse before they perished from hunger and the cold.

The feeling of weary mental confusion that stole over him then was welcome; and, weak from the agony he had suffered, he made an effort to rouse himself from the torpor that, Nature-sent, was lulling the pangs in his injured limb, but let his eyelids droop lower and lower till the distant light was shut out, and then cold, misery, and despair passed away, for all was blank.

The specks of golden light were beginning to show on the high peaks, and gradually grew brighter till it was sunny morning far up on the icy eminences, chilly dawn where the two sheepskin-covered figures lay prone, and night still where the fire was blazing by the pine-forest, and the great body of the enemy had bivouacked.

The two motionless figures were covered by a thick rime frost, which looked grey in the dim light, not a crystal as yet sending off a scintillation; and tiny spicules of ice had matted the moustache and beard of Bracy where his breath had condensed during the night, sealing them to the woolly coverlet he had drawn up close; while a strange tingling sensation attacked his eyes as he opened them suddenly, waking from a morning dream of defending the fort and giving orders to his men, who fired volley after volley, which, dream-like, sounded far away.

He was still half-asleep, but involuntarily he raised a warm hand to apply to his eyes. In a very few minutes they were clear, and he began breaking and picking off bit by bit the little icicles from his moustache.

It was strange how it mingled still with his dreams—that firing of volleys; and the half-drowsy thoughts turned to wonder that there should be firing, for he must be awake. Directly after he knew he was, for there was a sharp rattle in the distance, which came rolling and echoing from the face of the great cliff across the gulf, and Gedge jerked himself and said sleepily:

"That's right, boys; let 'em have it."

"Gedge!" cried Bracy hoarsely.

"Right, sir; I'm here," was the answer; and the young soldier rolled over from beneath the *poshtin*, rose to his feet, staggered, and sat down again.

"Oh, murder!" he cried. "My poor feet ain't froze hard, are they?"

"I pray not," said Bracy excitedly.

"'Cause I can't stand. But, hallo! sir; what game's this? They're a-firing at us, and coming up over the snow."

"No, no, it can't be!" cried Bracy wildly. "No tribes-men could fire volleys like that."

"Course not, sir. Hoorray! then the Colonel's sent a couple o' comp'nies to help us."

"Impossible!" cried Bracy. "Hark! there is the reply to the firing. Yes; and another volley. I almost thought I could see a flash."

"Did yer, sir? Oh, don't talk; do listen, sir. There they go. There must be a big fight going on down there."

"Then friends have attacked the enemy in camp—advanced upon them so as to catch them before daylight."

"Oh! they might ha' waited till it was light enough for us to see, sir. Mr Bracy, sir, don't, pray don't say it's reg'lars, because if it ain't I couldn't stand it now. I should go down and blubber like a great gal."

"It is a force of regulars, my lad," cried Bracy, whose voice sounded as if he were choking. "Friends are there below in the valley. I know: the Colonel must have been badly beaten at the fort."

"Oh, don't say that, sir."

"It must be. They have been too much for him, and he is retreating with our lads trying to make for the Ghil Pass. That is the meaning of the gathering last night to bar their way."

"Oh Lor'! oh Lor'! and us not able to fire a shot to help 'em. Be any use to begin, sir, like for signals to show we're here?"

"No," said Bracy sadly; "our single shots could not be heard."

"Not if we fired both together, sir?" cried Gedge wildly. "I'll load for you."

"How could they distinguish between our shots and those of the enemy you can hear crackling?"

"Course not, sir. I'm a poor idjit sometimes. But oh! why does it keep dark down there so long when it's getting quite light up here? We can't see what's going on a bit."

"No; but my ears tell me pretty plainly," said Bracy excitedly.

"Mr Bracy, sir."

"Yes?"

"We aren't worse, are we, and all this a sort o' nightmare before we loses ourselves altogether?"

"No, man, no. Listen. They must be getting the worst of it."

"Our lads, sir? Oh, don't say that! There must be a lot of them, by the volley-firing. Don't say they're being cut up."

"The enemy, man. Can't you hear how steady the firing is?— Splendid. I can almost see them. The enemy must be retiring stubbornly, and they're following them up."

"Yes, sir; that's it," cried Gedge wildly. "Go on, sir; go on."

"Their officers are holding the men well in hand, so as not to come to a charge in that broken country, and withering the crowd with their fire to make them scatter."

"Right, sir, right. That's it. Oh, if we was only there!"

There was a pause—the two men listening.

"The enemy's firing sounds more broken up, and is getting feebler."

"Yes, sir; I can make out that," panted Gedge. "Oh! I say, don't let the lads get out of hand and follow the beggars where they can get hold of the bay'nets and use their long knives."

For another half-hour the pair lay listening to the engagement going on, till it seemed as if the daylight below would never come. Then the darkness gave way, to display far below a cold grey mist, through which clouds of smoke were softly rising; and Bracy brought his glass to bear upon the fight still raging furiously, and looked in silence till Gedge turned to him:

"Oh, do say something, sir! Our lads—they ain't being cut up, sir, are they?"

"No, no, I think not, my lad; but I can hardly make out what is going on at present. Ha! it's gradually growing lighter there. The enemy are not where they were last night, and the troops are there."

"Then they've took the beggars' camp, sir?"

"That does not follow," said Bracy, whose eyes were glued to his glass.—"I can make out the white-coats now. They have divided, and are upon the rising ground all round. Our poor fellows must have fallen into a trap."

"No, sir; no, sir, they couldn't, sir," cried Gedge; "they'd have seen that fire and known there was an enemy."

"Yes, I forgot the fire," said Bracy. "Oh, if the sun would only shine down upon them now!"

"But he won't, sir; he never will when he's wanted to. He won't shine there for an hour yet."

"Yes—no—yes—no," panted Bracy at slow intervals; and Gedge

wrung his hands, like a woman in trouble, whimpering out:

"Oh! who's to know what that means, with his 'Yes—no—yes—no'? Mr Bracy, sir, do—do say that our lads are whipping the beggars back."

"Yes," cried Bracy excitedly; "I can see now; the hill-men are scattered and running towards the mountains."

"Hoorray!" yelled Gedge. "Hoorray! Hoorray! Hark at the steady volleys still, sir! Hoorray! Who wouldn't be a soldier of the Queen?"

"Ha! Who indeed?" sighed Bracy.

"And it don't matter, sir, now?" said Gedge.

"No; not so much, my lad; but they'll be harassed like this all the way to the Ghil Pass."

"And drive the beggars back, sir. But don't you think we ought to make one try to get down to them, sir? Same as I said last night?"

Bracy was silent as he kept on using his glass, with the valley below growing clearer—so light now that, the young soldier could begin to see something of the fight with the naked eye, and he joined in the eager watch downward for a time before repeating his question.

"I fear not, my lad," said Bracy, with a sigh. "The enemy are cut in two; one body is retreating down the valley in the direction of the fort; the other, widely scattered, is making for the snow-slope."

"Not coming this way, sir?" cried Gedge.

"Yes, as far as I can see; and our men are steadily in pursuit, firing wherever a crowd collects."

"That's the way to do it, sir; but that's cutting off our retreat."

"Yes."

"Well, then, sir, we must lie low till the enemy is cleared off. They won't come up here."

"No; they must be making for the track we crossed—the one below there, where we saw the men going towards the valley-bend."

"That's it, sir, and they've got their work cut out; but our lads won't follow 'em right up there."

"No; they will only follow till they have scattered them as far as "possible."

"And then go back, sir, and leave us where we are."

"Yes," said Bracy sadly.

Gedge was silent for a few minutes, during which they still watched the scene below. Then he broke out with:

"It's all downhill, sir."

"Yes, Gedge," said Bracy drearily; "it is all downhill now to the end."

"You ain't listening to me, sir," cried the lad. "Do put that glass away, sir, and we'll have a try."

"A try? What! to get down below? You try, my lad; but there is the terrible risk of being cut to pieces by the enemy if they see you."

"Don't begin that again, sir, please. You know I won't leave you, but let's have a try."

"I am helpless, my lad—as helpless as a figure half of lead."

"But I ain't, sir," cried Gedge. "The sight of our lads below there seems to ha' woke me up. I'm ready to die game; but I want to make one spurt for life first."

"Why, Gedge," cried Bracy excitedly as he lowered the glass from his eyes, "they're not our fellows after all."

"What, sir!"

"No; and there's a detachment down yonder coming from the east. I can almost see that they're doubling to get up in time."

"From the east, sir? Then the Colonel ain't retreating?"

"No.—Hurrah!"

"Hoorray!" roared Gedge, joining in.

"They're the Ghoorkhas, Gedge. They must be a thousand strong."

"Then one o' the messengers must ha' got to them after all."

"Yes; that must be it, Gedge; and they surprised the enemy's camp at dawn."

"That's it, sir!" yelled Gedge. "Hoorray! hoorray again! Then there is life in a mussel after all."

"They've scattered this force, Gedge, and the fort will be relieved, for the bravo little fellows will cut their way through all."

"Yes, sir. Now then, sir, you needn't hardly move. There's a bit o' slaty stone yonder as'll do, and all I want of you, sir, is for yer to sit still upon it, and nuss the rifles while I steer you down to the truck."

"Right in among the enemy, my lad?"

"Right through 'em, sir. They're on the run, and won't dare to stop to go at us. I never heard of a nigger as'd stand a moment when a Ghoorkha was coming after him with his crooked knife."

"Let's try," said Bracy, setting his teeth. "Life is sweet, my lad."

"Even without sugar, sir. Why, bless your 'eart! there's a lot of it in us both yet, sir. This here's nothing to what we've been and done."

Wild with excitement now, Gedge fetched the heavy slab of stone, almost as much as he could lift, drew it close up behind Bracy, and placed his arms under the young officer's shoulders.

"Now, sir," he said, "you set your teeth just as if the doctor was going to use his knife."

"What are you going to do?"

"Draw you right back on to this stone, sir. I must hurt you a bit, but I can't help that."

"Go on," said Bracy; and the next moment he was drawn back upon the stone, with no worse suffering than a fit of faintness, for his leg was numb with the cold.

"Right, sir. Now your rifle and mine across your legs. Stop; my *poshtin* first. May want it again. Got the cartridges handy?"

"Yes."

"Then I sits here between your legs, sir. Just room, and I can steer and put on the break with my heels. Ready, sir?"

"Yes."

"Then off."

The surface of the snow was like glass with the night's frost, and the stone began to glide at once, just as the first gleams of the rising

287

sun lit up the spot where such terrible hours had been spent; and the next minute, with a strange, metallic, hissing sound, the pair were gliding down the slope at a steady rate, which Gedge felt it in his power to increase to a wild rush by raising his heels from the surface upon which they ran.

"All right, sir?"

"Yes, all right. Go on."

"Ain't it wonderful, sir? Why, we can get down to the track long before any of them can get up to it."

"Stop, then, to let them reach it and retreat."

"If you order me to, sir, I will; but they'll never try to stop us; they'll scatter to see us coming down like this. Why, in less than an hour, sir, we shall be all among the Ghoorkha lads, and then hoorray for the fort!"

"Go on, then. I trust to you."

"Right, sir," cried Gedge excitedly; and in spite of several risks of overturning, he steered the novel toboggan sledge down the gigantic slide, with the wild, metallic, hissing sound rising and falling on the keen wind that fanned their cheeks, and a glistening prismatic, icy dust rising behind them like a snaky cloud.

Chapter Thirty Five.

The Idea Tamed.

Onward, swifter or slower, they moved as the undulations of the mighty snow-slope ruled with the rough track crossing at right-angles far below and gradually growing plainer, the white-coats of the fleeing enemy, the kharkee jackets of the advancing line of Ghoorkhas, and the pulls of smoke from each discharge coming nearer as if in a dream. The excitement of the wild rush seemed to madden Gedge, who, as he found out that he could easily control his rough chariot of stone, let it glide faster and faster, his eyes sparkling, and the various phases of the fight below sending a wild longing to be amongst it thrilling through his nerves.

"Oh," he shouted, "if there was only a hundred of us coming down like this to take the enemy front and rear! Are you all right, sir?"

"Yes, yes; but beware of the rocks down below there by the track."

"Right, sir. Wish they weren't there, though, and we could go right on; charge through 'em in no time."

He had to speak without turning his head, and Bracy did not catch half his words. But it was no time for speaking; and, forgetting for the time being his injuries and partial helplessness, Bracy began to share in his driver's excitement, and watched the movements going on below.

The height to which they had climbed had been great, and some memory of the labour they had gone through in the ascent came back as they swept rapidly down, till in an incredibly short space of time they neared the rocky track, with its rugged pinnacles and masses standing right up out of the snow.

Gedge saw that the enemy was still far below the track; and as he checked the way on the stone by gradually driving in his well-nailed boot heels, he looked to right or left for a spot where there would be a clear crossing of the track, free from projecting rocks, so that a stoppage would not be necessary. There it was, lying well to the right, narrow but perfectly practicable. For, plainly enough, he could see that there had been a snow-slide burying a portion of the track, and if he could steer between a couple of rocks, not ten yards apart, the glide down could be continued without a pause.

"It's all right, sir," he cried. "Signals is clear, and we don't stop at that station. Hoorray! Her Majesty's mails. Fast express."

It was on Bracy's lips to cry, "Take care," but he nipped them together and sat fast, feeling their pace slacken as if, to carry out Gedge's simile, they were easing down to run through a station.

Nearer, nearer, with rough crags half-buried in the snow on both sides and seeming to close in upon them as they glided down, with the narrow pass between the two rocks unaccountably growing for the moment closer together. But directly after, by clever steering, Gedge made a curve in their descent, brought the stone opposite the opening, and then let it go.

Their way rose a little as they approached the track where it was buried in the snow, but directly after the descent was steeper; and as soon as Gedge felt sure of his course they dashed through the opening at a greatly increased speed. Then he shouted in his wild excitement as they tore down towards the enemy, who were toiling upward, slipping, and even crawling on all-fours in places, while their active little pursuers were striving their best to overtake them, but pausing at times to fire.

Pursued and pursuers were still far below, but Bracy saw that it was only a matter of a short time before they would be amongst them; and now, for the first time, it was evident that their descent had caught the attention of the hill-men striving to reach the track, some of whom stopped short to stare, while a party of about twenty immediately bore off to their left as if meaning to intercept them.

"What's it to be, sir!" panted Gedge. "Charge through 'em, or stop and let 'em have it? They'll be 'twix' two fives."

"Stop!" shouted Bracy. "They'll try to check us, and slash as we come; and if we strike against even one we shall be upset."

"That's right, sir. Be ready with the rifles. Mine's charged, I think. 'Nother five hundred yards right for that lot o' twenty, and then slide off and open fire—eh?"

"You don't want your orders, Gedge," said Bracy dryly. "Quite right."

Gedge did not hear him, for, as they rushed down

A couple of shots were fired, and the missile whistled by their heads.

over the icy snow, he had his work cut out to check his awkward car, as it nearly mastered him, his heels gliding over the smooth surface and refusing to cut in. Forcing them down, though, the speed began to slacken, till they neared the ascending group of savage faces of those who had borne off to intercept them; and as the car was brought to a stand a couple of shots were fired, and the missiles sent whistled by their heads.

"Can yer roll off, sir, and lie on yer face?" cried Gedge as he snatched his rifle, threw himself down behind the stone, and opened his cartridge-pouch.

"Yes. Look to yourself. Fire sharply, or they'll be upon us."

"Or our bay'nets," said Gedge through his teeth.

The next moment he fired as he rested upon his elbows, and a shot from Bracy rang out, with the result that two of the group below

291

them dropped, and a yell came from the remainder as they made a rush to reach them. But their running powers were exhausted, and at the end of twenty yards they resumed their heavy climb, with their feet breaking through the crust of frozen snow.

Crack, crack! from the English rifles, and one more dropped in his track, while another sprang wildly in advance for a few yards, before pitching forward upon his face and lying still.

"Fire steadily," said Bracy hoarsely, "and we may cheek them."

"Right, sir. Quick, too, for the beggars on the left are closing in to help."

A couple more shots were fired, and another man went down, and then there was a yell of rage and an order from one of the party, with the result that all dropped upon their faces, checked, and began to fire at the pair crouching behind the stone, made to look bigger by Gedge's *poshtin* lying in a little heap on the top.

"It's all right, sir; they couldn't hit a haystack. Their hands are all of a tremble with climbing. We're right enough. I hit that chap."

Proof was given, for one of the enemy started up, dropped his long jezail, and fell backwards.

"Keep on firing steadily, Gedge," said Bracy huskily. "I must open upon that group on our flank. They're coming on."

"Then we're done, for, sir," said the young soldier. "But mind this, sir; I die game, though you did call me a coward last night."

"I did, Gedge, and it was a cruel lie, my lad. Fire away. I wish I had your pluck. Look here."

"Yes, sir.—One for you," growled Gedge as he fired again.—"I'm listening, but I can't look. Hit him, sir?"

"Yes," said Bracy. "Look here."

"Can't, sir."

"Then listen. When it comes to the worst—one grip of the hand, my lad, before we go."

Crack—crack!

Two more shots in answer to the scattered fire of the enemy, whose bullets whistled over their heads, seeking billets in the snow around.

"Won't be long, sir, I'm afraid," said Gedge. "No, I ain't afraid—not a bit. But those chaps are coming on faster. 'Tain't climbing, sir, now."

"No; they'll be upon us before five minutes have passed. Turn your rifle upon them, my lad, for two or three shots, and we may check them too."

Before Gedge could change his position a scattered volley from below somewhere rattled out, and the flanking-party coming on needed no checking, some of them falling dying or wounded, while the remainder threw themselves down and began firing, some at their pursuers below, the rest at Bracy and Gedge.

"Hoorray, sir! Didn't I say there was life in a mussel? The Ghoorkhas are at 'em. Look, sir, there's about a dozen of 'em lying down to cover the advance, and another dozen coming on with their knives. Let's show 'em how to shoot, sir. It'll help the little chaps, too, when they charge."

It was as Gedge said; and as shot after shot was sent with good aim, the party of tribes-men in front was lessened by half-a-dozen before the little Ghoorkha party came up within charging distance and made their rush.

"Fix bayonets!" cried Bracy. "The enemy may come at us;" and the little, dagger-like weapons clicked and clicked as they flashed in the sunshine.

But Bracy and Gedge got in a couple more shots before their foes sprang up to charge them. Then a couple more dropped as they came on, while a volley from below rattled out and made their attack feeble and aimless, though they reached their goal, one to make a slash at Gedge as he was pinned by the lad's bayonet, while two more struck at Bracy. Then the Ghoorkhas were upon them, racing over the snow, their crooked knives flashing, and the remaining enemy were fleeing for their lives, scattering far and wide, with their pursuers overtaking man after man, whose white-coats made blots on the glistening snow, and many a terrible stain. Then a whistle rang out as an officer came up to the stone at the double, sword in hand.

"Hullo, here!" he cried; "who, in the name of wonder, are you? I couldn't get up in time. My boys didn't do that?"

Bracy's lips parted, but no sound came.

"No, sir," panted Gedge; "it was the straight knives did it, not them pretty little blades."

"I'm glad of that. I was afraid my boys had made a mistake. But who are you?"

"Private Willyum Gedge, in the 404th Fusiliers; and here's my lieutenant, Mr Bracy, sir. We was coming from the fort to fetch you."

"Ah!" cried the officer. "How is it with them there?"

"All right, sir; but hard pushed when we come away. Ain't got such a thing as a doctor about yer, have you?"

"Yes, yes. My boys shall carry you down. All right," he cried as a bugle rang out from below with the recall; and by that time the little group were surrounded by some twenty of the active Ghoorkhas, for the most part with a begonia-leaved kukri in hand, laughing, chattering, and ready to dance with delight around the two British soldiers they had saved.

Meanwhile their officer was down on one knee rendering first aid to the wounded, the knife of one of the enemy having slashed Bracy's thigh, which was bleeding profusely; and a havildar of the Ghoorkhas was cleverly bandaging Gedge's left arm, chattering to him merrily in broken English the while.

"Try and swallow a drop more," said the officer to Bracy, who was reviving a little, and smiled his thanks, his eyes wandering round directly after in search of something, till a movement on the part of their rescuers enabled him to see Gedge, to whom he feebly held out his hand.

"Much hurt?" he said faintly.

"Tidy, sir. Smarts a lot; but I don't mind, sir. Say you've not got it bad."

"Bad enough, my lad; but we've won."

Gedge turned to the officer with a wild, questioning look in his eyes, for Bracy sank back, half-fainting.

"A bad, clean cut; that's all," said the officer, smiling encouragement.

"But it ain't all, sir," cried Gedge passionately. "He's badly hurt besides. Crippled in the leg."

"Ah! and you fought like that! Well, we must get him down to the doctor; he is not far below. Ambulance party here."

"Beg pardon, sir; why not lay him on the stone again, and let him slide down easy? I can ride, too, and steer."

"I don't understand you, my lad," said the officer, looking at Gedge as if he thought him wandering.

He soon did comprehend, though; and the little Ghoorkhas cheered with delight as, with Bracy lying upon the sheepskin-coats, the stony sledge went gliding slowly down the slope, half-a-dozen of the little fellows forming its escort, and ready to check it from breaking away, till the end of the snowfield was reached, and the two sufferers were soon after being well tended by the doctor in the temporary camp.

This was near the fir-wood hold by the enemy the night before—the enemy, after heavy loss, having been scattered far and wide.

Chapter Thirty Six.

How the Fort was saved.

It was on the third morning after Bracy and Gedge had been with the Ghoorkhas, who were in camp in a natural stronghold of the upper valley, resting before making their final advance to the fort. Gedge, with his arm in a sling, and a frost-bitten foot, which made him limp about the little tent they shared by the doctor's orders, was looking anxiously down at his officer, who lay perfectly helpless, appearing terribly thin and worn, but with a bright look in his eyes, which augured well for his recovery.

"Yes, sir; you look a deal better," said Gedge in answer to a question: "and, of course, the doctor ought to know; but I don't think you ought to be so weak."

"Wasn't it enough to make me weak, my lad?" said Bracy in a faint voice. "Why, I have hardly a drop of blood left in my body."

"Course not, sir; and you do eat and sleep well."

"Yes, my lad; and if we can only cut our way through these swarming wretches, and relieve the fort before it is too late, I shall soon begin to mend. It is horrible, this delay, and no news."

"No news, sir?" said Gedge, staring. "Didn't the doctor tell you?"

"The doctor? I have not seen him this morning."

"But he's been here, sir. He said you were in such a beautiful sleep that you warn't to be woke up, for it was doing you no end of good."

"But he said something?" said Bracy anxiously. "Have we had news?"

"Tip-top, sir. One of the little Ghoorkha chaps got back soon after daylight—one of the three that was sent different ways."

"But the news?"

"He got into the fort, sir, and brought a despatch from the Colonel."

"Yes, yes," said Bracy breathlessly.

"They was all well, but hard up for everything, 'speshly ammynition; but they could hold out for three days; and as soon as we come up he's going to make a sally and attack the Dwats in the rear.— Oh, sir, it is hard, and no mistake!"

"Thank Heaven!" cried Bracy softly. "There, my lad, I can lie and rest now."

"Yes, sir, that's the worst of it."

"It is hard—the worst of it?" said Bracy wonderingly. "What do you mean?"

"You and me, sir, having to lie up and be out of all the fun."

"Oh, I see," said Bracy, smiling, and with the careworn look seeming to die out of his thin face. "Well, I think we have done our share."

"Did you hear the firing last night?"

"I? No. Was there an attack?"

"A big un, sir; but the enemy was driven back everywhere, and left a lot of dead behind. I never see such fellows as these little Ghoorkha chaps is to fight."

"If they can only cut their way through to the fort, Gedge, there will be nothing then to fear, for Colonel Graves will hold the place, against any number that can be brought against it."

"And they will, sir," cried Gedge proudly; "nothing can stop 'em. They've got so much dash and go in 'em. There's going to be a big fight to-day, for the hills seem dotted with white-coats as far as you can see; and in an hour's time I hear we're to advance, so as to get the job done before it's dark."

Gedge's news was correct: and in an hour the column was in motion, the order coming to advance in skirmishing order, with ample supports, and no following up of the enemy was to be attempted, the sole object, being to reach the fort before night, and trust to the future for giving adequate punishment for all that had been done.

The orders of the officers were splendidly carried out, and the gallant regiment advanced along the right bank of the river as fast as the front was cleared, but at a severe cost, for the hills and patches of forest and rock swarmed with the enemy, and but for the abundance of cover the attempt must have failed. But by a series of rushes and their deadly fire the brave little fellows won their way on till well into the afternoon, when farther progress seemed impossible, the enemy's leader holding a patch of cedar forest most determinedly with a dense body of men. All this Bracy knew, for Gedge, in spite of his wound, was active enough, and kept his officer well furnished with accounts of their progress; but his face looked grave as, in obedience to Bracy's question, he told him all.

"Yes, sir," he said, "we're in a very tight place; and the Colonel here is looking a bit down in the mouth. The little chaps are raging about being kept back, and if he'd let 'em go they'd kill till they couldn't lift those head-choppers of theirs; but as soon as one's shot or cut down a dozen seems to spring up, and the place swarms with white-gownds, as if they'd quite made up their minds to kill us to a man before we can get to the fort. There, sir—hear that?"

"Yes, I hear," said Bracy, breathing hard. "It means an attack on the rear."

"That's it, sir. We're surrounded; and if it weren't for that rushing river being so full they'd come swarming over, and we should be done."

Further conversation was put an end to by the order to advance, after a brief halt to rest and refresh the men, the Ghoorkha Colonel seeing that the enemy must be dislodged from the forest in front at any cost. It was a desperate business, and could only be achieved at a terrible loss, for the river and precipitous rocks on either side put a stop to all idea of turning the enemy's flank. A bold dash was the only chance, and this was about to be attempted, while the rear of the regiment was being terribly harassed by the enemy closing in.

The last arrangements had been made, and the swarthy little fellows, so long held in by the tight rein, were trembling with excitement as they stood together in shelter, with fixed bayonets and kukris, waiting to make the rush. The bugle was being raised to the holder's lips to sound the advance, when a thrill of joy surged through the British leaders' breasts, for the help they needed came in the nick of time.

A sharp volley was fired from behind the dense patch the enemy was holding, and the Ghoorkhas cheered wildly as the bugle rang out; and then as volley after volley followed from beyond the trees they literally flew over the broken ground, not a man stopping to fire, but raced into the wood, hewing with their terrible knives, and driving the enemy out like a flock of sheep right on to the fire, and soon after upon the bayonets of Colonel Graves's men. It was only a matter of ten minutes, and then, fleeing to right and left, the enemy was springing up among the rocks or plunging into the river to escape the tierce little regiment they had sought to destroy.

Ill news flies swiftly, and the sight of their fellows streaming scattered up among the hills disheartened those who were making a savage attack upon the rear. A couple of volleys from the two companies who formed the rear-guard turned their hesitation into flight, and amidst tremendous cheering the advance was continued, with Colonel Graves's men clearing the way; and, merely harassed by a few distant shots, the column readied the fort whose walls were lined by non-combatants, women, and the weak garrison left behind. The men marched in cheering and counter-cheering, intoxicated as they were with success, while even the wounded carried on litters and mules, and the brave fellows who persisted in tramping on in spite of injuries terrible to bear, added their feeble cries to swell the jubilation of the scene.

But the wildest, most exciting moments were when, in the bright evening glow, the rear-guard of the little Ghoorkhas marched in, proud of two burdens they carried shoulder-high in litters, singing and cheering and waving their caps, as if they bore the greatest triumph of the relief.

One of those they carried lay prone and helpless, his sallow face quivering slightly from time to time with the emotion which attacked him as he was borne into the court—most painfully perhaps when his face was recognised by those at the windows of the buildings and on the walls. It was then that his name was shouted, first by shrill women's voices, and then thundered out and half-drowned by the cheers.

The other burden carried by the brave little Ghoorkhas would not lie, but insisted upon sitting; and somehow, in the midst of the wild excitement of their reception as the heroes who had brought back the help, Gedge seemed to go quite mad with boy-like joy. For as soon as he appeared, bandaged and damaged as he was, Mrs Gee called out his name. A burst of fresh cheering arose then from the men of his company who were near, and as their shouts arose and were echoed by those around, "Bill Gedge! Bill Gedge!" the poor fellow sat up as high as he could upon the little Ghoorkas' shoulders, threw himself into one of his favourite nigger minstrel attitudes, with left arm outstretched and right hand seeming to thump with all his poor strength upon the imaginary banjo held against his breast.

"Welcome, welcome back!" cried Colonel Graves a few minutes later, as he forced himself through the crowd to where Doctor Morton was excitedly superintending the carrying in of his two old patients to the officers' ward.

"Thanks, thanks, Colonel," said Bracy in a feeble voice. "I did my best, sir, but I only failed."

"Failed!" cried the Colonel proudly. "Why, the fort is saved."

Chapter Thirty Seven.

"For Valour."

299

There is little more to tell, for, after this last repulse and the strengthening of the but by doubling its garrison, the enemy's ranks melted away once more, the white-coats, terribly lessened, vanishing like snow from the hills.

Two days later long processions of unarmed villagers were bringing in stores for sale; and before twenty-four more hours had elapsed a deputation of chiefs from different tribes were suing for peace, the Empress Queen's authority being acknowledged, and the fort and its approaches became safe, so that it seemed hard to realise the truth of the great change. But change there was, the various hill-tribes round apparently accepting the position of being under the stronger power, and devoting themselves to the arts of peace.

It was while getting slowly over his injuries that Bracy's quarters became the favourite resort of many of the officers, even Colonel Wrayford, once more himself, often coming in company with Major Graham and the Doctor. But the chief visitors were Roberts and Drummond, the three young officers exchanging notes as to what had taken place during their separation.

"I never knew such a lucky chap as you are, Bracy," said Drummond on one occasion. "You seem to get most of the titbits and all the fat."

Bracy's face assumed such a peculiar aspect of perplexed wonder as he carefully shifted his injured leg so as not to jar his wound while moving, and he directed such a questioning look at Roberts that the latter burst into a roar of laughter.

"What is it?" said Drummond. "Have I said something stupid—a bull?"

"More like the bleat of an innocent calf," said Roberts—"eh, Bracy?"

"Oh, all right; chaff away, old chaps. But, I say, I hear that there are a lot of supplies coming up the pass—mule-loads and loads. There's sure to be a bullock-trunk for me, and I shall be able to get out of you fellows' debt."

"Our debt?" said Bracy. "You don't owe me anything."

"Oh, don't I? What about those boots?"

One morning, when Bracy was getting on towards convalescence,

Gedge, who was acting as invalid servant, entered the homely room holding out one arm.

"Why, Gedge!" cried Bracy; "the sergeant's chevrons?"

"That's right, sir," cried their owner proudly. "Youngest sergeant in the ridgement, Colonel says, and that he was proud to give me my promotion."

The young soldier held out his arm, upon which the regimental tailor had sewn a patch of very shabby cloth, bearing the three stripes of the sergeant's rank, the thing itself being a weather-stained rag.

"I congratulate you, my lad, with all my heart."

"I knew you would, sir. Ain't much to look at, sir, to some people. We shall get fresh togs served out some day; but I don't believe the noo stripes 'll shine out half so bright as these here do, sir, to me."

Bracy sighed.

"Can't help feeling as proud as a dog with two tails—ought to say three, sir, because that's the number of the stripes. But somehow I don't feel as I thought I should."

"I suppose not," said Bracy sadly. "I feel the same, Gedge. We did not fetch the Ghoorkhas."

"No, sir," said Gedge, grinning; "but we brought 'em back, and I don't see how any two could ha' done more than we did. But I didn't mean that, sir. I meant about Sergeant Gee. I thought it would make him as waxy as could be; but as soon as parade was over, and the boys had done cheering me for my promotion, I got showing off, for old Gee was coming up to me, and I was getting ready to give him back as good as he give me. But what d'yer think, sir?"

"I don't know, Gedge," said Bracy, smiling.

"Knocks the wind outer me at once."

"What do you mean?"

"Comes up to me and offers me one hand, and claps t'other on my shoulder. 'Glad to welcome so brave a brother,' he says, 'to the sergeants' mess.' My! I was took aback, sir, and couldn't say a word; and if next minute his missus wasn't shaking hands too with the tears in her eyes, sir—real uns, for I counted four as tumbled out and fell spat on the front of her dress. 'Willyum Gedge,' she says, and then she stops short with her lower lip dithering, and she couldn't say another word, only stood shaking her head, while the boys cheered again. Think Sergeant Gee meant it, sir, or was it only showing off?"

"He meant it, my lad. Gee has a great deal of harsh tyranny in his ways of dealing with those under him; but a braver and more honest man never joined the regiment."

"I'm glad o' that, sir," said Gedge. "Then, as he did mean it, why, of course we're going to be friends."

"Ah, Sergeant, you here?" said Colonel Graves, entering Bracy's quarters. "One moment before you go. I have mentioned you in my despatch for displaying signal bravery in protecting your officer upon two occasions."

"Me, sir? Oh, thanky, sir, but I—"

"Silence!—Bracy, my dear boy, I came to tell you that I have spoken so of you that if they do not give you the Victoria Cross I shall say there is something wrong."

"For me, sir?" cried Bracy, with his pale, thin face flushing faintly. "Impossible, sir. Oh, I have not deserved all this!"

The Colonel's eyes did not look quite so bright as usual as he warmly shook his young officer's hand.

"Let me be the best judge of that," he said. "You have always been one of my smartest officers, and in this last dangerous expedition you showed the will and did your utmost. It was fate that helped you in the last extremity to perfect the deed."

The day came when the simple little much-prized decoration was pinned on Captain Bracy's breast, and the motto never shone upon a truer heart.

"For Valour," he said softly as he looked down upon his breast. "Was it really well deserved?"